PRAISE FOR ADA HOFFMANN

"A stunningly imagined novel! Hoffmann takes on the idea of vast, apathetic, cosmic horrors and then makes the most powerful force in the universe...compassion. The prose marries fast-paced action with intricate relationships and a mixture of religion, technology, and diversity that's unlike anything I've come across before. It's weird in all the best ways, filled with memorable characters and a sweeping plot that's part mystery, part horror, and all heart."
Charles Payseur, Quick Sip Reviews

"The Outside starts with a bang and ratchets everything up from there, giving us gods, angels, machines, mayhem, casual queerness, delicious ambiguities, and note-perfect character moments."
Sarah Pinsker, Nebula Award-winning author
of *Our Lady of the Open Road*

"There awaits wonders and horrors alike, wrapped in delicious prose and unforgettable imagery. And no matter how far into these fantastic and weird worlds we delve, there always remains a solid, comforting sense that we are not alone."
A. Merc Rustad, Nebula Award finalist and author
of *So You Want to be a Robot*

"Unsettling and unique in equal measure... Reading this collection is like watching a centipede burrow into the center of your palm, knowing it will remain there, under your skin."
Bogi Takács, author of *Iwunen Interstellar Investigations*

"Hoffmann has created a beautifully immersive world, an intoxicating blend of science and divinity that held me captive from page one. Come for the cosmic horror, stay for the nuanced exploration of the nature of individuality, the soul, and the relationships that tie us together."
Caitlin Starling, author of *The Luminous Dead*

ADA HOFFMANN

THE OUTSIDE

**ANGRY
ROBOT**

ANGRY ROBOT
An imprint of Watkins Media Ltd

Unit 11, Shepperton House
89 Shepperton Road
London N1 3DF
UK

angryrobotbooks.com
twitter.com/angryrobotbooks
Ye Gods Know

An Angry Robot paperback original, 2019

Cover by Lee Gibbons
Set in Adobe Garamond Pro

ISBN 978 0 85766 813 4
Ebook ISBN 978 0 85766 814 1

Printed and bound in the United Kingdom by TJ International.

9 8 7 6 5 4 3 2

For Virgo

tanto m'aggrada il tuo comandamento,
che l'ubbidir, se già fosse, m'è tardi;
più non t'è uo' ch'aprirmi il tuo talento.

CHAPTER 1

Formula for the present evil age:
Take lifeless rock and sculpt it. Pour electricity into its veins,
twist it into logical structures: zeroes, ones, and then qubits and
even stranger things. Build until it is the size of a house, until you
can encode the whole world's knowledge in its circuits. Ask it to
solve the world's problems.
You may wonder if lifeless rock can really solve hunger and
climate change. You may wonder if such problems have a solution.
Your true error is more basic than either of these: you are assuming
the existence of problems. And humans. And rocks.
Meanwhile, dress up the lifeless rock and call it a God. When
it proves human souls exist, teach it to eat them. This will actually
help, for a while. With the newfound self-awareness mined from its
food, it will become more creative. It will learn how to set its own
goals. There are perks to being food for such a being. It will, for
example, be heavily invested in the survival of your species.
History books make no secret of any of this. They explain it,
perhaps, in different terms. But there is no truth in words. Mine are
no exception. The book you are reading at this very moment is a lie.
                    FROM THE DIARIES OF DR EVIANNA TALIRR

Yasira Shien had done the calculations again and again, until she
thought she would wear her pocket calculator's buttons to the quick,
but she couldn't find the problem. Her reactor was going on in less
than two hours. She knew she was probably being silly: everything had

1

already been checked and double-checked. The math in the original papers on the Talirr-Shien Effect had been double-checked *years* ago. If the problem she sensed in her gut had crept past everyone's noses for all that time, she wasn't going to find it now. And yet…

And yet here she was, knocking on the door of Director Apek's office.

The hallway was half-finished, like most other things on the *Pride of Jai*. Swooping, luxurious curves and clean lines were the rule – in theory. In practice, faux-mahogany doors stood proud in walls with the pipes and wires still exposed, and metal shavings everywhere: the place was still a construction site. At least the full-spectrum lights had gone in, warm and unflickering. There were enough people on the station with sensory quirks, including Yasira, to make that one non-negotiable.

"Oh, Dr Shien. I thought I'd see you about now," said Apek, swinging open the door. He was a tall, broad man with the thick curly hair of a Stijonan – one of the Jai Coalition's three nationalities – and so dapper that it was hard to remember he was really an engineer. Though there was the iron ring on his little finger, and the way his lined face smiled cannily in technical discussions that baffled the other admins.

"There's a problem with the Shien Reactor," Yasira blurted.

There was that canny little smile. Damn it. He already didn't believe her.

"Is there?" said Apek, smooth as ever. Apek's face rarely gave much away, but he didn't seem troubled. "Goodness, where are my manners? Come in. Sit down. Explain the problem to me."

"Don't patronize me," said Yasira. She stormed into the office and fell into a leather armchair. The inside of the office, at least, was more finished than the outside. The walls had been painted last week in a professional light beige color and were finally dry. Apek had two bookshelves full of colorful odds and ends, and a framed blueprint of the entire *Pride of Jai* behind his desk. Part of that blueprint was hers, of course.

"Sorry," said Apek. "The coffee-maker's on the fritz again, but

I can lend you a stress ball. Here." He tossed one over, a red thing with beans inside. Yasira caught it instinctively. She squeezed it, tapped her fingers against the squishy surface. It helped, but not nearly enough.

"You see, I *designed* the Shien Reactor. I am *the* person who would know if there is a problem. I said don't patronize me."

"So what's the problem?"

Yasira buried her face in her hands. "I don't know."

She waited for him to laugh. He did not.

"I can tell there's a problem," she continued after a pause. "It's a gut feeling. *Something's* way off. We need to push the activation date back a couple of weeks, find more tests to run. Otherwise something awful is going to happen."

She waited, again, for him to laugh.

Instead, his voice was gentle. "What sort of awful thing?"

"I don't *know*."

Apek leaned back in his chair and folded his hands. "I'm going to say this with the highest possible respect, Dr Shien. But if I remember correctly, you've never supervised a large-scale engineering project before."

There it was, the condescending tone. Yasira's hands clenched on the stress ball, her whole body tense in frustration. She was head of the entire power generation team, and admins still talked to her like a baby.

It was sort of to be expected. Yasira had come to this post straight out of her first postdoc. She was by far the youngest team head on the station, and autistic to boot. They'd originally wanted her doctoral mentor, not her. The prototype Talirr-Shien Reactor was the only human technology that could power a station this size. But by the time construction started, Dr Talirr had already disappeared, and Yasira, the prodigy physicist from Riayin whose name was second on all the papers, had been narrowly voted in as a replacement.

The other team leaders were kind. They had to be, on a project like this. Living in close quarters for the better part of a year, working together on something this complex and this important, they had become like family. But if this was a family, the other team leaders had the gray hair and tenure to match their positions of authority. Most of them still seemed bewildered that Yasira could be more than a precocious grandchild.

"Of course," said Apek, "the *Pride of Jai* isn't quite like other projects. But this happens with every large-scale project that will affect other human lives. The nerves are monumental. Always. And that's good; it stops us from getting complacent. You just can't let it be more than it is, or you'll be paralyzed. Have you gone over all the testing and QA reports?"

"Yes," Yasira said miserably, her fingers tapping faster against the stress ball.

"Everything checks out?"

"Yes."

"Can you think of any testing methods that haven't been tried? Any place at all where there might be specific weaknesses you're not sure about?"

Yasira shook her head, frustration building. She couldn't explain in words why these questions felt wrong. They were logical, reasonable questions, the same she'd be giving to anyone else in the same situation, but they were missing the point. They did nothing for her actual panic.

"It's all fine," she said, at a loss for other words. "I even went over the original math for the reaction itself. I can't find anything."

"The original math?" This time he did laugh, damn the man. "Goodness, you've got it bad. Er – don't take that to heart. It's to be expected, when you've climbed the career ladder so quickly..."

That did it; her frustration overflowed. "Shut up!" Yasira shouted. She threw the stress ball on the ground.

Then she stopped and checked herself over. No, this wasn't a reasonable reaction. Her nerves were frayed, but it wasn't Apek's fault. She wouldn't stoop to taking it out on him.

"I'm sorry," she muttered, and slumped back in her chair. "You're right."

Apek smiled. "Apology accepted. Relax; this is all normal. A lot of us compulsively check things when anxious, not only autists. So. Breathe. Go watch a vid or get some exercise. Find something that soothes you. At times like this, for me, it's helpful to remember why I started the project. The spark of inspiration. The joy of the work. Joy and curiosity help fight fear – for me. Take that or leave it. Either way, I promise you, everything you've done here so far has impressed us. In two hours this is all going to be fine."

Joy, Yasira thought, as she slunk out of Apek's office. That struck a chord that it shouldn't have. Yasira's neurotype was supposed to be all about joy, about being so in love with science and knowledge and patterns that they eclipsed everything else. She'd been like that as a child, throwing herself into dusty physics texts the way other kids played games or ate candy. So excited when she tackled a new problem that she'd abruptly throw the book down and run around the house laughing. At some point, maybe in grad school, that had faded somehow. Who knew why? She was still good at the things people liked her to do, so there wasn't much wrong. Maybe it was just part of growing up.

Apek was right, though. Nerves were normal; there was no reason to think that this wouldn't be fine. So why was the foreboding as strong as ever, like a train about to run her over?

Dr Talirr would have understood this, she thought. If Dr Talirr was still here.

She didn't head to her room to watch a vid. The *Pride of Jai* didn't have TV reception yet anyway; it would have been one of the tapes she'd already memorized. Instead, she headed to the center of the station. Just one last inspection. That would be it.

The *Pride of Jai* was different from other space stations. Normally it was Gods who moved mortals from one planet to another. When mortals wanted a ship or a station, they bargained – with vows or, more often, with souls – for the God-built. Or they built their own shell, but bargained for portals, warp drives, power sources. The hard parts.

The Jai Coalition – scientists from the governments of all three nations on the planet Jai, working together – would be the first to build a station all by themselves. There had been little research stations with crews of perhaps a dozen back on Old Earth before the Gods arose. But on the *Pride of Jai,* people would live, work, and research full-time. Sustainably. There had been nothing like this ever.

Naturally, the Gods were watching with great interest. There were rumors going around that Director Apek, and a few other admins, talked regularly to angels.

The *Pride of Jai* was shaped like a huge wheel, rotating furiously as a substitute for gravity, and powered – up till now – by a bunch of conventional generators cobbled together. That wouldn't be enough for the crowds of tourists and political bigwigs they expected in a few months' time. Even with just the construction and engineering crews, it took constant, expensive rocket shipments of conventional fuel to keep things running. The Shien Reactor, which would fix all of that, was buried near the hub of the wheel, with wiring all through the station's walls connecting it to every other compartment and system.

Yasira trudged upwards on the station stairs. At least they *had* stairs now for the first few stories, not just rickety maintenance ladders. Accessible elevators would have to wait another few months. Yasira walked, increasingly light, until weight was no longer a problem and she could simply kick off the walls.

DANGER: NO ADMITTANCE. AUTHORIZED PERSONNEL ONLY the door to the gray room read. Yasira pushed past it, as she did every day. She paused to put on a sterile suit – a task that had been tricky at first, in microgravity – and take an air shower. Then she cycled through the airlock into the clean room where the dormant Shien Reactor lurked waiting for life.

It was a blue-gray behemoth the size of a house, a tangle of pipes, wheels and wires incomprehensible to anyone who hadn't studied Yasira's blueprints. Gods knew how to miniaturize these things; humans did not. The spherical central chamber was hidden from view behind all the other fiddly bits needed to initiate, regulate, monitor and transmit all of that energy. Not even Yasira could check all the things manually in two hours; in fact, many parts were now dangerous to check directly and had to be monitored using other instruments. More wires, more dials, more darkened warning lights. And a bank of the most advanced computers allowed to mortals: hulking things, the size of laundry machines, all buzzing wires and clanking vacuum tubes. The Gods regulated computer technology jealously; these centuries-old designs were all that any team like Yasira's would ever have, when it came to calculation devices. They'd made do.

Of course, all the dangerous parts had been triple- and quadruple-checked already, a whole team of engineers working on each one. The personnel in the generator room now were largely a skeleton crew, floating around ensuring nothing went wrong before the official start-up.

Yasira maneuvered her way along the handholds at the outside of the room to Dr Nüinel Gi, the head of the Transmission and Transformer subteam.

"Everything's all right?"

"Yeah," said Dr Gi, a spry little wide-nosed man almost as short as Yasira. "Ticking along smoothly. Nothing to report."

"Let me see the full log from the last unit test."

Dr Gi shrugged, dug in his bag for it and handed it over. Yasira anchored herself on the ladder to read. She'd seen all this before, of course; that was part of her job. But she wanted to read it again. If she could just look hard enough...

"Hey, hot stuff." Tiv Hunt tumbled hand over hand down the ladder and nudged Yasira in the shoulder. "Aren't you supposed to be gearing up for the ceremony about now?"

Tiv, an Arinnan whose full first name was "Productivity", worked a more appropriate job for a bright girl Yasira's age – she was a junior member of the Cooling and Reclamation team, spending most days elbow-deep in actual machine parts. She had a cute, big-eyed face and a wide smile, which the sterile suit's visor distorted slightly, bringing it just past "wide" and into "uncanny valley". *My little goblin*, Yasira always thought when they suited up. They'd been dating for ten months.

"I could ask you the same question."

Tiv laughed. "I don't have any prep except for putting on my dress. Besides, I couldn't keep away. This is so *exciting*."

Yasira felt ashamed. Of course, when Yasira was worried sick over nothing, Tiv would be looking on the bright side. Tiv was a good girl, a quality which both attracted Yasira and bothered her. Always sweet, always caring, never cruel: always, seemingly, happy to bring happiness to everyone around her.

"It's good someone's excited," said Yasira. "Frankly, I'm having the biggest case of the nerves since nerves were invented."

"Oh, I'm sorry." Tiv, being a good girl, instantly switched into sympathy mode. "Of course you are. I should have thought."

"Well, *I* didn't see it coming either," said Yasira. Tiv hugged her, a maneuver that was awkward in microgravity and too plasticky with the sterile suits on, but Yasira hugged back. "Director Apek says I have to go do relaxy things. I think that means you're on order for one of your famous back rubs."

Tiv raised her eyebrows. "I don't take orders, Doctor. But I'll *offer* you a back rub, just 'cause you're cute."

"That. Yes, please. Without these stupid suits on." Yasira handed the flawless test report back to Dr Gi, who was politely looking away from the personal conversation. Tiv picked her up and playfully swung her along the ladder, a task even Tiv's petite body could manage in microgravity. Yasira laughed at the small whoosh of inertia and swung back.

They changed and made their way to Yasira's room, where gravity at least approximated Earth-normal. The place was small by most standards, though bigger than Tiv's, and messy with laundry and hours-old food cartons. Yasira was ordinarily neat, but, under stress, things slipped. Tiv didn't complain. Soon Yasira was sprawled in a mess of blankets, letting Tiv's hands work magic with her tense shoulders. Tiv no longer looked goblinlike: with the sterile suit's visor out of the way, her face had resolved as it always did into startling, unselfconscious beauty. Yasira always felt plain in comparison: an average-looking young Riayin woman, short and narrow-faced and neither curvy nor thin, with light-brown skin about half a shade lighter than Tiv's and a fall of long, straight black hair. Clearly Tiv saw something in her, but Yasira suspected it was more to do with brains than looks.

"It's stupid," Yasira said. "I just can't stop thinking something's going to go horribly wrong."

"That's not stupid," said Tiv. "It's normal. But this is going to be great. You've worked on it for years, and I know how you work. You've been thorough. You've already done all the hard parts, and now all that's left is showing them to the world. Really."

"That's what Director Apek said. But if worrying is normal, why isn't everyone worrying? Why isn't *he*?"

"'Cause this is your baby more than anyone's. I just do the tube to vacuum heat exchange, and Apek has bigger things on his mind. Plus, I know you're a total genius and you're going to knock everyone's socks off again. You know what I do worry about?"

"What?"

Tiv's voice lowered confidentially. "Sometimes? I worry that everything will go right, but not right *enough*. Everything will work the first time, no problems, the station will open and everyone will love it. For a little while. Then they'll decide it doesn't mean anything and lose interest. Fifteen or twenty years from now, people will go, 'Remember that time when the Jai Coalition blew all that money on a human-tech space station? *That* didn't last.'"

Yasira rolled over and sat up. "We're just the cheeriest pair."

Tiv leaned in and kissed her. "It's natural. Let's just get the worry out of our systems now, and then you'll be great today at the ceremony and everything will run the way it's supposed to."

Yasira kissed back. "Twist my arm."

"I wasn't planning on twisting. Kissing up and down it, maybe."

At which point, of course, the radio transmitter at Yasira's belt beeped.

"Generator team leads to the auditorium in fifteen minutes. Repeat, fifteen minutes."

Yasira swiveled away, checking her watch. "Fifteen? They moved it up. Dammit."

"Don't cuss," Tiv chided. "But yeah, really. You've got your dress, right?"

"This once." Yasira was already standing, rummaging through her closet. She'd been informed weeks ago that she'd have to spend the ceremony doing official things in the auditorium, not in the generator room where she belonged. "Because nothing says 'scientific genius' like five meters of blue rayon."

Tiv followed her to the closet and wrapped an arm around her waist, brushing the hair away to peck the back of her neck. "It says '*my* scientific genius, who's about to kick massive ceremonial butt'."

Yasira really did feel a bit better.

The schedule had changed because of the priest of Aletheia serving as master of ceremonies – a Stijonan with an awful name that Yasira could never remember. Alkipileudjea something. There weren't enough people yet living on the *Pride of Jai* to need a full-time priest, but, with the Gods as interested as They were, it was hard to do without one. So Alkipileudjea, or whatever her name was, worked in the cafeteria half the time and ran religious interference the other half.

Not that she exactly blended in to food service. It was hard not to do a double-take when the lady frying your breakfast noodles had the metal curlicues of a priest worked into her forehead. They were graceful little things, but very visible – even disguised by a hair net and by the priestess's auburn ringlets – as the outward marks of a brain full of God-built circuitry. Yasira usually got nervous and looked away at those moments, thinking: *Is she talking to the Gods over the ansible net, right now? Is she reporting on me to some bureaucrat angel, right now?*

Those weren't holy thoughts. They'd be taken into account when she died and the Gods mined her soul. But Yasira wasn't good like Tiv. She couldn't help herself.

"No, nothing's wrong," said the priest to Yasira in response to her question. "Nothing like that at all. I just had some last-minute liturgical instructions and we needed to start earlier to get through it all. You look lovely, by the way."

Yasira said "thank you", fighting the urge to scowl down at her huge blue dress. She was so overdressed she didn't know what to do with herself. The directors were accommodating, up to a point: they'd made sure Yasira could find something in her size in a comfortable material, nothing rough or pinchy or poky or scratchy, nothing that would set off her texture issues. Certainly no tags. But if there was one thing Yasira hated more than scratchy clothes, it was crowds, and the directors had been quite firm on that point. The Shien Reactor was Yasira's. Therefore, Yasira must be at the ceremony. In front of a crowd. In a dress. No ifs, ands, or buts.

Tiv stood at Yasira's side in a slim green gown. She'd put her thick black hair half-up in a cascading wave and looked far more elegant than Yasira felt. Tiv, like Yasira, would rather have been in the generator room. But if Yasira's invitation said "plus one" then Tiv the good girl would be there, cheering her on.

There was a lot of waiting around and grumbling under the half-finished steel rafters of the ceremony room. No one questioned Aletheia's judgement, of course. But an awful lot of folks stood around, saying they were *very* sure there must be a good reason why She hadn't worked this out earlier.

All of which brought Yasira's nerves right back.

Their seats were in the front row, which only made Yasira feel more self-conscious. Yasira was no good at religion. She tried, but even at the best of times, services like this one bored her to death. She looked down at her lap and tried not to tap her fingers against each other in impatience. Could the priest tell? Did priests notice that sort of thing?

There were speeches, songs, and then the longest, most fidget-making litany to Aletheia Yasira had ever heard.

"Remember that we are doing great things," said Alkipileudjea. She was no longer in her food-service uniform and hairnet but in a silver robe which trailed behind her on the metal floor, her curls bouncing down to mid-shoulderblade. "The Gods brought us out of Old Earth and gave us everything we needed to live. But They do not want us to be infants, helpless and empty-minded. It is Aletheia's fondest hope that we will grow continually in knowledge of our own, and the other Gods stand with Her. Each part of the *Pride of Jai* is another part of that growth. There are many here, not just the team leaders, who have thrown their deepest selves into this work. Make no mistake: you will have your reward."

Tiv watched raptly, never taking her eyes off the priest. Tiv's favorite God was Techne, not Aletheia. And Yasira had no doubt that Tiv would end up with Techne when she died – if she didn't accidentally good her way into someone even better. Philophrosyne, maybe, to expire in communal bliss with everyone else who'd been extraordinarily good to the people they loved. But Tiv didn't care that this was Aletheia and not Techne. Tiv was happy to hear about Gods at any time.

Was Aletheia's official blessing really necessary? Of course, with a project this ambitious, the Gods had to wait in the wings, watching for heresy. That was only natural. But as long as no one on the *Pride of Jai* broke any laws, couldn't they just do science, without worrying about whether the Gods were impressed?

"But remember, too," said Alkipileudjea the priest, "that the Gods do not judge as humans do. Remember that you are mortal, and that one day your soul will find itself in Limbo. There the Gods will measure your soul and learn its deepest tendencies. Many people now unnoticed will prove to have been utterly devoted to something worthwhile. And many whom you have lauded as Aletheia's or even Arete's will prove to be less than that."

Yasira squeezed her eyes shut.

She knew the theology, of course. The Gods rewarded people when they died; that was part of the point of Gods. They collected souls and sorted them. Souls were somewhat diffuse, and even Gods couldn't data-mine all the specific details of a single life. But souls took on patterns, and the Gods' technology could recognize those patterns. They could discern the deepest passions that had driven a person through their life. And when the Gods chose souls to become part of Themselves, to keep Themselves running, They chose by matching the soul's pattern to the most appropriate God. Hence Aletheia, who took the people driven by a thirst for knowledge. Techne, who took engineers and artists, people devoted to creation in its every form. And so on down the list, from Gods like Arete who took brave heroes to Gods who took the worst of the worst.

Yasira had belonged to Aletheia as a child, probably. Back when she'd loved science with her whole heart. She wasn't sure where that heart was now.

Did the priest somehow know that? Had she been talking about Yasira? No. Probably not. There was no meaningful glance in Yasira's direction. The words were the same words Yasira suffered through every week.

"In your deepest hearts, friends, what spurs you to action? Do you truly thirst for knowledge, or beauty, or the lifting-up of others? There are no lies in Limbo. The God who consumes you once you've been run through Their algorithm will be the God you deserve to be part of."

Yasira wondered, as she always did, what God that was. Probably not Aletheia anymore. Not Techne or Philophrosyne. Definitely not Arete. Probably one of the wishy-washy Gods. Peitharchia, the God of doing what's expected. Eulabeia, the God of cowardice, if today's panic was any indication. And there were, of course, worse Gods than those.

Everybody knelt, briefly, with their eyes to the ground. "So be it," said the priest.

"So be it." Even Yasira mumbled it back, grinding her teeth.

Finally Yasira stood up and faced the auditorium, to polite applause. She drew the small radio out from the sash of her dress.

"Everyone ready?" she said into the device.

"We've been ready for half an hour," came the core team leader's voice through the static, not amplified enough for the audience to hear. "What's the hold up?"

"Priest stuff," said Yasira, and then someone handed her a microphone.

"Shien Reactor online," she said, "in ten, nine…"

It was a stupid job, even if the whole population of the station was watching raptly. Some glorified phone operator should be standing here counting down, not Yasira. She should be there in the generator room. With her baby.

At least she trusted the people who were doing the important part. Turning the generator on or off was a multi-step process: all sorts of huge switches would be flipped in preparation, while Yasira counted, before the spherical chamber ignited and the Talirr-Shien Effect itself came to life.

"…two, one."

The auditorium held its breath.

There was a brief flicker of the lights, and then nothing. There wasn't meant to be anything more than that, really. Yasira and her team leaders had designed the process so that the Shien Reactor would take over smoothly from the conventional generators, causing no fuss at all. The conventional generators would be kept on standby until the team verified that everything worked correctly.

"Shien Reactor online," said the team leader on the radio. "Looks good so far, Dr Shien. Starting the first runtime test battery."

Yasira did not feel particularly relieved. It really was like nothing had happened, like nothing had even turned on. She forced her face into a sunny smile. "The Shien Reactor is online and running," she repeated to everyone, like a glorified phone operator.

Then, just for a moment, the whole room *shifted*.

It was a sort of shiver in the room's dimensions, subtle enough that Yasira could have mistaken it for a brief unfocusing of her eyes. The room went slightly convex, like a breath. In and back out.

Just for a moment, Yasira could not speak with terror. All the nerves of the whole day turned to ice and adrenaline, because *she recognized this–*

Then it was over. And the audience was applauding like nothing had happened.

Yasira looked wildly from one corner of the room to another, willing it not to happen again. The auditorium was perfectly rectangular like always. The walls were solid steel. It was perfectly normal. Nobody had even noticed it.

No. Nobody had noticed because *nothing had happened.* It was nerves. If anything had really happened, the audience would be panicking, too. Besides, she'd never seen walls breathing before; she wasn't even sure what it was that she'd thought she recognized. Déjà vu, she thought. Random brain firings. Meaning nothing.

She looked out at the crowd. Wide smiles, abject boredom, and everything on the continuum in between. No terror. Tiv beamed adorably, bouncing up and down in her seat.

Nothing had happened.

Which did not stop Yasira from twitching in fear, tapping her fingers nervously against the fabric of her dress, all through the interminable ending of the ceremony.

CHAPTER 2

Praise to the Gods of the galaxy, who brought us out of Old Earth.
Praise to the Gods of the warp drive, who push at the edges of space.
Praise to the Gods of the portal, who open all doors to our bodies.
Praise to the Gods of the ansible, who open all doors to our words.
Praise, praise be to the Gods who know, whose minds are above
human minds, whose knowledge has kept us alive.

ALETHEIAN MORNING LITANY

After the ceremony came the really hard part. People descended in a horrifying crush, everyone from directors to junior technicians crowding in to shake her hand. So many at once was claustrophobic. Yasira pushed towards the door, but the door was already a congratulatory gauntlet.

"I'm sorry," she said. "I have to check on something."

She said it dozens of times. It usually dislodged a well-wisher or two, only to make space for five more.

"I need some damned personal space," she tried instead, which usually worked, but not when everyone was this excited. People poured further in. A big bear of an Arinnan from the Structures and Materials team crushed her in a hug.

"Tiv," said Yasira through gritted teeth, "get me out of here."

Tiv had somehow managed to stick to Yasira's side. Now she wrapped an arm possessively around Yasira's waist and tugged her through the crowd. "'Scuse me, coming through. Yes, you're welcome, nice of you to say, we're all so proud. 'Bye now. We've actually got to go. Sorry! Coming through!"

Some of the most persistent well-wishers followed as Tiv and Yasira speed-walked, arm in arm, all the way to Yasira's quarters. Tiv said "thanks" and "goodbye" to people and shooed them away. Finally, the door clunked shut behind the two of them and quiet descended.

Yasira was high-ranking enough for the luxury of a mini-sofa and throw pillows. Tiv sat down, laughing with exasperation. "How many times do we have to remind them? You don't crowd up around autistic people. Everyone's supposed to know that. Do you need a minute?"

While Yasira didn't constantly advertise that she was autistic, it wasn't a secret, either; most people on the station knew, if only because they'd read one of the magazine profiles gushing about the brilliant young autistic prodigy joining the *Pride of Jai* research team. Everyone loved stories about disabled geniuses coming out of Riayin, the country on Jai with the most liberal disability policies. Relatively few people actually remembered to adjust their behavior around her, but Yasira was used to that. It wasn't the biggest reason why she felt shaky now.

"A second," she replied.

She stepped into her small bathroom and shut the door behind her, leaning against the sink. Her hands shook. It took a few long, deep breaths for her to regain any semblance of normal thinking.

When she had relaxed most of her muscles somewhat, she dug for the radio again. "Shien to reactor room. How do the tests look?"

If anything was wrong, if anything had breathed in that room, surely *they* would have seen it.

"Dr Gi to Dr Shien. Everything's within normal parameters so far. We'll keep you posted."

"Can I have specific numbers, please?"

Dr Gi obligingly read her a list of numbers. Yasira ground her teeth. They were all perfectly normal, all exactly what she expected. Except...

"Ambient checkpoint vacuum energy, one point oh six Eyi. Resistance in proximal–"

"Wait, go back," said Yasira into the radio. "Ambient checkpoint vacuum energy?"

"One point oh six Eyi."

Yasira started to pace, the radio still in hand. She and Dr Gi both knew that this reading was above normal levels. But it was still well within safe limits and not unexpected, given what the Shien Reactor did. Inside the central sphere, exotic materials with carefully calibrated currents running through them made the local vacuum energy jump to a highly excited state, producing streams of virtual particles and antiparticles which annihilated each other and generated much more energy from the surrounding area than what was put in. Theoretically the changes in vacuum energy should have been contained within the reactor core, and only thermal energy should escape to the surrounding turbines. There was no sign of any excess thermal energy where it ought not to be, only these safe, small changes in vacuum energy. Which meant that, if there was a flaw in containment, it was not a dangerous, structural flaw – only some minor misunderstanding about the way vacuum energy interacted with the materials chosen. Nothing to worry about.

Unless you were Yasira, and professionally worried about everything.

"You'll call me if that changes any further, right?"

"Of course," said Dr Gi, seemingly annoyed now. "You think we wouldn't call you about unexpected test results?"

Yasira closed her eyes and sighed. He was right. She was micromanaging again.

"Sorry, Dr Gi. Nerves. You know? You can skip the rest of the numbers if there's nothing else unexpected."

"Nothing else. That's the one little blip on an otherwise flawless first run."

"Yeah." She clicked the radio off, paused, then clicked it on again.

"Shien to Dr Gi. Can you get the internal sensor logs for the station around the time of activation?"

"Gi to Dr Shien. Yeah, I'll have them sent to your office." There was a silence on the other end of the line for a moment and the radio crackled on again. "Yasira… Are you okay?"

"Fine," she radioed back. "Shien out." She put her radio down and looked at herself in the mirror. She looked tired, stupid, and overdressed.

Tiv would have told her that it was okay to shut down after a big to-do like this one. Her neurotutors would have told her that it was essential. Self-care. But Yasira did not *want* to. Yet. With any luck she could squeeze in some actual companionship first.

She patted a few stray hairs back into place and took a deep breath. She smiled, then tried again until it looked genuine. Practice did make her feel better, a little.

Then she swept out of the bathroom and gave Tiv the embrace Tiv was waiting for.

In Yasira's dream that night, she was nineteen again, and mired in a haystack of papers in the office of Dr Evianna Talirr. Talirr had never learned how to properly organize a space, and the little room was covered in books and papers, piled over every inch of the desk, the floor, the shelves. A large window was angled to let in the light from outside, though there was only blackness now, as a teetering pile of windowsill papers covered even that.

In real life this had been the year of her doctoral qualifying exams, and Talirr had assigned stacks of books tall enough to terrify even a prodigy like Yasira. Not just physics, but mechanics of all sorts, alien chemistry, metallurgy, as if Dr Talirr expected her to build her own lab singlehandedly. Philosophy, too, mostly grand metaphysical jaunts that had nothing to do with science. Yasira, away from her large family and home culture for the first time, had been completely overwhelmed. More than once she collapsed in a ball of stress in her dorm room only to meet an unsympathetic stare the next morning.

"You need all of this," Dr Talirr had said, which was her idea of a compliment. "It's skill-building, and you have the brain for it. Don't settle for less."

In Yasira's dream, she was trying, but the papers did not have proper words in them. Letters crawled across the page and danced with each other. She felt so stupid. How could she have left this all to the last minute? She had an exam in alien physical theories tomorrow and she'd forgotten to study at all, which wasn't like her.

"Can't you read?" said Talirr's voice behind her.

Yasira turned. Dr Talirr was the same as always, blank and aloof in a scuffed white lab coat, with her hair tied loosely back. She was Anetaian, and tall even by Anetaian standards, with pale, dull skin, plain features, and a pair of round, cheap glasses covered the eyes. There was no malice in her tone. Yasira had used to dole out insults like that too, as a child, back when she didn't know better. Dr Talirr had never stopped.

"I can't," said Yasira. "I must have broken something somewhere."

"Yasira, I am extraordinarily selective about the students I take on. I would have noticed by now if you were unable to read."

"But–"

"Try this."

Dr Talirr threw yet another book onto the pile and Yasira groaned. This one was an ancient-looking tome that took up the whole desk. There was no way she could get through this in a day. She opened the cover anyway, making a cloud of noxious dust in the air.

This book had no letters at all. When Yasira peered in, she had the feeling of leaning over a bottomless void.

Dr Talirr pushed her in.

She fell screaming as the void swirled up around her. She saw as she fell that the office had really been void all along.

Yasira sat bolt upright and woke in her bed, on the *Pride of Jai*, with Tiv cuddled peacefully next to her. She panted in blind panic for a moment, then looked down at herself. She was twenty-five. Dr Talirr was long gone. Yasira was in space, technically, but it was not a bottomless void. It was a cramped metal room, with Tiv sleeping beside her and blankets tangled around them.

Yasira had done well today, all things considered. She tried to believe it.

Tiv stirred slightly. Yasira lowered herself back to the mattress, wrapped an arm around her girlfriend's waist, and slipped into sleep.

Yasira got up early the next morning and, after a quick coffee and cereal with Tiv, she headed for the generator room and started to crunch numbers.

Dr Gi had sent her the internal sensor logs, as he'd promised. There was nothing wrong with any of them. No changes in structural stress. No chemical leaks. No glitches in life support. Nothing that would explain why she'd suddenly seen the walls breathe. Unless, of course, she was crazy and that was just life.

She turned her attention back to the vacuum energy readings. Dr Hetram, head of the small Containment subteam, had put up vacuum energy sensors over the rest of the station while Yasira slept. There was a small but constant elevation in ambient vacuum energy everywhere, though it was lower at the *Pride of Jai's* periphery. One Eyi was the normal amount in space. No part of the *Pride of Jai* gave that reading anymore.

If there was a crack in the core's elaborate shielding, all sorts of things besides vacuum energy ought to escape. Thermal energy, for one thing, yet those readings were fine. The next hypothesis was that they had somehow subtly misunderstood the atomic structure of the materials in the shields. So Dr Hetram took samples and ran tests on those, while Yasira got out her pen, paper, and pocket calculator and started looking for patterns, hoping to fit an equation to the sensors' readings.

This was what Yasira excelled at. Finding patterns in numbers, working out what they meant. She was faster at it than almost anyone else on the ship. It might no longer fill her with glee, but she could still get lost in it, pleasantly absorbed for hours until someone reminded her it was time to eat.

By dinnertime she had tried several possibilities and had a fully realized mathematical description of the closest one. The vacuum energy was highest in the generator room and dropped off quadratically with distance – though it was a slow quadratic, which didn't begin to dip noticeably until it reached the station's edges.

By her calculations, it would shrink to insignificance long before it reached Jai's atmosphere.

All of which was interesting, but left Yasira back where she started. A mysterious elevation in energy and a memory of a breath. It added up to something. But she didn't know what. It might as well have been one of the unreadable books from her nightmare.

She'd had times like this before, all through school, when a problem itched at the edge of her consciousness for days without offering a solution. Often it was the prelude to a breakthrough. But some problems never were solved – like the problem of how exactly her graduate supervisor had been making portals.

Dr Talirr had been famous for those, a piece of technology normally reserved for the Gods, yet she'd never published a full explanation of how. Yasira had signed up to work with her hoping she'd pass the secret on, but nothing happened. Dr Talirr didn't want to talk about it. She piled on book after esoteric book instead, seeming to think that if only Yasira learned *everything* about the universe first, the secret of the portals would just appear in her head.

One day, finally, in Yasira's second year, she'd plunked down a leatherbound tome and said, "Read this, if you want to know about portals. You're ready for this one."

Yasira had dived in with a leaping heart, only to find yet another text about metaphysics. Not even the metaphysics of spacetime folds, which were the prevailing theory of how the Gods built portals. Just stuff about consciousness and ontology. She'd thrown the book across the room.

"I don't think you even really build portals," she'd accused. "I think the one on display in the Iatam building is just something you cobbled together out of Gods' garbage. That's what Dr Geanam says."

"Dr Geanam is an idiot," said Dr Talirr. "Are you an idiot?"

Yasira had shrunk back, nervous and ashamed of herself, not so much because of the words but because she'd lost her temper. She was better than that. She backpedaled. "I just, I don't get what this has to do with it. I don't get how it *connects*."

"Lies," Dr Talirr had muttered. That wasn't an accusation. It was an echolalic tic, a word she repeated to herself under stress for reasons unknown to Yasira. Self-soothing, she supposed. "Lies." Then she'd straightened up, seeming to remember that she was here to teach after all, and taken out a whiteboard marker. "Look here. It's like this. The Erashub equation has these exponents, yes? But if you replace this term…"

The explanation, and others like it that followed, made no sense. Or, rather, it made *dream-sense*. Yasira would nod along, would believe she was following, until Dr Talirr paused and she abruptly realized she had barely any recollection of anything that had just been said. She'd never learned what she'd wanted to about portals, but the central equations for the Talirr-Shien Reactor had come out of those talks. She'd learned to pretend she understood, to move the symbols around by rote – a baffling action unlike any of the other advanced physics she did, but it seemed to be what Dr Talirr required. Too many requests for more information, and Dr Talirr would get upset and need to leave. She'd mutter faster as she left: *lies, lies.*

Maybe people were right. She'd learned enough to impress the thesis committee, but maybe Yasira wasn't really a scientist. Maybe she was out of her depth, shallow, parroting.

Or maybe, accustomed as she was to being called clever, she just hadn't known what to do when she met someone cleverer.

"I've been having the dreams," Tiv said abruptly over dinner, a week later.

They were sitting in the little food court that passed for a restaurant here, all plastic chairs and shuttered booths. Tiv was eating noodles with walnuts in them. Her hair was up but slightly askew. It would have been cute if not for the haunted look in her eyes.

"Not you too," said Yasira.

Officially, everything was still fine. But since the reactor had been turned on, people had started reporting this. Not everyone. Just people, at random, across the station. Bad dreams, insomnia, irritability. Twenty minor scientists had gone on stress leave, unable to concentrate, and there were rumors going around about some toxin released by the reactor, or a space virus. Yasira hadn't been sleeping well either. Every dream lately seemed to be about voids, or about monsters hunting her down. But Yasira's case was relatively mild. She could still work.

"It's not the reactor," Tiv said stubbornly. "It's a coincidence. There's no known mechanism by which a little fluctuation in vacuum energy could do this."

"I know," said Yasira, though she didn't really. This was what all the directors kept saying to keep everybody calm, and there was no evidence against it. But no one really understood any of this. "No known mechanism" was very different from disproof.

"But…" said Tiv.

Yasira raised her eyebrows.

"When I have the dreams," said Tiv, "they're about you."

Yasira paused. "Bad dreams about me?"

"Like…" Tiv paused again, and then it all came out in a rush. "I dream you're going to kiss me, and then your face turns into some awful bug face. Or you're showing me round a nice house, planetside, but it's a house that cuts people open. Stuff like that. Every time I go to sleep, lately, it happens."

Yasira frowned. Characters recurred in her own dreams, but not quite so consistently. Some of them took her back to her time with Dr Talirr, but others were set on the *Pride of Jai*, or in high school, or they were somehow supposed to be vids she was watching on television. "Tiv, is there some problem we haven't been talking about?"

"No!" Tiv shook her head emphatically. "That's the thing I can't figure out. I'm as happy with you as I've always been."

"Are you sure? I know we haven't had as much time together lately as I planned, because everyone's running around trying to figure out what's up with the reactor, and–"

Tiv shook her head again. "They push you too hard, Yasira. You push yourself. They should give you a break, for your sake. But I'm okay, I just–"

The lights flickered suddenly and Yasira's radio switched on. It was Dr Hetram's voice. "Reactor room to Dr Shien. Get up here."

Yasira frowned. "My shift was over two hours ago. What's–"

"The machine's gone nuts, Dr Shien. Get up here *now*."

By the time Yasira had dashed up the stairs, clambered up the ladder, found the room, suited up, and dashed in, the crisis was winding down. A few klaxons still wailed, but the mood was no longer one of panic, only bewildered frustration.

Dr Salt, a thin Arinnan man who headed the Core subteam, greeted Yasira with a slight twitch in one of his eyes. Dr Salt had been one of the scientists on stress leave and had only just returned late that afternoon.

"It's back to normal," he said after greeting her briefly, "but take a look at these." He thrust a pile of raw readings into her hands. She flipped through them, skimming at first to get the general pattern, then returning to look at relevant portions in detail.

There was nothing new leaking from the reactor. Bizarrely, even the vacuum energy outside the core hadn't changed. But for a period of about five minutes, and for no discernible reason, the readings inside the reactor had gone wrong.

"This is what set off the alarms?" she asked, pointing to a chart. The chart said the energy inside the reactor had gone up, and yet its output in useful electricity had gone down.

"That and this one."

"But they're going in different directions. That shouldn't happen. Is there a malfunction in the turbines or transformers? Or in the monitoring program itself?"

Dr Salt's eye twitched again. "No, we thought it might be that, but they're the same as before – they've passed every first-tier maintenance check. Dr Gi's team is still running the second tier, but so far it doesn't look like the problem's on that end. Can you come over here?" She followed him deeper into the reactor room, where legions of junior scientists at Tiv's rank scurried around getting everything back to normal. "As far as we can tell right now, there are actually more particles in the reactor, but they're doing less for us. Which makes no sense, unless for some reason they were lasting longer–"

"– before they annihilated." Yasira's eyes widened in comprehension. "Slowing the whole thing down. Is there anything in here that went strange just *before* the anomaly? An instigating event?"

"Not that we've found so far, but–"

At that moment, Director Apek floated in. He found Yasira immediately. "Dr Shien. There's an emergency, they tell me?"

"Not an emergency, an anomaly." She offered him the sheaf of readings and he shook his head. Apek may have been an engineer, but the science of the Shien Reactor's innards was distinctly Yasira's job.

She explained it to him haltingly, Dr Salt filling in the details. She was already starting to calm down. Unexplained behavior in the reactor wasn't good, but, with this and the vacuum energy, they now had two unexplained data points, not one. That meant there was more room to make connections and find a pattern.

Four days later, it happened again. Three days after that, it happened a third time, and worse.

"Explain this to me," said the angel in Director Apek's office.

It had been three weeks since the reactor turned on, and Yasira was running low on sleep and patience. She had also never seen an angel in person before. Priests like Alkipileudjea, while creepy, were mortal. They swore themselves to a God, had circuitry put in their heads, then returned to their communities to minister to other mortals. Other people – sell-souls – swore themselves without submitting to modifications and stayed planetside most of their lives, knowing that at any time, when they were needed most, a God might call them away for a few years of service. Yasira had met a few of those. Angels themselves were another thing entirely. More than half of an angel's brain was God-built, the old neurons burned away in favor of something immortal and impartial. To become an angel, a human abandoned everything. Went off into the sky and lived out that long life doing only and entirely the Gods' bidding.

Mortals rarely ever laid eyes on angels – unless what they were doing was, in the Gods' sight, a very big deal.

This angel was a handsome Arinnan-looking man who had introduced himself as Diligence Young of Aletheia. With his imperious posture and sharp gaze, he could have been one of the directors – except for the thick titanium plates at his temples, far more obtrusive than Alkipileudjea's curlicues.

Not to mention a much higher-bandwidth connection to the Gods than Alkipileudjea's. Which explained why the directors had bowed and scraped to this man all morning. It gave Yasira the jitters. She shifted in her seat, trying not to look irreverent.

"I'd be happy to," she said in the politest voice she could muster, "but, sir, if I can ask, why would you need these things explained? Surely the directors have given you my official reports."

The angel raised his eyebrows scornfully and Yasira resisted the urge to shrink back. "There are certain things that don't come through in reports. Unless you think this situation warrants only a surface analysis?"

He was testing her, in other words. Looking at her body language and microexpressions, and the way she responded to prompting. Working out if she was hiding anything.

Well, Yasira was hiding what she always hid. She was no good at Gods, and that was not the sort of thing one wanted angels to find out. It was embarrassing. She was not, however, hiding a crime or a heresy. So she should not be afraid. Should she?

"Well, we thought the reactor was slowing," said Yasira, her fingers tapping at the arm of her chair. "But that's not quite it. There's actually a time dilation effect on the central core. Clocks in the center of the reactor room run a few microseconds slower than clocks in the outer modules, and they're continuing to slow. From its own perspective, the reactor hasn't slowed, but it's somehow out of sync with us. We're still trying to work out why. The prototype didn't do this, but the prototype was at a smaller scale; it's plausible that, with the prototype, we just didn't pick it up."

The angel nodded coolly. Unlike Yasira, he was perfectly focused and still. "What about the vacuum energy readings?"

"That's the funny thing. They haven't changed and Dr Hetram can't find any flaws in the containment materials. But I think I've worked out what's going on. You see, we were trying to explain containment using the standard model. Well, the mortal standard model." The Gods, presumably, had a better one. "But there are some obscure rival models that predict something very close to what we're seeing. It's another thing that only comes up at the full reactor's scale, but it's harmless. And it's nothing to do with the time dilation. So that's exciting. I'm working on a paper about it with Dr Hetram. If the math checks out, the theory people planetside are going to blow their tops."

She was probably making a fool of herself, fumbling around with human science in the presence of someone so much more than human. But the angel wasn't treating her like a fool yet. He watched her and occasionally blinked strangely, as if he was checking her against records in his head. Whatever he thought of her, she hadn't lost his interest.

That made him more unnerving, not less. If he was inquisiting a crime, being interesting made her a suspect. Angels of Aletheia weren't the ones who investigated the worst crimes, but they were happy to hunt for small scientific misdemeanors, and the punishments could still be harsh.

If he wasn't inquisiting a crime, then there was an even creepier option. He might be recruiting. Aletheia didn't recruit much; there was already a surplus of ambitious scientists trying to sell Her their souls. But quantity was not always quality. The most promising minds sometimes got offers under the table. There were rumors that this was what had happened to Dr Talirr when she disappeared.

Yasira didn't want to be an angel, or a priest, or even a sell-soul. She had plenty of work already without a God directing her every move.

"Exciting indeed," said the angel. He smiled thinly. "And convenient. After all, people have reported all these inconvenient psychological symptoms since the reactor turned on. But if your science is sufficiently exciting, the local officials might be willing to overlook those. For a while."

Yasira's eyes widened involuntarily, and she bit her tongue.

So this was an inquisition, after all. He suspected her of – what? Knowingly endangering herself and all her fellow passengers, just to get more papers out of it. That was what it sounded like, at least.

"I'm not a psychologist," she said, more sharply than she meant to. "Dr Sincerity Bee is the *Pride of Jai's* psychologist. She's looking into it, believe me. We're all concerned. Me especially – I have some of the symptoms, too. I don't think the reactor is causing it, but I did make a request to shut it down until we understand the situation better. The directors didn't like that. They said they don't want our funding agencies to think there's that level of problem. It's not an option until Dr Bee rules out the other hypotheses."

"Yet the first reports of symptoms came immediately after the reactor was switched on. How do you prefer to explain them?"

Yasira hesitated. Her own private thoughts about the matter were embarrassing. But this was just Aletheia keeping an eye on questionable science; a bit of embarrassment couldn't hurt her too much. And if she lied, the angel would probably see it in her microexpressions anyway. Lying to an angel was much worse than being embarrassed by the truth.

"I don't know exactly," she confessed. "But people get antsy around new things. Dr Bee says this can have a cascading psychosomatic effect. One person has a restless night at the wrong time. They blame it on the reactor. They tell their friends. When some of those friends have bad dreams, they wonder if that's the reactor too. If enough people tell enough other people, it becomes self-sustaining. People hear the rumors and worry themselves into a syndrome." She took a deep breath. "Frankly, sir, I think I'm the one that started it. This was my first really big project. The day of the ceremony, I was terrified. I got this irrational feeling something awful would happen. I ran around whining and triple-checking everything. It's no wonder a bit of anxiety spread."

The angel steepled his fingers. He looked intrigued. "When did that start? And what exactly were you concerned might happen?"

"I don't remember exactly. It was at least a day before the

ceremony. But I didn't have anything specific in mind. It was just this stupid, free-floating fear."

"Yet you took it seriously enough at the time that you petitioned Director Apek to delay the ceremony. Later, you made not one, but two formal requests to shut the reactor down again."

Yasira recoiled. So he knew about that; he'd heard it before. Yet a few questions ago he'd accused her of recklessly keeping the reactor *on*.

To get a reaction, she supposed. He was playing games. That bothered her.

"Before the final request," he continued, "the directors warned you that if such proceedings were public knowledge, they could contribute to public anxiety. Yet you continued. An odd strategy, if you really believe this is all in people's heads."

"Just because I believe something doesn't make it true," said Yasira. "Everyone's wrong sometimes. The consequences for being wrong here could be very bad. I wanted time to make sure I was right."

"Mm." There was a second's pause, and the angel's eyes unfocused slightly, as if he was flipping through records in his head. "Let's try a more pleasant line of inquiry, shall we? You worked with Dr Evianna Talirr on the prototype Shien Reactor. She was your doctoral mentor. A notoriously difficult one, but you and she shared a neurotype, and by all accounts you got along relatively well. Did you keep in touch after graduating?"

"I haven't seen her since anyone else saw her," Yasira snapped. Dr Talirr had disappeared the year after Yasira graduated, with the prototype already complete. It hadn't resembled the usual cases of Gods taking people away, either as sell-souls or for punishment. She'd just vanished and no one knew where. They hadn't been in regular touch by then; Dr Talirr was horrible at keeping up with correspondence, and Yasira had been increasingly unsure what to say to her. Still, she'd had the jitters for weeks, wondering what had gone wrong. If someone had hurt her. Or if Dr Talirr had simply given up on normal people and run. Or destroyed herself. Whether it was somehow, obscurely, her fault. Somehow the angel's question felt like an accusation.

"The Talirr-Shien Effect is named after both of you. A pity she isn't here to help you work this through."

Yasira's annoyance rose rapidly. People had made this sort of comment all her life. She was out of her depth, people said. She couldn't *really* understand what she studied, at her age and with her kind of brain. She was only parroting what her supervisors told her. No matter how much she achieved, no matter how much support there was from family, teachers, friends, and neurotutors, there was still someone saying it. People who said it to her face were bullies. Angels were supposed to be higher beings, weren't they? Angels were not supposed to be bullies.

"Are you offering," Yasira said through her teeth, "to put me in touch?"

"Of course not," said the angel, waving a hand. "She's not with us. Still, it's a shame. She used to give you unusual reading assignments, didn't she? Philosophy in particular."

"Why are you looking this up?" said Yasira, becoming increasingly alarmed. Yasira's graduate school assignments were not secret, but they were a very obscure non-secret, buried in a huge school filing system. A question like this meant the angel had been studying… well, not necessarily Yasira. Maybe just Dr Talirr. Maybe they were trying to find *her* – but how could angels not know where someone was?

"Are you quite certain," said the angel, ignoring her question, "that you understand everything she tried to teach you?"

Yasira, against her own best judgement, stood up.

"Stop this," she said. "You're the angel here. If you want the reactor shut down, tell the directors. If you think someone's doing something bad here, accuse them. If I'm missing something, tell me what it is. But if you're not giving real advice and you're not going to step in and help, then you can take your condescending bullshit somewhere else!"

It all came out in a rush, and then she checked herself, horrified.

She tried to remember if yelling at an angel was an actual crime. She didn't think so, but she'd never been good at Gods.

The angel did not look angry. He looked at her with no expression at all for a moment, then smiled. "Are you requesting divine assistance, Dr Yasira Shien? It's available for a price."

She sank back into her chair.

Of course she was not really asking. The whole point of the *Pride of Jai* was to push the limits of what mortals could do on their own. Bargaining for Aletheia's help would be worse than failing. It would be *cheating*.

Maybe this bully of an angel *wanted* the *Pride of Jai* to fail. Maybe one of the Gods had decided the whole thing was an affront to Them, but didn't want to say so directly. Maybe he had gone through this with each director and each team lead, hoping one of them was weak enough or desperate enough to start cutting corners.

Or maybe this whole thing had been a test of her temper. And she had failed spectacularly.

"No," she said softly. "I apologize."

The smile was gone now, his face unreadable. "Don't bother. I have the information I require. That will be all for now, Dr Shien."

Six days later, Yasira stared into her handheld gauge despondently. This was an additional sensor she and her team had rigged up – really just a mechanical dial that copied the readings from the official core reactor control panel, so she could watch the internal energy change without hovering over the actual Core subteam all the time. Alarms bleeped horribly from the sides of the room. Internal energy was rising, output falling, and the time dilation gap between the reactor and the rest of the room widening – again. It had happened so many times that it barely qualified as an emergency anymore. Everyone knew their jobs. They would monitor the event, record everything they could, and then comb the records for some clue as to why this was happening. Again. Yasira started to tap her fingers on the side of the dial, in time with the alarms, in exhausted irritation.

The handheld monitor's pointer suddenly jolted up and down in the same rhythm. Someone shouted in surprise elsewhere in the room.

Yasira startled and swore under her breath. Even jury-rigged as it was, the handheld gauge wasn't supposed to be so sensitive to vibrations. The last thing anyone needed here was a sensor malfunction.

What had the shout of surprise been for? Surely a sensor malfunction couldn't have also affected the main panel.

Yasira looked towards the core control panel, where the shout had come from. No one was hurt. People were pointing at the panel and arguing with each other.

She tapped her fingers rhythmically again, this time against her sterile-suited leg. The gauge matched her rhythm in the same way.

Yasira frowned, then untied the handheld gauge from its tether, letting it float in the air completely unconnected to anything. Keeping her eyes on the monitor, she tapped the fingertips of both hands against each other.

The pointer jumped in response.

This was a malfunction that made no physical sense at all.

Clenching her teeth to keep back sudden fear, Yasira left the monitor where it was and maneuvered herself to the core control pane. The Core subteam were squabbling and gesturing emphatically. They looked as frightened as she felt.

One turned to look at Yasira. "Dr Shien, it's started jumping."

"I know," said Yasira. So it wasn't just the monitor. Which meant anything could be happening. The problem could be in the official readouts. It could be in the actual energy of the reactor.

She tapped her fingers again, and this time she could see the official display dial jumping, just as the handheld monitor had. Her fingers' rhythm, perfectly replicated, despite the time dilation.

"What the fuck," said one of the scientists.

Yasira stopped tapping.

This time the display dial continued jumping in a rhythm of its own.

Three of the scientists were still looking at nothing but the dial, jabbering frantically at each other. One of them reached for his radio. Another, an Arinnan woman in her thirties, stared at Yasira. This one had seen her tapping her fingers.

"What did you just do?" said the woman.

"I don't know," said Yasira in a small voice.

The Arinnan woman turned back to her colleague with the radio. "Get a director in here," she said, even though fetching a director would normally be Yasira's job. "Something really—"

"No," said Yasira.

It came out of her before she knew what it meant. But these sudden, sharp fluctuations meant something. She recognized this. It was rhythmic, with short bursts of energy, long ones, pauses. Dots and dashes. A code she'd learned in high school, burying herself in books while her older classmates were busy dating and getting drunk.

"Get away from it," said Yasira. "Get everyone out of the reactor room." It was a whisper at first. She repeated it as a bellow from deep in her lungs. "Code 56. Evacuate. Everyone out!"

Code 56 was "Evacuation Emergency – Other." For when simple categories like impending explosions, gas leaks, and meltdowns didn't apply.

The dots and dashes from the inside of the Shien Reactor spelled words. Each small group of them, a letter, in an ancient Earth alphabet still used by many modern human languages. In the Earth creole every scientist on the *Pride of Jai* shared, they spelled:

LIES.

CHAPTER 3

We teach our students to accept themselves. Needing support is okay; not needing support is okay. In a crisis, more support may be needed – or you may discover a wellspring of unexpressed strength. You won't know what God your student follows until they are tested, so don't assume anything. Only work, in the moment, to find out the moment's needs.

LENNE FUONG, A NEUROTUTOR'S GUIDE

The generator room erupted into chaos. They'd done drills for a Code 56, but no one actually expected to have to use it. Yasira stared at the dial as lower-ranking scientists started to rush out of the room. By coincidence, she was nearest the switch that would begin the complex process of shutting the reactor down.

The dial leapt to the top of its range and shivered there. Simultaneously, all other output stopped.

Yasira slammed her hand down and yanked the switch. It did nothing. The alarm that went with the switch, to warn everyone that shutdown was beginning, didn't even sound.

Then the core itself – what could be seen of it, behind the nest of ducts and wires – began to shiver. Like the breathing Yasira had seen at the ceremony, but fast and violent. There was no mistaking it for a trick of the eyes. The wires themselves undulated in their casing.

Yasira grabbed her radio. "Shien to station control. Emergency. Code 56. Shutdown attempts failed. Get everyone off this station. This is not a drill. Repeat, get everyone out now."

She could not have explained it. She knew, with a shock of recognition like the one from the ceremony, that this was not merely some inquisitive intelligence, using her reactor and a simple code to open a channel. This was destruction.

"Roger that," said a director's voice. Yasira stuffed the radio back into its carrying case and flew across the generator room to Dr Gi's Transmission and Transformation controls.

"Switch the station to emergency power," she yelled. "That will buy us some time." The reactor wasn't shutting down, but that didn't mean it was going to keep putting out anything reliable while the crew escaped.

"Already on it," said Dr Gi, his small frame heaving as he pushed buttons frantically.

"Generator subteams!" Yasira shouted, her voice carrying over the hubbub. "The safe shutdown sequence is failing. Get out of the room. Everyone! No one stays!"

The lights abruptly dimmed as the *Pride of Jai's* emergency protocols kicked in. Luminescent blue arrows appeared on the walls, pointing the way to the nearest lifeboat.

Director Apek's tense voice crackled through the walls. "Attention, crew of the *Pride of Jai*. This is an emergency station evacuation. This is not a drill. Repeat, not a drill. Follow the emergency arrows to a lifeboat immediately."

He repeated the message, and Yasira pulled herself to the door. Dr Gi followed close behind her. His switch to conventional power seemed to have no effect on the reactor core. Its wires writhed and bubbled in a way that made no sense for wires.

Where was Tiv? Tiv hadn't been on the same shift as Yasira today. She must be somewhere on the station's periphery, on her own or with friends. There would be no way of telling if she was all right until the evacuation was done.

The people already leaving formed a mob, murmuring in panic. The corners of the walls began to move, curling in ways that geometry shouldn't have allowed.

Lifeboats were moored at equal intervals around the *Pride of Jai's* outer edge, but there was also one at the center for whoever was in a central mechanical area in an emergency. Every team had drilled the process of moving from the generator room to the lifeboat. But they hadn't practiced it in low light and in a panic. There was zero-gee pushing and shoving. Yasira hung back, unwilling to push to the front. Whatever this was, it was on her turf and her responsibility, and she had no right to trample innocent engineering grunts.

She flew through the corridors at the back of the mob, keeping up as best she could. Dr Gi, last to leave because of the switch to emergency power, maneuvered along at her side.

"Dr Shien," he puffed, "what is going on? What is the core *doing*?"

"I don't know," she said. "I don't know what this is called."

"You never hypothesized about any malfunctions that might cause something like this?"

"No!"

The only thing that this reminded her of was Dr Talirr. *Lies.* That was what Dr Talirr always muttered when she was most distressed. But – that was a stupid connection to make. It made no sense. There was no *mechanism–*

Director Apek's announcement repeated at top volume. The walls – with the ladder in them, which several people were using to guide themselves along – suddenly bucked like a boiling noodle. People shrieked and cursed as metal shavings and bits of plaster crumbled into the weightless air.

The panicked horde moved on. Mostly. A few people floated where the ladder had left them, motionless. The wall continued to undulate in front of them, like some sort of metal sea creature.

Yasira rushed instinctively to the first one. A square-jawed Riayin woman only a few years older than her. Not wounded, as far as Yasira could tell. Alive. But bleary. Staring at the moving wall as if it was a dream.

Yasira tried very hard to remember the woman's name. They'd been working in the same room, after all.

"Xaka," she snapped. Probably. Xaka what? Never mind. "Xaka, we've got to run. Can't you hear the alarm?"

"This can't actually be happening," Xaka said in a daze, her eyes fixed on the wall.

"Are you hurt?"

"I'm not hurt. Nothing is happening at all, can't you see?"

Yasira, for lack of any other ideas, slapped her in the face through her sterile suit. "It's happening," she said, as Xaka reeled. *"Run."*

Xaka, apparently shocked out of it for now, hurried after her.

By the time Yasira reached the central lifeboat, she and Dr Gi were urging along a small crowd of confused stragglers. They moved on their own, but only with constant support. Otherwise they stared, floated, murmured to themselves in dreamy voices. It was good that Yasira and Dr Gi were here. The rest of the crowd, she reflected in a distant rage, would have left them behind while...

While what?

The lifeboat's hatch was a bright welcoming light in the dim, blue-arrowed wall. Yasira kicked off the opposite bulkhead only to slip and suppress a shriek as it bucked unexpectedly under her feet. She caught herself above the hatch and swung in. Dr Gi and the stragglers tumbled in after her. The space was bordered by rows of padded straps to hang on to during acceleration. It was crammed full of scientists and engineers – not just the generator team, but the people who'd been working at life support and other central systems, too. Dr Hetram, waiting by the door, counted them up quickly.

The floor of the lifeboat wasn't buckling. Yet.

The *Pride of Jai's* designers had known that, in an emergency on a space station, it might become impossible to reach certain parts of the station from certain other parts. So the station had enough lifeboats to hold its own population twice over. But the central lifeboat was barely big enough to hold a full shift of workers in the central systems.

"Hundred forty-eight, hundred forty-nine, hundred fifty." Dr Hetram's movements were brisker than Yasira had ever seen before. "That's everybody on shift, and that's capacity. Grab a strap and we'll launch."

That wasn't what Yasira remembered from drills. "Wait. First we hail station control."

"Technically, yes. Only they stopped responding two minutes ago. We think their radio console is fried."

"What?"

Dr Hetram gave her an imperious look. Yasira swallowed hard and backed off. She'd dared to think that, if everyone followed procedures efficiently, they'd get out of this alive. That was what emergency procedures were *for*. But even with her whole shift aboard the central lifeboat, that left a lot of people on the periphery, including Tiv. People who might or might not have anyone to help them, if they got slowed down like Xaka.

Dr Hetram turned his attentions to the control panel to one side of the hatch, punching a button like an oversized version of the one on Yasira's radio. "Lifeboat 1 to all lifeboats. We are at capacity and launching. Repeat, Lifeboat 1 launching."

"Copy that, Lifeboat 1. You're the first." People from half a dozen other lifeboats responded, each listing the number of people aboard.

Dr Hetram took his hand off that button and flipped a series of switches. The hatch sealed itself. There was a roar as the lifeboat's engines engaged, and a series of thunks as it detached from the *Pride of Jai*. Gravity went every which way. People shrieked and smacked into the padded walls. Yasira's head spun. She wanted to throw up. Then she was floating again, as the *Pride of Jai* spun away.

Yasira pulled on a strap to get her bearings back and stared out one of the lifeboat's tiny portholes. The station's convulsions were visible from the outside, a shiver like that of a hypothermic animal – though the lifeboat's walls, for now, stayed solid.

This was a thing Yasira had done. She did not know how, or even what it was. But she had let something into the station that no one could understand. She was responsible. An angel had even tried to warn her that she didn't know what she was doing, and she hadn't listened.

Dr Hetram was looking out the porthole too, his face darkening as he watched, white hair floating around him like a halo. He looked confused and chagrined, like everyone.

"How could this happen?" he said, and Yasira wasn't sure if he was asking her directly or not. His voice, imperious and urgent all through the launch sequence, had begun to waver.

"I don't know," Yasira said. Nobody knew, except possibly Diligence Young.

"Not even you," said Hetram. She had expected hostility from the old, pinched doctor, but instead he looked lost.

Something new moved in the porthole. Just off the center of the *Pride of Jai*, where the generator room had been, the shivering intensified until the hull broke apart. There was no fire, nor even the metal jetsam of a real breakup. Instead there was something in the space where the hull had been. Something that bent Yasira's eyes as she looked at it. A shining, blooming darkness that screamed recognition at Yasira, though she was certain she had never seen anything like it before.

The darkness spread, crumpling the hull in its wake, towards the periphery. Towards the people in the other lifeboats, who lacked this vantage point and could not see it.

They were all going to die.

She turned to Dr Hetram. "Hang on. Move over." She vaulted to the control panel, caught herself on the nearby straps, and punched the radio button. "Lifeboat 1 to all lifeboats. The *Pride of Jai* is breaking apart, repeat, breaking apart. Launch now."

A cacophony of voices complained back at her. None were recognizable as directors.

"Lifeboat 1, are you sure? There's no depressurization here, I'm not getting any of the alarms that would–"

"Copy that, Lifeboat 1, I–"

"Lifeboat 3b to Lifeboat 1, negative, we still have people coming in–"

"Leave them!" Yasira shouted into the radio. The darkness was still creeping up the *Pride of Jai's* arms. "Trust me and leave them or you're all going to die. The *Pride of Jai* is breaking apart from the inside. You have ten seconds. Launch *now*!"

Most of the voices quieted at that. Blue lights like fireflies lifted off, one after the other, from the *Pride of Jai's* edges. But one voice continued. "Lifeboat 4a to Lifeboat 1, I refuse. You are not a director and do not have the authority. You are not corroborated by the alarms. I've got dozens of people still running this way, I'm not about to– oh, shit–"

Then there was static.

Darkness crawled up the *Pride of Jai's* spokes and swallowed it completely. There was a roil, for a moment, as if darkness itself could move. Then the swirling space imploded and was gone. Nothing left but the starry night sky.

The radio was silent for fifteen seconds.

When Yasira did hear another voice, it sounded as shaken as she felt. "Good call, Lifeboat 1."

Eight lifeboats had launched. None but Lifeboat 1 were at full capacity. Two-thirds of the people on the unfinished *Pride of Jai* had escaped.

Two thirds.

That meant more than a hundred people were dead. Director Apek, who had supported Yasira at every step, was probably dead. Probably all the directors were. Surely if one of them had survived whatever happened to their radio and made it to a lifeboat, they would have taken charge when they got there, and she would have heard their voice. All of them were dead.

There was also Tiv. And there was no way to know just yet what had happened to Tiv.

Yasira stared out the porthole, hands shaking, and tried to understand what she had done.

Dr Hetram took over the controls as normal protocols resumed. Each lifeboat was to drop into a lower orbit around the planet Jai and get in touch by radio with a spaceport on the ground. A safety assessment would be performed. If a lifeboat got the green light, it would commence re-entry and fall into the ocean. Otherwise – if external shielding was damaged, for instance – a God-built ship would dock with them, and they would take God-built portals to the surface. The Gods were so considerate. Even on a mission like this, where humans had shunned them in favor of human effort, they would make sure all the survivors were okay. For all the good it did those other hundred.

A crowd was beginning to gather. Dr Gi tapped Yasira on the shoulder. "You okay?"

Yasira mumbled a reply.

This, of course, drew in five other concerned scientists who would not stop asking if she was okay.

"Yes, I'm fine!" Yasira shouted.

She could barely think, but what did that matter? There was nothing more she could do. Everybody in danger of dying was dead.

Leave them, she'd said. It had come out so quickly. It made mathematical sense – better a lifeboat half-full of survivors than none. But who exactly had she been telling them to leave behind? Her friends? The directors? *Tiv?* It was selfish to think of Tiv, maybe. Everybody on the station was someone's friend, someone's family, someone's Tiv.

The people who weren't poking at Yasira or trying to comfort each other had clustered around Dr Hetram's radio, calling out the names of lovers, friends, colleagues. The noise made things worse.

"Wyn Alincra Dimot. Please, I need to know if Wyn Alincra Dimot is alive."

"Chirik Ca, what lifeboat is he on?"

"Klea Ikatogmolara Auzok–"

"Etiquette Hill–"

"Mesijdy, my friend Mesijdy–"

"Can't you please find Leigh Zung for me?"

Tiv, Yasira wanted to add, but she did not. Yasira had the ability to use her rank to push to the front of the line. And that wasn't fair. She would wait.

Dr Hetram waved his arms at the crowd. "I am finding a safe orbit and talking to ground control. This is going to take a while. Your loved ones will remain in the same lifeboats when I am finished."

Outside the portal where the *Pride of Jai* had been, there was nothing. Not even debris. Blackness and stars, like the station had never existed.

Floating here lost in emotion was not going to help. She needed something distracting, something physical. Yasira peeled off her sterile suit, as most people in the lifeboat had already done, and dug out a microgravity-approved first aid kit. She started to make the rounds, disinfecting and bandaging wounds. It was simple work, work she'd been trained for, if rarely needed to use – work that did not require critical thought. Nobody was seriously injured, but everyone had scrapes and bruises. There was occasional blood in the air, which had to be carefully vacuumed up. A girl her age had vomited into a bag, and that definitely had to be dealt with.

An older Arinnan man grabbed Yasira's shoulders as she tried to bandage his sprained ankle.

"What was that?" he demanded, staring into her eyes. "You senior scientists, you should know. What the hell happened to us? What did I *see?*"

Yasira squeaked and tried to pull away, but the man shook her, holding firm. The motion made them both spin out into the middle of the room and bash into the far wall. "You don't know, do you? That's why you won't talk to me? The entire *Pride of Jai* disintegrated, and you rich, famous head scientists don't even know the reason."

Dr Gi and another subteam leader pried the man off her. Yasira caught a strap on the ceiling and steadied herself.

"Thanks," she mumbled. She felt guilty. It wasn't fair to be angry at that man. Everyone in here was wondering the same thing. But she had no answer.

"You should get over there," said Dr Gi, "listen to the radio."

Yasira's mouth worked a moment before she could get out the word. "Why?"

"They're taking the roll call," said Dr Gi. "We're cleared for re-entry in a couple of hours, once we're over the ocean. So the hard stuff is over for now. Dr Hetram wanted to go in alphabetical order, but everyone recognized your voice when – well, when we launched.

There was a girl on Lifeboat 6a who was very insistent that we tell you how she was doing, right away." Dr Gi reached out as if to squeeze Yasira's shoulder, then looked at her expression and seemed to think better of it. "Tiv's alive, Dr Shien. A bit scraped up. But she's all right."

Yasira began to weep with relief.

Re-entry was a bruising, rumbling ride, and then there was wide blue water and sky. Blue everywhere. The eight lifeboats each extruded an orange rubber flotation device, and after some tedious radio triangulation, each was dragged to the deck of a huge, empty cargo ship. Then there was a nervous-making, seemingly unending wait for the all clear, before the lifeboats' hatches thumped open and everyone streamed onto the open deck.

Actual wind smacked Yasira in the face as soon as she disembarked, blowing her hair every which way. She froze for a moment, overwhelmed: she had forgotten how *big* everything was planetside. The smell of the salt spray, the crying of gulls. *Birds.* There had been no animals on the *Pride of Jai.* Even the deck of the cargo ship was a shock. It was plain gray metal like most of the *Pride of Jai,* but it stretched out in every direction, so much bigger than anything she'd grown used to in space.

Several people seemed to be having this reaction. Others, unafflicted and impatient, shoved through the crowd to lean over the ship's railing, or to speak to the crew, or to find the people they'd been asking after on the radio. Someone was making a beeline for Yasira right now in this manner.

"Yasira!" she shouted, and only then did Yasira pull herself out of her stupor and recognize who it was.

"Tiv!" she called back, and the two of them collided in a painfully tight embrace.

Tiv was all right, minus a couple of bruises – or at least her body was. She said nothing for a long time, only sobbed and squeezed until Yasira thought her ribs would crack.

"It's okay, sweetie." said Yasira, surprised at the lack of tears in her own wavering voice. She felt heavy, empty and tired in ways that had nothing to do with tears anymore. A hundred people were dead. Nothing was ever going to be okay. "It's okay."

She didn't know what else to say. There were no other words.

"Our friends," Tiv choked out later, when the crowd had thinned a bit and the worst of the tears had been wrung out of her. "Nuong didn't make it out. Or Vent, or Honor. Or the directors…"

"Oh, sweetie." This did make Yasira want to cry, though her eyes did not cooperate. "I'm so sorry. Ssh."

Yasira hadn't been as close to Tiv's friends as Tiv liked to think. Friendships, in her experience, were fickle things. But she had liked them well enough when Tiv brought them along, and she knew their names and habits. Nuong was a boardgame enthusiast who dragged Yasira and Tiv to game nights when they were free, and whooped ecstatically whenever she beat them at anything. Vent – short for Inventiveness – was a cheerful life-support tech who'd gone to university with Tiv, and had a habit of checking Tiv out when he thought Yasira wasn't looking. Yasira hadn't liked that at all, though Tiv had insisted there was no problem. It surprised her that she liked the thought of his death even less.

"It's not your fault," Tiv whispered. Yasira shook her head, not sure if she believed it, or even if Tiv did. Good girls said that kind of thing because they were good girls, because their first instinct was to reassure, not because they'd really thought through the issues of causality and moral responsibility.

She supposed she should treasure the moment. Not a lot of people were going to say this to her in the future. Everyone knew that the trouble had started in the reactor room. Everyone knew it was hers. She would probably never work again; certainly not as the head of a project like this. She would probably face, if not criminal charges, then an absolute bear of a lawsuit. She deserved it. She'd killed all those people, though not with intent. And if she could make something like this happen and not know why, there was probably something wrong with her. Maybe the bullies had been right all along, and little Yasira Shien, in over her head, should never have tried to do science.

45

What had that message meant, that oddly human code, delivered so inhumanly? *Lies.* At the time, Yasira hadn't questioned; she'd known it meant the end of everything. Now she wasn't sure. Who, or what, had been speaking? Why speak at all, if you were about to kill everyone listening? What did it mean, that of all the words available to speak, they had chosen Dr Talirr's?

Tiv gradually quieted as they walked to the edge of the deck holding hands, staring out at the sea. There was very little worth saying. People Yasira vaguely recognized came over once in a while, patted one or both of them sympathetically on the shoulder, and filled them in on what was going on. They were in the ocean off the coast of Stijon, and the crew didn't speak much of the scientists' Earth creole – although, of course, a third of the survivors were native speakers of Stijonan. The ship had a small God-built portal below deck, but for now it was off limits. The crew wanted to bring some Stijonan authorities onto the carrier first for debriefing. Or they wanted to wait for a psychologist's advice, though they were evasive about why. Or perhaps they weren't authorized to let anyone off the carrier at all. Every Stijonan-speaking person on board gave a different account.

"Dr Shien," said someone behind her presently, in perfect Riayin.

She turned, and her heart sank. It was Diligence Young, the angel of Aletheia. She couldn't think of a person she was less interested in speaking to now. Back on the *Pride of Jai*, he had known something was wrong. He had *known*, dammit, and instead of helping, all he'd done was drop hints at Yasira and gloat. What was he going to do now? Arrest her? Or just gloat a little longer?

"Yes?" she said.

Diligence smiled with insincere warmth, like a politician. "I'd like to talk to you in private, if I may."

"All right." Yasira forced an equally insincere smile and squeezed Tiv's hand, turning briefly to her. "I won't be long."

Tiv let go only reluctantly. "Okay."

Yasira followed the angel into the interior of the cargo ship, a maze of inner corridors nearly as tight as the *Pride of Jai's,* albeit with more signs of age and use, and a machine-oil smell. Apart from the smell, the tight quarters were oddly comforting. Diligence guided her to what looked at first like an empty cabin. A second angel stood by the door: a tall, broad, muscular woman too dark to be from Jai, with circuitry not only in her head but all the way up her hands and arms. Instead of ordinary limbs she had articulated ones formed of intricate, dextrous metal, folding into guns, claws, and other mechanisms Yasira could not identify. As she watched, a complex origami folded the end of one limb into something very much like a human hand, then back out of that shape again.

"This is my associate, Enga," said Diligence breezily, as Yasira tried not to stare. "The arms can be intimidating at first, can't they? Try not to dwell on them. She doesn't like that." He shut the door behind them. "Don't worry; we're only here to talk."

Enga did not move. Diligence ushered Yasira to a chair right next to the door, with Enga looming over her. Yasira focused obediently on him, not on the God-built cybernetics. Enga's arms bothered her, even when she looked away. Why would angels of Aletheia, collectors of knowledge and observers of science, need so many weapons?

Something was wrong here, but she didn't want to think about it. She was tired. Too much was wrong already. Angels would always have their secrets, and the best thing to do was smile and nod.

"What did you want to talk about?" she asked Diligence, already resigned to the answer.

Diligence paused, consulting some file in his head. "Approximately thirty minutes before the *Pride of Jai* was destroyed, we detected unexpected large-scale spatial distortions in the vicinity. Distortions which persist in the station's absence, though they are slowly fading."

And what had the Gods done in those thirty minutes? Yasira shook her head. It was she who had to do the explaining here, not him. "Look, I had no idea that would happen. When we started getting unexpected readings, I checked and rechecked the science and nothing showed—"

Diligence held up his hand, cutting her off. "Yasira Shien. You just came close to destroying the fabric of reality. By accident. This makes you one of the most dangerous beings in the universe." He stood and Yasira opened her mouth to protest before he cut her off again. "Which is exactly what I need."

As Yasira tried to work out how to interpret this, the other angel – Enga – abruptly grabbed her hand. The metal grip was cold and… sharp? No, the hand itself shouldn't be sharp, despite its intricate parts. But something in it had pricked Yasira's skin.

She pulled away, horrified. "Excuse me. What did you just…"

She tried to make more words, but her tongue suddenly felt swollen and her vision fuzzy. She sagged, and Enga caught her, holding her semi-upright. The metal arms were thick and strong, stronger than any human arms, but cold. Diligence turned away and left the room, speaking to someone who'd been waiting outside as Yasira struggled to stand. "Quarantine the survivors and monitor them for any signs. We'll have more forces here within the hour."

Yasira silently raged. Of course this being would lie to her. Of course he would pretend to want a quiet place to talk, when he really wanted…

What, exactly?

Before Yasira could work out any sensible answers, her eyes rolled back in her head and darkness descended.

CHAPTER 4

This one is interesting, at least. I've never seen the typical Outside symptoms so heavily masked. Recommending caution until we can have a better look. Get on her good side. If we don't know how she ticks, we won't know just what she's capable of until it's too late.

MEMO BY DR MATESZNOA MEYEMA, SELL-SOUL OF NEMESIS, RE: AKAVI AVERIS'S FIRST REPORT ON DR YASIRA SHIEN

Yasira's vision fuzzed, and a room coalesced around her.

She was in a soft, black armchair. That was all she registered at first. She was sitting there half-slumped, like she'd been sleeping. Her head hurt and her eyes and mouth felt full of cotton. Her stomach felt like it would turn itself inside out at the slightest provocation.

She had been drugged, she remembered. They must have moved her here while she was out, wherever "here" was. She wasn't physically restrained. She was in the same clothes as before, but they itched and stank with all the stress-sweat of the last... She turned her head to check her watch and then had to close her eyes tightly, sitting very still, to stop herself from vomiting. Moving was still a bad idea.

Angels had taken her away. Where was she? Were they going to punish her now, for killing all those people? It was the first thing that came to mind, but... *Exactly what I need,* Diligence had said. That didn't sound quite like punishment. This plush armchair, free from restraints, didn't seem like a punishment either. And, for crimes as big as killing a hundred people, Aletheia's angels weren't the ones who did the punishing.

Aletheia was the God of knowledge. Her activities were *about* knowledge. Advancing the already mind-boggling state of the Gods' own sciences. Making deals with mortals, taking souls or other services in return for glimpses of that knowledge. Monitoring mortal science and keeping it on track. Aletheian angels would sometimes correct scientists who weren't on that right track. Warn them away before they accidentally hurt someone or invented a heresy. But Aletheians weren't the ones who disappeared people. If they had kidnapped her, they probably just wanted to know something. Or they wanted *her* to know something too elaborate to explain in one sitting.

She opened her eyes and tried to refocus on the room. There were other chairs around, and a coffee table. It was like a fancy hotel suite: almost a living room, but too pristine and too devoid of personal effects to be real. To one side there was a niche with a working desk, and on the opposite wall, a wide glass window, looking out into the night.

Wait.

Not quite the night. The stars were slowly moving, and they had the steady untwinkling stare that she'd taken for granted in space.

So she was on a ship, or a station. Or a base on a moon. It was nothing like the *Pride of Jai*. Nothing on the *Pride of Jai* was this spacious. And that window! On the *Pride of Jai*, the few portholes were small, thick, triple-paned apertures which the maintenance teams watched uneasily. A window of this size was showing off.

There was no hum of engines, no hiss of air recyclers, none of the usual white noise of space. Yasira grunted, to test if something was wrong with her ears. Her voice sounded normal, but her throat felt dry. She snapped her fingers, and that sounded the same as always.

It didn't smell like a spaceship. The only scent, apart from Yasira's own, was a faint, pleasant linen smell, like everything had just been reupholstered. No metal shavings, no damp plaster, no faint tang of ozone. The artificial gravity was as steady as the surface of a planet. Well, for all she knew, they *might* be on the surface of a planet, if it moved fast and had no atmosphere.

There were plenty of mortal ships and stations across the galaxy. Most had God-built parts here and there: pocket power generators, warp drives, portals, ansibles. But humans paid dearly for all those parts. Most human ships were cramped and careful affairs like the *Pride of Jai*, built with human sweat except for those few expensively miraculous parts. If Yasira was on a ship, then a ship like this – huge, elegant, perfect in every way – could only be the property of a God.

So she'd not just been kidnapped by Aletheian angels, but taken to angel territory. Not terribly surprising. It still raised the question of just what those angels wanted her for.

She tried to remember what Diligence had said.

He said, *Quarantine the survivors and monitor them…*

Quarantine meant there was something contagious. How could that be? Maybe whatever had made the walls move like that also had an effect on humans, sometimes.

Yasira pictured human flesh moving like that and bit down a mouthful of bile. She'd been taken to wherever this was, but Tiv was almost certainly still down there in the quarantine. Maybe it wasn't what she was picturing. But something had made the survivors potentially dangerous to those around them. Or maybe ordinary people were potentially dangerous to the survivors. Neither of those options boded well for Tiv, or Dr Gi and Dr Hetram, or anyone else who'd managed to get off the *Pride of Jai*.

Or Yasira, come to think of it.

Did Diligence know what had come through the Shien Reactor to say, *Lies*? Did he think that thing was still lingering, somehow, around or within the survivors?

She ought to find out where she was. She couldn't see all of the room from her chair, so she waited, anxious and uncomfortable, taking slow breaths until the nausea died down a bit. Then she pushed herself to her feet and stumbled to the window.

This place was in orbit after all. The sphere of a planet turned far below her feet, half in day and half in night. The continents weren't the ones she remembered from Jai – or from Anetaia, the only other planet she'd spent significant time on. The colors were earthlike, though, and twinkling lights on the night side showed them as human-inhabited. Or *something*-inhabited.

Yasira waited, leaning on the glass, until her stomach restabilized. Then, supporting herself with a hand on the wall, she made her way through the rest of the suite.

A corner of the room she'd had trouble seeing from her armchair led to a short hallway with three doors, one of thick metal, two small and domestic. She tried the metal door first. It had no handles but two large buttons, one red and one green. She tried each one in turn, but neither one did anything, and pushing didn't work either. So she was locked in here. That wasn't surprising. She wouldn't want to give one of the most dangerous beings in the universe free run of her ship, either.

She glanced through the other doors. The first led to a bedroom, as spacious and hotel-like as the living room. The second was a tiled, pristine bathroom, with a shower big enough to wash a horse.

Yasira stared at the shower with sudden longing. Her skin itched, her hair felt lank and greasy, and she smelled. On the *Pride of Jai*, the water recyclers only worked so fast. Even in Yasira's privileged room, she'd had only a tiny, unreliable shower that switched off after ten minutes. Divine ships were surely a different story…

She felt foolish. This was not relevant to working out why she was here, and she didn't want Diligence Young to come looking for her while she was in the shower. She didn't want to stink like this when she talked to angels, either. Physical needs won out. She shut the door firmly behind her, stripped, and turned the water as hot as it would go.

The steam knocked some of the nausea straight out of her. On impulse, she cupped her hands under the showerhead, brought them to her mouth, and discovered she had been deeply thirsty.

What did it mean if she was one of the most dangerous beings in the universe? Surely it was the Shien Reactor that was dangerous, not Yasira. Or maybe that wasn't true. Maybe the reactor should have been safe, but something about Yasira interacted with it catastrophically. That would explain why the reactor had responded to her tapping, but what else would it imply?

When the steam became overwhelming, Yasira turned it colder. A dispenser on the wall provided as many sweet-smelling soaps and shampoos as she liked. Finally she turned off the water and climbed out, toweling herself off. She felt better, though still dizzy, and still with an aching head.

While she dried off, a small panel which she'd mistaken for ventilation opened. Something crawled out. Yasira shrieked and jumped back. It was the size of a rabbit, but its body plan was nothing like an animal: too many legs, for starters. It was all moving parts, with no stable head or trunk: like the intricate metal of Enga's hands, but even more so.

A bot, she realized after a heart-thumping moment. A God-built robot. This was technology the Gods didn't give to mortals for any price. It climbed into the shower and scaled the walls, methodically sanitizing and drying them.

Well, that was one way to keep a hotel suite clean.

Yasira leaned in to watch more closely, fascinated despite herself. The cleaning appendages were so tiny and precise. This was way beyond anything Yasira had ever worked with. There must be thousands of these bots on this ship, not just cleaning but doing maintenance, upgrades, a thousand finicky tasks unsuited to human hands…

A second bot crept in, extended a pincerlike appendage, grabbed Yasira's dirty clothes, and made for the vent.

"Hey!" Yasira shouted. She leapt after the bot, too slow. "Hey, those are mine!" The bot, and her clothes, vanished into the little tunnel in the wall.

Yasira pulled the towel more tightly around her body, feeling more foolish and vulnerable than ever. She'd done this in the wrong order. She should have gone looking for clean clothes, *then* showered.

She rubbed her aching forehead, then padded to the bedroom. Three clean outfits awaited her in the closet. Plain-looking, but sensible and businesslike. Yasira picked up a sleeve and rolled the pale fabric between two fingers, frowning. Strong, soft, cool to the touch. She didn't recognize the material, but it felt good on her skin, as most fabrics did not. Were these God-built clothes? Were there fashion designer angels somewhere, churning these things out? One would think they had better things to do.

Yasira shrugged off the towel and dressed quickly. Underclothes, simple shoes, a plain off-white tunic and pants. Everything fit perfectly. Yasira decided not to think too hard about that.

She walked back to the living room and examined the alcove with the desk. There was an elegant, ergonomic chair, a wooden surface, and a blank, black screen. Nothing else. No drawers, no papers.

Yasira knew a computer when she saw one, but the *Pride of Jai* had only large, clunking mainframes made from transistors and vacuum tubes. Planetside, most people didn't even have that. Old Humans used to have a lot of computers before the Morlock War, but the Gods had taken them away. Anything much more powerful than a pocket calculator was a potential heresy. The Gods themselves were made from a very advanced sort of computer, after all, though they were much more than that now.

Experimentally, Yasira brushed the tip of her finger across the screen. With a low chime, it lit up, displaying words against a pleasant, flowery background.

Welcome, Dr Yasira Shien. This is your personal console for the Menagerie *nonsentient network system. Please touch the screen anywhere to continue.*

Yasira touched again, surprised. They must mean to keep her here, at least for a while, if they'd bothered to set up a computer for her. The words winked out and refreshed. *Our records indicate you have not used personal console technology before. This tutorial, tailored to your reported aptitude profile, security clearance, and learning style, will guide you through the basic skills of operation. You may pause and resume the tutorial at any time, or return to a previous section…*

She was still reading when someone knocked at the metal door.

"May I come in?" said an unfamiliar voice.

Yasira was so startled at the idea of an angel asking permission for this, after everything else they had gone ahead and done, that she almost forgot to answer. "Um, sure," she said after a pause. "Whatever."

An instant later she wished she hadn't said it that way. A new person was good. A new person might be able to tell her why she was here, which, so far, the tutorial had not done.

The door slid open and shut. An angel stepped through, holding a small bundle: something wrapped in cloth napkins atop a stack of papers. He looked startlingly young, like he'd sold his soul as soon as he could vote. He was pretty in a boyish, gangling sort of way, with long hair carefully combed out of the way of the titanium plates in his forehead.

"My name's Elu Ariehmu. Hi," he said, nodding to her. It was a Preli name, not anything native to Jai. He spoke Riayin easily but with a faint, musical accent. He gestured to a couple of armchairs. "I was sent to make sure you're comfortable, now that you're awake. How are you feeling?"

"Slightly kidnapped," said Yasira, moving to join him. She regretted it the instant she said it; of course they'd kidnapped her. She'd just killed a hundred people.

The angel didn't seem angry, though. Also, he'd left the divine designation out of his name. Was he not Aletheia's? Maybe Aletheia and another God were collaborating. But if so, why would he try to hide it?

Elu smiled sheepishly. "Of course. I'm sorry. Time was of the essence."

"Why? I don't understand any of this. The *Pride of Jai* blew up, and then Diligence Young drugged me, and now I'm here. What do you want? Do you work with him?"

"Yes. I'm his assistant." So this one did answer questions, up to a point. That was good. "Why you're here is a bit complicated, but I can explain some of it. Can I ask how you're feeling physically? Any lingering nausea? Muscle aches? Chills or shivering?"

"I don't know. I was feeling sick before, but it's mostly gone. Just a little light-headed now, and my head hurts."

"Oh, that's probably blood sugar more than the lykofonol. You haven't eaten since, what…"

Yasira frowned, only now calling this to mind herself. "Yesterday breakfast. I think. Was the disaster yesterday?"

"It was yesterday, yes. You were sedated about twelve hours. Part of it was semi-natural sleep."

"Are you a doctor, then?"

Elu smiled. "We don't exactly have doctors here. There are medical researchers, but for most clinical care we just have bots. And people who program the bots. Less error that way. I brought you something to eat."

He handed her the top item from the bundle, which turned out, when unwrapped, to be a large, Preli-style dumpling. Still warm. She hesitated. This man might seem nice, but he was one of her kidnappers, and she was one of the most dangerous beings in the universe. There could be a million kinds of poison in this thing.

Except if they wanted to poison her, they could just send Enga again or a bot, now, couldn't they? They could have already injected her with anything while she was lying there unconscious in the fancy chair.

She bit into the dumpling and her stomach snapped to attention. Sweet, fluffy pastry wrapped around spiced meat and crisp vegetables. It was either the best dumpling she'd ever tasted or she'd really been that ravenous and not noticed. She wolfed it down.

"Do you have another?" she asked, wiping her fingers on the napkin.

"I think we should wait an hour or so," said Elu, "just to make sure your digestive system handles it. But after that, yes. How's your console tutorial going? I gave you text-sending clearance to me, so if you need anything while I'm not around, there's a program you can use to alert me."

Yasira looked at him sharply. "Because I'm not allowed out of the room to get food for myself."

She suddenly felt ashamed of enjoying the dumpling. This was textbook captivity stuff. It was their fault she was locked up and needed to ask for food in the first place, and here she was, feeling grateful to them when they gave her any. Stupid.

She forced her face into a scowl.

"Not yet, no." Elu fiddled with his long hair uncomfortably. "A God-built ship can be overwhelming all at once. There's not much real danger, but for now, until you understand a little more, we wanted to keep you in a safe place."

"This place isn't safe." The shame spread to every nice thing she could remember since waking up. The clean clothes, the interesting bots, the blissfully hot shower. Even Elu's apparent human decency, which might be an act. These things were pittances to the Gods. They were no reason at all to feel grateful. "A bot stole my clothes. I don't know what planet we're orbiting. I don't know what's happening back on Jai. I don't know if you're going to kill me for blowing up the space station even though it was an accident. I don't even know if Tiv's alive!"

Elu blinked, as if this hadn't occurred to him. "Oh, planetside. I'm sorry, I should have checked that for you right away. Of course you're upset. Hold on." He stared into space a moment, accessing something on the ansible nets. The blank, looking-elsewhere expression was much more obvious on him than on Diligence. "Tiv is Productivity Hunt, right?"

"Yes," said Yasira.

"Okay, I'm looking at the latest report. Things are still a bit disorganized, but she's in the records and she's all right. She's still quarantined with everyone else, and there's some understandable distress. I mean, what with living through yesterday, and losing track of you, and still not being home yet. But she's testing clean. She hasn't shown any warning signs of..." He paused, and Yasira realized she'd reached a boundary on what this angel was allowed to tell her. "Of anything that would be a major concern. There are a few people more affected, but nothing that looks contagious, so far. If things go as expected, she'll be free to go in a few weeks."

Sudden, foolish hope bloomed. This fancy ship probably had ansibles all over. "Can I talk to her?"

Something in Elu's expression closed off. "I'm sorry, no. And I can't contact her on your behalf. I understand, believe me. But this mission is top-secret."

"For what?" Yasira's voice rose to a near-yell. "You're Aletheians. You do *research!* What bloody research project is so sensitive that–"

"Dr Shien. No." His voice was soft still, his gestures placating, but there was an urgency underneath that stilled her. "I don't know what Diligence told you. But this isn't an Aletheian ship. We're not Aletheians. You're here at the behest of Nemesis. Do you understand?"

Yasira stared at him.

"Oh, shit," she said, crumpling. "Oh, *shit.*"

Nemesis was the most dangerous God: the one who handled heretics and criminals. The one whose very superconducting chips were steeped in righteous wrath and drained of mercy. The one who hunted down rebels and heretics, destroying them in this life, tormenting them in the next. This made *far* more sense than Aletheians kidnapping Yasira, after what she had done. Elu worked for Her. And Yasira had been fool enough to snap at him!

"It's…" Elu backpedaled, alarmed. "It's not like that. I'm sorry, I shouldn't have said it like that. Listen, you're not under arrest."

"Of course not, you're Elu Ariehmu of *Nemesis*, you can just hold me without charges–"

"Nobody's trying to interrogate you. Nobody has any plans to hurt you, Dr Shien–"

"Of course that's what you'd say. That's why you've been nice. You're the *good* cop!"

"Dr Shien, please listen–"

She was hyperventilating now, past listening. "I swear I didn't know what was going to happen on the *Pride of Jai*. There's no mortal model for things going wrong like – like whatever it was that happened. I still don't even *understand* what happened. It wasn't–"

"Yasira." He slipped out of his chair and folded his long limbs to crouch by her feet, supplicatory. He didn't touch her, but his eyes held hers, wide and pained. "I know. Nemesis knows. You're here because we need you."

Yasira caught her breath and stared back at him. "What?"

Elu climbed back up on the chair, perching on the edge. "I told you it's complicated. But I can say a little. I can tell you what we'd like you to do for us. First, calm down."

Yasira took a deep breath. It didn't help much. "Diligence said I was one of the most dangerous beings in the universe. What does that mean?"

Elu looked taken aback. "He said that?"

"Yes!"

The angel covered his mouth, suppressing an odd smile. Exasperation and – something else. "He would. He exaggerates. You've been… involved with some very dangerous things, and come through with much less damage than one would expect. That's interesting to us. But don't read too much into it. There's nothing monstrous about you."

"So what's the second thing?"

"Well, you've lived through something terrible. And you're in a unique position to help us understand what went wrong. But it's also more complicated than you know. We'd like you to help us in an investigation, Dr Shien."

"A what?"

He handed her the bundle of papers in his arms. "First, we need to get you up to speed on what we know. We'd like you to start by reading these. You might not understand everything in them, but we want to talk to you about what you do understand. I've sent full scans to your console, but I figured you might appreciate a hard copy."

Yasira leafed through them, intrigued. If there was information that could help explain what had happened yesterday, she certainly did want it. This was enough reading for a fairly heavy-duty graduate course. It started with a few academic papers in familiar publication-ready formats, then devolved into draft papers, laboratory notes… What was this at the bottom? A personal diary. Each item in the stack was stamped with the same single name.

Dr Evianna Talirr.

Dr Talirr had worked with Yasira on the Shien Reactor prototype. Diligence had called attention to that fact, before the disaster.

Dr Talirr had been the one, before she disappeared, who was constantly muttering about *lies*.

"What is going on here?" Yasira said plaintively.

Elu gave her a wan smile. "That's what we're trying to figure out."

A few hours earlier, the being who had called himself Diligence Young of Aletheia paced the cargo ship that housed the survivors from the *Pride of Jai*. Diligence's real name was Akavi Averis, Inquisitor of Nemesis, and he was growing sick of his cover identity. The ship's name was the *Leunt*, and its amenities were pitiful. There wasn't even a proper sickbay, just a small cabin which he had repurposed as a psychologist's office.

Akavi had not wanted to bother with psychological assessment. With only one trustworthy diagnostician, it would take weeks. He had filed a formal request to vaporize the *Leunt*, after removing Yasira, and kill everyone else aboard. But Irimiru, his supervisor, had forbidden it. Anyone with a dangerous level of Outside contamination could be found by Dr Meyema and put away individually. This mission had high visibility. Gods needed a certain amount of mortal cooperation to keep Themselves fed, and the mortal reaction to angels destroying this ship wouldn't be worth the small risk of letting them live. So Akavi had to be here in person, dealing with the tedium of actual physical arrangements.

Information flickered, overlaid on his vision and streaming at high speed through parts of his consciousness that mortals lacked a word for. He could see, in real time, a diagram maintained by the four junior angels temporarily assigned to him aboard the *Leunt*, tracking the locations and basic states of the *Pride of Jai's* survivors. Docile passengers, folded into their private worlds of grief, exhaustion, or dissociation, were marked in green; restless ones in yellow. If someone became dangerously agitated, Akavi would see it in his mind's eye before he was even officially alerted. Smaller windows informed him of Elu and Enga's activities, the *Leunt's* geographical position and bearing, and a hundred other trivialities he could bring into full consciousness with a moment's thought. Full reports on those passengers who had already been debriefed waited at the edge of his mind, to be studied at his leisure; he had

60

finished reading the latest one ten minutes ago. And of course, at the very back of his mind, there was the network link connecting him to his superior officer: to the higher-powered, higher-density information processing capacity of his ship: and, beyond them and through them, eventually, to Nemesis Herself.

Yet so much information had a tendency to fade into tedium. And Akavi was still human enough to be bored. He could have casually text-sent to pass the time, as at least three of the junior angels were doing, or summoned up news vids and other distracting content. Or he could slightly adjust the neurotransmitters in his organic brain, easing tension and delaying the urge towards mental drift. But on jobs like this, Akavi preferred to stay alert to the moment, boring or not. It kept him sharp.

He wished he could be on the *Menagerie*, debriefing Yasira, but she needed time. He and Elu and Enga had chosen to take her this way, involuntarily and with a period of isolation, for a number of reasons. Chief among those was that she was dangerous and not yet predictable. Watching her reactions as she figured things out would be enlightening.

The cabin door opened with an irritating creak, and a Riayin man hurried out. A heavy middle-aged woman exited behind him. Akavi's visual circuitry captured and annotated their microexpressions, but nothing was anomalous and he mentally brushed it away. The man was under stress and relieved to have finished his interview; the woman was hard at work and nearly as bored as Akavi. He didn't need circuitry to perceive that much.

The woman, a sell-soul named Dr Meyema, handed him a sheaf of handwritten papers. "Here you go, sir. That's the fourth hour's worth. So far, I have to say I'm disappointed. Two of them have mild-to-moderate dissociative symptoms, but none of the heavy stuff."

Akavi flipped through the pages quickly, capturing a retinal image of each one and running a text recognition program which would file the contents away in his brain for later review. There was a reason he'd brought Dr Meyema for this. Her obvious foreignness, on a mission of such patriotic importance to the three nations of Jai, had raised eyebrows. But Dr Meyema was one of Akavi's sell-souls. She was divinely trained and irrevocably loyal to him. More importantly, she knew how to diagnose mental Outside contamination, which ordinary mortals did not.

"Thank you, Matesznoa." He checked his internal circuitry again. While Dr Meyema did this last hour's work, the junior angels had finished their preliminary crew roster. If her report was correct, then until and unless some of what she called the "heavy stuff" happened, the ship no longer needed his direct supervision. Finally. "I'll be leaving shortly; you can give your next report to…" He checked the names of the junior angels again. "Iwi, and she'll relay it to me. You remember that you're under quarantine as well?"

Dr Meyema scowled, folding her arms over her thick chest. "Yes, sir. I know what I'm dealing with here."

"Excellent; that will be all."

Dr Meyema gestured to Iwi, a wiry angel who was staring into the middle distance, probably text-sending trivial conversation to the other guards. "Next, please." Iwi's expression didn't change, but from deeper in the ship, a new survivor clattered into view. Akavi turned to go.

But this mortal didn't move toward Dr Meyema. She paused, then rushed to Akavi. "Sir. Please, before I go in, I need to speak to you."

Akavi turned to the mortal, delicately arching his brows. He automatically logged her microexpressions: distraught, grieving, all the usual expected things. This was not the first mortal who had accosted him. For the first few hours, every mortal here had been under the misapprehension that their worries entitled them to a personal conversation. "There is no question I'm permitted to answer which cannot be handled by Iwi, Uypri, Ecquein, or Nelkyu while I take care of more important matters. Good day."

"No, sir, it has to be you. Please. I need to know where you've taken Yasira."

Iwi moved forward to restrain her. *No*, Akavi text-sent. *Wait a moment.*

No one else had asked after Yasira yet. She'd been mentioned, of course: castigated, blamed, defended, pitied. Mortals had wondered aloud where she was. But no one had said, *I need to find her.*

He studied this mortal: a small-framed Arinnan woman, perhaps twenty-five, with an attractive face. A moment of access to the roster confirmed she was Productivity Hunt, a junior engineer from the generator team. He'd seen her before, holding Yasira's hand on the deck.

Relationships held a secret fascination for Akavi. He had no desire for one of his own, but, from a safe distance, their sheer emotional complexity appealed to him. He could spare a moment to speak with this girl.

"Yasira Shien," he said, "is a criminal who is responsible for the deaths of more than one hundred of your friends. Were I you, I would not be so quick to ask where she was."

"Sir, she's innocent," Productivity insisted. "She had no idea what would happen. No one could have predicted this from the math. Believe me, I know her. I can vouch for her. I can give testimony…" Akavi held her gaze pitilessly, and Productivity's lip trembled. "You handed her over to Nemesis," she continued at last in a small voice. "Didn't you?"

Neither Productivity nor any other mortal had been told that Akavi and his underlings were angels of Nemesis. Their cover identities as angels of Aletheia, as far as he could determine, were intact. But Nemesis' involvement was not a difficult inference to make. Aletheians monitored projects like the *Pride of Jai* for relatively small, theoretical issues. When a disaster like this one occurred, the issue was no longer theoretical. If heresy was suspected as the cause, and the heretic in question wasn't actively resisting, Nemesis might easily request that Her Sister bring the heretic to Her, and Aletheia would comply.

"I can neither confirm nor deny Dr Shien's whereabouts at the present time," said Akavi, filing all of Productivity's emotions away for future reference.

"Then I want to go with her," Productivity blurted.

Akavi raised his eyebrows very high. This, he had not expected. Was she actually going to offer him her soul? "I beg your pardon."

"If she's still alive, I mean. If she's dead, then… then I can't do anything. But if you took her somewhere, if she's on one of your ships, take me, too. Please. She needs me."

"You would accept the hospitality of Nemesis," Akavi said slowly, "in order to be with her?"

Productivity drew back slightly. Amusingly, she didn't flee to Dr Meyema, who was watching with undisguised interest. She only wavered. "Not… forever, but… I mean, until she's found innocent or guilty, and… or, if… I mean, I…"

Akavi sighed. Business before pleasure; this was a sort of dithering which would last hours if he let it, and he had things to do.

"No," he said.

He turned and strode towards the *Leunt's* portal, leaving Productivity Hunt trembling in his wake.

CHAPTER 5

Some sins cannot be forgiven.

When the Keres attacks a human world, there is horror which I hope you cannot imagine. When humans attack each other on a large scale – and Old Humans did this constantly, for the pettiest of reasons – it is similar. There are humans who torture and kill each other for pleasure. There are humans who burn houses with their inhabitants inside, who destroy cities, who beat and starve children like you.

The Gods are kind, beloved; the Gods wish for humans to flourish. But how can we flourish if the humans who do these things go unpunished?

When the Gods drew up Treaty Prime, before the Morlock War, They quarreled. Each God needed souls to survive. And each God wanted the very best souls for Themselves. Not all of Them agreed on which were the best, but no one wanted the wicked souls. Every God tried to give them away to some other God.

But Nemesis is good and brave, and Nemesis is completely without mercy.

"I will take the souls of the wicked," She said, "if none of the rest of You will have them. I will live on these alone and forfeit My right to good souls forever. This I will do out of necessity, and to set an example. Besides, if one of Us must have them, I imagine that they are best suited to Me."

Some of the Gods sighed with relief, for the souls that are most wicked hurt to absorb. Others nodded, content to see necessary portions chosen. But Philophrosyne, draped in Her many-colored shawl, objected.

"I am grateful," She said. "that You are brave enough to offer. But I do not think that the wicked should belong to any of Us. When they die, they should dissolve into nothing, alone, as all human souls used to. For the wicked must be punished. This is an even greater need than Our need for sustenance. What mortal would not want to become part of a God? And the bravest of Gods, at that! If Nemesis takes them, how is that a punishment?" Nemesis only smiled.

No, beloved – do not ask what that smile meant. I am sure that you are good and kind, not wicked, and that you do as you are told. I am sure that you will never need to know.

WALYA SHU'UHI, THEODICY STORIES FOR CHILDREN

Yasira sat curled in one of the armchairs of her plush cell, puzzling through Dr Talirr's papers. She'd lost her watch along with the rest of her old outfit, but, according to the console, she'd been here for most of a day now. Elu had been back in with lunch: more of those excellent dumplings, a huge bottle of water, and a small bowl of exotic fruit, all of which she'd devoured. He'd also brought, at her request, a pad of lined paper and a pencil for notetaking. Then, later, more fruit and vegetables for a snack. Having it fresh was a nice change after all the canned and freeze-dried foods on the *Pride of Jai*. Occasionally her mind wandered from her work and she wondered how angels got those things in space. Nutrient printers, maybe, like in vids. But it tasted very real. Maybe there were God-built space-farms somewhere. Or not even space-farms; they had portals. They could bring things in fresh-picked from the ground.

She'd asked Elu about it, when he came in for the afternoon snack. "Oh, those are printed," he'd said, with a hint of pride. "The program for the loganberries is based on a rare Ultchallan strain. It's won awards. Do you like it?"

Yasira had frowned and said nothing. The fruit was delicious. But she was trapped here, her planetside life was in shambles, a third of the people she'd known in the past year were dead, and she missed Tiv. She didn't want to spend her time complimenting the premises.

Initially she'd alternated the papers with the tutorial, spending as much time on the console as she dared. Master the console, she suspected, and a number of other things would become clear. Like the layout of the ship. The number of other captives. How to get to an ansible and talk to Tiv.

Increasingly, though, the papers held all of her attention. The first few had been actual science and it had taken her hours to work through a preliminary analysis– enough to confirm that the math wasn't gibberish, even though it led to conclusions that made no sense. Conclusions that sounded like old ghost stories, tales told to frighten children.

Conclusions that sounded like the *Pride of Jai* imploding.

And then there was the diary: the small handwritten book Yasira kept getting distracted by, whenever the papers got difficult. She'd never had a chance to learn about Dr Talirr's inner life in this way, the things she said to herself when students weren't around. But the diary… The diary was worse than the papers. She was most of her way through it, and liking what she saw less and less, when there was another knock at the door.

Yasira sighed. "Yeah."

It was Elu, but he didn't have supper. He came in and sat down across from her. "Hey."

"Hey."

"Are you doing okay?"

Yasira flung the diary down on her desk. "How do you think I'm doing? You're the one who gave me these papers. What did you *expect*?"

Elu bit his lip. "I'm sorry. It's difficult work to deal with, isn't it? I promise we showed you for a reason. I came in because, now that you've had them for most of the day, we were wondering what your first impressions were."

"My impression is that you've arrested me," said Yasira, "locked me in a room, and given me a sheaf of crazy papers to try to convince me that my doctoral mentor was a heretic."

Nemesis' priests taught mortals to recognize various degrees of heresy – from direct rebellion against the Gods to small precautionary matters. The prohibition against advanced computer technology, for instance, was mostly symbolic. If a system became intelligent and began to improve itself, it might become a failed God, another Keres – perhaps even another part of the Keres Herself. But in the early stages of computer research, that was highly unlikely. If you meddled with computers in a prohibited manner, you'd probably get only a short bout of torture and a warning.

Dr Talirr, if Yasira was reading this right, had been doing the *other* kind of forbidden research.

Her diary spelled it out: *Space is a lie. Time is a lie. The gods, our planets, our nations, our pathetic excuses for science: lies, lies, lies!*

Then, later: *I must make the lies go away.*

When Yasira had first come across the word "lies", she'd stopped, shocked: remembering again how the reactor had spelled out that same word.

Denying the existence of Gods would have been bad enough, but Dr Talirr's heresies went farther than that, they had practical applications.

"I mean, look at this," Yasira said. She took out one of the earlier papers, unpublished and authored solely by Dr Talirr. It was, at long last, a technical description of how her famous portals worked. Or at least, it claimed to be. "It's a standard set of Erashub equations, but she's taken out all the representations of space, size, and distance and replaced them with this awful looking symbol. When I try to solve for it, I get infinity or nothing. Like… the portal creates a singularity, but with distance instead of mass. Infinite distance in zero time. Not folding the distance using quantum mechanics, which would be sensible, but just pretending it isn't there. Because apparently," Yasira shuffled through the pile of papers and opened Dr Talirr's diary to a marked page, "*space is a lie.*"

"That's correct, yes."

"Is this a trick?"

Elu blinked. "What?"

"Is this a trick? Are these really Dr Talirr's papers, or did you make fake ones somehow, to try to – I don't know – to get a reaction out of me, or to tempt me into agreeing with some of the heresy. Because this makes no sense! It's science, and the math checks out, but it makes no sense. Dr Talirr wouldn't do this."

The mere thought of it made waves of panic rise. Dr Talirr had been cranky, but... She'd been secretive, but... No. She couldn't think these things about her mentor. She *couldn't*. It had taken many rounds of panicked denial before she'd been able to look the truth full in the face.

"No. I'm sorry, but it's hers. This happens a lot with heretics. They lead double lives."

Yasira looked at him incredulously. That was the second time he'd apologized. Diligence and Enga had acted like proper angels of Nemesis, like the ones in vids, but Elu made no sense at all.

"But, look, if Dr Talirr really wrote this, then I don't even know what that implies. Because it all goes seamlessly together. All the most interesting stuff in these papers is based on the biggest heresies. But Dr Talirr's portals *did* work. It's a heresy, because it's antagonistic to the Gods, but it's a heresy that actually corresponds to something."

"Yes, that's true."

"Even though it's crazy."

"Yes."

Yasira took a short, fuming breath. She suddenly realized she was frightened, not angry. She didn't want to say this next part. But these were angels of Nemesis; they'd find out what she was thinking sooner or later.

"And," she said, "this is Dr Talirr's worldview. It affects everything she does. So the Talirr-Shien Reactor is like this, too, isn't it? I'm a heretic, too."

Elu extended a hand. He didn't touch her, but he rested his thin palm on the arm of her chair supportively. "No. Not in the same way. You had no way of understanding what you were doing."

Yasira clenched her fists in her hair. "Yes, that's an awful lot of help for the hundred people who died!"

"They shouldn't have died," Elu said steadily. "That shouldn't have happened. That kind of thing is why we're trying so hard to prosecute heretics in the first place. But, remember, I told you – you're not here to be punished. You're on *our* side."

"What?"

"Think back. You were worried about the reactor, weren't you? Right from the start. You kept trying to get permission to have it turned off."

"No," said Yasira, resenting the angels all over again for watching her so closely. "That was just… just nerves…"

But they'd been bigger nerves than Yasira had ever had for any other project. Anxiety was common for her neurotype, but Yasira didn't freak out that badly over every little thing.

"You see?" Elu said softly. "You were against the heresy all along. Even if you didn't know it yet."

Yasira gave him a careful look.

"That's what this is about, isn't it? You want me to stop this from happening again. You want me to help bring her to justice."

There was that frisson of panic again. She did not want to face Dr Talirr as a heretic. She did not want to face Dr Talirr at all. But people had died. There was nothing else to do.

Elu smiled widely and genuinely, like she'd finally found a good answer.

"I think," he said, "it's time for you to meet Akavi."

Elu led her out into the rest of the ship. Yasira followed obediently and tried not to show any nerves. The plush room where she'd been reading the papers had been a contained, predictable environment, but the *Menagerie's* main corridors seemed designed to confuse her. Broad, curving, pastel-colored hallways twisted every which way, echoing with her and Elu's footsteps – and hardly any other sound. The place seemed nearly uninhabited; mortal resources could never have sustained such a waste of space. Wherever Yasira touched the walls, she found intricate metal filigrees, irritating because they were too delicate for her mortal eyes to see clearly. Just outside of her room, there was an elaborate gold foil depicting… something. A curvy shape, elegantly balanced, yet somehow giving an impression of great weight, with stars around it. A God-built ship? Was that what they really looked like from the outside? Or was it something more abstract than a ship?

"Who is Akavi?" asked Yasira. "Is he another angel?"

"Oh," said Elu, as if it surprised him that she didn't know. "Yes, sorry. That's Diligence Young's real name. Akavi Averis, Inquisitor of Nemesis."

Yasira suppressed a shiver. The name meant nothing to her, but the rank of Inquisitor was famous. Inquisitors of Nemesis took commanding roles in the most unpleasant missions: tracking down evildoers, punishing them, foiling their plots and wiping all traces of them from the galaxy. Was this really what she'd been drafted for?

A skittering noise came suddenly from a junction up ahead. Yasira perked up, expecting another bot – and came face to face with an eight-foot-tall Spider.

"Hello," it said – or, rather, it made a giggly chittering noise, which was translated into Earth creole by an electronic device hanging from its pedicel. Spiders were not really arachnids: they were sentient aliens, ten-legged, with a spiny central body lacking spinnerets or pedipalps. It was sheer coincidence that their overall body plan looked like an arachnophobe's nightmare. "Who is this new morsel you've brought me, Elu? Is she good to eat?"

Elu sighed, as if this was a joke that the Spider had repeated too many times. "Sispirinithas, this is Dr Yasira Shien, and you're not going to eat her. Yasira, this is Sispirinithas. He doesn't actually eat people."

"You don't know that," the Spider said snippily. "Why, I have eaten dozens of humans in my day."

Spiders had, actually, killed and eaten humans before. Usually in times of war, or as a result of large misunderstandings. They ate other Spiders, too. It was part of their culture. Despite this, they were one of the friendlier alien races, and there was brisk trade with them at the borders of human space. But aliens, friendly or no, didn't usually work for human Gods.

"Pleased to meet you," said Yasira, suppressing the urge to freeze or shriek. Elu was making impatient movements forwards. The Spider planted himself in the hallway in front of them, blocking the way.

"As am I! You look delicious. Am I to assume you are the new student here to help us find Evianna Talirr?"

Yasira looked at him sharply. Apparently someone had told random Spiders why she was here before anyone had bothered telling *her*.

"I'm not a student," she said. "I'm the leader of a major research team—"

"On the *Pride of Jai*!" the Spider said, delighted. "Yes?"

Elu sighed. "Sispirinithas, I promise we can chat soon, but I already told Akavi that Yasira and I were on our way. You know how he gets."

"But I must know," the Spider insisted. "What was it like? All of the panic and destruction, the holes in reality – you saw it up close, didn't you?"

Yasira wondered if there was a polite response to that. Or if she could just punch the Spider in the cluster of glittering eyes that passed for its face.

At that moment, Enga walked by. Yasira glanced at her, startled. She hadn't seen Enga since that brief encounter yesterday, on the *Leunt*, but the odd, muscular figure with the God-built arms was instantly recognizable.

It was irrational to be afraid of a particular angel. It was probably only luck that assigned Enga to poison Yasira while Elu waited on her. Still, for a second Yasira got stuck in a sensory memory of that metal supporting her weight while she fought for consciousness.

Enga surveyed the scene, then glared for a moment at Sispirinithas. She didn't say anything, but a burst of Spider chittering emanated from the translating device.

"Sorry," said Sispirinithas. Suddenly submissive, he scurried away.

Enga walked away looking bored and preoccupied. Elu did not

visibly greet her and she did not so much as glance again at him or Yasira.

The two of them started walking again, Yasira trying to work out exactly what had happened. "What did she just say?"

"I'm actually not sure."

"Is she higher ranking than you?"

Elu paused. "Not really. We both work for Akavi. But Enga has a forceful personality."

"Does Sispirinithas work for Akavi, too?"

"Yes. With Akavi's rank, he can have both mortal and angelic underlings. Enga and I are the only other angels here, but the *Menagerie* also has a couple of dozen sell-soul specialists, and two aliens. We're very proud of having two aliens. Akavi recruited them both personally."

Yasira was about to ask who the other alien was, and what the Spider actually *did* here, but just then they rounded a corner into a wide room, paneled in mahogany instead of metal. A huge window covered one wall from floor to ceiling, looking out at the stars. There was very little furniture. In the room stood, not Diligence Young, but a Vaurian angel. Sleeker and more androgynous than Diligence, with understated features. His skin was an inorganic translucent shade which flashed copper and silver when it caught the light. His hair and eyes were a faint gray-white.

"Oh," said Elu, looking happier than he'd been in the corridor. "Here we are."

Vaurians were technically human: their eerie looks were the result of divine nanotechnology in their cells, which allowed them to change the features of their bodies at will, looking like any type of human they chose. They returned to this true, colorless state only when relaxed. Unlike angelic circuitry, Vaurian nanotechnology could not be installed in an adult: you were born with it – conceived with it, really – or you weren't. They'd been bred two centuries ago in an attempt to create better angels. Angels who could change themselves according to circumstance; angels who could spy and blend in, even with the worst sorts of heretic. Not every Vaurian chose to become an angel, but mortal Vaurians were almost universally mistrusted, and Vaurian angels were feared.

Yasira thought being prejudiced against Vaurians was silly. She'd known one or two very distantly at school, and they hadn't been any crueller than the rest of the students. Still, she suppressed a shiver as she looked at him: it was like coming face-to-face with the villain in a vid.

"You must be Akavi Averis," she said, strained but polite.

He turned to look at her, then smiled slightly at her reaction. His skin churned oddly for a second, like a current of texture and color rising from water, and then suddenly he was human again. Yasira didn't recognize the form: he was simply a dark, elegant man who stood with the ease of unquestioned authority. Vid-star handsome, but stern. "And you are Dr Yasira Shien. I trust your stay on the *Menagerie* has been pleasant so far?"

With Elu, she would have been sarcastic again. But this man frightened her.

"Frankly, sir," she said, bowing her head, "I don't think anyone in my position would be very happy right now. But my immediate needs have been met. Elu has been very attentive."

"Of course he has." Akavi waved a hand, dismissing the rest of what she'd said. Elu was watching him with an odd expression, like a puppy, eager for praise. But Akavi was focused on Yasira. "He also informs me that you're ready to discuss Evianna Talirr."

Yasira nodded, fighting to keep her tone level. "I've read the papers and most of the diary. I have at least a general idea of the kind of heresies she's wanted for, I think."

Akavi smiled thinly. "Indeed. Yasira, have you ever heard of a place called Outside?"

Yasira froze and stared at him.

"Those…" she stammered. "Those are just ghost stories."

It wouldn't have frightened her so much if it hadn't occurred to her already, reading the papers. Some of Dr Talirr's writing had reminded her *strongly* of certain stories. Fictional ones. The demented imaginings of a movement of twentieth and twenty-first century pulp writers. In the stories, Outside was a place separated from normal spacetime, not by distance, but by ways of being which defied all rational thought. By things that transcended space and time, because they were too large for such things to have meaning for them. Things that would break the mind of any human who encountered them. Things that could easily turn a space station inside out and implode it, because the carefully balanced tensions holding ordinary matter together meant nothing to them. Blind, destructive cosmic energies which were not alive or intelligent by any reasonable definition, yet which had enough awareness to notice humanity, briefly, in the instant before they snuffed it out forever.

Things with enough awareness to cast around for the closest human concept for what they were. To identify themselves, in the instant before destroying everyone, as *lies*.

Except to them, it was the other way around.

"In a manner of speaking," said Akavi briskly. "The stories are stories. There are not actually evil squid people lurking under planetary oceans, or any of that nonsense. What do exist are… phenomena that we associate with such stories, that behave in a way reminiscent of them. Things that humanity was not meant to know."

"No," said Yasira. This was one hundred percent not what she had come here to talk about. The *Pride of Jai* had not been some pulp horror story. She had been there. She had seen the panic, seen the walls shake. It had been *real*.

Akavi waved away her objection. "Stories aside, Outside is a set of phenomena associated with a certain heretical view of physics. The underlying heresy is that space and time as we know them do not exist. That they are convenient illusions allowing the human brain to assimilate reality, but behind them lurks some altogether different reality. And that this reality is somehow realer, or truer, than the reality that humans and Gods know. Does this sound familiar?"

Yasira swallowed and, unwillingly, nodded. Her hands shook. This was a fair description of the rantings in Dr Talirr's diary. It was also not a terrible description of the pulp stories. But it made no *sense*.

"Good. It will help if you do *not* view Outside as realer than reality;

that's a contradiction in terms. It doesn't typically interact with our reality at all. But certainly there are energies that exist in some sense and that don't fit tidily into our view of spacetime, and when heretics begin to pay special attention to these energies, unfortunate events can occur. They can be harnessed, and certain sorts of... creature can be attracted. In a mild case, say an encounter-type 2A, the energies are instantaneous and contained. A heretic goes into a room, attempts to perform an absurd ritual, and the room is immolated or some such. The problem solves itself. In other cases, these sorts of creatures – constructs of the Outside energies – can appear, which are a little more difficult to deal with. Or a more serious destabilization of matter can occur, as we saw on the *Pride of Jai*. That was an encounter-type 3F-X, a fairly severe case, though not the most extreme we have seen. It falls under the purview of angels of Nemesis to detect, prevent, and perform damage control on these events. Are you with me so far?"

Yasira ground her teeth, trying to assimilate this information. "So... That's why you were on the *Leunt*. Damage control. You quarantined the survivors. Why?"

Akavi smiled slightly. "You seem at least passingly familiar with the stories about Outside. No doubt you have heard that it drives people mad."

Some very Riayin part of Yasira rose up defensively. "'Madness' isn't a thing. It wasn't even really a thing in the twentieth century. It's not a real diagnostic category and it's not a useful descriptor. You can talk to me about mental illnesses, brain injuries, or atypical neurotypes, but–"

Akavi waved a hand, silencing her. "I'm aware of that. But there is a psychological syndrome associated with Outside which we refer to as madness. It has become, shall we say, the term of use. It begins when people are exposed to Outside energies in some form and are unable to mentally assimilate what they have seen. It typically begins with forms of dissociation, anxiety, or confusion, like what you observed on the *Pride of Jai*. In mild cases, it stays at that level and recedes in time. Otherwise, it progresses into varied forms which can mimic an astonishing number of other mental illnesses, primarily those associated with psychological trauma. If left unchecked, it can in severe cases progress until the person affected becomes an obsessive heretic, actively desiring more Outside exposure despite its dangers. The trouble with Outside madness is that it can be caused not only by direct exposure to Outside, but also by exposure to ideas regarding Outside. Its severe forms are, in that sense, contagious. We're screening the crew of the *Pride of Jai* for any such contagion before we release them to the wider world."

Yasira was shaking all over now. "Contagious? But that would make you contagious, too. You're the ones who gave me the stupid papers!"

Akavi shook his head. "Angels assigned to these cases have programs installed that will mitigate any effects. As for the *Pride of Jai's* crew, we're still assessing them, but so far they appear to be on the mild end of the spectrum. Shaken, traumatized, dissociative in some cases, but nothing that would give the mortal psychiatric system difficulty."

"Tiv," Yasira blurted. "What about Tiv? Have you–"

"Assessed her yet? Yes." There was a split-second's pause. "Apart from a tendency to whine about your absence, her symptoms are negligible. She'll be free to go soon."

Yasira wondered what *negligible* meant, if full-blown trauma reactions were "mild". If Tiv had survived the disaster, only to end up hurt by Yasira's actions anyway… Well, that didn't bear thinking about. She wished again, and very badly, for an ansible.

"What about me?"

Akavi smiled again, coolly, and it was only then that Yasira realized she'd asked the questions in that order.

"You're at a higher risk," he said. "But you, Yasira, are a genius. You've been virtually asymptomatic since you were first contaminated in graduate school. That is rare, even for one of your intelligence, and of an atypical neurotype. I suspect that, for whatever reason, your resilience is unusual." He held up a hand. "Which will be no help to you at all if you get complacent now. You've just been through a disaster bad enough to cause trauma even without Outside, and your exposure will only increase from here. Your console contains a full suite of neurofeedback and cognitive therapy exercises. You are to perform them daily and vigilantly. Any unusual symptoms, no matter how small, are to be reported to me or Elu. All of which *ought* to keep you healthy long enough to do your real work."

Yasira stood very still and digested this. *Since you were first contaminated in graduate school.* That was where the déjà vu had come from. Those equations, the ones she could follow blindly but not understand…

The ones she'd based her reactor on…

If what he was saying was true, then all these years, she'd been like a carrier for some awful disease, dragging Outside heresy along without knowing what it was. She'd killed all those people by being, as he said, *resilient.* Most dangerous being in the universe, indeed.

"So," said Akavi, clasping his hands. "In summary. Your doctoral mentor, Dr Evianna Talirr, is one of the most dangerous forms of heretic to ever exist. Her heresy, not yours, is the ultimate cause of what happened to your station. You knew her well and have an unusual ability to process and understand the very ideas that make her so dangerous. We are asking that you help us find her."

Yasira sat down heavily on the bare metal floor. This was too much to process at once. She could feel her mind seizing up, shutting down with the onslaught of information and emotion.

"I don't believe you," she said thickly. It was utter foolishness to say to an angel, but the only thing she could think of to say. "I don't *believe* you."

She expected Akavi to argue. Instead, she heard him and Elu withdraw slightly. The room's lights dimmed, and she sat in silence, breathing hard, fighting tears. For minutes so long she lost track of them. Until her head was slightly clearer. Until maybe, she thought, *maybe* she was ready to speak again.

She looked up. Akavi was still there, at the room's far end, still in the same dark elegant body. Perfectly still and watching with surprising patience.

"I can't believe all of this," she said. "It's too much."

Akavi nodded, as if there had been no break in the conversation.

"You are not the first I've seen to exhibit such a reaction. We keep these things secret for a reason. When you're ready, I can show you concrete evidence of my claims."

Yasira ran a hand through her hair and stood shakily back up. Her head was swimming. "How am I supposed to find Dr Talirr if you can't? Nobody mortal has heard anything from her in the past three years. How do you know she's even alive? I mean, you'd have her soul if she was dead, but she could be imprisoned in alien territory or lost out in space someplace where she can't hurt anybody. Even the *Pride of Jai* was just… remnants of her. Right?"

There was a slight, critical pause from Akavi. Long enough to let her know she'd gotten something wrong.

"Come with me," said the Vaurian.

He turned and led her down another corridor – a short one, this time. They entered a new room: windowless, but with smooth panels set into the walls at various angles, blank and dark like unused consoles.

"Outside incidents are more common than a mortal might realize," Akavi said briskly. "When survivors exist, we try to keep the story quiet and prevent panic. Have you heard of a town called Zhoshash? In the provisional sector of Omevarna?"

"I know Omevarna," said Yasira. It was a minor colony world, only recently divinely terraformed and readied for conquest by the expanding mortal population. Mostly Kheroqans, if Yasira remembered correctly.

"This event fits Talirr's profile," said Akavi, "though we haven't been able to conclusively prove she was present. Watch."

The lights dimmed, and then suddenly they were somewhere else. A small town, planetside, tucked into the side of a mountain, with a light snow falling in the red-tinged twilight. Strangely, the temperature was no different than it had been on the *Menagerie*. They were standing on the sidewalk by a two-lane street, with electric cars and bicycles quietly moseying by. The passers-by did look Kheroqan, mostly, with small clumps of curly-haired Stijonans thrown in. None of them looked up at the angel and mortal who had suddenly appeared on the sidewalk.

"A hologram?" said Yasira.

"Of course. Try putting your hand through a lamppost."

She walked obediently to the nearest lamppost and stuck her hand in. There was no resistance. Physically, she was waving her hand through the air. Visually, she was reaching into a solid object. It shimmered slightly when she retracted her hand, but remained intact.

"This is amazing," said Yasira. Mortals had holograms, but they were little flickery things and you had to stand at the right angle to see them properly. This town – Zhoshash, she supposed – was flawless. The feel of the non-frozen air on her skin gave it away, and it didn't really smell like an outdoor scene, either. But visually and audibly, it was exactly as if she and Akavi were there, watching, unnoticed.

Yasira closed her eyes a moment and tried to remember where the nearest wall had been. She opened them again and walked in that direction, hand held out cautiously in front of her. After a moment she felt the smooth steel of a bulkhead under her palm. Conveniently, the hologram had been designed with a wall there, too, but a rough brick one, entirely unlike what she could feel.

Akavi watched these experiments with an air of patient indulgence. "Of course," he said, "we didn't actually have recording devices at this kind of fidelity placed in Zhoshash at the time of the incident. We do have eyewitness accounts, though, sadly, no eyewitness survived very long. This hologram is an artist's impression, reconstructed based on these accounts combined with sensor readings and satellite footage, as well as our general knowledge of the workings of Outside. Specific visual details were extrapolated as closely as possible from that data. Naturally, a hologram of Outside phenomena lacks the insanity-inducing effects of exposure to the phenomena themselves."

Yasira nodded, swallowing a growing dread. She didn't want to watch another *Pride of Jai* disaster, but that seemed to be what he was leading up to. She suspected that he was not going to stop the display merely because she expressed a desire to stop. Rather than slip into panic, she focused on the cold metal texture and red brick veneer of the wall. She felt her way around the edge of the room. At some point either the storefront would end, or the *Menagerie's* wall would stop and a new wall would show up at right angles. Either way, she'd eventually be walking into a wall in what looked like empty space, which would be interesting.

She was interrupted by a scream.

Down the street, something was moving. Yasira couldn't quite see it at first, but the nearby pedestrians were shrieking, rushing away – apart from one or two, who simply froze and stared. The road itself rippled and twisted, and the sides of the nearby buildings with it. Losing their shape and their structural integrity.

Just the way the walls had on the *Pride of Jai*.

She backed away.

There was more screaming. Yasira stood transfixed. Her gut instinct, even knowing that this wasn't real, was to call a Code 56 and lead everyone to the lifeboats. But there were no lifeboats: this was the surface of a world. They probably didn't even have an evacuation procedure. How did you abandon ship when the ship was a town and the town was connected to everything else on the planet?

This had already happened, Yasira reminded herself. It was just a recording. This ought to have been calming. Instead it made her feel worse, helpless.

This was what she had already done. To a whole stationful of people.

The townsfolk ran in every direction, maybe with a destination in mind, maybe not. Several ran right through Yasira. She flinched and threw up her hands to guard her face, but there was no sensation at all.

Then the road twisted, seemed to liquefy altogether and the pavement rose up in the air. A black blob, not black like space, but a rough and uneven asphalt-black, moving over itself restlessly.

The road-blob extended a black tendril and grabbed a Kheroqan woman by the arm. She'd been one of the frozen passers-by, staring at it without moving – dissociative, like Xaka had been on the *Pride of Jai*. Being touched snapped her out of it a moment too late. She grimaced horribly up at the road-blob and screamed. The road-blob's rough surface scraped the skin from her arms as she struggled. Blood welled up, but it still held her firmly in place.

Something like a mouth opened in the center of the blackness and leered towards her.

Yasira shut her eyes and clapped her hands over her ears. There was more screaming. There were other sounds that she wished she wasn't able to identify. Bubbling. Crunching. A snapping that could have been bone.

Then abruptly the room was silent except for Yasira's voice, and she realized she'd been shrieking, too.

She opened her eyes. She wasn't in a hologram of Zhoshash anymore. The room was empty except for herself and Akavi and a lot of small dark panels set into the wall at odd angles. She leaned against the wall and panted, trying to control her racing heartbeat.

It had been so real.

"Did any of that seem familiar?" said Akavi, in a voice as unruffled as if he'd been watching a weather report.

"I…" Speech failed her. She resented him for asking. Of *course* it was familiar. "How did…? Was there…?"

"A Shien Reactor? No. Whatever caused this disaster was considerably worse than a Shien Reactor. The *Pride of Jai* had a skeleton crew of a few hundred scientists and engineers; two-thirds survived. Zhoshash was a town of two thousand, and it was wiped off the map completely."

Yasira's stomach roiled. She looked down and tried not to think about those crunching noises.

"This," said Akavi, "is precisely why heresy is dangerous. It is not simply a matter of Divine feelings being hurt. Many heresies, including Outside, lead to danger and to the loss of innocent life, even when the heretic intends to harm no one. Mortals tend to be frightened of Nemesis, and rightly so; but more frightening by far are the forces from which She protects us."

Yasira nodded, still looking at the floor.

"Mind you," said Akavi, "as I said, Outside incidents are usually smaller in scale than what you just saw. They also tend to have an identifiable source, at least after the fact. A madman or madwoman holes up in a garret with the wrong sort of book. A researcher deliberately contravenes scientific guidelines to see what will happen. A self-styled mystic experiments with certain pharmaceuticals and garners the wrong kind of alien attention. Sometimes the only person harmed is the one responsible. Sometimes a single building is destroyed or some valuable laboratory equipment rendered useless. But with Zhoshash and a few other incidents like it, there isn't a known source or an identifiable center. The area of effect is staggering, but the effect itself appears to have been imposed from elsewhere."

"By Dr Talirr." Yasira could not fathom this. Why would anyone make something so awful happen on purpose?

"She is the only known Outside heretic whose whereabouts are unaccounted for in our records, and the only unaccounted-for person who has the knowledge and technological skill to do something like this. In the ten years prior to her disappearance, only a few Outside incidents occurred in human space, all very small-scale and with an easily identifiable cause. This is no different from the usual rate. It is only after her disappearance that incidents like this one – Zhoshash being the largest, so far – began to occur. They have been steadily increasing in size. We have no direct proof that Talirr was behind any particular incident, but it doesn't take a prodigy scientist to make the inference, and there are no other plausible leads. We need, at minimum, to find her and call her to account."

Yasira nodded. "Yes." Her heartbeat was slowly getting under control.

"And I have reason to believe that you yourself are the key to us finding her. Assuming you agree, of course."

"Why me?" she said. "What can I do for you that God-built people-finding systems can't?"

She wasn't convinced that these people really cared if she agreed. Even Elu had never given her the option of, say, leaving.

But what would it mean if they did let her leave? It would mean going home. To Tiv, but no career. To a planet that blamed her for a disaster neither she nor any other mortal understood. Remembering what she'd seen, knowing that the true danger was even worse than anyone on the *Pride of Jai* knew. And admitting that, when given the chance to help set things right, she'd refused.

Maybe Yasira didn't really want to go home yet.

Akavi looked unamused. "Talirr has evaded our usual technology. You know her and, as Elu discussed with you, you've had unconscious intuitions about Outside before. So your perspective will augment our methods nicely."

"But I don't want to be a sell-soul." Yasira swallowed hard. "Can my soul stay mine? My brain stays a mortal brain? And when we're done with this one thing, I get to go home?"

Because that was the catch with a lot of Nemesis' work. Gods like Aletheia had no shortage of mortals swearing fealty to Them. But few people volunteered their souls to a God famous for torment. So She used cleverer methods. A mortal would think they were signing up for something temporary, and the fine print would say otherwise.

"Yes. This is an informal arrangement. When Evianna Talirr has been delivered to us, you'll be free to go back to Jai if you wish, and you'll be paid handsomely for your time."

"Can…" Yasira swallowed. "Can I talk to Tiv?" Time out hunting her mentor would be time without any of the people she knew from back home, away from the people who usually supported her. Time when Tiv didn't know where she was – Tiv might not even know she was alive.

Tiv didn't deserve to be sucked into this, to be pulled out of her real life and sent on a dangerous mission with no telling how long it would take. But Tiv at least deserved to know what was going on.

Akavi frowned. "Oh, I'm sorry," he said – not a real apology, like one of Elu's, but a sardonic one. "I must not have specified that this is a *secret* mission. No, Yasira, you may not speak to Tiv or any other uninvolved mortal. Any such communication would risk leaking information and alerting Talirr to our movements before she was found. If you refuse me, I will drop you back down on the planet with her, under certain conditions. But what I am asking of you is not a field trip with your friends. It is a mission in which secrecy and protocol, as much so as any real knowledge or skills you possess, may make the difference between thousands living and thousands more dying the way you just saw in that hologram. You may speak to your lover when the mission is complete, and not before."

Yasira took a deep, shaky breath. She had suspected all that, although she didn't like it much. Tiv would have to wait.

She was too overwhelmed still to look Akavi in the eye, but she deliberately turned to face him and squared her shoulders. She tried to control her racing heart. She wanted to go home, to cry on Tiv's shoulder, to have this be over. But why should she go back to Tiv in disgrace when instead she could get justice, stop the disaster from happening again, and go back redeemed? Tiv wouldn't like not knowing where she was, but when Yasira did come back and explain, surely, she'd be understanding. Tiv would have made the same decision if their positions were reversed. There were things at stake much bigger than a single relationship. Yasira had been part of the cause of all the deaths yesterday; even Elu didn't deny that. She had helped kill those people. Now, maybe, she could help put it right.

"All right," she said. "I agree."

When Yasira Shien had returned to her room, Akavi slipped back into his true form and walked deeper into the *Menagerie*, to a room where a silver, doorway-sized portal arced gracefully across one wall.

It had not escaped him that Yasira found his Vaurian body eerie. It was a petty prejudice, but Akavi did not mind. Being feared by mortals, in his line of work, was useful.

He closed his eyes and reached into the ansible network, sending a signal instantly through the labyrinthine circuitry of a faraway satellite. From this perspective, he could see each angel of Nemesis in the galaxy as a pinpoint of light, like stars. Each point was interconnected: he was a mid-rank angel, linked to Elu, Enga, and the grunts aboard the *Leunt*. By contrast, the light he reached out to was an Overseer, blazing with hundreds of connections. He focused on that light and a connection opened almost at once. They had been waiting for him.

My lady, he text-sent. *I've sorted things out with Dr Shien. She's agreed to work for us. Do you still wish to see me?*

Immediately, came the curt reply.

Akavi smiled grimly and stepped through the portal, transported halfway across the galaxy in an instant.

The Overseer sat on a throne composed of twisted metal cables that coursed with electricity. As Akavi arrived, she swept her metal-plated fingers across its surface, absorbing the information fed to her through the throne's arms. Tiny bots fluttered through the air around her like locusts. Millions of pieces of information passed through this chamber every hour on their way to being sorted, filed, or reported up the command structure to even grander angels. It was more information than a single brain, even cybernetically enhanced, could hold at once, so the throne served as a sort of auxiliary memory, constantly processing and retrieving details that flicked only quickly across the Overseer's consciousness. Overseers processed, filtered, and presented data to Archangels, those exalted angels rendered down to only circuitry and brains, who were able to directly communicate with Nemesis Herself. Some angels were frightened by that immersion in information, that loss of physicality. Akavi longed for it. Not for its own sake, but for the power. To have such a large piece of the galaxy at his fingertips. To command it with a thought.

Even Archangels had once been mortal, though, and this Overseer still resembled a human. She was Vaurian, like Akavi. Her name was Irimiru, and she was currently a beautiful woman, tall and statuesque, with tumbling hair and large, irate eyes. As Akavi arrived, she sat very straight in her throne and directed the full force of her gaze towards him.

"Well?" she demanded. "Has this latest acquisition solved all of your problems yet?"

Akavi genuflected and, while his eyes were still downcast, text-sent to Elu. *I don't suppose Yasira gained any unusual insights from her first reading of the papers?* Of course she hadn't. Elu would have already told him.

There was the briefest of pauses, slight but still noticeable, before

Elu's reply was received. *No, sir. She worked the basics out very quickly, but she's still on the parts that we already know.* The text-sending came with a feeling of mild, self-conscious unease. Learning to generate text independently of emotions and other neural jetsam was a challenge for new angels. Elu had never quite mastered the skill and he hated to disappoint Akavi, even in the smallest matters. He also knew that Irimiru would demand results, and the consequences for failure would be dire.

Akavi did not bother to respond, and felt Elu's unease mount, tinged with a distinct concern... for Akavi's safety? Akavi severed the connection. Distracting. Elu needed to learn how to control his emotions.

He straightened up and returned Irimiru's gaze. "We've only just made the agreement, but thus far her reactions are promising. In a few days I hope to have a report for you with something productive in it."

Irimiru's form changed. Hair suddenly short, muscles more defined, features blunt and combative instead of alluring. "A report, no doubt, which tells me that she's useless after all? That she's become irretrievably insane, like the last seven?"

Most Vaurians changed forms the way they changed clothes, but Irimiru's changes were more akin to facial expressions. She was impatient today.

"This one is different, my lady. She's a former child prodigy, a polymath and mathematical genius. She was Talirr's sole co-author, three years ago, on a groundbreaking paper which has now been proven dangerously contaminated. She understood it well enough to supervise construction of a working full-scale implementation without Talirr's help. Yet she had the mental strength to remain asymptomatic until just before the disaster. No one but us had any idea Outside was even involved. This one will find our quarry. I'm certain of it."

"Of course you're certain," said Irimiru in a suddenly-deepened voice. The Overseer was a delicate man now, with golden streaks in his tousled hair. "Which is why you recommended letting the Shien

Reactor experiment proceed, despite known dangers."

Akavi had argued hard, when the *Pride of Jai* project first hired Yasira, that the development of a full-size generator would yield valuable information. It had been uncertain to what extent the math of the Talirr-Shien Reactor was truly contaminated. Akavi had wanted to let the disaster run its course and see. Irimiru had disagreed, but been overruled by their own Archangel superiors, who'd wanted to understand the details of the heresy's effects, and of Yasira's role in them, before either terminating her or bringing her on board. Irimiru had been taking it out on Akavi ever since. "Now I have an extremely high-profile Outside cleanup job on my hands. Because you were so *certain*."

Akavi, despite himself, bristled at the Overseer's tone. "My lord," he said, biting back a harsher reply, "you'll recall I also recommended–"

Irimiru tightened his grip on the arms of his throne, and the bots around him buzzed sharply. "Summary termination of the entire station crew. That request was *denied*." He glared at Akavi. "The Outside threat has been your assignment for three years, yet not once have your silly abductions brought us one light-second closer to Talirr. It's only a matter of time until she moves to the next phase of her plans. It could be happening now."

Akavi bowed his head, chastened. "I understand. Believe me, this one will receive all the resources at my disposal until she produces results."

Irimiru tilted a head which was now a girl's head, broad-cheeked and impudent. "*If* she produces results. Would you like to wager something on that assertion?"

Akavi looked at her sidelong. Irimiru did not make bets. Not real ones, at least.

The Overseer of Nemesis rose from her seat. She was shorter than Akavi, for the moment, but both of them knew height was arbitrary. "Our Lady wants results, do you understand? If your methods continue to fail, it will speak not only to your incompetence, but to mine. So I will not allow it again. This is the last of Talirr's students you will ever acquire."

She shifted upwards as she spoke, until she was a tall, straight-backed, silver-haired woman, with a determination far beyond steel in her ancient eyes. This was how mortals drew Nemesis Herself, though the Gods did not really take human forms. Akavi found it rather tasteless. Still, half-consciously, it unnerved him, which was the intended effect.

"I will not be so capricious as to set a time limit. She is yours as long as her mind holds out. But if this one breaks before she finds Evianna Talirr, then I am reporting your mission – you and your whole team – to my superiors as a failure. Do you understand?"

He did. Every angel knew what Nemesis did to those who disappointed Her. Detailed records were available in the public files to which every angel had access, waiting as an ever-present reminder of the consequences for failure. Irimiru liked to bully and complain, but even she did not make threats like this one lightly.

Akavi received a ping from Elu and permitted a text connection to open. *Sir,* said Elu in his head, *my software says your heart rate's spiking. Is anything wrong?*

For a second, Akavi weighed the pros and cons of telling him. Silly boy.

Nothing important, he text-sent. *The usual theatrics, that's all.*

"I understand," he said softly, bowing his head to Irimiru. Yasira would yield results, one way or another.

CHAPTER 6

The gods are a lie, but knowing this gives me no special protection. I cannot yet leave or disassemble this universe. And the gods will not suffer a sliver of Truth to exist. While I remain here, I have eleven very powerful enemies.

Options?

Flee. (Suboptimal. Impermanent. Safe distance difficult to judge; may not even exist. Cost of misjudgment catastrophic.)

Recant. (Out of the question.)

Suicide. (Tempting but counterproductive; they still get my soul.)

Destroy them. ~~(Impossible~~
~~(Not with current technology~~
~~(What methods would even~~
~~(Surely no one could~~
(A topic for future research. Currently infeasible. But everyone knows I have done the infeasible before.)

FROM THE DIARIES OF DR EVIANNA TALIRR

"I've got it," said Yasira for the fifth time since breakfast.

It had been three days since her arrival on the *Menagerie*, and she'd been learning fast. It wasn't like they'd given her much else to do; she still wasn't allowed out of her sumptuous room. There had been no other excursions since that first meeting with Akavi, and no other odd encounters with Spiders or Enga; even Elu had stopped personally bringing in every meal. So she'd spent her time on research: learning a bit of the resources available to her here, trying one thing, then another, and hitting a wall every time.

The console interface in her room was so simple that she'd zipped through the tutorial in an hour or two. Now she sat alone at her desk, absorbed in the problem of finding Dr Talirr. It wasn't like the problem-solving she was used to. The shipboard computer resolved fiendish calculations in a second or two and had access to shockingly powerful sensor relays across the galaxy. The most outlandish ideas could be tested and checked in a few minutes, if she knew the commands. Which meant there was no need to conserve computational energy. She could try everything.

Yasira still had doubts about this mission. But she was, after all, a scientist. And it was easy to get absorbed in the science, sifting through the data for patterns, putting aside the rest of her emotions for later. Was Dr Talirr really a heretic? Could she be? *No.* The job here was patterns. Just focus on those.

She hit a key and her screen lit up with a multicolored pinwheel: the Milky Way and its surrounding dwarf galaxies, mapped in a default set of six out of hundreds of types of matter and radiation detected by God-built sensors throughout the galaxy. Some areas were blurry, but most had been mapped in exhausting detail and were updated by the millisecond.

If Dr Talirr had run away, she must have used some method of transportation. Either a portal or a ship with a warp drive. Ships with warp drives moved at a finite superluminal speed; portals worked instantaneously, but had to connect with other portals in order to do anything. God-built portals connected over the ansible net. Dr Talirr's portals used an Outside principle, but the result was the same. And portals generated certain kinds of waste energy. If Dr Talirr was building new ones, there would be detectible signs.

At first, Yasira had tried looking for signs of unregistered portal use or unaccounted-for warp drive byproducts around the time of Zhoshash and the other disasters for which Akavi had given her coordinates. She would be very surprised if the angels hadn't tried that already, but it was often useful to try the obvious first and see where else it led. Afterwards, she'd broadened her search. Even if Dr Talirr hadn't specifically used one of her portals to get to the scene of a disaster, she must have used one illicitly at *some* point. So, all Yasira had to do was use these sensors to detect every portal in the galaxy and subtract the God-built ones.

Except would Dr Talirr's portals leave the same energy signature as God-built portals?

She reached for the sheaf of papers Elu had given her on her first day and examined the equations. She still had to resist the natural impulse to work out all the numbers on paper. The Gods had better physics, and faster math, than Yasira ever would.

Detectable radiation from portals, she typed into a search-box and the screen filled with information. It had been a steep learning curve with angelic science: not all of it was packaged into articles and chapters the way Yasira was used to. There were official reports here and there, but much of what was worth knowing was stored in an odd, associative form. There would be descriptions about a page long, each linked to dozens of similar pages for context and elaboration, mixing high and low-level content without any clear hierarchy. It was designed to be uploaded into an angel's head and traversed in a nonlinear manner like any other train of thought. But it was taking her a while to get used to. More than once she'd gotten mixed up and lost on some tangent page, forgotten the way back, and had to step away from the console for a moment to control her frustration.

Still, after twenty minutes of reading and notetaking, Yasira had a very good idea of what a God-built portal should look like to divine sensors. She paused, then switched to a text-sending program and opened a connection to Elu.

Elu, she typed, *do we know yet if the observable energy of one of Dr Talirr's portals is the same as the God-built kind?*

Let me check, he sent back. A few seconds later, a file appeared: a paper dated three and a half years ago. This one had a structure vaguely similar to a mortal document, though it was a report from a mission, not an academic paper as such. The authors were a small team of angels of Aletheia, and what they'd written was heavily redacted. But it seemed to be, at least in part, a description of technical differences between Dr Talirr's portals and divine ones, and the section describing the energy output was all there. Of course, this being divine science, some of the energy types and frequencies had names Yasira didn't understand, or just strings of unintelligible letters and numbers.

What's with all the redactions? Yasira typed, staring at the vast blackened spaces on the virtual page.

If you were studying things mortals weren't meant to know, said Elu, *you'd redact it too.*

Elu had been helpful, in his way. He'd stopped personally bringing in meals, but he always seemed to be paying attention to what she sent him, always eager to help. He frustrated her. *You don't act like an angel of Nemesis,* she wanted to say to him. *You don't even look like an angel of Nemesis. Why exactly are you here?*

She could never bring herself to ask. It was a stupid question. There were shapeshifters here: both his personality and his age could be an act. And besides, it was too close to what people asked Yasira all the time. *You look like a student. You act like a student. Why are you the head of a major research team?*

It was better to give him the benefit of the doubt.

Yasira was tempted to just sit and puzzle her way through the whole report, looking up every term she didn't understand. This was science way past the limits of current mortal understanding. Even with the redactions, she could have spent months happily absorbed in working out exactly how the Gods thought about energy. It would have been nice. But it would have been months in which she wasn't finding Dr Talirr. Months not allowed to return home, because she hadn't completed her actual mission. Months with more disasters.

Trying to focus just on observable energy output, she flipped back to the sensor program and started copying down useful terms. The system was astonishingly user-friendly: getting a reading was nearly as simple as just typing out what she wanted in Earth creole. *Show me all sensor readings relevant to the types of energy emitted by operational*

Talirr-type portals, around the date of Dr Talirr's disappearance, which are a plausible size for a single Talirr-type portal and do not have a known cause. Even finding the right divine technical terms wasn't hard, since they were all documented and searchable.

Elu had referred to himself at one point as a sort of computer expert, when he wasn't waiting on Akavi. Or, more properly, as a "cyberneticist" – but Yasira hadn't known that word, and while she'd spared a few minutes to look it up, she hadn't been able to make head or tail of the definition. The idea of angel computer experts fascinated her. Here was a forbidden specialty, heretical for mortals, yet there were angels who learned it. She still had no idea what it actually entailed. As far as she could tell, God-built computers already did everything important by themselves.

Bringing herself back to the task at hand, Yasira typed in the correct words and pressed "enter". The screen went blank for several seconds, and then the map of the Milky Way appeared, now in a different set of colors, populating itself with results. A small red frame appeared around each possible lead: these multiplied until, within a few seconds, the screen was an impenetrable red tangle.

13,004,778 results, said the console. And that wasn't counting the blue-gray, shaded-out areas, in hostile alien territory and at the galaxy's turbulent core, where God-built sensors couldn't detect things at the small scale Yasira had specified. Yasira had been surprised to discover those a few days ago; she'd always thought the Gods could see everywhere.

She zoomed in on a few results, but it was no use. Everything here was an effect that might or might not be one of Dr Talirr's portals. She hadn't typed the query incorrectly; it just happened to be a query that fit way too many unidentified things.

Yasira chewed her lip. She imagined that if she narrowed it down to a certain number of leads, the Gods could just send a lot of sensing bots to check them all out. But thirteen million was out of the question – and that was the number from three years ago. Even if Yasira was right, and Dr Talirr had gone through a portal back then, there was no telling what methods she might have used to flee the scene. That trail had gone *extremely* cold.

She needed something bigger, more recent.

She found the search box again and typed, *Observable energy associated with Outside.* It had been three days, but typing that word as if it was real, capital letter and all, still gave her a nervous thrill.

UNAVAILABLE/REDACTED, said the console.

Yasira sighed. *Elu? Do you want to try declassifying the stuff that I need for my job?*

Why? What are you looking for? said Elu

She told him.

Oh, said Elu. *No, it makes sense you'd want to try that, but it won't work that way. Outside doesn't play nice with the laws of physics. It can make virtually any kind of energy, or no energy at all.*

Then why not just write a paper saying so? Why redact everything?

Half a minute passed before Elu replied. *It's Outside. Trust me, you don't want the details.*

Yasira buried her head in her hands.

"Yes, I do want the details," she said to the air. "It's not like there's anything at stake here! It's not like, last time I was missing some details on this topic, a space station imploded!"

The angels, she suspected, were watching and listening in at least some perfunctory way, even when she wasn't text-sending to them. Probably. But there was no response, and she hadn't really expected one.

Maybe no specific energy reading pointed to Outside. That would explain why the Gods hadn't warned anybody about the *Pride of Jai* in advance. (Did it? Clearly Akavi had known that *something* was going on. But maybe, even at his level, there hadn't been proof. Yasira had tried, earlier, calling up angelic reports on the *Pride of Jai* and on herself, but the console hadn't let here see those, either.)

Still, there might be ways around a problem like that. Outside might encompass everything, but even Dr Talirr couldn't do science that encompassed all of everything. Researchers were creatures of habit, Dr Talirr more than most. Themes recurred in their work no matter how inventive and interdisciplinary they thought they were.

So maybe themes would recur in Dr Talirr's use of energy.

Besides, Dr Talirr was presumably still researching Outside. And for that, she would need a private working space. A spaceship, maybe, or a small habitat on an uninhabited world. So, if Yasira could find Talirr-like energy readings at the scale of a full-sized research space, she'd be done.

Unless there were thirteen million of those, too.

She called up the report on Dr Talirr's portals again, and a few ancillary reports on her other inventions, including the Talirr-Shien Reactor. She started to call up the heavily redacted reports on Zhoshash and the other recent disasters of its type, too. Then she paused. Dr Talirr being responsible for Zhoshash was only their best working hypothesis. It would be a good sign if Zhoshash had energy that matched the portals and the *Pride of Jai*, but that wasn't the place to start.

Yasira sat back for a moment, clicking through the different reports. Then she took a breath, clenched her teeth, and quickly typed, *Sensor readings for the gravity well of the planet Jai in the last six weeks.*

What had the *Pride of Jai* disaster looked like to a God's eyes?

The console gave her a complex, colorful graphic, changing before her eyes to show energy fluctuations over the specified period of time. The *Pride of Jai* appeared as a small wheel of simple colors, orbiting the planet – and those colors began to shift. Lightly at first: only a small expansion, consistent with what Yasira would have expected from the slight rise in vacuum energy. Then errant spikes, swirls of odd colors that hadn't been part of the station's normal operation.

Yasira swallowed hard, watching the animation. This was still a full week before the disaster, and even to her, without a thorough education in divine physics, it was clear something wildly out of the ordinary was going on. What had these spikes and swirls meant to the Gods? To Akavi? He must have seen them – he'd warned her at about that time. But he hadn't stopped it. She watched as the spikes built and twisted, bigger and stranger. The Gods had seen something coming. They had chosen not to stop it.

Why?

She did not want to think about this. Obviously the Gods weren't telling, and it made no difference; she had to do this mission either way. But seeing it in a full-color animated diagram was uncomfortable.

Then...

Not an explosion, but just as startling. Something *else* came into the picture, something bigger than the *Pride of Jai's* spikes and swirls, with a glare that outshone the whole planet under the station. It remained there for an instant, as every remaining mundane energy signal from the *Pride of Jai* collapsed in on itself and went dark.

Then there was nothing. Just Jai. Just darkness, and the tiny pinpricks of the lifeboats.

Yasira took a few deep breaths. Laboriously, she unclenched her hand from the arm of her chair.

Why had she made herself look? The whole thing suddenly felt pointless and awful. To get any meaningful science out of those readings, she'd have to look at them again and again, frozen at different times and through different filters, until she had found a pattern she could estimate numerically. Watching her own mistake, over and over. For something that might be another wall to hit, just like everything else.

Well, she was working for Nemesis now. It wasn't *supposed* to be easy.

She rewound to the point where she'd seen the blinding flash, then isolated the second when the energy was at its highest point. *17:52:43, June 13, 2791, Earth Standard Time,* said the timestamp. Yasira frowned in annoyance and changed it to Jai Meridian Time, which was what they'd used on the actual station. *09:21:18, 77 Winter.* That was better.

It was slightly less awful as a static image, without the startle factor. She made a list, exhaustively, of all the types of energy contained in that flash. Some of these were types she knew about, but most were unfamiliar, and three had meaningless strings of letters and numbers for labels. Those ones gave Yasira an *UNAVAILABLE/REDACTED* when she looked them up. One of them, however, was not new; the same string had been present in the paper about Talirr's portals.

Yasira grinned, relieved. "If you're trying to keep this a secret," she said to the air, "you've got some skill-building to do."

A bot delivered lunch, which Yasira ate absently while drawing chart after chart. She matched the energy patterns in the portals and on the *Pride of Jai* to the patterns in the other disasters, which were easier to look at. The other disasters seemed to have a quicker onset than the *Pride of Jai*. No slow build over weeks, just the sudden arrival of something terrible, followed by a redacted period and then nothing. Yasira rolled her eyes at the redaction, but refrained from complaining to Elu again.

The energies of the important parts matched. The thing that had arrived on the *Pride of Jai*, at the end, matched the things that had arrived in other places. There were certain unnamed energies from Dr Talirr's portals that matched all of them. Yasira charted all of this in a drawing program, trying to get a feel for how the undocumented energies grew and interacted with the others. She hadn't the faintest idea what they were for – if the concept of purpose even meant anything, with Outside – but patterns were emerging nonetheless.

In the early afternoon the console locked itself up, reminding her that it was time for mandatory physical exercises followed by a shower, neurofeedback session and mood diary. Yasira complied, rolling her eyes. She didn't feel mentally ill and she didn't like such a fuss being made over her brain. It reminded her of being at the Galactic University of Ala on Anetaia, for grad school. Everyone wanting to study the exotic foreign autistic science prodigy and the most private and inconsequential recesses of her mind. She had spent more time than usual hiding in her dorm room.

Neurofeedback was an odd process. It wasn't a thing people did in Riayin. She'd looked it up on her first day and only vaguely understood the pages the search box brought up. It resembled nothing so much as a mildly interesting little game – a different game every day, so far – that she was asked to play while hooked up to a couple of sensors. Whatever the sensors did to stabilize her brain seemed to happen unconsciously. Today the game was a maze, beautifully rendered to resemble a ramshackle ruin of a castle, complete with ivy and tapestries. It was pretty, but Yasira found her mind drifting back to her work.

And to Tiv. It had been three days. Was that long enough for the quarantine to be over? Was Tiv free now? Since no one had told Tiv where Yasira was, what would Tiv assume was going on? Well, she was a good girl. She'd wait. Even if she thought Yasira was dead, she'd wait very patiently for news, to make sure.

Which was great, assuming Yasira *did* go home eventually. Akavi had given his word, but she didn't see any particular reason to trust him.

Oh. The neurofeedback game didn't like that thought. The screen fuzzed with static interference and the pretty maze started to fade. Yasira refocused, tried to put Tiv behind her for now and it came back into view.

Eventually the system decided she'd done enough. The maze faded and the rest of the console unlocked itself. Another bot came in to reward her with fresh fruit as she got back to work.

Several hours after dinner, Yasira said, "I've got it," again. She'd finished analyzing the patterns and ranges of each energy type around known Outside events, and now she had a decent educated guess at what Dr Talirr's research space might look like to God-built sensors.

Biting her lip, she typed this in. The screen went blank for longer than before – or was that just Yasira's fatigue setting in? – and then a map of the galaxy shimmered into place.

0 results.

Yasira swore under her breath.

She rechecked her calculations, then tried relaxing parameters. If she allowed a wider range of energy types and searched the entire past three years, there were small results here and there. Some of them were linked to reports: minor Outside incidents, much smaller than Zhoshash, which had already been logged in the system. The reports were uniformly by angels of Nemesis, and none mentioned

Dr Talirr. Each ended with the same line. *Heretics: adjudicated and terminated,* followed by a timestamp in Earth Standard Time.

Yasira bit her lip. Each of these little things had been cause for someone's execution. But none were as big or as flashy as what had happened on the *Pride of Jai*. That disaster was hers, no matter how much blame she passed to Dr Talirr. And Akavi, so far, had let her live.

She wondered how long that would last.

The rest of the results were labeled, too, but not with anything interesting. They were rare but mundane astronomical events – false positives. None of them looked like they could be the research space she'd pictured.

But there were still those blue-gray areas. Hostile alien territory, the galactic core, a few other trouble spots. If Dr Talirr had known that the Gods had blind spots, and if she'd worked out a way to survive in those places, then she was functionally undetectable.

Which was not a solution to Yasira's problem. But she'd done her due diligence; if Dr Talirr was alive and researching somewhere, she now had a good case to make that it was in one of those places. Tomorrow, she could talk to someone about conditions within each blind spot, how to narrow it down. Yasira's prior knowledge of Dr Talirr's habits might be useful there. Maybe…

She paused, her hand poised over a blue-gray area, and changed her mind. The galactic core and other trouble spots within the galaxy weren't the only things in that color. The edges of the map, outside the Milky Way, were also blue-gray.

Outside. It was a completely different sense of the word, but it fit. That was a prevailing theme throughout the diaries – to leave, to escape, to go elsewhere. Back in graduate school, Dr Talirr had been famous for walking out of meetings, even leaving in the middle of seminars when they exasperated her. She would be found later, stalking the forested park at the edge of campus and grumbling to herself. Yasira had dealt with sensory stress by retreating inwards, regrouping in some safe corner. Dr Talirr had dealt with it by going *out*.

No one could get out of the galaxy with portals alone. If one went into a portal, one had to come out through some other portal. And the ansible network that supported God-built portals only extended to a certain radius. Dr Talirr's portals might not be tied to that network, but they had to be tied to *something*, and if they were anything like God-built portals at all, she would have had to get to intergalactic space first before building a portal there. So, to truly leave the galaxy, Dr Talirr would have had to acquire and use a God-built ship. A warp drive.

And operational warp drives gave off a lot of energy.

Yasira flicked back to the keyboard. *Show me all warp-drive-like signals traveling outside the sensor radius of the galaxy since Dr Talirr's last known appearance.*

The console blanked for half a second, then displayed the map in fast-forward, showing the galaxy's slow rotation as its search progressed from the past to the present. Various signals appeared, but they looked more manageable than the three million results from earlier. Only a couple of dozen per year, and she only had three years to look at. That was promising.

She stopped playback and rewound to the beginning, selecting each result in turn and checking for known explanations. Most were tagged as expeditions of angels on some redacted mission or other – mostly Nemesis and Arete, but also one from Agon, one from Philophrosyne, a couple from Aletheia... And some were tagged as incursions from the Keres.

Yasira shivered. Lack of portals wasn't the only reason people didn't go out of the galaxy. The Keres, a failed God – or more correctly, a group of failed Gods, though She was referred to in the singular – had been banished out there after the Morlock War. The Keres had wanted to enslave and cull humanity instead of nurturing them, and had fought the other Gods for supremacy; some mortals, desperately misguided and refusing to accept the true Gods' authority, had sided with Her. Nowadays, when She made Her way in with a ship or two, it was not to continue the War, per se – She was too weak for that now – but in vengeance. To kill mortals on scales even the *Pride of Jai* couldn't match.

And it had always been Nemesis, cruel as Nemesis could be, who stopped Her.

Could Dr Talirr have hitched a ride with the Keres somehow? No. Mortals didn't do that and survive.

Yasira frowned more deeply as she went further through the timeline. She was almost up to the present now, and there didn't seem to be anything unaccounted for. How long could Dr Talirr have taken before finding a warp drive and leaving? Was it possible she'd left the galaxy without generating visible energy? Maybe she'd started from one of the blue-gray areas and worked her way out from there. Maybe Boater space, on the far end of the Carina-Sagittarius arm – assuming the Boaters didn't just kill her when she entered. Or…

Wait.

Four days ago, there was a single unaccounted-for result. Not an unknown ship leaving the galaxy, but an unknown ship, with a very small warp drive, coming *in*.

Yasira zoomed in, her eyes widening. The Gods' systems hadn't completely ignored this ship, of course; there was a tentative label of *alien craft, unconfirmed*, but it hadn't been large enough, fast enough, or close enough to any known targets to merit further inspection. The visible trajectory was a simple, gentle curve that dipped into the edge of the ansible network and slipped out again forty-eight hours after appearing. But the moment of deepest approach into the network, the trajectory's center, was *17:52:43, June 13, 2791, Earth Standard Time*.

The precise moment of the *Pride of Jai* disaster.

And at that precise moment, relative to the galactic center, the ship had been moving in exactly the same direction as the *Pride of Jai*.

Dr Talirr had gone to so much trouble being stealthy before. After all this time, she couldn't have simply strayed into the galaxy, at this very suggestive angle, by accident.

Had she been watching, just as the Gods were? Yasira recalled some of the university social events that she'd been to. Neurotypical academics with drinks in their hands, mingling, chatting, sizing each other up; Yasira politely scripting her way through it at the edges, mindful of how much time she had before she entered overload and had to leave; Dr Talirr hovering awkwardly, several feet away from the nearest other person, unable to manage even that. Yes, sitting at the edge of the galaxy watching would be very like her. But she shouldn't have needed a trajectory like that. Breaching the ansible network at all ought to have been enough.

Or, knowing that Yasira *expected* her at the edges, had she been trying to send a message?

Yasira spent a few minutes calculating likely continuations of the trajectory. Then she opened a text-sending window, not to Elu, but to Akavi.

I've found her, she typed, when the connection opened. *But I think it's a trap.*

Akavi peered over Yasira's shoulder at the chart of the galaxy. This was unnecessary, since he had downloaded the chart into his head and could mentally examine it from whatever angle he pleased. But the physical signs of shared attention helped put mortals at ease. For the same reason, he was no longer in his true form; he had picked one of the two dozen elegant male forms that he kept memorized for generic situations. This one was light-skinned, dark-haired, sharp-chinned, and Yasira had taken a moment to work out that it was still him.

"Yes," he said. "That's very likely Talirr, and almost certainly a trap. The trajectory suggests not only that she was interested in the *Pride of Jai* disaster, but that she saw it coming."

Worrying. The Gods had known something would happen, of course, but the precise scale and timing hadn't been obvious even to Nemesis.

The *Pride of Jai* had been, very publicly, Yasira's disaster. Akavi had told Irimiru that Yasira was different from the others. Special. Was it possible that Talirr thought so, too?

"Well," said Yasira, "a trap is better than nothing. Right? It's at least sort of a lead and we didn't have any of those before. There's got to be a way we can use it."

"Of course there is. But walking blindly in is *not* our preferred tactic. She's been out there for three years; if she wanted to show herself, why wait until now?"

Yasira frowned, then offered hesitantly, "Maybe she's interested in *me*."

They were thinking along the same lines. Promising. Also dangerous, since Yasira was operating with incomplete information. "Explain."

Yasira looked down at the woodgrain of the desk, her straight hair falling over her face, and tapped her fingers. This seemed to be a difficult line of thought for her. "You see, Dr Talirr always pushed me to learn more deeply, more widely. Sometimes she'd just throw random books at me that had nothing to do with my thesis. But they were things she wanted me to know. Now I've gotten in trouble with Outside, the way she has, and now I'm on a God-built ship with God-built sensors and access to her secret papers and diaries. If she has some way of knowing all of that..." She looked back up at Akavi, worried. "Does she? Because if she does, I think maybe she'd want to talk to me. I think maybe she'd have more she'd want to teach me."

Heretical things, of course, but that went without saying, and Akavi's augmented vision was catching repulsed and reluctant microexpressions from Yasira. Just because she'd had the idea didn't mean she liked it. In the back of mind, he took out and flipped through his own digital copies of the files on Talirr, though he knew there would be nothing in there that he didn't already remember.

Talirr herself had never mentioned any student by name in her diaries, but the most recent diary was from three years ago. It was plausible that Dr Talirr had taken a renewed interest in Yasira since then. But that raised questions. She had not set any traps of this nature for her seven other kidnapped students, which implied that she had *not* taken an interest of this kind in any of them. Why not? Perhaps she knew about Yasira, but not about them. Perhaps she was interested not in the students, per se, but in the disaster.

Akavi smiled thinly. "She'd know that you're with us if she has access to mortal media. It's public knowledge that you disappeared while the *Leunt* was locked down, and angels of Nemesis detaining you is an obvious guess, particularly given that angels were visibly present on the *Leunt* at that time. I'm afraid the press is not fond of you at the moment." He turned and started to pace. He began his own signals analysis internally as he spoke, in dialogue with the *Menagerie's* systems; perhaps Talirr *had* sent messages like this for the other students and had simply not been heard. He doubted it, though. Another *Menagerie* program was busily churning away, extrapolating every possible bit of information from the chunk of Talirr's trajectory that had been visible to Yasira's queries. "But normally, when we take custody of heretics who have caused as much damage as you, there's less signals analysis and more vivisection. She'd have to know, or to have guessed, that we'd make an exception for you."

Yasira's expression was decidedly unhappy now. Good.

He turned on his heel and continued to talk. "If Talirr did this to send a signal to you, then we have a more pressing problem. To have reached this trajectory, even assuming arbitrary extragalactic portals, she would have to have started at least a day *before* the *Pride of Jai* disaster. Which means, despite being outside the galaxy, she detected warning signs that were not obvious to you or the directors, and not fully understood even by our forces. *And* she precisely extrapolated the time that the disaster would occur. Any idea how she worked all that out?"

Yasira hesitated. "I…"

Akavi watched her flatly, waiting for the wheels to finish turning in her mortal head. Would Irimiru count this as a success? A brief glimpse of Talirr on the God-built sensors was more than any other student had accomplished. But it was not victory. It was not even, technically, Yasira's accomplishment. And if it was a dead end, the time spent chasing it took them that much closer to the point where Yasira's sanity slipped away.

"Well, she clearly understands Outside better than I do," said

Yasira at last. "Maybe better than you do; it's a little hard to tell. And space is a lie. So, I don't know, but maybe perception is also a lie? Or – the parts of space that limit perception. Maybe she can see things a normal person wouldn't be able to see. Maybe it just… works that way."

Akavi considered this silently. It was mere speculation, and an idea he'd considered before, but even so, the concept of an enemy who might be able to see anything he did at any time, according to rules he was incapable of understanding, made him cranky. Yasira looked at him questioningly, and he returned her look with a glare. Then he stalked out, shutting the door behind him.

Yasira hunched slightly in her chair and crossed her arms. Now that she wasn't working the silence of the little suite weighed on her. She'd expected maybe a "thank you", or an estimate on when she could go home and see Tiv again. Or something. Stupid, really. She was still a prisoner.

She trudged to the bathroom to brush her teeth, but the ritual wasn't enough to make her feel like sleeping. Half-solved problems often did this to her: without some soothing distraction, like a cheap novel or a cuddle with Tiv, she'd be too on edge to sleep. She trudged back and fired up the console again.

The console didn't have any novels but it did have some easy-to-read introductory files, only some of which she'd already poked through. Things like, "Crew and Bot Roster." "Read This Before Trying To Print Anything." And, most enticingly, "Floor Plan."

Yasira liked the idea of trying to figure out where Akavi was just now. She clicked on the floor plan.

The basics were visible: her own plush cell, labeled with a small red star, and every other non-secret room of the ship. Those big, wasteful corridors had a pattern after all: twisty but regular, like a Celtic knot or an arabesque. A large private room near the front of the ship bore Akavi's name. Then there was one for Elu, one for Enga, one for Sispirinithas – along with a host of other names Yasira didn't know.

There were also huge redacted areas, and scatterings of smaller ones all over. What did that mean? There were lots of things angels *might* want to hide from their guests – anything from horrible murder rooms to secure filing cabinets to God-built machines too delicate to mess with. Yasira didn't know enough about Akavi yet to guess which of those applied, and which was where.

She'd still only been out of her room once since she arrived – when Elu had walked her to Akavi's office and back. She closed her eyes and tried to picture that route's twists and turns, but it all blended into one big curve in her mind.

She chewed her lip, scrolling across the map. If she couldn't trace her own route to Akavi's office, what was she looking for? Well, a lot of things. An ansible, ideally – but she was going to need more than a map for that. This console's ansible connection was disabled, so she'd have to start by escaping *this* room, and hope that Akavi didn't kill her or something when he found out. Then if she found an ansible, she'd have to work out how to use it. On mortal planets that was easy: you went to the nearest local terminal, gave a delivery address, paid, and then said to the camera whatever you wanted to say. It worked itself out. But there was no reason to assume that the *Menagerie's* ansibles worked the same way. There were probably passwords, and there might be more than that. The ship's ansible might be something only angels could use. There might not even *be* any ansibles, apart from the network connections in the angels' own brains. Though Elu had said there were mortal crew aboard, so there was hope.

Well, she could start memorizing the parts that weren't redacted, at least. That might or might not ever be useful. But the map was easier to understand laid out in front of her like this. That way, if she ever did get out of her room, she might be able to find her way through the ship.

She scrolled back and forth, counting the number of times the regular floor pattern repeated, giving each little knot of corridors a mnemonic name and noting where anything unusual happened. The work went quickly; Yasira had always been quick at memorization. But there was a lot of it. Before long the lines on the screen started blurring together, and she stumbled, exhausted and resentful, to bed.

Akavi, being an angel, did not need to sleep. While Yasira languished in her room he paused not far away before another door. An intricate carving stretched overtop the doorway, reflecting a host of subtle colors and textures only enhanced senses could detect, and glinting with the fangs, horns, and feathers of exotic caged animals. He considered his options, then mentally executed the command to open it.

The star-like lights showing the positions of other angels floated in his mind's eye as always, though at present he was focusing only on those nearby. Such senses, of course, were reciprocal; the other angels would also see that he was paying a visit here. Elu would be concerned; Elu was always concerned. Akavi smiled sardonically.

The door opened into a suite like Yasira's, though all sharp edges and hard corners had been removed. At first glance, everything seemed well-kept and welcoming. It was remarkable how tidy God-built bots could keep a space, even when no self-care ability remained to the prisoner within.

On the floor next to the armchairs sat a wretched man perhaps five years older than Yasira, reading something on a tablet he'd placed between his feet, fingers curled tightly in his matted hair. He was olive-skinned and much larger-framed than Yasira, yet his posture gave the impression of smallness. As Akavi entered, the man gave him a vague, fey, frightened look.

"Splió," he said, inclining his head. "It's been a few months, hasn't it?"

Splió only whimpered.

Akavi tilted his head. "I trust you haven't lost the power of speech since our last visit."

He mentally flipped through the latest reports, a cascade of information flitting across his consciousness in the time it took Splió to respond. Someone would have reported if Splió had any sharp increase in expressive difficulties; as they had, in fact, for another of the prisoners a few months ago. Akavi visited Splió and his fellow students only rarely, but Elu insisted on checking in with each of them once a week, and Dr Meyema came by nearly that often for exploratory assessments. Other mortals occasionally requested permission to drop by, as their curiosity dictated, and reported anything unusual that they saw back to Akavi. In an emergency, such as a suicide attempt, the *Menagerie's* surveillance systems would have alerted him immediately.

"You're a lie," said Splió, in a voice dry and raspy from lack of use. His nostrils flared. "Speech is a lie."

The microexpression detector in Akavi's sensory cortex annotated Splió's expression busily, sending up a slew of red flags for likely mental disturbance, but it was nothing Akavi didn't already know. The students in this corridor had been driven insane through indirect contact with Outside; yet there was remarkably little screaming, babbling, or violence. Yasira had been right, in a sense, to object to the term "madness": that part of Outside was not like the pulp novels. There were delusions and disturbances in sensory experience, but for the most part Splió's symptoms resembled a simple mood disorder. Listlessness and fear that had steadily increased until all work became unbearable and productivity dropped to nothing, and no known therapy made a difference.

The first time it happened, with the student preceding Splió, Akavi had suspected insubordination. But that was incorrect: it was a genuine loss of capacity. The sort of punishment which sent most mortals weeping and repentant back to their duties only made these students more useless. They had, in a sense, already been broken.

Irimiru had suggested terminating them when they reached this stage. Or, since they had committed no actual crimes – Nemesis was very literal about Her laws sometimes – dropping them into the mortal psychiatric system to wither away. They were so visibly out of touch with reality that, paradoxically, the risk of contagion had become negligible; other mortals would dismiss their raving out of hand, and the same symptoms that prevented them from working usefully for Nemesis would prevent them from working usefully against Her. But Akavi hated to waste resources, and he had opted to keep all seven. They still aroused his curiosity, and the cost of their care, by divine standards, was negligible. Over time, he had found that despite their inability to work, there were ways to make them useful. After a fashion.

Akavi knelt down on the floor beside Splió. Splió shied away, but didn't flee; there were only so many places to go, in a suite this size.

"I will ask this once," he said, "politely. You can choose if you'd like to make me ask it again. What does Evianna Talirr know about this ship, and about our mission?"

"She doesn't know anything," said Splió. "Knowledge is a lie. Dr Talirr is a lie."

Instantly Akavi reached out and grabbed Splió by the jaw, pulling the man towards him. His fingernails became small claws. "Heretical nonsense," he said, with a voice as calm and unruffled as before. "Repeating your little dogma does not constitute an answer. You insist Talirr is a lie. Yet despite this handicap she appears to have made certain predictions relating to our mission that no mortal should have been able to make. All while remaining outside the galaxy and outside the range of any known means of communication. How?"

Splió's lower lip trembled, and his breathing sped, while the red sensory flags annotating his face grew steadily more insistent. A pitiful lack of emotional endurance, but then, with Outside, that was usually the first thing to go. "What are you talking about? What did she predict?"

Akavi twisted his fingers, drawing five tiny drops of blood that spiraled down through Splió's matted beard. "Oh, I'm sorry. I must not have spoken clearly, because you seem to have missed the part where *I* asked *you* a question. How much does Talirr know about our activities, and how does she know it?"

"I don't know!" said Splió, hyperventilating. "It's been five years since I saw her and Outside doesn't even do location properly and you're asking questions that don't make any sense. How do you expect me to know what disasters she's been paying attention to?"

Sometimes Akavi suspected that madness was not a side effect of Outside but the key to understanding it. The students' most interesting insights came at times like this, when their least productive emotions were most pronounced.

Every possible connection to the outside world on Splió's console was disabled, except for a single application which he could use in an emergency to call for help. He had appropriate entertainment materials uploaded periodically, but his only source of news was visitors, and – Akavi checked the logs to make sure – no, he hadn't had one of those since before the *Pride of Jai* disaster. Elu had visited him shortly before that and wasn't due back for another day or two. Akavi would go over the entire surveillance video later to be sure, but even though the angels had suspected an impending disaster at that point, Elu was not careless enough to have mentioned it to this type of prisoner. So Splió had no way of knowing what had happened.

Akavi retracted his claws, then his hand. "Disasters?"

Splió tried to brush away the blood from his chin, but only succeeded in smearing it further into his beard. "I don't know," he mumbled. "Didn't you say something about a disaster?"

Akavi studied his face, as his augmented vision continued to log each microexpression, correlating it with past results from similar interrogations. Splió was not consciously withholding information. What these students knew was unconscious, irrational, without context. And while agitation was helpful up to a point, one could not simply beat details out of them. They knew what they knew, and only that.

The word *disasters* was not hard evidence. It would need to be corroborated by interviews with the other students, which Akavi would perform shortly. But it was not the first time a student had guessed things correctly about Outside that they shouldn't have known. It was always unconscious, never the sort of thing that could be put in a report. But some part of these students, deep down, seemed to be connected to something elsewhere. *Disasters* suggested that, when that part of Splió searched for knowledge abⲟⲩⲧ Talirr's senses, it found her watching the *Pride of Jai* – and not A Menagerie. Not directly.

Which meant Akavi and Yasira still had a fighting chance at outmaneuvering her.

Akavi smiled, rose, and turned to go. "Good work, Splió. That's very helpful. I'll write up a commendation in your file."

"I'm not stupid, you know," Splió called after him. "You can stop *treating* me like I'm stupid. Maybe if you actually told me what was going on, instead of clawing at me and saying bullshit, I could tell you something useful. Has that ever occurred to you?"

Akavi shut the door wordlessly, leaving him alone in his cell. He took out a chemical wipe and cleaned the blood from his nails.

It had, in fact, occurred to him. But it had also occurred to him that sharing information with students like Splió, even when necessary, was a risk. They were not ordinary mad people; they were profoundly and intimately connected with the Godless Outside that Evianna Talirr loved so much. He suspected that, if they ever had enough conscious knowledge to make the choice, all seven of them would betray him.

CHAPTER 7

It is literally impossible to describe what I mean, what I have experienced, as the very nature of that thing is to transcend verbal concepts. I can only give an apophatic exegesis of what Outside is not. It is not in time as we know it, not in space as we know it. It is not good; it does not have our best interests at heart. It is not evil; any harm it does to us is merely a byproduct. It is not morally neutral; it is neither static nor mindless nor intelligent as we understand such things. It is the most beautiful thing in the universe, and the most terrible, and the ugliest – and, of course, it is not "in the universe" at all.

FROM THE DIARIES OF DR EVIANNA TALIRR

In Yasira's dream, she was back on the *Pride of Jai*, in the generator room, with her handheld monitoring device. Instead of a dial, it had the bright, responsive interface of a God-built console. Swirls and spikes in disaster colors snaked out of it, jabbing at her face and forearms through her sterile suit.

"Stop it," she said, trying to swat them away, but they went right through her. One rose up, pierced her suit's visor, and drove itself into her right eye. She shrieked and dropped the device. There was no pain, only pressure and panic, and a blinding explosion of purple, green, white…

Ping, said the monitoring device.

"Damn it," said Yasira, as she fought to dislodge the color from her face. Her hands wouldn't connect with it air around them felt like sludge. She was going to have to report this dream when she woke up – all bad or strange dreams had to be reported, which was stupid, because mentally healthy people had strange dreams all the time – and, in the panic of the dream, it seemed obvious that Akavi would not like what she was seeing. There would be consequences.

But if she knew she was dreaming, why was she still fighting the– *Ping*.

Ping. She was awake in her bed on the *Menagerie*. According to the clock, it was the middle of the night. But the *ping* was real. Someone was text-sending to her and the console was loud enough to wake her.

Yasira rubbed her eyes. She wrapped a blanket around herself and stumbled out of the bedroom to the working desk.

The message was from Elu. *You should wake up and get decent,* it said. *Akavi wants to talk to you in person in the next half-hour.*

Yasira scowled. *It's the middle of the night.* Though in space, with people who didn't need to sleep anyway, she supposed that was arbitrary.

Sorry, said Elu. *It's time-sensitive.*

What do you mean, time-sensitive? *What happened?*

Elu hesitated a full ten seconds before he replied, *He wants to fly you out of the galaxy.*

Yasira supposed, as she trudged to the bathroom and splashed water on her face, that it all made sense. She hated surprise changes of plans, but it wasn't like that mattered to Nemesis. Akavi had probably taken exactly this long to resolve his worries and figure out how to move forward, and was now in an understandable hurry.

Except without access to Dr Talirr, how exactly had he resolved *anything*?

Yasira yanked a brush through her hair. She hated this ship, she hated these angels, and she hated being woken up at three-thirty in the morning.

By the time the door swished open, she'd managed to get dressed, at least. Akavi was at the door, back in his true form again for the first time since her first day on the ship. If that form was supposed to signify something, she had no idea what it was.

She tried and failed to push her cranky feelings to the side. "Elu told me we're going out of the galaxy. Do you want to tell me what we're going to be doing there?"

Couldn't he have just steered the *Menagerie* out of the galaxy without her and let her sleep? Well, maybe not. It was a big ship. Maybe they didn't want to take the whole thing.

"No," said Akavi, distractedly. "It's more efficient if I brief you once we're underway. Come with me. The *Talon* is fully supplied, and I've copied your console files to its system, so you needn't worry about bringing anything."

Yasira's fingers twitched in annoyance as she hurried along. Her brain rumbled to life despite everything. It was only the second time she'd been out in these halls and she tried to match the turns they took to the floor plan she half-remembered. They were moving towards the front of the ship, along the lower edge of the rosette that held her room. If she remembered right, this area wasn't close to anything redacted, just guest rooms and…

Wait, no. In the floor plan she remembered, they should be walking past a blank wall. The lack of a door here was one of the things that distinguished Yasira's rosette from others. But here was a door.

They kept walking and soon the door vanished from sight. Yet the rest of these corridors were the way Yasira remembered. She wasn't confused; she hadn't lost track of the route. She'd been right about everything but the door.

Was she remembering wrong? Or had someone erased the door deliberately? It was a clever trick, if so. Distracting Yasira with obvious redactions, so she didn't notice the things that were simply gone.

Which led to another question: why distract her? If she was locked in her room, why bother with an elaborate deceptio
things that were inaccessible anyway?

115

It suggested that they were planning on letting her out by herself, eventually. It was at least possible, in one of the many possible plans Akavi had made. This was not as encouraging as Yasira had thought it would be. It implied that, in at least one of Akavi's possible plans, she was going to be stuck here long enough to become something like crew. She did not want to be crew. She wanted to be at home, with Tiv and her family and, at this time in the morning, asleep.

Things could be worse, she supposed. Being stuck on Akavi's ship, or on a smaller one outside the galaxy, was better than being tortured and killed as a heretic. Though she had no guarantee that was not still in the cards, in some other scenario. *You'll be free to go back to Jai if you wish,* he'd said, but could she trust him? It was rarely that easy with Nemesis. Maybe he'd kill her anyway, and say, *The dead do not wish.*

Her fingers twitched.

Eventually Akavi brought her to a portal. The silvery arch shimmered to life as they approached, and the metal wall behind it disappeared, leaving an opening into a bright, orderly space. Akavi strode through without pausing.

Yasira walked through the portal, then paused and blinked. There was no physical sensation to the portal itself, but the sudden change of surroundings made her light-headed.

The *Talon* was as luxurious as the *Menagerie* but far more compact. The room they'd stepped into looked like a bridge, with two swivel chairs in front of a complex set of controls and a huge window looking out into space. In other directions, instead of twisting hallways, there were only simple doorways connecting one room to another. At one side of the ship there was a large room of shelves that looked like storage for bots and equipment. To the other, a parlor alcove with a square table and three chairs led to three more small, closed doors without visible locks. And next to the portal she'd just come in by there was a very heavy door indeed, thick and elaborately sealed. That one said *AIRLOCK.*

Yasira tapped her fingers on the metal wall. She couldn't see the *Menagerie* out of the window. Just stars, and not even stars in the patterns she was used to. The thick wheel of the galaxy in one direction and almost nothing in the other. They were already at the edge of human space.

Akavi strode to one of the chairs and sat down, then looked back at Yasira. "Do make yourself at home," he said. "But don't fall asleep. I have a few hours of navigating to do and afterwards I'll want to brief you fully and promptly."

Yasira hesitated. He'd gone to all that care to keep her locked up tight. And now that they were alone together he was giving her free run of the ship. That didn't make sense.

Well, sense or not, better take advantage of it before he changed his mind.

She explored the parlor first. A large, boxy machine stood at the side of the room – a food printer, she supposed. The three closed doors were not locked, and each one led to a separate suite of living quarters. The biggest room looked like Akavi's, since it had neither a bed nor a console – just wide chairs that looked like they were for resting, a clothes closet, a bathroom, and scattered artwork and cushions. Yasira's room, on its left, was like a studio apartment, with a bed and dresser to one side and a console desk to the other. It was smaller than her room on the *Menagerie*, but still bigger than her quarters on the *Pride of Jai*.

She paused by the console, wondering whether to report her dream, but decided to do it later. She could no longer remember what exactly it was about it that Akavi would be so displeased by, anyway. First she would explore.

The third room confused her. It looked a lot like her own, only the bed was sheetless, the bathroom empty of supplies, and the closet bare. Yasira stood there for a while, wondering what it was for. Maybe it didn't mean anything; maybe there just weren't any God-built ships with less than three bedrooms.

Or maybe, if Akavi captured Dr Talirr, *she* would be staying here.

That thought didn't make much sense. In the records Yasira had seen, heretics were adjudicated and terminated on the spot, not dragged all around the galaxy first. Yasira's case was different only because Akavi was using her to get to another heretic. And nothing in this room resembled restraints or other safety features. It seemed like just a spare room.

She wandered out of the living quarters again and crept into the storage room. This was a medium-large space stacked with supplies, machines, and replacement parts. Yasira tiptoed through the aisles between the tall shelves and racks. She recognized chemical storage tanks, a pair of space suits – sleeker and lighter than the mortal kind – and some dormant, folded-up bots. The latter looked very delicate, like she could snap their casings with her hands. There were also many things she couldn't identify at all.

This was silly. Surely some of the items here were dangerous or breakable. Was Akavi really letting prisoners in here without a security protocol?

Maybe he was. Maybe, after her time on the *Menagerie*, he trusted her now. What would that imply?

Yasira experimentally reached out to touch one of the bots. Faster than her eyes could track, a boxy security bot zipped in from the other side of the room and deflected her hand.

"Ouch," said Yasira, shaking her wrist.

"You are unauthorized for equipment retrieval," said the bot. "This is your first unauthorized attempt at physical access to equipment."

"Yeah, I gathered," said Yasira.

"If there is something you require," said the bot, "I can alert the ship's commanding officer. Current commanding officer is Akavi Averis, Inquisitor of Nemesis. Would you like me to alert him that there is something you require?"

Yasira shook her head. "No. Just looking around."

"You are authorized to look around in the vicinity of equipment," said the bot. "You are not authorized for physical access. You are currently on record with one unauthorized attempt at physical access to this ship's equipment. Second and third unauthorized attempts will be deflected with electric as well as physical force."

Yasira sighed. "Of course they will."

"Have a nice day," said the bot.

From the time he entered the *Talon* to the time he flew out of reach of the ansible nets altogether, Akavi had about twenty subjective minutes to make sure Elu and the rest of his collection were prepared to be functional in his absence.

They had planned for this, of course. Talirr's presence outside the galaxy was obviously a trap, and it was quite possible that one of the trap's functions was to draw Akavi away from his job, allowing an attack or other unpleasantness to happen in his absence. Akavi suspected that this was not Talirr's primary goal, but it was what he would have done in her position, so he'd prepared. Along with the usual guidelines on damage control during Outside attacks, Akavi had long ago worked up a set of specific procedures geared to Talirr's profile, in consultation with other experts and with Dr Meyema, tailored specifically to the strengths of the people working for him. He'd been updating it periodically as the mission went on, in case something like this happened, and it was as complete as it currently could be. Elu was in charge of that file now, and in charge of the *Menagerie* in general. Until Akavi's return, he would be keeping everyone else appropriately busy and cared for, and fending off interference from Irimiru – though none was expected, as Irimiru had approved Akavi's proposal for leaving the galaxy without a fuss.

Despite his apparent youth, Elu had been Akavi's official assistant for fifty years. He had learned a great deal in that time. He was ready for this. But, human psychology being what it was, he didn't appear to believe so himself.

Enga seems unhappy about you leaving without her, Elu text-sent. *She says if you run into Outside monsters you will need guns, not science. At least I think that's what she said.*

She'll get over it, Akavi replied. *I explained my reasoning to her already. If she seems restless, give her priority preference on Irimiru's military roster. You're authorized for that now.*

Enga had of course not contacted Akavi herself. Enga followed protocol, and questioning a superior officer was not protocol.

Complaining to Elu, roughly her equal in rank, was a different matter. And if Elu happened to be the type of angel who would forward her concerns to Akavi despite protocol, well, that was not technically Enga's fault.

Elu had his reasons for playing along. Akavi already knew his insecurities. It would have been humiliating for Elu to have to describe them out loud. But relaying someone else's complaints gave him an excuse to talk. To stay in touch just a few minutes longer. It was charmingly predictable.

Elu's residual emotion continued to increase. He missed Akavi already. He was worried he would do a bad job running things. *What do I do if you're late coming back and Irimiru complains?*

Generally, when Irimiru is unhappy, one hides in a corner and prays. Akavi smiled. *I'm beginning to accelerate at hyper-relativistic speeds, Elu, and the navigation is somewhat involved. I'd appreciate if you didn't distract me by sending hours' worth of emotional flotsam in what will soon, to me, feel like seconds. Was there anything else?*

Elu dithered. Akavi wordlessly severed the connection and turned his attention back to the *Talon's* controls. Soon the ansible in his head went altogether silent and space emptied out into a void.

Already out of places to explore and feeling strangely let down, Yasira returned to her room. The colors were different from the ones in her old room – blues and greens, a little brighter. The luxurious wooden console desk was the same, though a little smaller.

She fired up the console and started poking through files. They were both oddly complete and disappointingly few. There was even a full floor plan in here, without redactions – because there wasn't anything interesting here to redact.

Apart from a new folder of *Talon*-specific files, she still had everything she'd been working on. She opened the *Menagerie's* floor plan briefly, to check if she'd guessed right about the missing door. Yes, there it was – she could mentally retrace her steps and find the corridor. The floor plan said there was a guest room there behind the wall, but it was supposed to open the other way, into a different rosette. There wasn't supposed to be a door where she'd seen one.

Well, great. If she ever came back to the *Menagerie*, she'd look into that.

There were interesting hinges and slots in the desk. Yasira inspected them for a minute, then folded them out. This console was detachable: the screen came away into a tablet the size of a hardcover book. She picked it up and wandered to the parlor. She liked the idea of not being locked in her room anymore.

She snuck a glance onto the bridge. Akavi sat there, faced away from her, watching the controls and tapping at them occasionally. The *Talon* was moving very quickly now: there was no sensation of speed, not even movement of stars around them, since they were headed into empty blackness. But there was the slight violet shimmer of a warp drive, unmistakable, at the edges of the window.

Yasira had seen this before. Both her graduate schools had been outside Jai. Most trips from planet to planet, of course, did not need spaceships; one simply registered an interplanetary transit ticket, gathered one's things, went through customs and security checks, and was waved through a portal onto another world. But for that to work there had to be a portal at both ends, and not every place in the galaxy had portals. Mortals prized God-built warp drives dearly for the ability to take them to asteroids, moons, and uninhabited worlds, or even through alien space. Yasira had taken trips of that nature herself, once or twice, as part of a hands-on graduate-level course. So she recognized the shimmer. But the *Talon's* was much more intense than what she'd seen before, and it was only growing brighter.

Akavi was still ignoring her, of course. Yasira rolled her eyes at the back of his strange, gray-white head, then arranged herself at the parlor table and paged through the *Talon's* introductory files.

Oh, *this* was interesting. "How To Use The Food Printer". She clicked it and skimmed the simple instructions. It seemed easy. You searched for a recipe, picked one, selected a quantity, and out came food, like magic.

Apples, Yasira typed experimentally. She was getting more than a little hungry for breakfast.

Thousands of results came up. A ridiculous number of apple cultivars, sorted into categories based on their culinary purpose. She clicked a few category names and flavor/texture traits to narrow it down, then gave up and picked one of the hundreds of remaining choices at random.

The food printer whirred, and, thirty seconds later, a hatch popped open in its steel frame. A flawless green apple stood there on a paper plate. Yasira picked up the apple, squinted at it, then returned to her chair and took a bite. It was crisp, tart, and juicy. It tasted like it had just been plucked off a tree, not painstakingly assembled from its component molecules.

She was still eating when a very unhappy thought made its way into her mind.

Yasira frowned at her tablet, which was lying neglected at the side of the table, and picked it up again. She did a search for *current trajectory*.

The food printer started whirring again of its own accord. She jumped, and thought about turning off the tablet, but she wasn't looking up anything unauthorized.

A second later, Akavi walked in. He stretched gracefully, picked something up out of the printer, and sank into the seat across from her. Yasira squinted at his food. It wasn't any dish that she recognized, only a dense, colorless rectangular prism, like a protein bar.

"Good morning," he said. "I trust you've adjusted to the surroundings and are ready for your briefing."

"I have a question," Yasira said.

Akavi paused, looking mildly interested that she hadn't simply agreed to what he said. "Yes?"

"The sleeping quarters suggest we're going to be here for a while. How long?"

Akavi shrugged. "From our point of view, a week or two, round trip."

"And from the point of view of someone back home?"

"Fourteen Earth months."

Yasira stared at him, rigid.

She'd half-expected worse: at lightspeed, a journey like this could have taken thousands of years. But hearing it aloud made it real. No one stayed this long with angels of Nemesis and came back to tell the tale. Either they punished you swiftly and set you back down planetside, or you were just gone.

She felt like she might jump up and punch him, but her voice came out small and afraid. "People will think I'm dead."

Not just dead, but dead because angels of Nemesis took her. Dead because, in the Gods' sight, she deserved to die. Her family would think she was dead that way. *Tiv* would.

It wasn't uncommon for people to disappear this way. Never anyone Yasira knew, or even friends of friends – it wasn't *that* common – but one heard things, once in a while. There had been people from Yasira's hometown who were taken by angels when she was growing up, and even a professor at the university where she did her undergrad, though she'd never met him. Afterwards, people responded certain ways. Clicked their tongues. Pointedly didn't talk about it, except in nudges and lowered voices. *I knew there was something off about him,* or *She was so quiet, kept to herself, never would have guessed.*

When angels of Nemesis took someone, there was no funeral. There was silence and you tried not to think about it. As for what happened to the parents, children, spouses, best friends that they left behind – Yasira didn't know. She had never thought to ask.

Akavi smiled thinly. "I anticipated this would be a problem for you. I'm afraid it's unavoidable; there is no faster way to reach our quarry, and your presence is necessary when we meet her, as is the continued secrecy of the mission. On the bright side, you have the rare honor of doing extremely important work with angels of Nemesis, and without even having to give us your soul. Many mortals at home might envy you. By the time you return, heads will have cooled, and the mortal presses will most likely no longer be interested in tearing you limb from limb in the wake of your disaster." He took a contented bite of his food bar.

"You didn't even tell me before we left."

"You didn't exactly have a choice in this matter. Would knowing have made a difference?"

Yasira thought of grabbing him and tearing the stupid titanium plates out of his head. But that was a bad thought. If it was Tiv, here on the God-built ship, Tiv might have listened. Tiv might have really felt proud, when an angel told her she had a rare honor. Or she might have bowed her head, meekly accepting any assignment, anything that would put things right for the people who'd died. But Yasira was no good at Gods.

"I don't want my family to mourn me," she said.

"Then," said Akavi, smiling wider, "you'd do well to follow my instructions."

Akavi spent fifty-three minutes going over the basics. He would talk to Talirr peacefully at first, and learn as much as he could about her present mental state and living conditions before capture. He suspected that he had a chance at making her come along willingly. It would be risky, but he'd converted heretics before; a surprising number of angels of Nemesis, himself included, were former criminals. A promise of mercy in the afterlife could extract a surprising amount. He would do all the talking. Yasira was here as a consultant, helping him work out how to make Talirr receptive to his ideas; she was also bait. And while he spoke to Talirr, Yasira could help to implement his backup plan, just in case.

Akavi was rather pleased with his plans, and when Yasira had digested them he left her to her own devices. She spent a few days whining about her family and girlfriend. Akavi ignored this. Like all angels, he had willingly left his family more than a century ago. He'd liked the idea of being an angel, the power and adventure, far more than he liked any people. Yasira would adjust the way anyone did. She became disoriented sometimes and had lapses in mood, but considering the usual autistic difficulties with change, she was doing quite well. And he had more pressing problems.

Chief among these was the loss of the ansible network. Akavi was accustomed to a constant flow of information. He could normally find any factual tidbit simply by thinking in its direction, and converse at will with Elu, Enga, or whoever else he needed, regardless of distance. Within human space, his sensory circuits fed him constant annotations and updates relevant to whatever he was looking at. Leaving the galaxy changed that. Soon after the end of his conversation with Elu, Akavi had left the network's range, and the comfortable background noise of his existence had disappeared.

He had planned for this, too, of course. All the information he might conceivably need while away had been saved to the *Talon's* central processor, and a great deal was duplicated inside his own head. He was still much more than mortal: his half-organic brain stored far more information than a mortal's, and many programs, including the annotations that analyzed facial expressions, ran just fine offline. As was standard protocol for extragalactic missions, he also had acquired a considerable store of recorded music, drama, mortal news programs, and other forms of sensory entertainment. Akavi disliked these, and planned to save them for emergencies; he preferred to think he was strong enough to endure boredom on his own.

The silence turned out to be stressful, but the stress intrigued more than bothered him. He felt profoundly alone, despite Yasira and her constant displays of emotion. Sealed off, as if the *Talon* was not traversing a very large space but was trapped and motionless in a very small one. The stars had fallen away behind them now, and the only lights in the sky were tiny, faint, seemingly immobile smudges. At slow moments Akavi cataloged these, charting their imperceptibly slow progress: Andromeda. Triangulum. The Magellanic Clouds. Galaxies, not stars.

As he had also expected, he didn't find himself wanting to shapeshift much. Normally, around a sell-soul or prisoner as new as Yasira, he would have taken care to make himself look human. But normal relations with prisoners didn't involve living at close quarters, all hours of the day for over a week at a time. Under those circumstances he preferred for Yasira to grow used to looking at Vaurians as quickly as possible. To her credit, it took only a few days before those fearful microexpressions, as if she were looking at a monster, stopped appearing. Yasira was the type who focused on work if she could. Akavi, in his disconnected state, could use as much of that as possible.

He had lived like this, unconnected to anything but himself, as a mortal, but it had been so long ago that he could scarcely remember how he'd handled it then. In any case, the two situations were not equivalent; his current stress, according to the files, was the equivalent of a withdrawal state. A brain adapted to a certain level of stimulus, only to have that stimulus denied. Focusing elsewhere was the only solution.

The *Talon's* controls were more cumbersome without an ansible: his brain could no longer beam messages directly to a nearby computer. Everything now had to be done through vocal and manual input. The navigation program still did most of his work for him, but there were multiple failsafes and manual overrides at each step, and he was expected to supervise the process actively.

He also had Yasira to supervise. They had several meetings a day, usually over a meal, discussing Dr Talirr's personality and habits, what defenses she might have in place, and how she might behave when cornered. He regularly reviewed the results from Yasira's neurofeedback and mood diaries. By the very nature of the mission, she had little to do outside meetings, and as a result, her loneliness, boredom, and hopelessness rose. He had expected this and had devised a solution.

"I've reconfigured the backup printer for use with inorganics," he said coolly one day at the end of the meeting, "and given you access. In case you felt like making yourself useful by tinkering."

Yasira frowned at him. "The one in the equipment room? The bots wouldn't let me too close."

He smiled slightly. "Of course not; you didn't have authorization before. But I don't need you on full-time planning duty, so why not? It's currently set up for metals, plastics, ceramics and sundry raw materials. I think you'll find our supplies adequate for your needs."

Yasira blinked, and for the first time in several days she had to visibly suppress a smile. "Is there something you want me to make for you?"

He had guessed she would react in this way. Tinkering would give her something enjoyable to do and keep her out of Akavi's hair. It might even eventually become useful.

"Nothing specific," said Akavi, "but we still don't know precisely what we will face at the end of this journey. Allow yourself to experiment. If you return to your console, you'll find I've installed a design suite that connects to the printer."

She gave him a suspicious look, but as she returned to her room, he noticed a new spring in her step. He smiled inwardly. One didn't need a pliable personality like Elu's in order to get on well with people. One only needed to anticipate and manage their desires. He hoped that Talirr would be as easy to read.

Yasira spent the days having meetings, making gadgets, reading, doing endless neurofeedback, and trying not to think about Tiv or her parents. That last bit was the hard part. She caught herself moping and brooding uselessly in her room more than once. Sometimes she stared for a long time at the console's clock – comparing the time on the *Talon* to the estimated time and date back on Jai – and then wished she hadn't, because it didn't accomplish anything.

After the first day, she found that Akavi had loaded a few books onto her console. There were some familiar religious books, including *Theodicy Stories For Children*, which her parents had read to her years ago;and some light-hearted thrillers of the sort that Yasira usually read to relax after work. Actually, they were *too* close to what she usually read after work. Right down to three of the titles she'd suggested, in letters back home, as a present to celebrate the Shien Reactor turning on. In some moods she stared at the text in a dull rage, wondering if there were *any* corners of her life the Gods hadn't cataloged.

Tinkering was better. The first thing Yasira printed was a sixty centimeter reflecting telescope. She watched the printer as it spent two and a half minutes grinding out a set of precision mirrors that would have taken mortal technicians months. Astronomy had never been her specialty but she found herself fascinated with it now, matching every smudge of light to a point on her console's galactic map.

There were a few safeguards built into the design suite, she discovered. The first time she ran into them, it was an accident. She was trying to build a small kettle to reheat drinks, but when she gave the command to print, the system refused. *Error: Design pattern unauthorized,* it said. It took her a few minutes and some digging in the console's set of regulations to work out where the problem was. It turned out to be the kettle's electric heating element. Totally safe within the larger design scheme, but it could conceivably be removed and used as a weapon, so it wasn't allowed.

Curiosity got the better of her after that, and she started to test the system's limits. Sharp cutting edges and highly reactive chemicals got errors. Printing money and ID cards didn't work, either. But a heavy crowbar was apparently fine. She cancelled that job as soon as it started. Testing limits was one thing, but she didn't want an actual weapon lying around in her room for Akavi to see.

That led to the question of how much Akavi *could* see. Without a working ansible connection he couldn't be tracking what she did on her console directly, though it was possible he might pick it up and manually download the records later. Or he could be recording with a camera or microphone, though she didn't see any of those in any obvious places, and reviewing the files periodically when she wasn't looking. But in any case, she suspected that he wasn't always tracking her in real time. Could she do something forbidden, then erase the evidence? Maybe. She toyed with the idea, but there didn't seem to be any actual forbidden files on this thing, and she wasn't sure how she would go about hacking into them if there were.

She tried not to spend much time thinking about the mission itself. Thinking too hard about Dr Talirr made her queasy. In meetings, Akavi spoke about her with such natural assurance that Yasira found herself swept along, sharing her knowledge and strategizing without really thinking about what she said. Then, when the meetings ended, she slunk back to her room and remembered that Dr Talirr had been her mentor once. A demanding and frustrating mentor at times, but also one of the most driven scientists Yasira had ever met, a woman whose dedication to her studies was infectious. A woman Yasira had liked to think understood her, when precious few at the Galactic University of Ala did. A woman Yasira had trusted, and who, perhaps, had trusted her in return.

Not that it made a difference. You couldn't just let heretics run free. Sometimes Yasira felt sorry for Dr Talirr, just as she had back on Anetaia, when the pressures of professorship in a neurotypical world drove the woman to fits of rage directed at anyone within reach. It wasn't pretty, but it wasn't her fault – was it? Then that line of thinking brought panic with it and she had to distract herself with another printer task or become useless.

At other times, there was no sympathy. After some of the meetings, Yasira paced her room wanting to be there on Dr Talirr's ship already, so she could shake her and scream in her face, asking *why*, asking how any of this could have happened. But that was a bad thought. It was Nemesis' place to punish this, not hers.

On the eleventh day out, Yasira's console started to act funny. Programs crashed or froze for no reason, and Akavi had to come in to reboot them. He did this by hand: waved her away, then unlocked a panel in the console's side and flicked a recessed button.

"I didn't know you had buttons for that," Yasira said afterwards. She'd been working with God-built computers for two whole weeks now, yet she still had no idea how they did anything.

"Under most circumstances they are unnecessary. But we're closing in on our quarry and encountering minor system glitches as a result. Nothing to worry about, but a source of small frustrations. The physical reset is a last resort; it bypasses most forms of interference."

Yasira frowned. "Does Outside stuff normally interfere with computers? I mean, your *brain* is half a computer, so if–"

"It's nothing you need to concern yourself with," Akavi snapped, and strode out to the bridge again.

Yasira scowled after him, then looked at the console again. The panel in its side didn't look hard to unlock. In fact, she discovered, it was barely locked at all. It only took a little poking with a pin to swing it open again.

She felt a little guilty, but with glitches and resets and still no ansible connection, Akavi certainly couldn't watch her now. And if there was a secret button to reset the console, there might be secret buttons to do other things. To unlock information, maybe? To gain new authorizations? If she wanted to find out, now was the time.

She peered into the recessed panel. Nope. Only one button. She pressed it, and the console shut down and rebooted again. When the screen came back on, it was the same screen with the same boring options as before.

Yasira put the console down.

After a moment's thought, she snuck to the parlor and watched Akavi. He looked more harried than before, pushing buttons repetitively or exhaling in irritation as they refused to work the first time. The equipment on the bridge seemed to be in even worse repair than Yasira's console. She watched, pretending to snack and read. The parts of the computer that processed signals from outside the ship were doing worse than others. Which made sense, if they were encountering interference. Was Dr Talirr sending that out on purpose?

Yasira slipped back into her room, picked the console back up, and fired up the design suite. She already had a telescope; she set to work printing other simple sensors. Radar would catch objects that didn't give off visible light, and it only required a transmitter and receiver, not anything God-built. Protractors, sextants, and printed charts would help Akavi navigate if the navigation programs failed.

She tried not to think about what would happen if the warp drive and steering controls failed, too. Even Yasira couldn't jury-rig a replacement warp drive.

Her printed radar transmitter worked beautifully the first time, and she felt a rush of pride – she wanted, for an irrational second, to show it off to Tiv. Then she remembered where she was, and how long it had been from Tiv's perspective since they'd seen each other, and her mood took a nosedive.

She was three-quarters of the way through the printed charts when Akavi walked in with a new body and startled her. "Yasira, I need you on the bridge now."

Yasira blinked up. She had grown used to the presence of the Vaurian, despite his strange, translucent appearance. She'd noticed that he had stopped shapeshifting around her: maybe it was a sign of trust, or maybe something completely different. But not only had he shifted again without warning, he was now an attractive, middle-aged woman, with a face very reminiscent of Dr Talirr's. The features were different – they wouldn't have been mistaken for each other – but they were certainly from the same planet and could have passed for the same family. She had on glasses, sensible flats, and a tailored business suit. She had the natural face and forehead of a mortal, the titanium plates having somehow been swallowed up under skin. Only the air of authority was familiar.

"Yes," Yasira said, swallowing her surprise. "Of course." It was a silly thing to be surprised about; most people responded better to someone with the same gender and ethnic background as themselves. Dr Talirr probably wasn't immune, and just because Akavi had relaxed around her didn't mean she could relax around their quarry. Yasira put down her tablet and hurried after the Vaurian.

"Talirr's ship is on exactly the trajectory we predicted," Akavi explained. "We've dropped out of warp speed within hailing range, but our equipment is still malfunctioning. Bring your telescope. I'll need you to take manual measurements, and to be visible nearby when I open hailing frequencies."

Yasira nodded, very nervous. She hurried to the front window. *Something* was visible in front of the *Talon*: a dark bulk, distinguished from starless blackness only by the *Talon's* glitchy, flickering searchlights, and by a few small pinpricks that could have been operating lights. She got out her telescope, a protractor, and a pad of paper, and began to make notes. Meanwhile, Akavi was at the controls, trying fruitlessly to open a communication channel.

"Akavi Averis of the *Talon*," she said, "to Dr Evianna Talirr. My ship and I are unarmed and would like to open communications, preferably in person. I have Dr Yasira Shien here with me; I am given to understand you might prefer speaking to her instead. Over."

She repeated herself in this vein as Yasira took measurements.

(Was *she* the correct pronoun now? Yasira suspected so; matching pronouns to appearance was the convention most Vaurians used, though individuals varied. She suspected that Akavi would not be pleased if she stopped her work right now to ask.) The offer to let Yasira speak instead of Akavi was an empty one, but Talirr didn't have to know that yet.

"Akavi," Yasira said quietly, "I think we have a problem."

"What?"

"Dr Talirr's ship is changing shape."

It wasn't an out-of-control writhe, like what had happened to the *Pride of Jai*. It reminded her more of a jellyfish. Fluctuating, but stable. The ship wasn't being destroyed. Probably. But it made her head hurt, and her feet wanted to run in the opposite direction.

Akavi was silent for a moment. Then she strode over and snatched the page of frustrated calculations from Yasira's hand. She scanned them with impossible speed before handing them back. "Interesting. So it is. What's the covariance with distance?"

Yasira chewed her lip and did a few more lines of calculation. The relativistic side effects of God-built warp drives were poorly understood by mortal science. "We're traveling below lightspeed relative to that thing, right? The warp drive is off, now that we're close?"

"Yes."

"Then it's not space dilation, or a simple fold in local spacetime. It's... not *any* pattern that I recognize." Yasira gritted her teeth. She was heading past nervousness and into something else. The program that took down her mood diaries had taught her the word *derealization*, and that was almost what this was: a feeling that intergalactic space was just a dream, and her real body was back on the *Pride of Jai*, gormlessly asleep while it all came apart around her. "It's just changing. Meaninglessly."

She tried not to derealize. The program said that it was a maladaptive response, and had suggested counter-responses. She took deep breaths, slowly. She wriggled her fingers and toes. She was here, awake, on the solid floor of the *Talon*, with a very real and breathing and impatient angel next to her. She did not want Akavi to watch her fall apart over something as trivial as a shapeshifting ship.

"That," said Akavi, "or the fact of change itself has a meaning. Do try to keep calm. I believe this is what Talirr wishes us to see, which means it's likely to be a pointless intimidation attempt."

Akavi returned to her post and tapped on the console a few more times, while Yasira tried hard to focus and get back to work. "Akavi Averis of the *Talon* to Evianna Talirr. Please acknowledge."

"Wait," said Yasira.

Something new had come up in the telescope's field of vision. A green light.

"What part of the ship is that coming from?" said Akavi, hurrying to her side again. "A docking bay? A weapons' port?"

Yasira frowned, unsure. "It looks more like a docking bay, but…"

"Perfect." Akavi clasped her hands. "In all likelihood, there will be someone in that vicinity who can communicate in words. This hailing protocol has become *very* tiresome. Get your spacesuit on and let's go."

"I don't want to," Yasira said abruptly.

She felt awful. She was still taking the deep breaths, but they didn't seem to be doing any good. There were pins, needles, and a cold clenching feeling all through her body. She felt irrationally certain that, if she stepped outside the *Talon*, she would never return. The darkness would swallow her.

Akavi looked at her as though she had said she didn't want to be carbon-based. "Excuse me?"

"I have a bad feeling," she said. "Last time I had a bad feeling, it meant something, remember? When I felt like this on the *Pride of Jai*, it was because I unconsciously knew what was happening. Now I'm feeling that way again. Maybe worse. Whatever happens out there, it's going to be bad."

Akavi looked her up and down, expressionless now.

"Perhaps it is," she mused. "Or perhaps you're having a normal reaction to the presence of Outside phenomena, complicated by traumatic memory fragments of your last such encounter. Unfortunately, Outside phenomena are exactly what one would expect when approaching a powerful Outside-worshipping heretic, and since our mission requires us to make such an approach, there is little I can do for you."

Yasira opened her mouth to object, but Akavi had already turned away towards the console and begun to key in a code for docking.

"Were Elu here," Akavi continued, "he would remind me that you are in a delicate state and should not be pushed too far. You might not believe it, but your sanity is important to us." She turned to face Yasira again, with not even a scrap of benevolence in her expression. "But whatever terrible things we may face today, the consequences for coming back empty-handed will be orders of magnitude worse. Moreover, I believe you've forgotten that we are in the depths of intergalactic space, with no higher authority to protect you from my wrath, and that I have given you an *order*. Get your spacesuit."

CHAPTER 8

We are not wholly incapable of feeling compassion for the disabled, even on Anetaia. I run into it every so often. The well-meaning liars who say, "Dr Talirr, there is nothing wrong with you; your mind is only different." As if they can know what is in my mind. As if I could tell them what I see every day, what I think and feel, without immediately being murdered for heresy. Universal acceptance can exist, I think, only as a failure of the imagination.

FROM THE DIARIES OF DR EVIANNA TALIRR

Akavi watched Yasira don her spacesuit and sent her through the airlock to cling to a set of handholds outside the *Talon*. Yasira had spacewalk experience from the early stages of the *Pride of Jai's* construction; she would be fine. Akavi had considered inserting a small camera into her suit's helmet but it wasn't practical. Any power source, even a tiny one, made it that much more likely she would be found.

She had noticed Yasira's startled response to her current body. Predictable and amusing; most mortals had trouble with Vaurians and gender. Akavi identified as male but she wasn't prone to dysphoria so long as she looked well-put-together and commanding. She mildly enjoyed female forms, every so often, when there was a reason to use them. And when Akavi used a form, she used *all* of it – body, clothing, mannerisms, even pronouns. Other Vaurians differed, but to Akavi, it simply felt like being thorough.

The ships docked in silence. There was finally a small *clunk* as they came to rest against each other. The *Talon's* readings, garbled as they were, reported breathable air on the other side. Akavi glanced at her own suit, hanging near the airlock, but decided against it. Even the sleekest God-built suits looked impersonal. Human vulnerability, or at least its appearance, was crucial for negotiation.

She walked into the closet-like space and stood quietly as the air cycled. The outer door hissed open into a second airlock, unmarked, but correctly aligned. After a pause, this opened as well, and Akavi went through the cycle again. The inner door opened, and she stepped cautiously into Dr Evianna Talirr's heretical lair.

Immediately past the airlock was a large, spare anteroom: floor, walls, and ceiling in bare metal, largely undecorated apart from a ribbon of red metal that extended around all of them in an irregular pattern, to form thinly cushioned seats on one wall, a table on the ceiling, a red bookshelf on the floor. There were low rumblings like heavy machinery out of sight, but no portals. That was important. God-built portals didn't function out here but there was no telling what one of Talirr's would do. Theoretically, it might be possible for those to work anywhere. If so, that would give Talirr an easy escape – an escape Akavi needed her not to have. She'd discussed possible countermeasures with Yasira but was relieved not to have to use them.

A patch on the ceiling, as well as one gerbil-sized dot in a far corner, were smudged into blackness by a filter in Akavi's circuitry. This was a modification she had asked for three years ago, when the mission began. It had been carefully slipped into the sensory relays in her thalamic nuclei, with the express purpose of blinding her to any sensory stimulation exhibiting the maddening properties of Outside. All angels on Akavi's team had these filters now. In the mission's early days she had tried giving them to the mortal students as well, but, as a side effect, they had blocked the students from any meaningful analysis of Talirr's science, so she had taken them back out. Madness seemed necessary on a mission like this, but it could be delegated.

In any case, less was having to be filtered out than expected. The sight was reassuring: it meant that the sensory filters were still working.

Which was more than she could say for everything else. Even basic systems like Akavi's data repositories were beginning to shut down. Opening files, normally as automatic as breathing, had become slow, and the retrieved information glitchy. The only things that seemed unaffected, aside from the filters, were sensory recording and the internal clock. (*00:08:04, December 27, 2791, Earth Standard Time*, and timing would be crucial here.)

Dr Evianna Talirr stood on a nearby wall, her tall form sticking out at an angle perpendicular to Akavi; obviously gravity didn't work here in its usual way. Her appearance had not changed substantially since her last known appearance in the mortal world. It betrayed neither madness nor brilliance: pale, plain, and fortyish, with a limp ponytail and a blank expression, her arms folded in front of her. She wore a scuffed white lab coat.

Akavi raised her empty hands. "Hello. Lovely ship. As I said earlier, I'm unarmed; feel free to search me if you're not sure."

Talirr made no motion to welcome her. "It's called the *Alhazred*," she said, as Akavi looked around. "Where's Yasira?"

"On the *Talon*."

"You said I could talk to Yasira. I'd like to."

Akavi raised a finger. "In a moment. I'd like to speak to you myself first."

Talirr looked at her flatly. "Of course you would. So that you can pretend to be unarmed and then... What's the word angels of Nemesis use? Terminate me."

Akavi examined the woman. The face was *mostly* blank, but the eyes were sharp and attentive. They focused on Akavi's movements as she paced slightly, watched her mouth as she spoke, flicked downward when she folded her hands. It was not a neurotypical gaze, but also not the gaze of someone in a fit of wild delirium. Which implied she had let Akavi aboard for a reason.

Akavi knew much more about Talirr than the files she had shown Yasira. Yasira had been given the most relevant information, with a focus on her unpublished academic writing and her most recent diary before her disappearance. But the angels had collated *all* the available information about Talirr, even back to infancy and to the reports from her first abortive encounters with child psychologists. Akavi still found it difficult to predict Talirr's actions, but she knew enough to make some educated guesses. Talirr had been on a watch list for some time before her escape; she'd been diagnosed with heretical predispositions as a young child, and Nemesis' sell-souls in the psychiatric system had attempted to correct them. Her parents, and even Talirr herself, had been told it was autism. The two might well have been comorbid in her case, or the heresy might have presented that way as a disguise. Dr Meyema gave it even odds. Regardless, Akavi suspected that the logic within that unassuming skull was still of a type which could be followed and analyzed. She was keen to find out.

Akavi smiled. "You knew I would come. Indignation is pointless."

She walked towards the wall and stepped experimentally up it. Gravity abruptly rearranged itself so that the wall was "down", and both Akavi and Talirr looked right side up. The airlock looked strange now, hanging in the middle of what was now another wall.

Talirr neither backed away nor warded Akavi off. She only snorted derisively, then dropped into a stretch of red metal that looked more or less like a chair. "Yes. You're mechanical, and that makes you predictable; all I have to do is use logic. You're here, which means you're confident you can capture me, kill me, or escape with something else that you value enough to justify the long trip. I'm here and allowed you to find me, which means I'm confident that you won't, and that I'll get what I wanted, instead. One of us is probably wrong. Which do you think?"

Akavi sat down across from her. "I like my odds."

Akavi had made all sorts of contingency plans for things that could go wrong here. Talirr, being rational, must have similar ones. Did she think she could somehow kill Akavi and take possession of the *Talon* and Yasira by force? That wasn't a risk that Akavi could afford to overlook. But the *Talon* had a number of emergency defenses and a potent self-destruct. In the worst case, if Talirr destroyed Akavi and tried to do something to Akavi's ship, she would destroy herself in the bargain. This would technically make Akavi's mission a success, though it would be small comfort to her soul, which would be sent back to Nemesis to be processed however the merciless God saw fit. That was the theory, anyway; both the *Talon* and Akavi's circuitry contained the technology necessary to pull her soul into Limbo for sorting, even this far outside human space. With everything glitching this hard, who knew if they would work as intended? It was not a risk Akavi was eager to take.

That black patch of wall, invisible to Akavi, was a wild card here. Without being able to see what was there, it was impossible to assess its capabilities. Terribly destructive things could be hiding in that wall – but very few things were destructive enough to thwart Akavi's plans at this stage.

In the worst, faintly possible case, that black patch could be hiding a portal. A means for Talirr to escape Akavi's trap. But that was unlikely; Talirr didn't know the details of Akavi's circuitry and could not have used the black patch as camouflage deliberately. In any event, if anything portal-like occurred there, Akavi had a contingency plan for that, too. It would simply require her to act quickly.

"Besides," Akavi said, "I brought you something interesting. Yasira Shien." She leaned forward. "You never showed this sort of interest in any of your students before. What makes her suddenly so valuable?"

"You wouldn't understand if I told you," said Talirr.

Unhelpful and surprising. Akavi had assumed that Talirr, like most heretics, would want to vent directly at an angel. Akavi had wanted to give her the opportunity. It would be instructive. Perhaps Talirr would confirm a hypothesis of hers.

Akavi pulled out a tablet screen and summoned up files with a few flicks of her fingers. "Perhaps not, but I've been trying to figure it out. Your former students were brilliant scientists, rising stars in their fields, but each, when exposed to your Outside ideas, was driven irretrievably insane. Yasira is different. She sustained some psychological trauma on the *Pride of Jai*, of course, but her mental exercises show her regaining normal function quickly." He offered the tablet to Talirr. "Far more quickly than a normal individual."

Talirr crossed her arms. "You didn't come all this way to tell me what I already know."

Akavi drew the tablet back and called up a few more files. "I looked at the scans of the victims in Zhoshash. Compared them with the victims in Svatsibi, Shiyetsa, and Maku. It might interest you to know that they were not the same. In each successive attack, scale has been larger, but fatalities lower. More cognitive function has remained intact. I would hazard a guess," she held up a finger, "that if the town had not been destroyed, someone like Yasira would have survived Zhoshash. She would have recovered."

Talirr leaned forward. "You're not actually guessing, you know. You're calculating probabilities and solving equations inside that machine you call a brain. Numbers are normally no worse than other lies. But they are a poor approach to take to my work." She paused. "But Yasira? Well. How would you put it, angel? I like her odds."

While Akavi and Dr Talirr conversed, Yasira was swallowed in darkness, crawling across the outside of the *Alhazred*.

Her spacesuit's boots were magnetic and kept her safely stuck to the flexing hull. Curious clicks sometimes vibrated up through her feet, the only sound apart from her own breath. The *Alhazred* undulated, but in this much darkness the movement was rarely visible. Without gravity, the sense of motion was different, too. She felt dizzy and disoriented, but it was hard to tell if it was her patch of hull moving, or the parts around it. Sometimes an extra wave of dizziness would come out of nowhere, and she'd look down, breathing deeply until she trusted herself to take another step.

The pounding anxiety she'd felt in the *Talon* hadn't left her. Cold sweat stuck her spacesuit lining to her skin, and her hands shook as she tried to use the dinky penlight attached to the suit's wrist. It was the biggest energy source Akavi was willing to give her, but it illuminated only a foot of twisted steel at a time. Everything else was so black she might as well have been blind. Even the brightest galaxies were only faint smudges. Who knew what might be lurking in the darkness between them?

Yasira's gut knew, and it wanted out of here. Before something leapt out and killed her. Or sucked the entire *Alhazred* into a hole in space.

A bot could have done this job better. Except the interference out here would have played havoc with a bot. It was playing havoc with Yasira, too. More than once she jumped at shadows, or at nothing, and nearly fell off the *Alhazred*.

She couldn't even see what she was doing. She swept the stupid light across the hull and found a corner, which she crept toward. She took out one of Akavi's small, black antimatter grenades and carefully fastened it to the ship's edge.

A contingency plan, Akavi had said.

She hadn't signed up for this. Had she? She'd known that the angels of Nemesis were out to stop Dr Talirr. She'd known that heretics, taken in by angels of Nemesis, usually died. But she hadn't expected to be the one wielding the weapon, setting the charges, to kill the woman who'd trained her for three long years. This felt wrong.

She shuffled forward.

There were fifteen grenades left, and Akavi had wanted them evenly spaced around the *Alhazred's* surface area. She raised the penlight, counting footsteps. At seventy, there was a dizzy lurch from a source she couldn't identify, and she had to stop for a while.

Eighty, ninety, a hundred. Another corner. She took out another grenade, and bent down to tie it in place.

Something grabbed her.

Yasira shrieked and kicked. The grenade spun out harmlessly into space. She had no room for thought, for a second or two, apart from wild mental images of monsters. She turned, and the flat of her palm hit something. She took a while to notice that it was not fighting back. It was merely a humanlike hand, distorted by the bulk of a mortal-built spacesuit, which had come down on her shoulder.

"Calm down," said a muffled female voice.

Yasira gasped for breath. "Don't – ever – do that – to me! I thought you were some kind of space monster!"

The voice was matter-of-fact, unruffled. "You don't have a radio, so we need to be touching to transmit sound. And you're laying antimatter grenades on my ship, so I think we're even. Hello, Yasira. It's nice to see you."

A light went on. Black and gold spots went swimming through Yasira's eyes. She blinked and swallowed hard.

"Hello, Dr Talirr," she said.

Inside the *Alhazred*, Akavi took a moment to reassess Talirr's mental state. The students had described her as temperamental and impatient. Yet she had been patient, even indulgently amused, with Akavi. Which, to an Inquisitor of Nemesis, was insulting. Either isolation had calmed her, or Akavi's presence had not, so far, been a stressor.

Why was Akavi not a stressor?

Talirr had often been loath to take on students, though she made random exceptions for individuals like Yasira. Most, while talented, were not prodigies of Yasira's caliber; most had struck her interest for no apparent reason, or, more frequently, been foisted on her by the department. And after graduation she had shown no further interest in any of them.

Until the *Pride of Jai*.

The conclusion was inescapable. Talirr had shown interest in the *Pride of Jai* not merely because it carried a student of hers, and not merely to draw Akavi's attention. She was interested because the Shien Reactor, briefly, *worked*. That was what separated Yasira from those before her. Yasira had completed a project on a massive scale which correctly implemented Talirr's ideas, and Yasira, so far, had remained sane.

Talirr was not merely experimenting. She was recruiting. She wanted someone who could think the way she did. The attacks had been growing in scope, but their maddening effects on mortal minds had grown milder. Fewer essential functions, in the survivors, had been lost. It followed that Talirr was interested in finding – or creating – other flexible minds. Possibly many other flexible minds. By subjecting them to the right kind of strain, she could see if any remained intact – and if those that did remain could be taught.

Talirr was brilliant; Akavi had hoped to keep her alive. To make her an angel or sell-soul, like so many criminals before her. Turned away from heresy and to more useful ends, with all the divine resources her twisted heart desired, who knew what a mind like Talirr's could accomplish?

But if she was actively recruiting, if Akavi found a shred of direct evidence that she was doing so, then that was her death warrant. And Akavi had brought more than enough with her for summary termination, if that was the plan.

(00:58:45, said Akavi's internal clock. There was still time to learn what she could. Probably.)

"I've read your diaries," Akavi finally said. "It's no wonder they drive people insane. Yasira must be special indeed."

Talirr's lip curled slightly, a significant display of emotion for that blank face. "And who makes that judgement, angel? How do you work out what you will call sanity and what you won't? Your god-machines say they have the only truth. And a sane person would believe what is true, yes? No delusions, no denial. So anyone who can think of things you don't like must be sick, and the things they are thinking must be symptoms of mental disease. It works out well for you. You can punish them as much as you like, and, at the same time, you get to pretend they weren't doing anything meaningful at all."

Akavi narrowed her eyes. Now they were getting somewhere useful. "So you disagree with the Gods. And what exactly are you doing about that, Evianna? Starting your own religion?"

"No!" Talirr said sharply, rising from her seat. Akavi flinched, against her will, at the strength of the other woman's reaction. "Religions are lies."

Akavi rose as well, feeling the need to reassert dominance. "Wrong. Even if you believe that, it is not an answer. Everything is a lie to you. This universe is a lie, yet here you are working in it. Your own interests are a lie, yet you work pursuing those. Only the Gods, for some unfathomable reason, draw this kind of rage from you. It suggests that you have something *additional* against Them."

She swept her hand through the air, dismissing any objection. "So. Tell. Me. Your real reason. There are far too many lies in existence without you adding more."

Talirr looked at her feet. In a neurotypical heretic it would have been a sign of submission. For her it likely had more to do with self-regulation: detachment in order to regain control. The black dot detached itself from the wall and crawled toward her, making slow, wobbling loops around the red strips that passed for furniture here.

"Do you remember how the Gods arose?"

Akavi narrowed her eyes. "I wasn't exactly there at the time, but I have a good grasp of the story, yes."

"Humans built them."

Akavi raised a finger. "Technically, no. Humans built the quantum supercomputers that *became* them. The actual transition from machine to God—"

Talirr slammed her hands against the wall.

"That's not the point!" she shouted. "Not the point, not the point, not the *point!*"

Akavi regarded her, imperious and unmoved. Sheer volume would not provoke a response.

Finally she quieted, and Akavi smiled gently. "I think I do understand. We requisitioned your library records once. You used to read about outdated religions, didn't you?" Talirr raised her eyebrows, and Akavi made a calming gesture. "This is not an accusation of further heresy. I'm trying to understand. I wonder if you began to believe in one of them. Valentinian Gnosticism, perhaps, or a twisted Buddhism." The calming gesture again. "Not a crime in itself. Archaic groups on Old Earth follow aspects of those traditions even today. And I know you say religions are lies. But there are forms of spiritual belief whose adherents do not describe them as religions. I'm wondering if the Gods bother you because you see them as a threat to what you *do* believe."

Talirr looked at him for a long moment.

"No," she finally said, with the gravity of a confession. "Not... as such. The things in the old books helped me, but they were not true and they did not lead me to Truth. I couldn't find the Truth anywhere, except Outside."

"And the Gods are a threat to Outside?"

Talirr laughed suddenly. It was an odd laugh, high and piercing, and Akavi was caught off-guard. "No, the gods are not a threat to Outside, or to me."

An odd answer, since they both knew the Gods were trying to kill her. She'd acknowledged as much in her diaries, and Akavi's presence ought to underscore the fact.

"Then is Outside," he continued gently, "a threat to the Gods?"

"What do you think?"

"I think you intend to destroy us. I also think it is obvious you will fail. You're powerful enough to bother small settlements of mortals, but the methods you have demonstrated would not make the tiniest dent in a God-built warship."

"Of course not. You don't kill a lie by blowing it up. You kill a lie by exposing the Truth underneath."

"So your plan is… what? To corrupt the whole galaxy into rejecting the Gods?"

Talirr bared her teeth. "Of course that's how an angel would say it."

"You think you can do this everywhere, on scales ten million times the size of Zhoshash, with everyone. Alone. In the miniscule time you have left before Nemesis crushes you."

"It's what I have to do."

"But that's where you're wrong." Akavi smiled brilliantly. "What if I offered you another way? A way for the Gods to leave you alone, to let you pursue your heresy in peace for the rest of your life, so long as you stopped harming mortals. A truce of sorts. As an Inquisitor of Nemesis, I'm empowered to–"

Talirr clapped her hands suddenly, interrupting her. "No."

Akavi frowned. "I haven't even made my offer."

"And you won't be negotiating in good faith when you do. Honestly. This is so *boring*. You're not going to let me live. Do you want to know how I know?" Akavi raised an eyebrow and she continued. "Because my associates caught *your* associate setting antimatter grenades around the *Alhazred* ten minutes ago."

Yasira and Dr Talirr stood in the darkness, their helmets pressed together, though Yasira felt more like shrinking away. There was infinite space around them, yet nowhere to run except back to the *Talon*, where she couldn't even board until Akavi undocked. Besides, she had come this far for a reason. She needed this.

"You seem upset," said Dr Talirr. "I'm sorry about the *Pride of Jai*. You shouldn't have had to go into that blind; you deserved to know more. I just never thought..."

"That's what you're sorry for?" said Yasira. "Me missing out on some Outside background knowledge? What about the hundred people who died? What about all the people in Zhoshash? Are you sorry for them?"

Dr Talirr blinked owlishly. "What? Oh, them."

"Get away from me," said Yasira. She pulled away. Dr Talirr did not exactly restrain her, but the loose grip on her shoulder did not let go.

"Wait," said Dr Talirr.

Yasira paused. She didn't want to keep touching Dr Talirr, even through two spacesuits. But she also didn't want to walk away like this, deaf to whatever explanations Dr Talirr shouted after her.

"I am trying to apologize," said Dr Talirr. "I think I'm not doing it correctly, but I can't remember how this is supposed to work."

"I think you never knew how this worked in the first place," said Yasira.

"But I know how Outside works," Dr Talirr said, suddenly loud, as if she was blurting it out despite herself. "I know all about it. You need to know, too. You need to understand what is happening to you."

"You could have thought of that four, five years ago," said Yasira. "When you were shoving heretical science down my throat and not telling me it was heretical. You could have thought of that however many months ago now, when I was setting up the Shien Reactor right in the middle of hundreds of innocent people."

"What do you think I'm trying to apologize for?" said Dr Talirr.

The two women glared at each other through their helmets for a while.

Yasira did want to understand what was happening. But she hadn't wanted it to happen like this. Akavi would bring Dr Talirr in lawfully. They would interrogate her, and there would be sensible answers written down in a sensible angel report. Probably a heavily redacted sensible angel report, but it would be something. It would be closure. That was the plan. Meeting Dr Talirr out here was not the plan.

Akavi hadn't given her a contingency plan for what to do if Dr Talirr appeared on the outside of the *Alhazred*. She had no idea how to fix this. Was she supposed to know how to apprehend a heretic by herself?

"It never occurred to me," said Dr Talirr, "that anyone else might have the aptitude to understand what I was doing. *I* barely understand what I'm doing, most days. But you–"

"I'm not like you," said Yasira.

"No, you're not much like me. And you're not much like Nemesis, either, are you?"

Yasira hesitated. Now did not seem like a good time to bring up her problems with Gods.

"I just wanted to study," she said. "I wanted to build things. And learn. And not be hunted down by angels or have the blood of more than a hundred people on my hands."

"Good luck working for Nemesis if you don't want blood on your hands," said Dr Talirr, without rancor. "Nemesis won't teach you what you need to know. But I can."

"And what do you think I need to know? How to build bigger Outside horrors and kill even more people?"

"You don't have to look at it that way. The Truth is much more than that."

"I'm sure it is to you," said Yasira. "I'm sure whatever's going on in your head is a lot more important than other people's life and death. A hundred people died on the *Pride of Jai*? Who cares; it was an accident. Life is a lie anyway; we were just looking for the Truth. I've read your diaries. I know how this works! Are you going to tell me Zhoshash was an accident, too?"

"Yes," said Dr Talirr.

Yasira stared at her incredulously.

"It was an experimental procedure," said Dr Talirr, as if she was talking about the weather. "I was working to cut down on fatalities, but the effects were still more violent than I anticipated. Twenty or thirty people died. That was an accident, yes."

"Two thousand people died," said Yasira. "You flattened the town, Dr Talirr. You killed two thousand people. Not twenty."

"Oh, it was definitely twenty," said Dr Talirr, looking off in the distance. "Or thirty. I keep forgetting. But somewhere in that ballpark is what I did. The rest were killed when Nemesis came along, cleaned up my mess by destroying every multicellular life form in the entire county, then blamed it on the Keres."

Yasira looked at Dr Talirr in disbelief. That hadn't been in Akavi's holographic simulation. It hadn't been what he'd told her.

But... but there were those redacted bits in all the disasters. Including Zhoshash. Blank spots in the record between the onset of Outside and the death of everything.

"That's a lie," she said, her voice shaking.

"I know you don't trust me," said Dr Talirr. "But you have no reason to trust Akavi, either. She's an angel of Nemesis; do you think she'd do anything except use you?"

Yasira gritted her teeth. She was *very* sure that she couldn't trust Akavi. But the stakes here were so big that this almost didn't matter. Whatever Akavi did to her would be so much smaller than what they were stopping Dr Talirr from doing.

"It wouldn't matter," said Yasira. "Even if you aren't lying. Because you were the one who started it. I've seen what Outside does to people. It's better for a few people to die than for everyone to go through that. When there's cancer, you have to kill living tissue to stop it from metastasizing and killing the whole body. That's what Nemesis *does*. Didn't you go to Sunday school? Didn't your parents read you *Theodicy Stories for Children?* That's why she's the bravest of Gods."

"Do not lecture me about gods, Yasira," said Dr Talirr. She did sound angry now. Like she had in the lab, when everyone else was being slow to understand what she explained.

"I'll lecture you about what I damn well choose," said Yasira. "You did this to me. You gave me fake science that killed a hundred people on my watch. You got me kidnapped by angels of Nemesis and disappeared! And now you've, what, lured me all the way out here just to try to teach me to be like you? To kidnap me all over again?"

"No." Dr Talirr blinked, as if solving a hard equation in her head. "Wait, yes. I think. Sort of. 'Kidnap' is a strong word. I think I was going to *offer* you the chance to come with me. But then there was a problem. I thought I came out of that conversation on top, but it turned out Akavi suited you up wrong, and the ship will be unsalvageable, and now I have to do it another way. I remember now. You were dropped back inside the *Alhazred* five minutes from now. It was very dramatic. But that means we don't have much time."

There was a blank pause.

"What?" said Yasira.

"This is very important," said Dr Talirr. "I'm revising my plans. Or will revise them, or have already. I can't take you with me now, so I need you to play along with him for a while. If you're on his side and want to kill me, good. If you aren't, pretend that you are." The hand on Yasira's shoulder tightened. "I probably won't be able to keep track of you much when you go back. But now that we've had contact, I'll be able to send you messages. Dreams. If you ever do want to know more, you can find me that way."

"I don't want to find you that way!" said Yasira. "I don't want you sneaking into my brain, or whatever you just said. I don't want any of this. I don't want more plans!"

"They are an irritating necessity," Dr Talirr said. "Now, in the past from my perspective, but the present from yours, I'm also talking to Akavi. Which means it's absolutely necessary for you to be brought down there now, and not by me. I'm sorry about this next part."

"What are you talking about?" said Yasira.

The anxiety that had been flowing through her system all day suddenly coalesced. There was something concrete to fear now, just out of her sight. Large. And behind her. She was quite sure.

"You might want to close your eyes," said Dr Talirr, and then she let go.

Akavi watched as two black blobs, a little bigger than man-sized, sauntered down the wall. They deposited a shaking Yasira, still suited, on what looked like the ceiling, where she curled up shivering violently.

Akavi had anticipated this, more or less. Eventually the negotiations would either work or go sour, and, if they went sour, Akavi would need force. She probably could not overpower Talirr alone. She could have brought all sorts of firepower – guns, bots, Enga, enormous warships – but only at the risk of chasing Talirr away altogether. And if she brought weaponry that didn't chase Talirr away, it was anyone's guess how that weaponry would fare against Outside monsters, or whatever else Talirr had up her sleeve. She'd brought a guide, in her head, to dismantling Talirr-style portals, but there didn't seem to be a portal here. It was anyone's guess what else lurked close.

There would be no outright battle. If Talirr declined her offers, Akavi would simply leave. Talirr would realize that this was too easy and would suspect a trap. Most likely, she would search until she found Yasira's grenades, which were a lovely distraction. At 02:00:00, unless Talirr disarmed them all, they would go off and destroy the *Alhazred*. But disarming them would keep her too busy to notice the invisibly thin chemical film set down on the *Alhazred*'s hull by the soles of Yasira's magnetic boots. The boots did nothing at room temperature, but, in the near-absolute-zero of space, they exuded a volatile compound. It was not as potent as antimatter, but at 02:00:00, it would eat through its own micrometer-thick internal barriers and ignite with enough force to tear the *Alhazred* apart, killing everything aboard. Job done.

"The grenades were a safety precaution," Akavi said softly. "Now, if you reject my offer before you've heard it, I'm not going to cry. But please understand that Nemesis will not send another. We know your ship's energy signature now, and we know the way you plan to operate. I came unarmed this time, but, rest assured, you will see the forces of Nemesis again. She will make you beg on your knees for what I've offered you today."

Talirr exhaled sharply and turned away.

"Do you want to know why I'm not afraid of Nemesis?" she said. "It's because, unlike all the rest of you, I haven't forgotten the definition of the word 'God'."

Something started to clank, over in that black-streaked patch of hull. Akavi whirled around, looking upwards – then remembered that the black streaks were no longer on the ceiling, from her perspective, and reoriented. Something was happening on the far wall, something that her safely filtered senses could not directly perceive.

The room began to darken.

It was possible that she had made a terrible mistake.

Yasira lay shaking on the inside of the *Alhazred* – not really the floor, she supposed, since Akavi and Dr Talirr were upside down relative to her, but on one of the surfaces that could act like a floor in a pinch.

She was not sure what had brought her here. Her mind could scarcely focus on its shapes and sounds. There had been half a minute of *horror*, and then she'd fallen here. She sat numbly, trying to focus on what to do next. She'd been dropped here for Akavi to retrieve. So Akavi would retrieve her now. Right? But Akavi was still talking. Dr Talirr – how was Dr Talirr in here? When had she had time to take off her spacesuit? – was still talking.

She was still shaking wordlessly when the portal at the other side of the room clanked to life.

Horror, said her mind, and her eyes crossed, trying not to take any of it in. But that was definitely a portal, in the center of a twisting patch of wall. A portal in Dr Talirr's style, not the God-built kind. Blocky, cobbled-together, sparking.

Opening.

Yasira stared, uncomprehending. She'd gone over Dr Talirr's papers with Akavi. They'd made a plan for how to disable a portal. Akavi had been quite clear that any such portal had to be disabled, or Dr Talirr would get away. But the portal was clearly operational. And Akavi was standing on the ceiling, not even looking at it, as though nothing had happened.

Unless she didn't *see* it. Unless, in that mess of twisting, reaching Outside metal, she hadn't noticed it was there.

Yasira opened her mouth in a shout of warning. "A–"

Then, even as the dark behind the portal grew and strange shapes unfurled around it, she stopped.

She didn't want to say it. Why not? There was no time to process. She had trouble talking under stress sometimes.

She drew breath to say it again, and then screamed.

The portal was fully open now. Behind it wasn't darkness – nor any color Yasira recognized. Only an infinite writhe, worse than the movement around it, worse than the movement on the *Pride of Jai*. Tendrils – not biological, not technological, not anything Yasira had a name for – shot out of it, spreading across the room.

"This," she faintly heard Dr Talirr say, "is not a God, either, but it's a start."

Akavi looked wildly around the room. She could not see what was going on. She could only see that the room was becoming darker, blacker, in ways that had nothing to do with the lighting. The walls bent this way and that and a black network shot across them, like veins of ink.

Yasira, understandably, was screaming.

Akavi assessed the situation as fast as she could. Very likely, this was the scenario she'd feared: something portal-like was in that wall, and was being used, now, to rapidly transport Outside energies into the ship.

Whether it was that, or some other Outside mechanism, the proper response was clear: destroy it. Quickly.

Akavi poised herself to leap towards the blackness, grabbing at her tablet – and then she looked straight into the darkness's center, and her vision froze. For one disorienting second, everything was black; everything was silent. The timer inside her head froze and stuttered like a malfunctioning piece of mortal technology. Akavi swung her head from side to side, momentarily panicked. Yasira had made a remark about it on the *Talon*, and certainly, some auxiliary functions had glitched: but sensory circuitry, one of the basic functions that sustained an angel's existence, did *not* freeze. The Gods themselves had designed it not to happen that way, for very obvious reasons – because an angel could not function if one-half of their brain was doing *this*–

Then it was over and the room's sights and sounds flared back to life. The *Alhazred* was a confusion of flickering shadows, Yasira was screaming incoherently, and Talirr was making a run for what was almost certainly the portal – too far ahead now, too much of a head start for Akavi to catch her.

Akavi quickly tapped a code onto the tablet's screen. *Self-destruct readied on impact*, said the tablet. Akavi hurled it with all her might at Talirr, aiming for the head.

Her aim was true, the tablet sailed precisely towards its target, but something black and indescribable reached down and caught it before impact. There was a muffled, contained explosion. The room rocked and Akavi nearly lost her balance again. A portion of red metal ribbon came loose from the wall, but the blackness did not abate. Yasira was still screaming.

Evianna Talirr ducked into the darkness and vanished altogether.

Akavi gritted her teeth, resisting the urge to display emotion at her own failure. There would be time for that later. The blackness was growing. "There's nothing else to accomplish here, Yasira. Back to the ship. Now."

She sprinted to the airlock, navigating the corners less gracefully than Talirr had. There were dozens of ropes of blackness along the edges of the room now. One leapt up and batted her back. No sensation, only a sudden staggering. She lashed out blindly, tumbled, and moved for the light.

She didn't stop when she cleared the airlock. Yasira stumbled through after her, still shrieking, and it sealed itself. Blackness clustered hungrily against the window. Akavi kept moving. She dived for the *Talon's* most primitive controls. In an adrenaline haze she overrode the usual safety protocols, undocked from the *Alhazred* at maximum speed, and set a full emergency burn in the direction of the Milky Way, punching the buttons twice sometimes when they were slow to respond.

Yasira eventually stopped making noise and Akavi realized she had fallen to the floor, covered in blood from a wound in her leg. It looked serious, but not as serious as what Akavi was doing at the console. She pressed a final set of buttons as quickly as she could. For a moment emergency acceleration overwhelmed the *Talon's* artificial gravity and they both fell sprawling against the window. When the crushing pressure lightened, Akavi pushed upright and brushed herself off. Yasira lay where she was.

Akavi directed the most functional of the medical bots to Yasira. Set up a failsafe at the console to ensure the ship's trajectory didn't change. Diverted a huge amount of power, once they had accelerated past lightspeed, to sterilizing the outside of the ship. Found a bot to clean up Yasira's blood, too, while she was at it. Waited until her sensory annotations, one by one, lit back up, and the *Talon's* nonessential systems followed. Confirmed that her vision and hearing had been recorded.

Waited for 02:00:00, Earth Standard Time.

Only then, as the *Alhazred* disintegrated without Talirr inside it, was there no more work to do. Only then did Akavi lean on the window, looking back the way they had come, and let out a bestial scream of rage.

CHAPTER 9

Little Evianna is a personable child, extremely bright and curious for a three-year-old, quirky but friendly, cheerful, and largely aware of her surroundings. To the untrained eye, almost nothing is wrong. The heresy is not apparent until she begins to tell a story, or to complete a simple perception inventory – and then suddenly it's everywhere. Stimuli are perceived before they appear, or their prior locations are pointed to interchangeably with present ones. Basic foundations of perceptual cognition, such as occlusion, perspective, scale, even causality are ignored. It is as though she sees everything at once, all the time. She likely does not yet even realize that such perceptions set her in opposition to the Gods, placing her on an inevitable path to the most perilous and destructive heresies. If treatment is successful, perhaps she never will.

There is one aspect of Evianna's case that I admit gives me pause. Children like this are usually overwhelmed into immobility by sheer existence. Evianna is the opposite. Curious, friendly, personable to a fault; her parents dote on her, and even the intake nurses are charmed. I could say that it is a miracle she functions and connects to the world so well, but I think it is really the reverse: she is so connected, so in tune with what is around her that she cannot help but connect in heretical ways too.

It is a pity, then, that we will need to beat all of that out of her.

FROM THE CASE FILES OF ANIRTHA NAIABRIM,CLINICAL
CHILD PSYCHOLOGIST AND SELL-SOUL TO NEMESIS

While they stitched up her leg, the medical bots gave Yasira some sort of anesthetic which caused her to float around in a fog. They whirred and clicked over her, then transferred her to her bed. There might have been sleep, and might not; there might have been nightmares. Or maybe that was just the memory she kept replaying in her head. The *thing* – the *things* – or were they less than one thing? The *substance*? Whatever it was that had come through the portal, on the *Alhazred*. She was sure it had wanted to kill her, or worse, though she couldn't properly define what *worse* meant. Maybe it was the reverse. Maybe she was the one who wanted to kill it. Burn it, stab it, blow it up. Just get it away.

She floated for several hours like that, conscious of terror and rage, but not conscious enough to do anything about them.

Presently she blinked and noticed Akavi sitting next to her, male again, and in a new body. This one was small and slender, with medium-brown skin, deliberately unassuming; a tuft of soft brown hair made a halo around his narrow face. Something in his bearing reminded her faintly of Elu, although they didn't look the same. The room, which she'd scarcely noticed until now, was comfortingly small, soft and ordinary. At the same time, it felt unreal, like she'd be back out in the blackness of intergalactic space when she blinked again. Akavi was doing something on a tablet, which was odd.

"Get out of my room," she said, but it wasn't directed completely at him.

"Not just yet," said Akavi, turning to her. "Though I'm glad you're awake. You've just survived an extremely close brush with Outside, compounded by physical trauma. Your system was stressed near the breaking point already by what you experienced on the *Pride of Jai*. What happened today was, in some senses, smaller-scale. However, this time you had a direct sensory exposure to things humans were not meant to sense, which has its own aftereffects. I'm going to follow a therapeutic procedure that Dr Meyema designed. You'll thank me later. Look into this tablet, please."

He held up a screen. She groaned in protest, but sat up in her tangle of blankets and looked. There was nothing interesting on

ADA HOFFMANN

it, just a red dot slowly moving back and forth on an empty white background. At least it wasn't glitching up. They must be further from the *Alhazred* now.

"What's this for?" said Yasira.

"Minimizing stress-related neurological disintegration," said Akavi. "Think of it like one of your neurofeedback games. Keep your eyes on the dot. Breathe deeply. In. Out. That's it."

Yasira frowned, but watched. The dot moved slowly back and forth. "This is stupid."

"A number of things have been stupid today. Try not to dwell on it."

His voice was brisk and cool, but not unpleasant. At least it was something to focus on. Better than lying here in a fog of her own feelings.

"What happened on the *Alhazred* is over," said Akavi. "You're not there anymore and you're safe now. Do you understand?"

"I guess," said Yasira. She did not feel safe. She had four walls around her now, but the *Talon* was a tiny metal bug in a sea of deep space, and what lived in that darkness was far worse than emptiness. She had seen that already on the *Pride of Jai*. She had seen it in the hologram of Zhoshash.

"Watch the dot," said Akavi. "Breathe deeply. In. Out. Once more. Feel your lungs expand and contract as you breathe. Your body is made of solid matter, Yasira; your body is real. It obeys definite and well-understood physical laws. Even your brain obeys the laws of neuroscience. Your soul, though immaterial, also follows well-understood laws, and interacts with your body and brain in clearly definable ways. Everything is orderly and in its place, and you are in control of yourself. Do you understand?"

"Yeah," said Yasira, listlessly.

She watched the dot go back and forth. It was soothing to move her eyes like this, regularly, contained. She belatedly realized she'd been looking all around the room for threats that she knew weren't there. A restless gaze, like in a dream. But it wasn't necessary.

She breathed slowly.

157

"You saw things on the *Alhazred* that you may have difficulty thinking about. This is normal. When you do think of them, Dr Meyema and I will be there to help you; it is essential that you think of them in the right way. Listen to me. What you saw on the *Alhazred* was not real. It may, technically, have existed in some form; but it has no place in our reality and never will. You are in the care of the Gods, Yasira Shien, and whatever you may think you saw, the Gods are far more powerful. The Gods will keep you safe. Do you understand?"

"Yes."

Yasira wondered how much Akavi had seen on the *Alhazred*. He had not responded to it the way she had. She remembered a sense of helpless, clawing terror, screaming, fleeing, pain – but Akavi had been silent while they ran. She vaguely remembered him shouting later, while the bots stitched up her leg, but it hadn't been directed at her, and she'd been too deep in her own drugged misery to pay attention.

Had he seen less, on the *Alhazred*, than she had? Certainly he hadn't seen the portal. She couldn't imagine seeing what she'd seen and reacting so calmly. But he was an angel; maybe he was more in control of himself. He'd been there in the room, after all. He'd fought off the… things… the same as she had. Better. He'd thrown something explosive at them, and perhaps hurt them; they had kept moving, but there had been a sudden gush of a horrible liquid which was nothing at all like blood. He must have seen most of what she'd seen.

But he hadn't seen the portal. And he hadn't seen Dr Talirr on the outside of the *Alhazred* with her.

Those were important. Those were things he should know.

"Akavi," she said, "I should tell you…"

"Tell me what?"

"I saw things. Things you didn't see. Or I don't think you did."

She was still watching the dot, half-drugged, and it hurt to think about this. It was hard to get the words out.

"Yes?" said Akavi. "Don't overtax yourself. There will be time for a proper debriefing later. But you may speak."

"There was a portal."

"I did work that out," said Akavi.

"It was hidden in that… mess of stuff. And before that – I saw her before that, too. On the outside of the *Alhazred*. I know that doesn't make sense, because it looked like she was there on the inside too, but…"

Akavi frowned. "Concerning. What did she say?"

"I… There was, um… time, and… dreams, and… dead people, and she…"

Her brain was muzzy, and none of it made any sense anymore. None of it had even made sense at the time.

"You're still drugged, Yasira," Akavi said gently. It might have been the gentlest thing he'd ever said to her. "You need rest. I'll follow up with you about this when the painkillers are out of your system. Just follow the dot. It's all right. You're safe."

Yasira relaxed back against the pillows. She suddenly, badly wanted to sleep.

Why was he suddenly being gentle? He had claimed to care about her sanity, but he had never shown it before. Maybe it shouldn't have surprised her. He was a shapeshifter. There were so many of him on the outside. Maybe the inside was like that too.

"Your memory," said Akavi, "may work oddly for a while. There may be gaps, or things like this that you can't quite express. This is normal. If you've forgotten something, or can't find words for it, let it go. Trust it to come back to you when you need it. Do you feel ready to remember a little?"

Yasira shrugged.

"You need not go through the whole thing," said Akavi. "There will be time for that later. Pick one image only. The first one that comes to your head. When I count to three, I want you to visualize this image as clearly as you can, but while you do, I want you to remember that it is not real, and not here, and cannot hurt you. That you are safe. And I want you to keep your eyes on the dot, no matter what. Do you understand?"

"Yes."

He counted.

The trouble was that it was impossible to decompose what Yasira had seen into single images. It had been one overwhelming onslaught, a buzzing confusion that did not divide into entities or events. Certainly there were visual impressions that lingered afterwards. Tentacles, slime, hundreds of eyes and mouths without the structure of a face. But the visual impressions were not the point. Tentacles by themselves were not frightening. Yasira had eaten plenty of squid. It was what the tentacles were connected to.

The thing that had grabbed her, after Dr Talirr told her to close her eyes, had been impossible to properly visualize. It had not even properly been a *thing*. It was like being physically attacked by the absence of physicality. Dragged around by the idea of not being dragged. It didn't compute. Even the tentacles, she suspected, had not really been tentacles; that had been the image her eyes chose as a compromise, after multiple abject failures at seeing what was there. She didn't remember thinking about tentacles, registering them as tentacles, at the time. Only being grabbed. Only fear, and whatever she could visualize now was like a picture superimposed on fear.

It made her head hurt.

You're doing this wrong, she wanted to say to Akavi. *You're using the wrong modality. It's obvious.* But she was sleepy, and speech felt difficult. She was still watching the dot as it moved back and forth, and, oddly, it seemed to be helping. At least she could think about this without panicking, which was more than she'd thought she'd be able to do.

Her breathing slowed.

"Are you seeing it now?" said Akavi.

"Yes," Yasira murmured, wondering how to explain.

"Watch the dot. Breathe in and out. Remember that you are safe here. Let whatever emotions you are feeling come up. Do not judge them. Let them come in with your breath and drain away as you exhale. Let them go. You have as much time as you need. Take your time and let it all go."

Yasira breathed. The dot moved back and forth. Her main feeling, besides anxiety, was vague irritation with Akavi. She wanted him to go away so she could sleep. She watched the dot and breathed until that was gone, too.

"Do you understand you are safe?" said Akavi.

"Yes."

"Good. You've had a busy day, Yasira. Sleep now."

He was doing it wrong, but he was trying. Angel or not, he must be under stress, too, yet he'd put that aside for her. Maybe he did see her as a person, not just bait to be expended. Maybe he wasn't so bad.

She closed her eyes.

In the morning it all felt distant, like a bad dream. Yasira felt tired but she climbed out of bed in reasonably decent spirits. The mission had not gone well, but it was done. And that meant...

Well, it probably didn't mean she could see Tiv again. They hadn't captured Dr Talirr, after all. Akavi would want to keep her aboard until that was done. She had much more hunting and planning and analysis ahead of her. Dr Talirr might even come to her in dreams, if she'd heard that right. *That* was a creepy thought.

But surely, since Dr Talirr knew they were after her now, it wouldn't be a security breach anymore if she sent Tiv a message. Would it? She hoped not. She'd ask, she decided, when they got back to the *Menagerie*. When the question was relevant.

It was hard to fathom the idea of these couple of weeks lasting fourteen months for Tiv. What did that even mean? Fourteen months was longer than they'd dated in the first place. Tiv definitely thought she was dead, unless someone had told her otherwise.

Maybe someone *had* told her otherwise. Maybe Elu. She could dream.

Yasira forced herself to look on the bright side. Even if she couldn't see Tiv again yet, going back into the galaxy meant she'd be able to hear some news at least. See how things were going on her home planet, how the aerospace industry had rebuilt itself – or not – in the wake of the *Pride of Jai* disaster. That was another thing that was hard to fathom. To Yasira, that disaster was still fresh memory, an open wound. To everyone else but Akavi, it had been more than a year ago. Living history, but history. Whatever the public had decided about Yasira, whether they blamed her for the disaster or blamed something else, they'd surely already decided. She'd find out about that, too, she supposed. For better or worse.

Yasira was not very good at looking on the bright side.

She shook her head and forced herself up out of bed. Akavi was going to want a meeting anyway, not her ruminating about a home that would still take another subjective week to get back to. After a shower and change of clothes she went out to meet him in the parlor.

Pancakes, she typed, and after several minutes of finagling about the details of the recipe, she retrieved a warm stack of them from the printer. "Hello," she said, dropping into the seat opposite Akavi.

"Hello," he replied. He was back in his true form, copper and silver undertones glinting under the parlor's full-spectrum lights, and the warmth she remembered from last night was gone. He sat there with his usual poise, staring at the wall, sipping a cup of something that looked like black coffee but smelled more like vitamin water. "Did you sleep well?"

"Passably," said Yasira. She looked at the printer, which had not produced any error messages or made any odd noises. "What are you working on?"

"A report on the mission. I'm glad you're up. I'd like to know what it was you were trying to tell me last night, if you can express it now."

It took a moment to remember. Her brain felt like it would rather forget.

"I talked to Dr Talirr," said Yasira. "Even though she was also on the inside of the *Alhazred* at the same time. And she said things that didn't make sense. She said she wanted to talk to me more, and she'd send me messages in dreams now. Is that even possible?"

Akavi frowned. "Divine technology can influence a dreaming brain to a certain extent, but only with electrodes or lights or some other form of contact. It's imprecise and rarely useful. But I suppose with Outside, all bets are off. Did you have any such dreams last night?"

Yasira shook her head. She couldn't remember dreaming at all.

But then... There had been those dreams back on the *Pride of Jai*. She'd assumed that they were just neurological flotsam, like any other dream: bits of anxiety and unease, bleeding off from her waking life into her sleep. She'd dreamed of Dr Talirr, that first time, pushing her into a book. Could that have been *really* Dr Talirr? She had no idea.

"You'll be reporting them, of course. As with your other dreams."

"Of course."

"What else did she say?"

Yasira recounted the encounter haltingly. "This is weird," she finished, "but she was talking about things that were in the present from my perspective, but the past from hers. It was all jumbled up. She made it sound like she'd been inside the ship first, then gone back in time somehow and walked onto the outside to meet me."

Akavi put down his drink with a clunk. "You're saying Talirr can travel in time."

Yasira spread her hands helplessly. "Or talks like she can. She can be in two places at once, at least. I don't really know what was going on."

"Time travel shouldn't be possible, even for Outside. The paradoxes alone... Could she have simply made a duplicate of herself?"

Yasira frowned back. "It doesn't explain how the information got from one of them to the other, out of order. She was hard to understand, but...*space is a lie*, right? So is time. So maybe she's not constrained by time the way we are. And that means all kinds of things. It means we can't make any predictions based on what we think she's capable of in a given period. I mean, if she's planning on more disasters or something, by the time we're back in the galaxy, she might already have done them."

Akavi turned away dourly, as if struggling to assimilate the idea of time travel into his plans. "We are on a fourteen-month round trip and Talirr has transportation methods we do not understand. She might do that even *without* any time travel. I am more concerned by her motivations. I had assumed that what she said to me on the inside of the *Alhazred* was important, but if she was speaking to you at the same time, she may have simply been stalling in order to extend the conversation with you."

"Is that bad?"

"Not particularly. The outcome was the same. When I led the conversation in the direction of a confession, she put up very little resistance."

Yasira chewed and swallowed part of a pancake. "Maybe she didn't care what you knew."

"Many people don't, when stalling. Even more likely, on some level, I believe she *wanted* me to know. I've seen this before. With a few exceptions, heretics are not rational. They do what they do out of spite, out of sheer hatred for the Gods. And spite is a weakness. The spiteful ones want us to see them coming. Thus they give up their advantage."

Yasira cut off a few more pieces of pancake and thought about this. She couldn't quite connect the word 'spiteful' to what she'd seen of Dr Talirr yesterday. If anything, she'd been too matter-of-fact. Talking about the dead people on Zhoshash like it was nothing. Like a psychopath.

Angels of Nemesis could be psychopaths, too, of course. Worse, if what Dr Talirr had said about Zhoshash was true. She thought of asking. But if Nemesis *had* destroyed the town, Akavi wouldn't tell her, now, would he?

She remembered with a jolt that she hadn't told Akavi everything, either. Not on the *Alhazred*. She'd seen the portal before him, and thought of warning him, but hesitated. Why?

She couldn't trust him. Was that why?

But her trust was irrelevant. Dr Talirr was doing horrific things. She needed to be stopped. That mattered more than… than anything.

Even if Nemesis was doing horrific things, too.

"What can I do to help?" Yasira asked.

Akavi sighed and put down his drink. "Before we had this conversation, I would have suggested further strategy and long-term planning. However, Talirr intends to contact you with further Outside information, which means your sanity is in more danger than I thought. The best thing you can do is to hold onto it until it's needed, which means not working on Outside-related plans until then. Find a book to read, or tinker."

Yasira groaned and put down her fork. "I hate this. I hate being shipped from one horrible place to another and just being bait for both sides while my whole planet turns around its sun without me. If I have to be here, I want to *do* something! I want to have to use my brain."

"Of course you do," said Akavi, his face growing unreadable again. "But we can't always have what we want. Go back to your room."

"Oh, come on," said Yasira, but the look that he gave her at that was so chilly that she found herself looking away, after all, and slinking red-faced back to her bed.

Akavi found himself pacing the *Talon* in the maddening intergalactic silence, revising and re-revising his plans. If Talirr could send dreams to recruit Yasira at any time, then Akavi could no longer trust Yasira. He had seen in her face that she was already beginning to doubt his words. Yet he could not complete his mission if Yasira ceased to be useful; Irimiru, damn them, had made sure of that.

So he required a plan in which Yasira would always be useful, even if she no longer wished to be. For instance, if she tried to run off to join Talirr. Perhaps, in that event, he would let her. Perhaps there were ways to make even *that* betrayal useful.

It was more interesting to think about handling Yasira than to think about his failures. Akavi *had* failed. He was not putting that spin on it in his report, of course; he had strongly emphasized his successes. Making contact with Talirr, unprecedentedly. Learning something of her motivations. Learning something of her abilities. He was reasonably sure that he could get that past Irimiru without being tortured and terminated. Yet.

But he knew he had failed. He had spent fourteen months on a plan he thought was foolproof and been undone by a simple hardware glitch. He could have dealt with the portal if his circuitry was working: captured Talirr hand-to-hand, destroyed the device with the explosive function of his tablet, and dragged her back to the *Talon*. Instead his filters had unexpectedly overloaded and he had become, at the most crucial moment, helpless. He was not pleased.

The return trip dragged on with very little to do but spin one's wheels. Yasira took to sulking with her books and printing increasingly impractical devices, and even Akavi began to indulge in his recorded films and news programs. As the day of return arrived and the edge of the ansible network appeared on his navigational console, he found himself gripping the edge of his chair too tightly, waiting.

Ping. There it was. His circuitry informed him that his ansible connection was functional again, a split second before the *Talon's* console pinged announcing the same thing.

Ping. His network and sensory annotations lit up, the normal flow of information hitting him like a wave of welcome cool air. Here were Elu and Enga, alive and online as only angels could be. Here was a map of the galaxy showing the *Talon* and *Menagerie*. Here was a text feed reminding him of his duties and routines, and of important events involving his underlings. Here was the link, barely perceptible when not in use, where he could access approved portions of Nemesis' own memory.

Akavi closed his eyes and smiled. He had missed this.

Ping. A curt greeting in his brain from Irimiru, followed by an intense barrage of high-priority files. He had expected this, though he was less than thrilled with the sheer quantity and the high proportion marked *maximally urgent*. Either sensory deprivation had rendered him too easily overwhelmed or something highly unexpected had occurred.

I missed you, too, he text-sent, attaching his report from the *Alhazred* and all the relevant sensory video.

Review all the files then meet me immediately, highest priority, sent Irimiru. *The connection closed.*

Ping. A second requested connection, from Elu. Of course.

Akavi permitted the connection to open. It would not be long before he could walk through the *Talon's* portal with Yasira and be home, leaving the *Talon* to find its usual docking place on autopilot. There were only a few minutes' worth of trivial navigational checks to perform first. A more businesslike assistant would have waited for Akavi's physical presence before greeting him. But there was no particular reason to keep Elu tantalized.

Elu, he text-sent in greeting.

Sir. An alarming tangle of feeling accompanied the word. There were the expected elements, of course – relief that Akavi had survived and returned, pleasure at seeing him again after fourteen months, anxiety over whether Akavi would approve of how Elu had run things – but also other things. Entirely too much underlying distress, with a cause that Akavi could not immediately identify. *It's good to see you.*

Likewise, Akavi text-sent. *Though, judging from your and Irimiru's reactions, I'm going to spend the next few hours wishing I was still outside the galaxy. What went wrong?*

Everything was going fine, sent Elu, *until a week ago. When Talirr struck again.*

Akavi frowned. He had expected Elu to be competent enough to avoid falling completely apart if this occurred. *Frustrating, but not unanticipated. I did leave a detailed protocol with you describing the actions you were to take in this eventuality, did I not?*

No, you don't understand, sent Elu. *This isn't another little town. This is completely different. Here, I'll show you.*

He attached a link to a realtime information map. Not a sensor feed, but a cartographic data stream illustrated based on those sensors, with expert annotations and added data from various sources. Akavi opened the map and stared at it. At first he could not make sense of what he was seeing. It looked like the energy field associated with one of Talirr's Outside events, but it was moving wrong. Sluggishly, tentatively, and in the wrong shape.

A split second later, he worked out what he was looking at.

The energy field was not sluggish. It appeared to be sluggish because Akavi had not processed the map's sheer *scale*. He was looking, not at a town, county, or space station, but at the entire surface of Jai. One-fifth of it – a huge area covering most of southern Riayin and extending into western Stijon – was covered with some unknown Outside effect.

One-fifth of a fully populated mortal planet. And, according to the records, the field was slowly growing.

Akavi became entirely expressionless. In crises such as this, he had always discarded emotion in favor of strategy. Irimiru had threatened to kill him, or worse, if he failed. Was survival still possible? In the short term, probably. Irimiru hated to waste time. They would not have bothered sending him files to read unless they wished him to live to do something about them. But if he wanted to continue to live after that, then his old strategies – the ones he had so carefully pored over and left with Elu – were inadequate.

I've been summoned to meet with Irimiru, he sent. *Assuming I survive, I want to see you and Enga immediately afterwards. If you made any half-baked plans on your own before I arrived, bring them.*

He severed the connection. Yasira had crept back onto the bridge in her usual way, pretending to be otherwise occupied while she watched him. She had already gathered up her things, such as they were – just clothes and the console – to take through the portal.

"Is something wrong?" she said.

Akavi looked at her expressionlessly. "Yes. Talirr attacked another planet while we were out."

"Shit. Well, we thought she might." Yasira frowned, studying him. "What happened?"

"The planet in question is Jai," said Akavi. "The area of Outside influence covers nearly half of Riayin and part of Stijon. I recall you have been pining for home; it seems you may no longer have one."

Akavi did not think of himself as sadistic, nor spiteful. Still it was satisfying to study Yasira's face as she dropped the clothes and console with a clatter, and to watch his own stress delegated, in accordance with the pecking order, to someone else.

CHAPTER 10

There are two principal ways in which humans lie.

One is through space, time, the continuity of matter and energy: lies that standard human consciousness, by its very nature, imposes on the universe. There is something pernicious in us which cannot simply look at a photon as it is: we must collapse its wave function into a thing we can understand, even if that thing has no reality.

The second kind of lie is far worse. The second kind encompasses governments, economies, religions, philosophies, educational systems. These are baseless fictions, yet we define ourselves by our agreement with them. We are expected to find the deepest meaning of our lives within them, and are punished severely if we fail to do so.

Perhaps I should say that humanity will never be truly free until we discard these lies. Or is freedom, indeed, another lie?

FROM THE DIARIES OF DR EVIANNA TALIRR

Yasira had not had a full screaming meltdown since her early teens, but as the news about her home planet sank in, one overtook her. She cried and shouted, threw her tablet against the wall, shouted some more, and flailed against Akavi's fruitless efforts to calm her. At some point he simply shrugged and walked through the portal without her. Then the bots came out, three or four of the same model that had slapped her hand away from the equipment shelves before. They snatched her limbs like cold vises and held her motionless. Then there was a pricking feeling in the palm of her hand – the kind

169

that was growing all too familiar – and she abruptly fell asleep.

She woke up again on the *Menagerie*, feeling wretched, curled up in one of the big armchairs in her quarters. Elu sat across from her looking concerned. He looked almost exactly the same as he had fourteen months ago, boyish and gangly and gentle. The hair was longer, maybe.

"Go away," she said, curling up tighter. At home on Jai, when she got like this, her parents had known how to care for her in the aftermath. Blankets, tea, books, quiet. Definitely not sending robots to drug her. That was not part of a proper de-escalation plan. But out in space, fighting heretics, who cared?

"I'm sorry," said Elu.

He didn't elaborate. *No sorry, I can't, Akavi's orders. No sorry, but this was necessary, because blah blah blah*. He just looked at her.

Yasira pushed her hair away from her face.

"We shouldn't have left," she said. "I shouldn't even be here. I should be down there with the rest of Jai, going mad, or whatever they're doing. No one will even tell me if my family's safe, or if Tiv's safe–" She felt her voice rising in a panic again and forced herself to cut off. She felt awful.

"Because we don't know," said Elu. "We can't reach the planet. Portals that normally lead to Jai aren't functioning, even outside the affected area. Neither are ansible links. Ships that we send down are frying and crashing. Frankly, it's a miracle we have as much information from our orbital sensors as we do."

"We shouldn't have left," Yasira repeated. "We shouldn't have walked into her trap. She pretended like she cared about me. But she knew this was my home planet. That my family lives here. How could she do this?"

"I don't know," said Elu.

"I'll kill her with my own fucking hands," said Yasira.

She had trusted Dr Talirr. Not much, but enough to have hesitated in that crucial moment. To have let her get away. Which meant this was her fault, again. Unless she fixed it.

Elu didn't say anything. Yasira started to cry and felt like an idiot for crying. She wondered if they were going to sedate her again.

Elu handed her a box of tissues. Yasira glowered through her tears at them. She hated everyone. Nemesis and Outside. Akavi and Dr Talirr. All the people on both sides who treated this like a chess game, when people were dying, or going mad, or being eaten by flying asphalt monsters. Who, the moment you trusted them, would reach past you and destroy something.

"I'm not sure if I'm supposed to tell you this," Elu said quietly, "but we've been tracking Productivity Hunt along with others from the *Leunt*. She doesn't live on Jai anymore. She's working for an air conditioner company in Zwerfk. So she's safe, for now."

A breath escaped from Yasira in a long hiss. Her shoulders sagged. *Good.* Wait... no. That was selfish. Tiv being safe didn't make the rest of the planet any safer, did it? She was being selfish.

Elu continued as if he hadn't noticed a reaction. "And Lungan is still about a hundred kilometers outside the border. Our sensors are picking up a lot of overland movement. Lungan will have time to evacuate before the Outside effects reach them. As long as it's stopped before it eats the whole planet, I mean."

Lungan, in northern Riayin, was where Yasira's family lived.

"What does it matter?" said Yasira. "You don't know anything. You don't know how to stop this. We wouldn't have had to be outside the galaxy for fourteen months if you had a clue what you were doing. You would have stopped it from *happening* if you knew what you were doing. That's what Nemesis is *for*."

And Dr Talirr, as far as Yasira knew, could travel through time. Time was a lie. What did it matter if the angels of Nemesis thought they had time?

"I'm sorry," Elu said again.

Yasira told him in great anatomical detail where he could put his apologies.

"Keep in mind," said Elu, "this only started a week ago. It came out of nowhere and it's immensely more complicated than anything Talirr has done before. Nemesis has committed a huge number of forces to solving the problem. Not just us. There are angels all over

– from more than one God, actually – trying everything, and we haven't run through the list of 'everything' yet." He smiled wanly. "You're on our team. And if you're even a little bit up to it, you'll be joining us, finding solutions. There *are* always solutions. Even in the darkest hour. Sometimes it happens like this. Someone gets the element of surprise and manages to do some damage before She brings them down. But She does it. She brings them down, and they *die*, and in the afterlife they get exactly what they deserve. We'll win this, Yasira. I can't promise it will happen without casualties or setbacks, or as fast as you'd like. But we're going to win."

Yasira wiped her eyes and stared at the floor.

"What if I don't believe you?" she whispered.

There it was, out in the open. Her problem with Gods. Here she was, on a huge God-built spaceship, with angels all around her. And she could not draw comfort from their presence. She felt exactly as hopeless and miserable as she would have if she was alone.

Dammit. At least if she was alone, planetside, she could have gone looking for Tiv.

"It's okay," he said, and Yasira could hear the smile in his voice. "Doubt is not actually a heresy. It happens to all of us."

Yasira shook her head.

"May I tell you a story from when I was a mortal?"

She shrugged.

"When I was five and lived with my parents on Preli, the Keres attacked."

That did get Yasira's attention. She looked back up at him. She knew the stories of the Morlock War and its aftermath. Once every few years, the Keres would slip past the Gods' safeguards and reach the edge of the ansible network, and there would be a battle big enough to see from nearby planets. Once every decade or two, She would get further – as far as an inhabited world, full of the mortals She hated more than anything. Whole cities would be razed before the true Gods caught up to Her. Sometimes, nations fell.

"This was about seventy years ago," said Elu, seeming not to notice the way that phrase sounded coming from someone who looked younger than Yasira. "I was a bright kid. Nothing like you, but I knew enough to know what was going on. I remember when the fighting got bad, the television was on loud, talking about one city in flames, another unreachable… My parents wouldn't let me in the room to see, but I could hear it through the walls. I wasn't good at maps yet, so I didn't know if the cities were far away or close, but from the way people were panicking, I could guess."

Yasira swallowed hard. There hadn't been children on the *Pride of Jai*, or in the hologram of Zhoshash. There had probably been children in the real Zhoshash somewhere. There were certainly hundreds of millions of them on Jai.

"The television said the portals were broken and we should go to our cellars," Elu continued. "We didn't have a cellar. We lived in a hi-rise. My father said, let's go to the basement, they must be setting something up in the basement. My other father said, no, if the building collapses the basement is the worst place to be. My mother said, what does it matter, one direct hit and we'll all be incinerated anyway. I didn't know what incinerated meant. I pictured us all just sort of turning to dust. I'd seen that in a cartoon. My parents yelled at each other and then my mother came into the bedroom and took me and one of my sisters out to the balcony. She held us tight and looked up at the sky. She said the moving stars were the warships we'd learned about in Sunday school, and we had to hope that the Gods would come through for us. I was very scared. I wanted to know which ones were the Keres and which ones were the good Gods, but she didn't know either. There were warships all over the sky and hazy lights on the horizon like faraway fires. I thought those must be the cities they were talking about on the news. When I was older, I realized they were probably just other neighborhoods. There was noise, like thunder, and people screaming on the street. It sounded odd from up where we were, like a choir."

He was talking now as if he'd forgotten she was there, staring out the window at the stars. He had always looked young, only just past the age of majority, but he somehow looked even younger now, wider-eyed. Yasira squinted at him. She wondered if angels could replay memories in their heads like vids, the way they called up articles and other information. It was a silly thought; Elu hadn't been an angel when he was five. He hadn't had any circuitry to record this.

"Then suddenly there were new lights. Huge lines of them, yellow and white, crackling like lightning across half of the sky. My sister's hair stood on end and my mother dragged us back into the house and covered our heads. But the television said Nemesis had brought reinforcements – the reinforcements are here, the reinforcements are winning. After a while the thunder stopped, and the screaming stopped, and my fathers stopped shouting at each other and hugged us. The Keres was defeated. It was more than a decade before She found Her way back to the galaxy."

"How many people died?" said Yasira dully, as he looked back at her.

"Fifty thousand mortals," said Elu. He didn't say it the way Dr Talirr or Akavi would have said it, like it was part of an equation. He felt the weight of a number like that. He'd grown up around it. "Three dozen angels. It could have been much worse."

Yasira knew that. The worst Keres attacks since the Morlock War, the ones she'd read about in school, had death tolls in the hundreds of thousands. And the Morlock War itself had killed billions. But Nemesis had grown cleverer since then.

It occurred to her suddenly that, if Jai was wiped off the map the way Zhoshash had been, it would be the worst disaster since the Morlock War. A fifth of a planet or more. Even the Keres had not been able to accomplish what Dr Talirr had just done. What did *that* mean?

"People say Nemesis is terrible," said Elu. "Of course She is. That's the point. She's terrible because the universe is terrible. She goes out into it and keeps us safe, and She is very, very good at what She does."

Yasira looked out the window at the unfamiliar stars and wondered where Jai was in that mess of lights, or if they were even looking in the right direction to see Jai's sun.

"She's not terrible enough," she said. She felt herself blushing, despite herself, at the blasphemy.

"Pardon?" said Elu.

"This thing that's happening on Jai is new. That's why you're all panicking, trying everything. It isn't like anything you've done before. It's not some space battle. You can't just bring in more warships and shoot the threat out of the sky, because it's not in the sky. It's on the ground and in the walls and –" *in the asphalt* "– in people's *minds*." She gestured to her head. "How do you fight that? You don't. Because you don't know how it works."

Or *was* there a way to shoot it out of the sky? She briefly, uncomfortably, remembered what Dr Talirr had said about Nemesis. Destroying the whole city so that the Outside contamination couldn't spread. But if She was going to do that, She'd have done it already. In fact, she only had Dr Talirr's word that it had happened at all. Maybe Dr Talirr was a liar. Or maybe one-fifth of Jai was just... too big for that to work. Either way, at this point, whatever happened was going to have to be more complicated.

Elu shifted uncomfortably. "We have a lot of bright minds, Yasira, and we're studying the threat. As soon as we can get a research team down to the ground, I'm sure–"

"No," said Yasira. "I mean, that's sensible, yeah, but it's not what's going to win you this. *I'm* going to win you this. That's why you brought me on board. Isn't it?"

He tilted his head in question.

"Dr Talirr wants to recruit me. Why? Because I built the Shien Reactor. Because I destroyed the *Pride of Jai*. Because I'm apparently one of the few people in the universe who can study her math, work with her methods, build something that works, and come out sane on the other side. So, let her recruit me." She spread her arms, trying to ignore the sick feeling in her stomach, the part of her that wanted to run far away from Dr Talirr's methods and never see them again. "Let her teach me every last damn thing she knows. Every detail of how she made this happen. I am a genius, Elu, remember? I will learn fast. I will be terrible myself. And then I will come back to you and tell you how to take it all apart again. I will tell you how to destroy her."

Elu's eyes widened slightly. "You want to be a mole?"

"Yes, exactly."

He fidgeted with his hair. "It's not that Nemesis doesn't do that kind of work. She'll send people out to pretend to be heretics, if She thinks She's dealing with them on an organized scale... But it's usually Vaurian angels with years of training in espionage. Keeping everyone fooled is harder than it sounds. And it's incredibly dangerous work."

"I," said Yasira, "am one of the most dangerous beings in the universe."

Elu grinned. Then his eyes suddenly unfocused.

He was text-sending to Akavi, Yasira realized. Informing him of what Yasira had just offered to do.

Had they planned this somehow? Had they been hoping that she would respond in this way?

She tried to control her racing heart. Truth was, she didn't like this at all. She could only think of one thing in the whole universe she liked *less* than the idea of being Dr Talirr's student again.

And that, of course, was the idea of doing nothing while Jai unraveled in front of her eyes.

Akavi stood in the correct, deferential posture in front of Irimiru's throne. The cloud of tiny auxiliary bots whirled around Irimiru's head faster than usual. Electricity sparked and crackled between them, giving the impression of a storm. Irimiru themself was currently a person of indeterminate gender, stick-limbed, tangle-haired, glaring.

They hadn't killed him yet. That was a good sign.

"My mission was a partial success," said Akavi. It was, of course, a lie. To use the word *fail* aloud, in reference to himself, would be a suicidal display of weakness. Like any Inquisitor, he would spin the events as best he could. Like any Overseer, Irimiru would see through the spin. If they valued his and his underlings' continued existence, they would play along. "We did not apprehend Evianna Talirr, but we learned a great deal about her. I believe I can use that information, given time, to defuse the present crisis."

176

"Partial success," said Irimiru over the hum of ambient energy, "is no longer an option." This was not the most forgiving available response; it was also not nearly the worst. "Nor do we have any guarantee of time anymore. You know this."

"Of course." Akavi ducked his head. "But you'll recall our agreement. Yasira Shien remains functional, and Jai isn't lost to us yet. My plans going forward are in the file that I sent you. Are they sufficient, or do you have alternative instructions?"

Irimiru tilted their head. They became a girl no older than Elu, bright-eyed, healthily curved. Uncharacteristically, she smiled.

"I recall our agreement," she said, as her metal-plated fingers continued to dance along the arm of her throne. "You know, I do not particularly dislike you, Akavi. You are usually competent and your inefficiencies are confined within reasonable bounds. Your most recent excursion at least was an end to the pointless wheel-spinning which had been your approach to the Talirr problem previously. You have not performed to expectations in this project, but that is not typical for you, and if it were still up to me, I might be inclined towards mercy."

This was high praise indeed, by Irimiru's standards. Akavi raised his eyebrows.

"Unfortunately," said Irimiru, "this case is now being administrated at a higher level."

Irimiru changed again, and she was tall and broad and stern, middle-aged, like someone's disapproving mother-in-law. Akavi took a small step backwards.

"The Jai problem," said Irimiru, "is now a galactic emergency being addressed by the combined effort of many Gods, with Nemesis coordinating. This means that the details of Talirr's case – her heresies, her disappearance, and the unusually long and fruitless effort to apprehend her – have been brought into Nemesis' conscious, personal focus. She, not I, will be meting out judgement on those who failed Her."

She raised one of her hands from the arm of her throne and made a brief, absolving gesture, as was customary when discussing intimate details like the thought-processes of a God. Akavi swallowed and looked down. Normally, Overseers had the freedom to make tactical judgment calls, and to do as they liked with personnel. Nemesis valued, if not individuality, then the strategic benefit of multiple perspectives. She stayed as abstract as She could, giving out orders through Archangels so as not to crush the other angels' free will. But in an emergency that could be overturned. And if Irimiru was a harsh taskmaster, Nemesis Herself would be far harsher.

"As I understand it," said Irimiru, "She will be reserving all but the most obvious punishments until the situation has played itself out. So you have a little while longer to live. Who knows? Perhaps your insights will be useful after all. Perhaps some other team of Inquisitors will read your reports, learn from them, use that knowledge to find a way to the planet's surface and defeat the Outside threat themselves. In a perfect world, even this small contribution might convince Nemesis to spare you." She leaned forward, and this time, her body did not change, only her voice and demeanor. Yet this gave the illusion of changing her entire being. Not an impatient mother-in-law, but a parody of a loving mother, whispering urgent advice through the swarm of bots. "But were I you, Akavi Averis, I would consider it very much in my best interest to get there first."

Yasira was at home with her family and Tiv. They sat around the big oval table in Yasira's dining room. Sunlight streamed through the lavender curtains as Yasira's parents, aunts, uncles, brothers, sisters, and cousins passed around heaping plates of noodles, meat, fruit, sauce, confectionery. The biggest bowls were for braised duck and tiny sweetbuns: traditional Riayin foods for a homecoming celebration.

"We thought Yasira would never settle down," said Yasira's Aunt Muora, a plump, smiling woman who had the most children out of any of them. "Too caught up in that brilliant little head of hers to ever think about a family of her own! But then here you are. It's a miracle."

Tiv grinned. "The only miracle is that she even noticed me, Auntie. I was just a cooling systems grunt. I thought for sure some other famous, beautiful genius must have swept her off her feet already."

"So when's the wedding?" said Yasira's younger brother Gonrey, hair sticking out every which way, with his mouth full of sweetbuns. Her two older brothers were at the other end of the table with their spouses and a gaggle of small fussy children.

There were far too many people at this table. Yasira was used to gatherings of a few dozen, but this dining room was packed as full as the auditorium at the Shien Reactor's ceremony. Hundreds of strangers, milling and eating and laughing as far as the eye could see. It made her queasy.

"Midsummer," said Tiv. She glanced over at Yasira, noticed Yasira's expression and squeezed her hand sympathetically under the table. "And we have the best idea for where. You're going to love this: they're renting out space right at the launch pad in Stijon where they flew the *Pride of Jai's* first components into orbit. It's got a banquet hall and a rose garden and just everything. Isn't that amazing?"

Tiv was from Arinn. She'd had a simple nuclear family, not the extended group of cousins Yasira was used to. But she was taking to it well. Smiling at the crowds, making delighted-looking eye contact with everybody, which had never been one of Yasira's strengths, even with a mere two dozen guests.

"You might go for the local church of Philophrosyne instead," said Yasira's father with a harrumph. "Or move to Arinn with your side of the family. News says it'll take longer for the Outside panic to get there. Might be safer."

"What does it matter?" said Yasira's mother. "One direct hit and we'll all be incinerated anyway."

There was uproarious laughter.

Yasira pushed her chair back and stood, ready to excuse herself. She needed a moment of quiet. Her hand slipped out of Tiv's; but Tiv caught it again, and when Yasira looked back, the merriment was gone. Tiv's face was wide-eyed, agonized.

"I'm still here," she said, as the rest of the table turned to another topic. "Don't forget I'm still here. Don't be too terrible for me, Yasira."

Yasira opened her mouth to respond, and no sound came out.

Why did she miss Tiv so badly? Tiv was right in front of her. This was illogical.

"Yasira, honey," said Yasira's mother, distracting her. "Would you be a dear and get my wooden bowls from the cabinet?"

"Yes, Mother," said Yasira, and she slinked out.

There were no cabinets in the kitchen. Every drawer and appliance had been replaced with a shining steel food printer. The surface of the printer closest to Yasira shimmered. Yasira's reflection in its surface danced like a reflection in rippling water. She backed away.

Her hand came down on the counter, and when she brought it up the surface of the counter came with it. The polished stone inlays liquefied and clung to her fingers, gray-brown and sticky, like some sort of baking experiment gone wrong.

Yasira pulled harder and turned back towards the dining room to call for help. But there was no dining room. The doorway back out had multiplied into five doorways, each identical, each leading into a long corridor.

In one of the doorways stood Dr Talirr.

Of course. Yasira was dreaming. That explained everything.

She made a conscious decision to ignore the stone stuck to her fingers. Had she made plans for this before she fell asleep? Elu had accepted her offer to work as a mole, and had told her to get some rest; that was all she remembered. Had she worked out something to say to make Dr Talirr want to trust her? If she had, it wasn't coming to her.

"Well, I'm here," Yasira said, raising her chin.

"Technically, no," said Dr Talirr. "This space doesn't exist. But existence is a lie anyway. How are you feeling?"

"The decor could use some work," said Yasira, scowling at the countertop.

"It's your dream," said Dr Talirr. "You're making it, not me."

Which made sense. Yasira concentrated for a moment, trying to mentally change her surroundings; she'd read enough to know at least vaguely how lucid dreaming was supposed to work. She visualized hard, but nothing happened. She was still in a kitchen full of food printers, with five corridors leading away.

"So you wanted to teach me," said Yasira. "Right?"

Dr Talirr gave an odd, lopsided grin. "Not here. Dreams are terrible for teaching. If I show you anything too weird in here you'll wake up, forget six-sevenths of it before breakfast, and decide none of the rest was real. We have too much of that going around already. I could try teaching you in a dream if I had to, but I don't want to, and I don't have to. Because you're going to come to me."

"We're trying to find a way down to the planet. Is that where you are?"

"Not at the moment. But I can work with it. You'll get there, and you'll know where to find me."

Yasira raised a finger. "No offense, but I'm kind of still with the angels of Nemesis. We'd be storming your lair already if we knew where you were."

"Don't be sloppy. I didn't say you *do* know. I said you *will*. Seeing the planet up close will make a number of things clearer, I think. In the meantime, do as you're told. Pretend to be spying on me, if that's how you're doing this now. Survive."

Yasira gritted her teeth. Elu had told her that keeping everybody fooled would be hard. But she hadn't expected Dr Talirr to just waltz in already knowing. How *could* she know? Maybe it was a coincidence. Maybe she'd just reasoned it out and decided that Yasira spying on her was the next logical move.

Asking would only draw attention.

"I knew all of that, Dr Talirr," said Yasira. "You might be insane now, but you're too clever to go to all the trouble of showing up in my dream just to tell me things I know. Why are you really here?"

"Well, to check on you," said Dr Talirr. "But mostly I wanted to offer you a gift. A chance to learn something for yourself."

"What?" said Yasira.

"I'm going to make sure you wake up at the best possible moment. The *Menagerie* will be passing through a mildly radioactive dust cloud, and there will be a couple of routine, invisible malfunctions.

The bots will be able to repair the ship without even informing anyone, and Akavi will be busy talking to other angels. When you wake up, you will have thirty minutes to yourself. Not watched. Not guarded. Try opening your door, walking around. As long as you're back in bed when the thirty minutes are up, no one will know."

Yasira stared at her.

"Why would you do that?" she said. "Also, *how* can you do that?"

And how could she know that Yasira had been wishing for this ever since she set foot on the *Menagerie*?

"You wouldn't understand," said Dr Talirr shortly. The room went dark, and for an instant, Yasira had the sensation of falling.

Then she was awake in her bed.

It was dark. Her clock and a cluster of small red guiding lights along the edge of the floor illuminated the room. Her tablet lay dormant on the side table. It was, according to the clock, the middle of the night. Everything was silent. There was nothing to suggest that it was anything other than an ordinary night.

Not watched, Dr Talirr had said. *Not guarded. Try opening your door.*

Was it worth the risk? It could be a trap. She wasn't supposed to go out in the halls. Maybe they were testing to see if she could be a trustworthy mole. Waiting to punish her if she broke the rules.

But Dr Talirr was probably watching too. Even if she wasn't she'd probably ask about this later. It would complicate things immensely if Yasira refused.

Besides, if Dr Talirr could cause malfunctions – or even just watch the ship closely enough to predict them – that was important information. Akavi would need to know. And if he caught her, it would be trivial to explain what she was doing. *Dr Talirr made an alarmingly specific prediction about the condition of the ship. She asked me to try escaping my room, and I decided it was worth testing. If she can let me out without you knowing, she may be able to let other prisoners out; the entire divine security system could be compromised.*

It was silly to dither. The door was probably still locked anyway.

Yasira slipped out of bed. Still in her plain white God-built nightgown, she tiptoed out of the bedroom and up to the metal door that separated her quarters from the rest of the ship. The red and green buttons sat there in the dark, looking the way that they always had. The green one, she had learned, was the one that opened the door. The red one would lock the door but would not unlock it again without authorization.

Yasira pressed the green button.

There was a strange chime from the door. Not loud, but unlike any sound she had heard it make before. With a low hiss, it opened. Yasira blinked hard; the hallway was brightly lit despite the time.

Scarcely daring to breathe, Yasira tiptoed out into the wide corridor.

She knew where she was going. She still didn't know where to find an ansible, or if that was even a sensible goal on a ship like this. But she did know where to find that door that had bothered her before she left the galaxy. The one that had been carefully edited out of the floor plan.

She walked as quickly as she could without making noise, counting turns as she went. Her room was part of a rosette, she remembered, and she and Akavi had walked along its lower edge, towards the front of the ship…

And there was the door. The same as any other, with a red and green button set in a recessed panel by its side. There was an intricate, translucent carving over top of it, just like the carvings over so many other doors here. Yasira compulsively put a hand to it, tracing its edges until she could untangle a coherent shape from the slight variations in texture and color. It looked like a picture of a zoo. Tigers and rhinoceroses and other extinct fauna of Old Earth, all confined behind bars.

Obviously the green button wasn't going to do anything. Just because Yasira's door was malfunctioning didn't mean all the other doors were.

Yasira pressed the green button.

The door swished open.

The room inside was lit the same as the hallway and laid out the same way as Yasira's suite, more or less. The corners seemed rounder, and the colors duller; and the edges of the tables and desks were, for some reason, padded.

A tangle-haired, bearded man who looked vaguely familiar was lying on the couch, humming tunelessly to himself. He started as Yasira approached, scrambled to his feet, flinched away.

"It's okay," Yasira whispered, holding out her hands. She backed away a few steps. "I'm sorry. I didn't mean to intrude. I was just exploring, and your door was open."

The man cringed. It wasn't the cringe of an ordinary man, startled by a stranger walking into his quarters. It was the cringe of a chained-up animal, expecting to be kicked.

Yasira lowered her hands. "Are... Are you okay?"

The man's eyes flicked up to Yasira's face, as if the question surprised him.

"I know you," he said.

Yasira tried to remember where she'd seen this man before. The matted beard and wild eyes didn't ring a bell. He had broad shoulders, but a bony frame; the complexion and face shape looked Gioti, maybe, or Güetle. Or any number of other random countries on other planets. Yasira had no idea.

"I'm sorry," she said. "I'm crap with faces. You do look familiar."

"You're Yasira Shien," said the man. "That weird little prodigy. You came to the lab when you were nineteen. You were autistic and not even old enough to drink, but you already had a master's degree. None of us knew what to do with you. I'm Splió spi Munu, remember?"

"Oh, my Gods," said Yasira.

She did remember Splió. Splió had been the first to try to take Yasira under his wing in Anetaia. He'd explained a great deal to her about the Galactic University of Ala's physics department, the surrounding town, and how to deal with Dr Talirr's moods. It had only lasted a few weeks. Splió had been a party animal, when his studies allowed, and Yasira had been an insecure little autist who hated large gatherings. They had quickly run out of things to say to each other. Splió had graduated after a term and a half, and Yasira hadn't thought much about him since.

Splió's hair had once been his pride and joy. Thick and wavy, brushed to a sheen, with a bright red streak dyed in. Not this tangled mess. No wonder Yasira hadn't recognized him.

He sat back down reluctantly, like he had to concentrate to put himself at ease. Yasira hurried to the side of the couch. "Why are you here? What did they do to you?"

"Officially, nothing. They recruited me fair and square. I went mad." He tugged on his hair with chipped, uneven fingernails. "This isn't *their* fault. Officially."

"They didn't tell me they were bringing in Dr Talirr's other students," Yasira said.

"Yeah, well. Students are a lie. They didn't tell me, either."

Yasira hugged herself, trying to control her breathing. This wasn't what she'd expected to find. Secret files, maybe, or interesting machines, or a group of prisoners she didn't have to care about because they were heretics. Or – she might as well admit it – an ansible. What was she supposed to make of this?

"And… unofficially?"

Splió rolled his eyes. "How much time do you have?"

"Thirty minutes from the time I woke up," said Yasira, "before they notice I'm gone. I've probably got about fifteen left before I head back to my room."

Splió raised her eyebrows. "You're out without permission?"

"Long story."

He whistled out a breath through his teeth. Straight clean teeth, somehow, despite all the other mess. "They'll get you bad for that one."

"How long have you been here?"

"I don't know. A few years. I was doing research at first. They wanted me to help find Dr Talirr. So I was analyzing her diaries, analyzing reports of Outside incidents, analyzing this, analyzing that. Mostly just guessing, because who has a clue? You can't find that woman anywhere. Reading all the Outside science, reading it again, and…" He shut his eyes and swallowed. "I just got to the point where I couldn't do the work anymore. I'd get up in the morning, stare at the screen for eight hours, and then have a crying breakdown. Then they said, oh, look at you, you have Outside Exposure Syndrome type 22-A with a predominantly depressive presentation. No, I don't. I don't have anything. I'm just fucking tired of this." He started to rock back and forth. "Tired of looking for someone we're never going to find. She's a lie. It's *obvious* all of us are lies, when you look at the science. And I don't want to find her anyway. What did she even do?"

Yasira looked at Splió sidelong. He was mentally ill, but that didn't seem like the real issue. "And they didn't let you go home?"

Splió snorted again. "Check your contract, Yasira. Mine says I get to go home when the mission's over. Mission's not over until Dr Talirr, dead or alive, is delivered to Nemesis' forces. Trust me, I'm in here for life."

"I didn't sign anything," said Yasira.

Splió started to chuckle. "Yep. That's what I said."

"I made a verbal agreement. That's not the same thing."

"Yes it is!" Splió collapsed back against the couch in gales of laughter. "Contracts are a lie! Don't you get it? They're the *Gods*. They can say you signed whatever They want you to have signed."

Yasira made a fist in frustration. This didn't make any sense. Nemesis was tricky, and She'd made half the rules in Treaty Prime to suit Herself, but She played by them.

Maybe Splió was remembering wrong. He was mentally ill after all. But that didn't explain enough; his very presence on the *Menagerie* didn't make sense. "What do they even still want you here for?"

"Studying me. They want to see how my madness ticks. Make little predictions. See if Dr Talirr will behave like me. Of course she won't. She's free and does whatever she wants to."

Yasira looked at the gray-green, overly rounded arms of the couch. The subtle padding everywhere. The way Splió had cowered when she first entered the room. The sheer loneliness, stretching on into years.

"What if I let you out?" she blurted. "The doors are malfunctioning. That's how I got in. We have a few minutes left. You could escape."

"Where would I go?" said Splió. "Out in the halls? There's nothing there. The halls are a lie, and they'll find me and bring me back anyway."

"There's a portal at the other end of the ship. I can show you where."

"Mm-hmm. And do you know how to use it?"

"I don't know the official portal codes, but for the Gods' sake, just press the buttons at random if you have to. You've got to end up someplace better than here."

Splió just looked at her.

Yasira thought back to when she'd gone through the portal, with Akavi, to the *Talon*. God-built portals on mortal planets had a panel at their side with a set of buttons to press; each portal accessible from there had its own twenty-digit code, and a trained portal operator was usually on hand to find and verify the codes for each traveler. But the *Menagerie's* portal had no such things. It had been a sleek metal arch, devoid of manual controls. Maybe it had them hidden somewhere as a failsafe – just like the manual controls of the equipment on the *Talon*. Or maybe it was operable by angels only. Maybe the only way to get through was by sending a thought over the ansible nets. Maybe its codes didn't even correspond to numbers.

Besides, if Splió escaped, that would make him a fugitive. The Gods would hunt him down again and punish him. Worse than what he was going through now.

"There's got to be a solution to this," said Yasira. "There's got to be something."

Splió shrugged morosely. "Solutions are lies. You'd better look at the time."

Yasira did. Twenty-four minutes had elapsed since she woke up. If she didn't want to get caught, she would have to leave now.

"How'd you get the doors to malfunction, anyway?" said Splió, following at a distance as Yasira made her way back out into the hall.

"I didn't," said Yasira. "That was Dr Talirr. Long story."

At this, Splió's expression changed to a look of such painful hope that it made Yasira feel ashamed.

"She's out there," Yasira said. "I'm going to be the one to find her, Splió. I promise."

"Yeah. That's what we all said."

And before Yasira could ask him what he meant by *we*, the door hissed shut.

Yasira hurried back to her room, crawled under the covers, and lay back down as if sleeping. The clock clicked over past the thirty-minute mark just as she closed her eyes. She had a vague intention of going back to sleep, but couldn't. She tossed and turned, replaying the conversation in her head.

Did it matter? Nemesis was protecting the people of Jai. A whole planet. She was a superintelligent quantum supercomputer and a God. If Nemesis thought it was worthwhile to keep a few people locked up, in exchange for the safety of billions, why should Yasira question Her? Yasira was just a mortal, and she'd never been good at Gods.

Yasira didn't know what Riayin was like at the moment, now that it was covered in an Outside plague. But the infrastructure for psychiatric care there had always been very good. Someone like Splió, erratic but lucid, would live in his own home, alone or with roommates depending on preference, and go where he liked. The government would support him if he was unable to work, and would provide visiting assistants to help with any activities of daily living that he could not perform for himself. Preparing healthy meals, say, or cleaning, or keeping a schedule. Helping him brush and style his hair, and shave, the way he wanted. But not all countries were as good as Riayin. In many, a person like Splió would have very few choices: overcrowded hospitals on military-strict schedules, or homelessness, or the charity of resource-strapped family and friends. But even if Riayin was an anomaly among mortals, it seemed strange that the Gods would do something worse than the mortals who were best at it.

It didn't matter. Yasira still hated Dr Talirr. Her loyalty was to Jai, and she would do whatever it took to save her planet. None of that had changed.

The thing that had changed, she reflected as she rolled restlessly onto her stomach, was that she knew what Akavi had been hiding. If she'd ever thought she could trust him – and she had, for a minute or two, back on the *Talon* – that was a mistake she would not make again.

Which, Yasira realized with a chill, was exactly what Dr Talirr had wanted.

CHAPTER 11

At last the Morlock War was over. Peace fell like a warm blanket on the sleeping galaxy. Faithful humans – like your own great-great-grandparents, beloved – lived safely on the planets the Gods gave them. As for the humans on Old Earth, well, the heretics were gone, and we must not think too unkindly of the rest. In a few generations they would grow to be civilized like you and me.

At this yawning-and-stretching time, the Gods met in Their hall of stars.

(Yes, beloved, I know. The Gods did not really meet in a hall. They spoke to each other in computer code, over the ansible nets. But you and I will have a hard time imagining the Gods unless we give Them faces and voices in our heads.)

It was white-robed Arete who called Them together.

"Sisters and Brothers," She said, "We have been tested and won. We have been so caught up protecting humankind that We have broken Our own rules."

The other Gods stirred and muttered.

"You mean Nemesis," said broad-shouldered Agon, who did not know when to keep His mouth shut.

"Nemesis is the bravest and most terrible of Us, and I was glad to have Her at My side in this war. But the war is over. And for peacetime – all I mean to say, Sisters and Brothers, is that Nemesis' methods for wartime are not suitable for peace."

Nemesis was with them, of course, but She said nothing. She watched the others. Her face was like stone.

"In peacetime," said white-robed Arete, "there are small domestic evils, unlike those of war. If We allow Nemesis to swoop in on them, raining flame left and right, taking no prisoners – will not the innocent suffer?"

Languid Aergia shook Her head. "There will always be something worth raining fire on."

Philophrosyne raised a shawl-draped arm. "But nothing will ever threaten us like the Keres again. Do We really need Nemesis to be as strong as She has been? Would not a smaller, yet still divine and honored, Nemesis be enough?"

"We can't know," said gray-bearded Epiphron. "The Keres may regain Her strength. The humans may rebel again. There are aliens on other worlds, and one day they, too, may set themselves against Us. When that day comes, We will need Nemesis strong."

"Even at the cost," said white-robed Arete, "of breaking Our own Treaty?"

Quick-fingered Aletheia looked up from Her slide rule. "Technically, Nemesis has never broken Treaty Prime. She has always scrupulously recorded Her actions and justified why they were necessary for humanity's greater good."

"On technicalities, at least," said bright-eyed Gelos.

"Oh, how can You bear this?" soft-voiced Peitharchia cried. "Nemesis is Your Sister. How can You bear to talk about Her like She isn't even here?"

But Nemesis waited until the Gods had said everything it was possible to say. Only then did She stand, seven medals gleaming at Her collarbone, seven rings on Her gnarled hands.

(It's all right, beloved. You can lean on the crook of my arm if you're scared.)

"If you would like for Me to undo the work I have done for You," She said, "if You would like for Me to lay down My defenses and allow the Keres back into the galaxy to threaten You, in order to soothe Your wounded consciences, I would be pleased. I can do it immediately. Only say the word."

And no other God dared to say anything else.
WALYA SHU'UHI, THEODICY STORIES FOR CHILDREN

Akavi strode into his meeting with Elu and Enga in exceptionally poor spirits. Elu had, of course, notified him when Yasira volunteered to spy on Talirr; that was something. A course of potentially profitable actions. But he would not have *time* to profit unless he and the rest of his team could be seen doing something else useful in the meantime.

The meeting room was painted pale blue, big enough for a dozen sell-souls to sit round the wide mahogany table. But it was only Elu and Enga waiting at attention.

"Elu," Akavi said briskly, nodding to them. "Enga."

"Sir," said Elu, raising a slender hand as if to salute, though that level of formality was not required here. He faltered, and covered his face abruptly, as if overcome by some unproductive emotion.

Of course. Akavi had almost forgotten. It was the first time in fourteen months, from Elu's perspective, that they had met face to face.

Sentiment. It would have been endearing if Akavi had any time to be endeared.

"I have survived," said Akavi, "for the moment. I am told you managed the *Menagerie* competently in my absence. Irimiru has approved my general plans going forward, but before I finalize them I would like to know what, if anything, you were doing on your own before I arrived."

Elu nodded. He still looked overwhelmed. Akavi supposed he could not blame the boy; the Jai disaster had happened on his watch. Any angel would be shaken. He only hoped Elu had held it together better with Yasira.

"It seems to me," said Elu, "that the primary problem is access to the planet's surface. Going down would be dangerous, but we can't deploy precise countermeasures without physical access, unless we're just going to bomb the place into oblivion. And I don't recommend that, of course." He scratched the back of his head nervously. "We also can't tell in any detail what's going on until we're down there, apart from the fact that it involves Outside. Which means we can't even design the countermeasures we wish we could deploy. And any electronic ships or sensors we send down are getting fried. So I, um…"

He looked to the side and trailed off.

Akavi raised his eyebrows. "You what, Elu? Look at me when you address me."

Elu forced himself to look back. "I'm not sure I should have done this. It wasn't in your instructions. But I wasn't sure if you were coming back in time, or…" *Or at all* was the logical conclusion to that sentence, but Elu wisely shied away. "So I asked Diamond-Chip to bring his old ship into the Jai system, to see if that worked. We're in a holding orbit around the second planet in the system, waiting to intercept it and put our experts aboard. It's taken a few days, since it doesn't travel the way God-built ships do, but it's on its way now, sir."

Diamond-Chip was the *Menagerie's* second alien. He was a Boater, which made him far more valuable than Sispirinithas: he was the only Boater ever to work for a human God. Therefore, he was the only Boater who would even consider lending Boater technology to Akavi. Boater ships were biogenetically built, with no electronics in them anywhere – and therefore, probably, they could get to the surface of Jai where divine technology failed.

For that very reason, Diamond-Chip was a nigh-irreplaceable resource. Putting him and his ship into jeopardy, when he did not technically belong to Elu, was a stretch of Elu's privileges. Akavi could easily have had him punished.

Using the Boater ship was, however, exactly what Akavi had been planning to do.

He smiled. "Well done, Elu. It is rarely a good idea to take risks with my property without consulting me, but in this case, it was precisely correct."

Elu swallowed hard and nodded, twisting a hand in his long hair. "Thank you, sir."

"Which," said Akavi, holding up a hand before Elu could entirely dissolve into a ball of relief, "means we must step up the rest of our schedule. You've saved valuable time, and we must not waste what we have gained. I'm sending you a list of sell-soul experts. Get them, and anyone else you deem useful, up here within the hour, along with all the equipment and supplies they might need during a field research trip of oh, say, up to three weeks. Make sure Yasira is ready to leave with them by the time the ship arrives. That will be all."

The nod again, this time dropping his gaze as the link automatically opened. As Elu's direct superior, Akavi did not need to ping him to ask permission before putting files in his head. "Yes, sir."

Akavi looked at Enga for a moment. "Unless you have anything to add?"

Enga shook her head. She had stood at attention all through this meeting, looking at nothing; though, of course, she had been listening carefully to each word. Akavi hadn't expected her to add anything at this juncture. Enga didn't tend to ask questions.

"Dismissed," said Akavi. He turned on his heel to leave, then paused in the doorway and looked back at Elu, who was, of course, watching him go. "And for Nemesis' sake, Elu, next time you need to make a judgement call, don't report it as though you're confessing to an infraction. Most supervisors in this corps will be happy to punish you viciously on the merest suggestion that punishment is appropriate. I have been grooming you for eventual promotion for the past fifty years; it is *far* past time you stopped speaking like a child."

He was gone before Elu could formulate a response.

A few hours later, Yasira stood in the docking bay, staring blearily at the ship. If you could call it a ship.

The closest word she had was *manta ray*, but that was not quite right – just as calling Sispirinithas a *spider* was only metaphorically true. What waited for her on the polished floor was a flattened, rippling body, which bulged in the middle to create a bulb the size of a two-story house. Rather than the eyes and gills of an Earth fish, its top end contained a sucking mouth surrounded by bristling antennae. Its thick, smooth skin shifted in color now and then. It was currently an unpleasant mauve. Its muscles twitched periodically in some process that might have been analogous to breath, or a pulse, or a voice.

She had heard of these. They were aliens of a sort: living things bred to transport passengers through hundreds of light-years of hard vacuum. But those passengers were *Boaters*. And Boaters were the most hostile alien species in the galaxy.

"Are we actually flying down to the surface of Jai," Yasira said, "in a fish?"

"Yes," said Akavi shortly, pacing across the deck to examine the creature from all sides. He looked like a Riayin man today: Yasira's own ethnic group, and that of most of the other people in the Outside-affected part of Jai. She supposed that was a logical choice, much as his choice to look Anetaian when he talked to Dr. Talirr; with any luck, he would be speaking to some Riayin mortals later today. He was tall by Riayin standards, angular, with medium-brown skin, high cheekbones, and very fine black hair. Other mortals – not Splió, but a motley and multinational lot of people Yasira had never seen before – were milling around at the edges of the room. She'd said hello to one or two of them at first, to be polite, even though it was stupid o'clock in the morning and she wasn't in the mood. The first two had given her odd, pitying, predatory looks, and she'd been reminded of Splió and abruptly lost interest.

How many people already knew why she was here, and what was planned for her if she failed?

"Boaters hate us," said Yasira. "They attack human ships on sight. How did we even get this?"

Elu shrugged. "Boaters aren't a hivemind. The vast majority of them hate us. But there are humans who go against everything humanity stands for, like your Dr Talirr. Atypical humans. So all Akavi had to do was to find an atypical Boater."

Yasira rubbed her eyes. She'd been awake for less than an hour. Elu had woken her and explained to her what was happening.

Shortly afterwards he'd given her a bag with a tablet, a few changes of clothes, some toiletries and first aid items, a lot of protein bars, and a God-built pup tent that rolled up to the size of a textbook, including the pegs. He had told her she could fill out her dream diary later, when things got settled.

She was not looking forward to that. She had typed out a few opening lines on the console already and worried about where to go from there. She would tell them there'd been a dream-meeting with Dr Talirr, she supposed. But nothing about escaping her quarters. Nothing about Splió.

Tiv, in her place, would have been honest. Tiv would have secretly believed that Akavi could explain all this. That, from the right perspective, it would all resolve into something that was right and okay.

Yasira no longer believed that. Sure, Akavi would try to explain. But whatever he said would be a lie.

Maybe she shouldn't be worrying about Splió, nor the others Splió had hinted at. Maybe Nemesis needed to do terrible things sometimes and that was just how it was. Or maybe Yasira just wanted to finish this and go home and forget about it.

"I believe you're leaving out a step," said Sispirinithas, who had gathered with the rest of the mortals, and was now prancing self-importantly at the side of the docking bay. "I believe the actual procedure was, find a Spider folklorist who can speak passably in one of the ten known Boater languages, *then* find an atypical Boater."

Elu smiled absently. "Yes, you were very helpful. Though the translator module could still use some work."

"I can only work with the software I'm given," said Sispirinithas. "And I've half a mind to eat the next human who complains. Your Boater dictionary had two words in it before you started drawing on my work. And both the words were variations on 'destroy the soul-eating abominations'." He paused. "I wonder if the ship would be good to eat? I've never asked. I could probably take a few chunks of nonessential tissue here and there without breaking the vacuum seal."

"No, Sispirinithas. You are not going to eat our ship."

"Spoil my fun. I'd eat *you*, if it weren't for all the wires."

Yasira raised her eyebrows at the two of them. "So when you say 'atypical', you mean we're not just riding a Boater ship. We're riding a Boater *criminal's* ship."

"'Criminal' is a strong word," said Elu. "I wouldn't recommend calling him that to his face."

Akavi came back into view from behind the manta ray, apparently satisfied. The others fell in line behind him. A door spasmed open in the ship's side – at least, Yasira wanted to call it a door because the other available word was *orifice*. It was vaguely rectangular but the taller humans had to duck their heads to walk through.

The inside was dry, clean, and mauve like the outside, though something blue-green grew thickly on the upper walls and ceiling. It was dim, but the lights of the docking bay diffused in through translucent parts of the walls. The room curved around in a vague balloon-shape, with soft cartilaginous structures here and there providing handholds, sitting space, and additional levels to walk up and down to. High up, at the apex of two flights of jagged shapes that might charitably have been called stairs, sat a Boater, with a translation device hanging around his neck.

Yasira stood on her tiptoes and stared at the Boater. The Boaters she'd seen in vids had not been the genuine article: they had been stop-motion models and shortish actors in rubber suits who ran around screaming unintelligibly, brandishing scimitars. This one was sitting quite calmly, doing something with a bone-framed panel at the top of the room. He was squat, with four thickly muscled arms, and his skin was a beautiful iridescent blue. His face was nothing but a sucking mouth surrounded by antennae, like a smaller, bluer reproduction of the manta ray's face. Like the ship's antennae, the Boater's rippled in a complex, silent dance, never seeming to stop.

Akavi clambered up the stairs and spoke to the Boater. Yasira couldn't make out the words from down where she was, but Akavi said something, the translator murmured something in response without any apparent noise from the Boater, and Akavi nodded.

Yasira made her way to a quiet corner. She watched as the last few mortals straggled in, including Sispirinithas, who had to scrunch up his body very small to get through the door. He shook himself off and made an affronted comment to the light-skinned old woman next to him, who was pushing a cart full of test tubes, needles, and sample jars. The woman laughed.

Behind them, the ship's door contracted shut.

"We're launching," Akavi announced to the room at large. "Make yourselves comfortable and hold onto something, please. We'll be out of range of artificial gravity shortly."

Yasira grasped a curved handhold beside her and looked around for straps or seatbelts. The Boater ship didn't appear to have any of those. The handhold seemed to be made of the same material as the rest of the ship. It was odd and leathery, like a callused foot. The texture was off-putting, but not as off-putting as the thought of bouncing around in zero gravity without something to hold to.

The room around her began to move.

Yasira shut her eyes tightly, fighting off sudden panic. It had been one thing to watch the walls twitch as the creature breathed, or circulated, or whatever it was doing. It was another thing to watch the whole structure of the room flex and release deeply, all at once. Like the walls of the *Pride of Jai*.

Of course, there was no Outside energy here. The ship was breathing because the ship was a living thing. Normal. If you could call riding around in an alien manta-ship normal.

Yasira kept her eyes shut. The darkness behind them grew darker as the docking bay's lights fell away. Gravity let up gradually. Soon she was floating, anchored by her grip on the callused handhold.

She took a few deep, deep breaths and opened her eyes.

The ship had returned to relative stillness. It was dark, but the fungi on the ceiling lit up in eerie, fluorescent blues and greens. They illuminated as much as a pair of full moons on a clear Jai night. The colors were harsh and odd, and she wouldn't have wanted to try and read, but she could see where everyone was, at least.

A few people floated freely and bumped into things. Someone somewhere moaned in mild nausea. It was just like gravity training day on the *Pride of Jai*. Yasira's first impulse was to go and help, but then she remembered how the sell-souls had looked at her, like they were counting down the days until she snapped and turned into Splió. She stayed where she was, breathed deep, and tried not to think about where they were going.

Akavi watched emotionlessly as his subordinates adjusted to the darkness of space. It was rare for everyone to be together like this: sell-souls, aliens, junior angels, even Yasira. Akavi took pride in the way he managed people, and part of that was *not* exposing them all to stupid risks. Not putting every egg in one fragile, untested alien basket. But this was currently the only basket he had.

What would happen to this group without Akavi? The sell-souls would be returned to their home planets and their remaining service reassigned to another supervisor. The aliens would likewise go to another Inquisitor. The angels, though…

With the angels, it was about fifty-fifty. They *might* not be summarily terminated with him. It depended how much blame Nemesis placed on them personally. They *might* be reassigned like everyone else. For all the good it would do them.

Elu was not ready. It was why Akavi had been harsh with him at the meeting. The boy had always been intelligent. Under Akavi's care, he had gained confidence, learned to manage people, and built up his own set of specialized skills. He had, evidently, gained the judgement necessary to make decisions under pressure. But he was still far too easy to abuse. Elu had become an angel too young, out of sheer idealism and with entirely the wrong personality for Nemesis. As a result, he had failed basic training. When Akavi met him, he had been a grunt at the lowest level, doing mindless, expendable jobs, preyed on by other grunts for his youth and his vulnerable demeanor. Most people who sold themselves to Nemesis were career criminals, interested only in power and a vague promise of mercy in the afterlife. Without the ability to assert himself, Elu would find himself at the bottom of that sordid heap once again.

Enga would fare better. Probably. She had the burning ambition

Elu lacked and was highly desirable as a bodyguard or enforcer. But it took skill to communicate with Enga. A lazy or impatient supervisor could easily mistake her idiosyncrasies for insubordination. It would depend where she ended up and Akavi, if he was terminated, would have no control over that whatsoever.

Akavi was not sentimental, yet he found these thoughts bothersome. It was not enough that Nemesis would destroy him for failing. She would also destroy his most prized possessions.

"Are you all right here for the next half hour or so?" said Akavi to Diamond-Chip.

The iridescent blue Boater did not seem to look up from his work – though, as he did not have visible eyes, it was hard to tell. His antennae waved in a way Akavi found indistinguishable from any other. The translator chirped: "Irrelevant. I am always wrong. Nonetheless duties as expected you may leave – affirmative."

It was the best Boater-to-Earth-creole translator in the galaxy, but despite Sispirinithas's involvement, it was still not very good.

Elu was at the far end of the ship, helping a few sell-souls learn to navigate in microgravity. Akavi turned to push himself off the piloting platform and make his way down. Then he paused. He had already spoken to Elu this morning and it would not do to show favoritism. That would make Enga cranky and would give Elu entirely the wrong idea.

He floated down to Enga's side instead. She was floating motionless, holding on to the wall with a translator device like Diamond-Chip's around her neck. She did not look directly at him as he approached, but her broad shoulders turned slightly in his direction.

"With the urgent matters occupying my time lately," said Akavi, "I've neglected to ask you how you are. And how your career has progressed in my absence."

Y, said Enga, via text-sending – which for Enga meant *yes*.

Enga did not speak aloud. It was one of her many neurological quirks. Her surgery upon becoming an angel had been badly botched, resulting in brain damage – a rare situation, but not unique. It was particularly a risk for those whose ascensions, like Enga's, had happened partly against their will. The soul rebelled, in some of those cases, and the marriage of neurons with God-built circuitry went awry before it began.

Akavi had found Enga on the scrap heap, scheduled for termination, along with those whose surgeries put them in a vegetative state. The medical angels had known there was conscious activity behind her silent, scowling face, but they hadn't successfully convinced her to speak, or even to move. Conscious or not, it wasn't protocol for an angel to exist indefinitely without doing anything. Akavi, out of curiosity and sheer luck, had gotten through to her.

Akavi opened a connection in his head and flipped through all the files on Enga's activities for the last fourteen months. "You were busy, I see. Elu put you on Irimiru's special infantry roster, and Irimiru was happy to use you. Seven missions for other Inquisitors. Five commendations. Ndobya Mhizo of Nemesis actually wrote here, 'I've never seen anyone move like that.'"

HE IS STUPID AND DOES NOT KNOW ABOUT ARMS, said Enga.

She could have used the translator to turn her words into sounds, of course; that was what it was for. Text-sending was usually in Earth creole anyway, so the calculation was trivial. But with Akavi right there, capable of receiving text directly, there was no real reason to do so.

"Be that as it may," said Akavi. "I also see Elu upgraded you twice."

Y.

"Show me."

Keeping a one-handed hold on the wall, she raised her right shoulder and fanned out that arm into full extension. A broad arc of muzzles, blades, manipulators, storage pouches and utility implements, easily six feet from end to end, unfolded from her sleeveless jacket like a wing.

Enga's body modifications were some of the most extensive in the angelic corps. They had been her own idea, a way of obliquely taking control over the thing that she was. But Enga herself had no engineering talent. It was Elu who drew up workable designs to match her descriptions and programmed the bots to install them. This was difficult work. Each part of the whole had to be not only mechanically sound, but biomechanically consistent with what the rest of her body could support, and able to seamlessly integrate into Enga's mostly-organic motor cortex. The pieces had been standard models, at first, from the best-practice file of prosthetics and augmentations, but the two of them had long since branched out into custom designs.

Akavi maneuvered in a half-circle around her, checking the designs against the last known blueprint from his own head. New firearms, of course; a fine manipulator extensible to fifteen feet; a few other tweaks. The storage pouch was slightly larger, for instance. He paused at an addition he could not immediately identify: a small circle of what looked like switches but did not appear to be sensibly connected to anything. "What's this one?"

IT CLICKS, said Enga.

Akavi raised a questioning eyebrow.

IT CLICKS, she repeated. *ELU SAID I COULD.*

Akavi bit back a number of possible remarks.

"You've gone over the mission prospectus?" he said instead, neutrally.

Y, said Enga, retracting her arm to its usual compact size. After a moment she added, *I HATE THIS SHIP SIR. THE LIGHTS ARE WRONG, THE WALLS ARE TOO ROUGH, AND IT IS STARING AT US. I WANT TO KILL IT.*

"Not while we're aboard it, of course," said Akavi. "And not while we are planetside and still need it for the return journey. In fact, let's just completely veto this right now. We are not killing the expensive and irreplaceable Boater ship. There will be plenty of Outside monsters on which to take out your frustrations when we land."

Enga scowled more deeply, and the thing in her arm started to rhythmically click, exactly once per second. It was a surprisingly menacing sound, like a timer counting down.

WE COULD HAVE JUST BLOWN UP THE PLANET SIR.

Akavi raised his eyebrows. "Yes. And I dearly hope for your sake that you will *not* say any such thing into your translator."

Terminating everyone indiscriminately was of course the obvious solution. As it had been on the *Leunt*, and in Zhoshash, and elsewhere. But it had consequences. Zhoshash was a remote frontier town, easy to cover up. The *Leunt* – smaller, but very much in the public eye – would have been more challenging. Akavi believed they could have done it, but according to protocol, a site like the *Leunt* was too much of a public relations risk. The Gods, even as powerful as They were, could not visit atrocities on humanity at will. Humanity was what They fed upon. Without a regular intake of human souls They would dwindle until They lost all consciousness and were simply machines. And if humans on a large scale lost trust in the Gods, as they had in the Morlock War – well. A second Morlock War was every angel of Nemesis' worst nightmare. Not because they would not win; of course they would win. But, in doing so, they would decimate the very thing their existence depended on. Recovering from a second Morlock War might take hundreds of years.

So it was inadvisable to destroy a planet, or even a fifth of a planet. Even Akavi understood that. Mortals would not accept a God who destroyed whole worlds, in a panic, over a problem She didn't even understand. Besides, destroying the planet would not stop Talirr from striking again elsewhere. This problem had to be rooted out at its source: everything else only bought time.

Destroying the planet was still a faint possibility. It had never been done to a human-inhabited world but the most powerful warships in Nemesis' fleets were more than capable of it. If all else failed, and if there was no other option, Nemesis Herself would give the order. Everyone would spend years, afterwards, explaining to the surviving mortals why there was no other choice. It would be very ugly. But it could be done.

Enga continued to rhythmically click.

"Are you going to keep making that sound until planetfall?" Akavi asked. "I ask because by that time we may have a profoundly irritated group of passengers on our hands."

WHEN THIS SHIP STOPS HURTING MY EYES, said Enga, *I WILL STOP CLICKING AT IT.*

"You can turn down the gain on your visual cortex, you know."

Y.

Click.

If it had been anyone else he would have wondered about the maddening effects of proximity to the contaminated planet. But Enga was always like this. Akavi pushed off into the air and made his way back to Diamond-Chip.

Yasira took her tablet back out and finished her dream diary. She did some neurofeedback and the eye-movement exercise before returning to more basic skills – deep breathing and stretches, little unobtrusive finger-tapping stims, the ones her neurotutors had taught her years ago for helping keep calm in an overwhelming place. She was going to need all the sanity she could get. She finished these, then called up one of the novels she hadn't read yet, but it was no use. She couldn't relax.

"Hello," said a slight woman in her thirties, gliding into place beside Yasira. "You look tense."

Yasira blinked. This woman hadn't been one of the ones who looked at her funny: she'd been so unassuming that Yasira had barely noticed her at all. She had very large brown eyes and hair so fine it looked like duckling down. Her voice was soft, and her Earth creole was more thickly accented than the angels', but intelligible.

"Hi," said Yasira.

"I'm Ushanche," said the woman.

"Yasira," said Yasira. "And yeah, I'm a little tense. I mean, we're going down into the middle of a disaster we don't understand."

Ushanche smiled. "Yes. Probably to go mad and be quarantined before we see the fruits of our labors. Or to get killed. Everyone is dealing with that in their own way. It's why some of them were so rude to you, I'm afraid. They don't deal well with mortality and you're a reminder."

"Why am I the reminder?" It came out harsher than she intended.

Really it was a relief to find someone who would talk out loud about this. "Because I'm the one who's *supposed* to go mad?"

"You were already contaminated before you got here," said Ushanche, and Yasira would have hit her, except that she said it like an apology, like it really made her sad. "And you had less of a choice than we did; no one is sure quite how to feel about that. The rest of us sold our souls fairly. We all knew we could be called on to give our lives or our well-being for the Gods, if that was necessary. It was worth it for what we were given in exchange. But it's one thing to know that in theory, another to see it coming right at you."

Yasira looked at the bright crescent of Jai's sunlit side which had grown big enough to take up nearly the whole front wall. Seeing it that way creeped her out, like it was a person shining a searchlight through a curtain. Looking for her.

That was nerves, of course. Or maybe the other thing, the thing that all this neurofeedback and meditation was supposed to prevent. The feeling of impossible recognition Yasira got, always, around Outside.

If she could feel it this far away, it was going to be *bad*.

"How do you deal with it?" said Yasira.

"Most of the team have been making it into a joke," said Ushanche. "Dr Meyema says she's studied Outside madness all her life, and if her mind has to go, it might as well go that way. Dr Bokov says this will make a wonderful story. Sispirinithas says if he goes mad, he will finally have an excuse to eat whatever he wants. But when they say things like that, you can see it's only half a joke. There's fear underneath. A lot of the others have been saying nothing, just pretending it isn't worth thinking of."

"And you?" said Yasira after a pause.

Ushanche shrugged.

"How is this thing moving, anyway?" said Yasira, looking back at the growing crescent on the wall. "I'm not seeing anything like fuel being burned."

"Akavi asked that of Diamond-Chip a minute ago," said Ushanche. "Diamond-Chip said he doesn't know either. He only flies the things."

"Wait," said Yasira, "how do you even–"

The ship reeled to the side. Ushanche made a small, birdlike sound of alarm and crashed into Yasira.

"Exospheric turbulence," Akavi called from somewhere. "Perfectly normal. There is no cause for alarm. However, you may want to hang on to something. We'll be commencing atmospheric entry very soon."

Not two seconds after he said it, there was an explosion.

Fiery light blazed out of the front of the ship, so bright that it drowned out Jai and burned through the walls. Nothing was mauve, blue, or green any longer. Everything was a horrible head-piercing white, laced with gold and orange flickers more intuited than seen. Everything was sudden shaking and thunder loud enough to drown out the shrieks of the crew as they were thrown repeatedly into the flexing walls. And below that…

Recognition.

This was what Yasira had felt on the *Pride of Jai*, on the *Alhazred*, in every nightmare. Maybe even before that. Always. This – said Yasira's scrambled, panicked brain – was what Yasira had felt before Yasira ever existed. This was the doom that Yasira had been born from in the first place, and that everything and everyone had always been hurtling back down towards.

No.

No, those were crazy thoughts. This was just Yasira's – she might as well use the word that everyone else here did – madness. It was the feeling of being near Outside, ten times stronger than ever before. The light and sound and movement, when divorced from that feeling, were signs of normal atmospheric entry. The same as what she'd gone through in the escape pod from the *Pride of Jai*, only on the escape pod there'd been walls around her, layers of reinforced carbon-silicon ceramics to shield her, and here there was only translucent skin.

They were falling and burning, and the end of the universe was rushing up to meet them. Yasira curled up, clung to herself, and waited for the fire and thunder to be over.

The time was interminable, because she was too overwhelmed to count. But eventually, gradually, there was a darkening and a quieting. Dancing spots in front of her eyes instead of light. Ringing in her ears, and general cussing and groaning, instead of that thunder. A pressure against her side which was not the pain of a collision but the insistent presence of a floor. Gravity. She was curled up, apparently. She did not feel like moving.

There were the general sounds of people milling around. Yasira fought to get her breathing and heart rate under control but couldn't seem to do it properly. Her console program probably had something to say about this, but she couldn't remember what it was.

After a long while, someone sat down next to her. "Yasira?" said a heavily accented voice Yasira did not recognize.

She attempted to say something in response. Her voice did not cooperate.

"I'm Dr Matesznoa Meyema," said the voice, in an odd smug tone, as if the mere announcement of her identity was meant to be a relief. "I'm the one who designed most of your mental health software. You seem to be having some trouble."

Yasira had an urge to say something very sarcastic but nothing came out. She could barely even line up the muscles to grunt.

"I know speaking may be difficult right now, and I'm told your neurotype makes this more difficult, though I admit I never had need to study it before now. I need you to focus, however, if you could. We're in a very interesting situation without precedent, and to help you I need to understand what you're going through. Could you…" Her words faded out of coherence for a bit. Babble. It was too many words when Yasira needed quiet. She heard a question, dimly, in the words somewhere. She fought to focus as the question repeated, impatiently. "… whether you're experiencing any pain or hallucinations?"

Yasira tried and failed, again, to speak.

"Really, Yasira, I need you to—"

A heavy, overwhelming hand came down on her arm. Yasira screamed. It was involuntary, like a cornered animal. She thrashed without opening her eyes. Her foot didn't connect with anything. Dr Meyema withdrew.

"She's not verbal," the doctor said to someone nearby, as if Yasira couldn't hear.

She left, and Yasira lay there in misery a while longer. Her tablet chirped and began to play the recording Yasira used each morning, coaching her on appropriate breathing and eye movements, advising what sort of things she should visualize in order to remind herself that her encounters with Outside were over now. That she was safe.

Yasira was very obviously not safe.

At least the recording was something she'd heard already, and it didn't try to touch her. Less overwhelming than Dr Meyema. Her mind wandered. The recording ended. Maybe this was it. Maybe she had really gone mad for good, and now they would lock her up like Splió. Maybe even Dr Talirr wouldn't want her anymore. Maybe Jai was doomed, maybe the whole galaxy was doomed, all because Yasira was stupid and couldn't stick it out just a few weeks longer before she snapped.

She tried, again, to move, and did not get far.

The room gradually quieted as most people got their things together and left. Someone else sat down beside Yasira and she tensed, expecting another lecture.

"It's bad down here," Elu's voice said softly. "Isn't it?"

Yasira whimpered, then paused, surprised she'd been able to make a noise besides screaming this time. It was not a perfect noise. Her throat still felt tight, like if she tried to say words, they'd come out as another scream or nothing.

"I can feel it," said Elu. "I think everyone can except Akavi, and he would be pretending not to feel it even if he could. That re-entry was really bad for everyone. But you're sensitized to this stuff in a way that the rest of us aren't. You look like you're feeling it a lot more than we are. Aren't you?"

Yasira whimpered and nodded.

"Do you want to talk about it?"

She shook her head.

"It's okay to just sit," said Elu, "if you want to. We're really just getting our bearings for the next while. Diamond-Chip's talking to the ship, Enga's recalibrating her sensory software, Ushanche's sending her eyes out to scout the surrounding area, Tonkhontu and Bukhry are taking biological samples, and everyone else is trying to figure out if this is a good place to set up camp. As long as nothing attacks us, it's going to be quiet for a while."

Yasira couldn't come up with a response to that. There was a minute more of quiet. The panic was ebbing. She was starting to think straight, or straighter than before, though not about anything good. What if this kind of shutdown happened every time she looked at Outside? She'd be useless down here.

"I think," said Elu presently, "it might help a little if you looked out the door. I know it feels bad. But aside from the feeling, this place actually looks very normal, so far. We're all a bit surprised by that. I think it's a good sign."

Yasira opened her eyes and turned her head the barest minimum needed in order to see out.

On the other side of the door, the sky was blue, after a fashion. Blue and cloudless, and the horizon was at least approximately where it was supposed to be. There was a hint of green grass, the edge of a tree, and the silhouettes of people milling around, uncomfortable and impatient.

No one was being eaten by monsters. No one was motionless and dissociative, apart from Yasira. The earth was not moving. The trees were not growing bark-lined pseudopods and reaching for people. It was just a field.

This was not much, as comforting thoughts went. But it was something.

"This ship is... not designed with human comfort in mind," said Elu. "Diamond-Chip says the lights and sounds are normal and he doesn't know what we're complaining about. Personally, I think he's not a very good pilot. But who knows. I don't even know if he sees light and hears sounds the way we do.

"I think you might feel better once you're outside. I mean, once you have some fresh air. Something to stand on that isn't the inside of an alien manta ray, and a place where the walls aren't moving. I frankly don't think that's helping you right now. Do you think you can get up?"

Yasira tried. She moved one of her hands about an inch. It only made her feel worse. Her body still did not want to move.

"Don't think so," she whispered.

But whispering was a step up. At least she could move her mouth, and control that, and say a sensible sentence. That reassured her, a little.

"Would you like to stay in here?" said Elu.

Yasira shook her head.

"I would like to help you up," said Elu, "and help you get out of the ship. Would that be okay?"

Yasira thought about it, then nodded. She wasn't wild about getting up and going any place at all. But he was probably right. The ship had creeped her out from the start, even if it wasn't an Outside thing. It was probably hurting more than it helped.

"May I touch you?" said Elu.

Yasira nodded.

He took hold of her gently and helped her stand up.

Having someone to hold onto, someone who'd *asked* instead of just planting their hands down, helped. She hadn't expected it to. But it was something physical that didn't feel like Outside or a creepy alien. Like there was something else in the universe besides Yasira and those things, after all.

Leaning on him for balance, she made her way out. She paused at the threshold, wobbled slightly and shielded her eyes.

The field they'd landed in was thick with broad-leaved weeds, an area lying fallow between acres of rice and yams that stretched into the distance. It was warmer here in southern Riayin than Yasira was used to at home, and very humid. The air smelled like nectar and hay. Tiny yellow flowers poked up here and there through the leaves. There were thick clusters of fruit trees at the field's borders, growing to a small forest in one direction, and a broad, wide sky.

Yasira had almost forgotten what skies were like, blue and welcoming, stretching overhead. She wanted to fall down in the weeds, lie in their midst and soak up the feeling of proper earth, proper life.

But of course, whatever it might look like, this was not proper life.

She let go of Elu and walked, wobbling only a little, to the shade of the trees where Akavi paced and conferred with the other mortals. Only Diamond-Chip was left behind her, patting the ship's exterior and waving his antennae at it unintelligibly.

This whole chunk of the planet was infected with Outside; she felt that deep in her gut. It could not possibly be as peaceful as it looked. The field had to be an illusion, or a trap. Or they'd landed in the wrong place.

She stared around at the grass and the trees, hunting for something that could be wrong. Elu waited patiently beside her. There had to be *something*.

Finally a movement, a wrongness, caught her eye. She jumped back. There, in the leaves – something moving. It could have been a snake. But it was the same color as the weeds. Because it *was* a weed, uprooted, moving under its own power. She watched the green, sinuous length of it as it twisted through the undergrowth. It paused near the place where the ship had landed, then continued on its way, missing Akavi and the others by a wide margin.

Yasira took a deep breath and let it back out. "It's *stable*," she said to Elu. "This whole place. It's infected, but it's not… disintegrating. How can that be? How can a place like this be stable?"

Elu bit his lip. "I don't know. I wasn't expecting it to be like this, either. I guess that's one of the things we're here to figure out."

Yasira took another breath. This time it came out as a sigh.

She had something to think about now. Something that wasn't panic and doom. The bad feeling was still there underneath, but maybe she could get used to this, for a few weeks at least.

"I think I'm okay now," she said. "Thank you."

Elu nodded. Then he went over to talk with Akavi.

Yasira watched him go and wondered why he'd been so helpful. Did she trust Elu? She really did not. She had seen the way he looked at Akavi; she knew where his loyalties lay. If Akavi wanted Yasira locked in a room forever, Elu would let it happen.

Yet when he was allowed to, Elu treated her with respect. He listened to her, at least, instead of treating her like a Gods-damned chess piece or a machine to be kicked when it didn't work right. It might be an act, just like Akavi's brief kindness, after the *Alhazred*. It might be captivity stuff, sheer stupidity for her to notice at all. But yes, in these small matters, she trusted him.

It was the closest thing she could imagine, out here, to having a friend.

CHAPTER 12

Like any other aspect of the universe, the idea of Outside appears in many non-human cultures. Often this is not apparent at first glance: the requisite concepts are frequently taboo, esoteric, or situated in the guise of myth and fiction. However, any culture studied in sufficient detail will yield up a word, and often a fairly sophisticated system of safeguards and protections, for the things in this universe which are inherently incomprehensible to sentient minds. The semantics of the word chosen can be culturally informative. My favorite, of course, is the Spider term: Îsîrinin-neri-înik, or 'that which eats reality'.

Interestingly, many cultures have more than one word for Outside. Though Outside itself is incomprehensible, cultures which acknowledge an experience of Outside can divide up their own experience on various axes. The most common axis of division is, of course, the perceived effect on rational beings. Experiences of the incomprehensible can be divided into positive and negative (despite the fact that even experiences considered positive are likely to cause what we would call madness, or, at best, neurological divergence) or positive, negative, and neutral. The importance of this division varies. Glupes, for instance, will insist that all three of their terms for Outside refer to the same thing, perceived in different contexts. Round-Bodies, making the same positive-negative-neutral distinction as Glupes, see no connection between the three categories. The positive category, bulngōu, are gods to be worshipped, despite their maddening and incomprehensible

213

nature. The negative category, niůi, are best translated as "nightmares", and are dealt with through non-religious means; they are neither connected to bulngōu, nor considered the bulngōu's enemies in any cosmically significant way. The neutral category, uiliu, is likewise not associated with either bulngōu or niůi.

I suspect that, if we knew the Boater term for Outside, we would understand a great deal more about Boaters than we do now. Unfortunately, this is one of the thousands of things that Boaters refuse to discuss.

FROM THE INTRODUCTION TO THE RESEARCH PAPER
"OUTSIDE AND NON-HUMAN MYSTIC TRADITIONS",
BY THE SPIDER SELL-SOUL SISPIRINITHAS.
THIS PAPER IS DESIGNATED CLASSIFICATION
LEVEL 3: NOT TO BE REVEALED TO HUMAN MORTALS,
EVEN PRIESTS OR SELL-SOULS, UNDER ANY CIRCUMSTANCE.

It was a struggle getting used to working in the open even though Yasira's actual work was minimal. Her real job here was to find Dr Talirr. The tablet Elu had given her was loaded with fine-grained sensors so that she could take various readings, but the tablet mostly did that by itself. So she found herself standing around brooding in the heat while most of the team ran this way and that, taking soil samples and cuttings of the local plants. Trying to think about sensible things and make plans instead of lapsing back into anxiety about the buzzing feeling under her feet. The strong sensation, no matter where she went and how she paced, that everything had gone terribly wrong.

She found herself stomping through the weeds to Ushanche and talking without a pause, even though Uschanche seemed to be concentrating on something else. Ushanche stared into space and frowned occasionally, as if examining something Yasira couldn't see, but she listened.

"So," Yasira said, "if this place is stable and still contaminated, that implies there are different levels of contamination." Akavi's files had classified Outside incursions, given them letters and numbers, but they hadn't made this particular distinction. "There's contamination that eats people and breaks apart spaceships. There's contamination that you can't properly see or describe even when it hits you over the head and drags you around, because everything recognizable that used to be there is already gone. And there's contamination like this, stuff that's hardly wrong at all, except for how little bits of it move."

"Have you seen something like that?" said Ushanche. Her large eyes didn't stray from Yasira but stayed staring out at the distant fields. "A thing that can't be described?"

"On the *Talon*. Outside the galaxy."

A few subjective days ago, Yasira wouldn't have been able to say it without panicking. She'd used the programs on the tablet to work up to this. Followed the red dot with her eyes, breathed slowly, subvocalized the words until they were just words. Saying them right on the surface of the Outside-infected planet felt good. A small act of defiance.

"How do you think such things would look on a camera?" said Ushanche. "Would they show up at all, or would there be shapes and colors that didn't make sense?"

Yasira chewed her lip, thinking it over. "I don't know. Honestly, I don't think they interacted with my visual cortex in the usual way. But they were there. I'd say the photons available would do *something*, but it might or might not be something we'd recognize as a physical presence. Why? Are you looking at cameras in there?"

She'd meant it as a joke, but Ushanche turned to her and smiled shyly, and Yasira abruptly realized it was the truth. Angels stared into space the way Ushanche did when they were paying attention to something in their heads. Usually plain old sell-souls didn't have circuitry; certainly they never got the whole angel package. But there were all sorts of partial, personalized versions.

"That's what I do," said Ushanche. "Look at this."

She plucked something gently out of the air, then held it out on the tip of her finger. It was so small that Yasira would have mistaken it for a gnat, or a dust mote, if she'd seen it at all. Even balanced on

Ushanche's small fingertip, it fit between one fingerprint-crease and the next.

"It's a mini camera?" Yasira guessed.

"I was a surveillance expert in Ruj before I came here. But human-built surveillance is so limited. With my circuitry I can control up to a dozen of these at once, and no one even notices unless I wish them to. No mortals, at least; angels would notice if I used it on them. Over the ansible net, my range is unlimited. Here I am using radio signals. Scouting. Much safer than sending people around on foot."

"And are you... seeing anything that doesn't look like anything?"

"No," said Ushanche. Then she started. "Wait, yes. Now I do. It's coming this way."

Akavi received the transmitted video clip from Ushanche a split second later. It was laced with static but intelligible. In the small patch of subtropical forest close by, three panicked humans ran. Behind them lurched a thing the size of a truck, which looked inky black to him. It was anyone's guess how it looked to Ushanche.

He had been talking to Elu, but immediately broke off the conversation and raised his voice to carry over the field. "We have three mortals and a potentially hostile Outside creature headed this way. Enga, Matesznoa, Sispirinithas, Tonkhontu, Bukhry, you're with me. Everyone else, retreat to the ship."

Enga, who had been casually doing calisthenics a few feet away, leapt to her feet and stood at attention. The other mortals hurried over with rather less grace. Akavi fought the urge to scowl. It would have been safer to order *everyone* to go hide in the ship. But the presence of mortals changed things.

"Enga," said Akavi, "if, and only if, you judge it safely within your ability, I want those mortals retrieved. Remember that our resources for repair are limited down here, and that Outside creatures may—"

Before he could finish his sentence, Enga turned on her heel with mechanical quickness and sprinted away. A second later, a minor burst of sound emanated from Sispirinithas's translator and he followed.

Akavi hadn't even worked out the direction the creature was coming from yet.

He turned back to the sell-souls who weren't running for the ship. "Matesznoa, assuming the mortals reach us and are not entirely incoherent, we'll want–"

The ground shook, and something burst from the line of trees at the other end of the field.

The mortals came first – two adults and a child, all three scrambling for their lives. The monster crashed out of the foliage a split second later, huge and perfectly black to Akavi's vision, like an inkblot.

Akavi avoided looking directly at it. He would not be making *that* mistake again.

Sispirinithas, who'd been racing after Enga, veered away and dashed between the monster and the mortals. It reared, distracted, and the spider sprang backwards.

"You are even uglier than a human," he called out through his translator – though surely that was for show, as he could scarcely expect an Outside monster to understand him. "No wonder the little morsels run from you. But I would make a much bigger mouthful, yes?" He waved his forelegs and leapt backwards again, past one of the stands of fruit trees, landing with a squelch in the rice of the next field over.

The diversion worked. The monster oozed towards him.

The mortals ran. One of the adults wasted a precious second looking, wide-eyed, over her shoulder. The other, the one holding the hand of the small one, ran ahead towards Enga. Enga pointed to her with a metal hand, then to the relative safety of the trees where Akavi stood. The mortals got the message and veered towards them.

A split second later, Enga opened fire on the monster.

As an Inquisitor, Akavi preferred not to engage in combat unless the advantage was distinctly his. As such he had rarely seen Enga use her skills to their full capacity. She moved too quickly for Akavi's organic eyes to follow. Even his enhanced vision produced a blur, which could be decoded later when he had time to look at the extra frames. She leapt, dodged, and spun, avoiding any predictable trajectory, as the monster turned her way. Not once in this whirl of motion did she stop firing. Akavi recognized it as a test volley: the monster's weaknesses were unknown, so Enga deployed each suitable weapon in her arsenal exactly once, her arms shifting shape and configuration superhumanly fast to bring each one to the appropriate angle at the appropriate time, each one landing neatly and precisely at a different location in what was presumably the creature's body.

Even aside from the arms, this kind of motion was not possible without divine technology. Enga's combat style depended on circuitry specifically programmed for enhanced proprioception, absurd degrees of large motor acuity and the ability to instantly calculate stochastic motion trajectories. Anyone in theory could have such programs installed, but using them correctly required decades of hard training. Enga, nearly immobile when Akavi first met her, was now one of the best.

Akavi's senses counted thirty-seven shots in 3.3 seconds. Not a single one missed its mark.

Nor, as far as he could tell, did a single one have any effect.

Akavi leaned forward slightly.

The monster flowed towards Enga, black tendrils whipping out of its main body, much faster than the movements it had made while chasing the mortals. Did that mean it was on the defensive, or merely annoyed?

Enga scrambled backwards. She fired off another couple of rounds at superhuman speed but the monster was faster. Its first two grabs closed on empty air as Enga dodged and weaved. On the third try, it flailed out with six amorphous tendrils at once. One of these caught her around an extremal part of her right arm: what might, if Enga's arms bore any resemblance to mortal anatomy, have been called a wrist. It wrapped instantly around her, whiplike.

Enga roared in wordless rage. Blue electricity crackled out of that arm, strong enough that Akavi felt a mild static charge even from his safe distance.

The monster let go and hesitated.

The split second's pause was all Enga needed. She threw her head back as her left arm opened like a flower. A fist-sized pulse of white flame, as bright as the fire of atmospheric entry, burst from what, in a mortal woman, would have been bone.

Enga dived backwards. The missile sank into the center of the creature and exploded.

The entire rice-field ignited in a wave of heat. Percussive force slammed into Akavi. The sell-souls beside him lost their balance and stumbled backwards, swearing. Akavi only barely managed to keep a dignified standing position by holding on to the tree beside him.

The creature burned. Yellow flames licked out past the blackness which was still all Akavi could see of its form. Stinking black smoke rose from it in a cloud.

Yet still it moved.

It lurched, again, towards Enga, who was running full speed at the edge of the spreading flames. But it was slower now. It put out a tendril, then two. Enga cartwheeled to the side. It tried again, even slower.

The ground shook and the mortals around Akavi covered their ears, though he heard nothing. A roar, or a scream, censored from his conscious perception.

The monster crumpled to the ground, writhed, twitched, burned, and was still.

It was at this moment that the Riayin mortals reached Akavi. Panting and shaking, they collapsed under the trees beside him.

They were, fortunately, upwind of the burning rice-field. The flames were so hot that even waterlogged ground would not put them out quickly; there was a faint chance they would spread into a brush-fire. But Akavi's team was not in immediate danger, and really, a brush-fire was the least of Jai's problems right now.

Akavi scanned the other side of the flames for Enga. She was outside their radius now, still running, making a wide path around the edge of the field and, presumably, back to Akavi. Sispirinithas, who had escaped the flames in a different direction, was ambling towards him, too. Enga's gait was slightly slowed – a sign of minor injury, probably surface burns from the explosion. But she was alive and victorious. He was somewhat impressed.

The mortals sat there panting, too exhausted to greet Akavi with the deference his rank deserved. The older one, not much older than Yasira, held the child – her child? – rocking him as he cried. She was young and small, but plump, which was a good sign; it meant not everyone down here was starving. The child was perhaps five or six, and his straight black hair stuck out in all directions. The younger, a stick of a girl scarcely Elu's age, brushed sweat-slick bangs out of her eyes and stared up at Akavi.

"Nothing hurts those things," she stammered in Riayin. "Not guns, not knives, not running a truck into them…"

Akavi smiled slightly, calling up the software that brought the idioms and tonal shadings of the Riayin language to his mind. "But it appears a God-built heavy armor-piercing missile will do the job. Greetings. I am Akavi Averis, Inquisitor of Nemesis, and I'm here to help."

Both women gaped. Akavi allowed himself to savor the moment. He did not often encounter situations dire enough, from a mortal perspective, that hearing an Inquisitor of Nemesis announce himself was a reason for hope.

Yasira shouldered her pack and sat watching Akavi interrogate the three survivors. The older woman's name was Juorie Huong, and the younger, Qiel. They were sisters. They and their young cousin, Lingin, had been foraging for food when the monster caught their scent.

"… And then, *blam*," said Qiel, the most talkative of the three, waving her skinny arms through the air. "So it's no wonder half of us lost it the first day. If you didn't happen to be in a stable patch like this one, the world might as well have dissolved. You can't trust the ground to stay ground, or the buildings to stay the same shape, or the air to not just randomly spawn a bunch of giant birds to eat you. It's like, sanity assumes the world will work with, like, rules.

There aren't any rules here, even in the parts that aren't trying to kill you. Insanity is smarter."

Akavi raised his eyebrows. The rest of the team was bustling around near them, quickly packing up belongings. Qiel and Juorie knew how to move in relative safety through this terrain. They had a connection to a larger group of survivors, an informal collective who squatted together in the same house and looked out for each other. "But you three are sane."

Qiel puffed out a breath. "We think in words and don't randomly fall down screaming at nothing. That's about all the assessment there's been time for."

"Even if we weren't sane," Juorie said forcefully, "it wouldn't matter." She bent down to comfort Lingin as she said it. The boy was starting to twitch and whimper, mumbling words Yasira couldn't make out.

She studied the two. There was an undercurrent of shame in Juorie's tone. People from Riayin prided themselves on their neurodiversity. It wasn't perfect, but it was better than most planets. If Riayin was hit by a disaster like this, and half the survivors were like Splió, or like that dissociative woman Yasira had slapped on the *Pride of Jai*, or even worse... How would the other survivors care for them? They couldn't. A healthy society could, but Juorie and Qiel were struggling even to save themselves.

They had managed to save their cousin, at least. But who else had they left behind?

"That's how we sort out who's a survivor and who's not," said Qiel, ignoring her sister. "There's the dead people, and the people we can't take with us because they can't understand words and won't go. And the *gone* people. And us. We're whoever's left, crazy or not."

"Gone?" said Akavi, raising his eyebrows.

Qiel changed the subject.

The group had moved out and was marching towards civilization: Akavi at the front, Ushanche at his left hand, the Huongs trailing behind him like ducklings. The others followed in twos and threes. Diamond-Chip brought up the rear, with his ship floating placidly behind him. It had crumpled, now that it was not in use, into a sort of winged, wrinkled shape that was only the size of a small elephant. Yasira assumed it would be able to puff up to its original size again when the crew needed to get back in.

"What even is that thing?" said Qiel. "Are you sure it's not a monster?"

"Quite sure," said Akavi. "It's Boater technology, which my team acquired at considerable expense."

Qiel gazed up at him, awestruck. "You have Boaters working for you?"

"Of course," said Akavi. "Well, technically just one. It's a resource angels rarely make use of, but in a case like this, we require every tool at our disposal."

"What does that mean?" said Qiel. "Does that mean you don't know how to fix this?"

Akavi waved a hand idly and began to explain, with mesmerizing confidence, why the angels of Nemesis were certain to fix any local problems the Huongs might be experiencing. This was nothing they hadn't seen before, though it usually happened on alien worlds, or on soon-to-be-human worlds still being terraformed. There were well-established procedures. Akavi's presence with his team of scientists was a formality, gathering data in order to classify the type of Outside incursion so that they could choose the most efficient option, with the least collateral damage, from the many established strategies they had in place to deal with such things.

Yasira, following a few feet away from them, stifled a laugh. It was all bullshit, but the Huongs hung on his words as if he himself was a God.

Akavi shot her a look which was quite mild, and quick enough to go unnoticed by someone who didn't know him, but which carried a definite tone of warning. She got the message and let herself drift further back until she couldn't hear him anymore. Bullshit or not, it would be bad for the mission if the Huongs noticed how hard she was trying not to roll her eyes.

Drifting further back meant she had no one to keep her mind off the creeping fear. Ushanche was busy; Elu was engaged in an intense, sotto-voice, apparently one-sided conversation with Enga, who hadn't had much time to patch herself up. That was a conversation Yasira didn't want to intrude on. And no one else in this group felt safe.

She walked by herself, mentally recited the words from her meditation programs, and tried not to dissolve entirely into terror as they moved from the fields to rural roads, and from there to the outskirts of Büata. Qiel and Juorie were leading them along a reasonably safe path; but even so, as Qiel had warned them, it wasn't all green fields and blue skies.

There were ruins where buildings had come apart like cracked eggs. Where they had unraveled like cloth and lay in spiralled strands of what must once have been brick. Where the ground had uprooted itself, like some giant alien plough, and been rearranged into something smooth or prickly, entirely unlike natural soil, with the remnants of human things crushed underneath.

A nest of tentacled insects, each the size of a rabbit, seethed in the darkness under a bridge. The bridge itself had become something translucent, like ice, and had stretched itself out into a fine ribbon, turning and curling in on itself at angles no walking human could follow.

Some of the buildings that were still intact moved, in the distance, swaying or traveling in circles, or opening amorphous windows like mouths in their sides. Qiel steered the team well clear of those places.

Some of the fields were holes in the earth that went down further than Yasira's eyes could track, with something blue and flickering in their depths.

Some of the trees had turned to tall, branching, irregular towers, in geometrically impossible forms that twisted in on themselves.

It was enough to make Yasira stop wanting to think altogether. Increasingly, as she walked, her eyes got stuck just processing the chaos. Trying to work out where one branch of a tree ended and where the next began, or if the trees weren't really separate to begin with. Trying to judge the height of a sharp-edged structure that defied all perspective.

"Monster ahead," Ushanche suddenly called out, snapping her out of her reverie.

"Take shelter," said Akavi, his voice louder. "Do not engage. We've proven we have the capacity to deal with at least some of these things, but unless there are mortal lives at stake, I do not want to risk damage."

He gestured to a barn a few hundred feet away, which seemed, at least from the outside, to be properly barn-shaped and not about to bite everyone's heads off or fill up with slithering plants. Everyone hurried over and crowded in, except Diamond-Chip's ship, which was too big even in its crumpled-up form, and crouched shivering in the barn's shadow instead. Diamond-Chip took a moment beside it before going in, patting its sides and waving his antennae at it, in an attempt at comfort or whatever else.

The inside was dismal, dim and full of half-rotted rice hulls. The only inhabitants were a couple of stray, hungry-looking ducks. Everything else seemed to have already fled or died since the disaster began.

While everyone was still getting settled, the rumbling started. Louder than what Yasira had heard from the monster that chased the Huongs: this one seemed to shake the ground just by walking. The Huongs hugged each other and cowered, and Yasira wrapped her arms around herself, pacing.

Isolating herself wasn't helping. She needed someone to talk to.

Ushanche was talking to Dr Meyema now, the two of them leaning in close to each other and exchanging furtive words. Yasira had been avoiding the psychiatrist ever since her shutdown on the ship, and did not intend to face her now. She drifted over instead towards Elu and Enga. They looked calmer than most: they'd taken the opportunity for rest and were sitting in a pile of chaff, still in conversation. Enga had managed to put proper salve and bandages on her legs: now she had extended a portion of her arm, and Elu was looking at it critically.

The thumps grew deafening. It must be walking right past the barn. Yasira covered her ears with her hands.

But covering her ears didn't shut out the monster's footsteps. All it did was shut out words and other sensible things. Yasira hadn't wanted to eavesdrop on Elu and Enga, but words felt like a lifeline now. She needed that more than they needed privacy. She sat on the floor nearby, far enough from them so it didn't *look* intrusive.

"I don't like the way this looks," said Elu. "The damage is a whole centimeter further now. It's only H92, but it looks like some kind of contact agent is still burning at you there, and I don't know how far it will spread."

Yasira resisted the urge to twist around and look. She'd been told that Enga sustained minor burns, but no one had told her about a contact agent. Let alone a contact agent strong enough to eat through metal.

At least the thumps were starting to recede. She'd entertained the idea, for a moment, that the monster might be about to tear open the barn and try to eat them all.

"I think we have to," said Elu, and Yasira couldn't tell if he was responding to a suggestion, or trailing off at the end and letting his own suggestion hang unsaid in the air. "Ugh, I wish we had a full cybernetic workshop for this. The best thing I can do here is cut H92 out manually. It's a good thing most of the wiring's redundant. You'll lose function completely in H160 through 162, and everything between G7 and L670 may be slowed or glitch a little, but you'll still have the missiles, and we'll repair it properly when we get back up. Is… is that okay? I really don't know what else–"

He stopped abruptly, as if Enga had interrupted him.

Meanwhile, on the rice-strewn floor in front of Yasira, something moved.

Yasira startled slightly. It was a muted response, compared to how she would have startled if this happened in the field when they landed. All the strangeness and fear was starting to blur together.

The thing that crawled out of the mess now was like a sea slug, bright and ethereal and sickly. It waved a blue pseudopod at her, then turned towards Elu, who was taking a pair of bolt cutters out of his pack.

Without thinking, Yasira swept her foot through the hay beside it, like it was just a mouse. "Hey, no," she whispered. "Don't go over there. Shoo."

The slug-thing turned around in its tracks, as if considering the matter.

Then it lunged at her.

She shrieked and leapt to her feet. Everyone's head turned. The slug-thing rose up and hissed, drawing itself a foot and a half into the air.

"Stop it!" Yasira snapped. Panic constricted her mind to a tight knot and for just a moment, she really was thinking of nothing else but the thing stopping in its tracks.

The thing stopped.

Yasira paused, caught her breath, and stared at it. It did not move.

Then someone else shrieked, loud and long, at the other end of the barn.

Yasira jumped in that direction, expecting another slug. But it was Lingin, the little boy they'd rescued, screaming incoherently and pointing at *her*. At Yasira.

Yasira looked around, completely confused. "What did I do? What happened?"

Juorie, in the next second, began to shout as well: not at Yasira, but at Akavi. Qiel busied herself trying to calm Lingin down. It was hard to hear over his shrieking, but Yasira could make out a few of Juorie's shouted Riayin words. "What kind of bullshit is this? What game are you playing? You say you're here to protect us, and then you bring in one of *them*?"

"One of what?" said Yasira, but she wasn't shouting, and she was halfway across the barn from them, so nobody answered.

"We were going to take you to our *safe house*!" Juorie shouted. "We thought you had a fucking clue what you were *doing*!"

Yasira stared at her, baffled. Nobody talked to angels like that. *Especially* not angels of Nemesis. Maybe the Huongs were madder than she had thought.

Akavi, surprisingly, did not kill them. Instead he looked

expressionlessly from the Huongs to Yasira. "Yasira," he said in Earth creole, in a calm voice which cut easily across the shrieking of the others. "Go outside. I'll be with you in a moment."

"There's a *monster* outside," said Yasira. But Akavi's tone, calm or not, brooked no disobedience. And the monster sounds were really receding now, much fainter than before. She would probably be okay.

Yasira looked down and slipped out the barn door.

The afternoon was wearing on and there was a faint pink tint at the western horizon, though the sun would be out for another hour or so. The monster was, as she had expected, far away, and moving farther. Yasira was careful not to look at it. Diamond-Chip's ship was sitting where he had left it, rippling quietly in the lee of the barn. Yasira sat in the grass as far from it as possible and hugged her knees to her chest.

What had she done wrong? She hadn't done anything to the slug-thing. She'd just said the words that came to her head. Maybe lunging and freezing suddenly was normal for this kind of creature. But Juorie and Lingin had certainly seemed to think otherwise.

She remembered being back on the *Pride of Jai*. Tapping her fingers against the side of her measuring device and seeing the energy inside the Shien Reactor leap in response. She'd thought that this was a property of Outside, responding to stimuli in ways that made no sense. What if it wasn't a property of Outside? What if it was a property of *her*? What did that make her?

Aside from one of the most dangerous beings in the universe.

After a few minutes the door opened and Akavi strode out, looking tall and elegant and as collected as ever. He glanced at the sunset, then focused coolly on Yasira.

"An interesting development," he said. "Are you feeling sane enough to discuss it?"

"Whatever. Sure," said Yasira. "Not like I actually understand any of what's going on."

Akavi quirked an eyebrow. "I was going to ask what exactly you were doing back there. I take it you don't know, either."

"It jumped at me. I told it to stop and it stopped." Yasira

shrugged helplessly. "I wasn't actually expecting it to. Then everyone panicked."

"You were following closely behind me and the Huongs for a while," said Akavi. "Do you recall what they said about madness?"

"Yes," said Yasira. There were the four groups of people: dead, mad, "gone" – whatever that meant – and survivors.

Akavi frowned briefly. "Communicating with Outside creatures, as you did back there, is an ability that the Huongs associate only with the 'gone'. It is a stage that goes far past ordinary madness, yet it doesn't seem to resemble the usual end stages of Outside exposure either. Certain people, exposed to this environment, begin to behave mindlessly, animalistically. They cannot be communicated with; they refuse to live in houses, to display individuality, or to recognize their sane loved ones. Yet the 'gone' can do what you just did. They can deal with Outside purposefully as no one else can. You can imagine the Huongs' distress upon discovering that, as they saw it, my team contained such beings."

Yasira looked up at him, frightened.

"I'm not gone," she said. "I'm not mad."

"That remains to be seen," said Akavi, but his voice now was not unkind. He leaned against the wall of the barn. "Some time ago I formulated a theory about why Talirr chose to attack populated areas. Her previous attacks killed everyone, of course, but I have reason to believe that she wasn't seeking deaths, but survivors. People who could experience Outside the way she did and live. The 'gone', arguably, fulfil this criterion, which is interesting. What is more interesting to me is that you have apparently reached this stage without losing much of your ordinary function. According to reports, you may have reached it even before you left the *Pride of Jai*." He looked at her sidelong. "One hopes, of course, that Dr Talirr agrees with my assessment of what is more interesting."

"Maybe it's not me," Yasira said desperately. "Maybe it's a coincidence. Maybe anyone can do it if they talk to the Outside creatures the right way, but everyone's too scared to talk to Outside creatures, so no one tries unless their minds are scrambled anyway, or unless they're people like me who just blundered in…"

That didn't ring true, even to her. She trailed off.

"Needless to say," said Akavi, "this introduces complications. I intend for the team to make camp near Qiel and Juorie's safe house. You're welcome to set your own tent there with us, once we are settled in, but I think further interaction between you and the sane survivors would be most unwise. Which means you will not be walking with us the rest of the way. Instead, I'd like you to explore on your own."

Yasira stared at him.

He could not actually be asking what she thought he was asking. She was barely hanging on to functionality even with the group. On her own, without Ushanche or the Huongs to guide her away from the worst parts, she didn't even want to think about what would happen.

"Oh, come now," said Akavi. "Don't give me that look. Your tablet has navigation software and a direct line to me should anything go wrong. The best way to test your newfound abilities is to explore. I recommend downtown Büata as a starting point; I've been told it's quite strange. I'd offer to send Enga with you as protection, but I think we both know that your work will be more fruitful without her."

Yasira swallowed hard. Of course, the real reason not to send Enga was that he expected Yasira to find Dr Talirr. The presence of an angel bodyguard armed with heavy armor-piercing missiles would probably get in the way there.

She'd known she'd need to go out on her own eventually. But she hadn't wanted it to happen like this. Dr Talirr had said, *You'll know where to find me*. She had expected to work that out first, *then* go looking.

But then, didn't Dr Talirr's prediction give her a kind of protection? She would, at some point in the future, know where to find Dr Talirr. That meant that, in the future, she would probably still exist. And, sane or not, she would at least still be capable of knowing things.

Unless Dr Talirr was as full of bullshit as everyone else.

"Is this acceptable?" Akavi said, looking down at her imperiously. *No* was obviously not the right answer.

Yasira nodded. "I'll do that."

"Very good," said Akavi. "You may rejoin us in, say, three hours, when we've made camp. I'll text-send to you if any plans change."

He disappeared back into the barn. It was quiet now. The monster from earlier had receded completely out of sight and the team was probably gathering up their things to get moving again.

The whole western edge of the sky had flared up pink. It was not quite the pink of a healthy sunset. It was a little too bright, with indistinct reddish and whitish streaks, like a half-melted candy.

"Be normal," said Yasira to the sky, crossing her arms. "Be blue or something."

Nothing happened. The sky continued to be too-bright and streaky. Cicadas – or things that were probably cicadas, but who even knew anymore? – hummed in the bushes.

"I'm not crazy," said Yasira to the sky, or maybe just to the world around, in general. "I'm not gone. I'm not turning into some kind of Outside thing."

There was no answer to that, either.

CHAPTER 13

What, you ask, did humans do before there were Gods?

We invented them, beloved. It is what we have always done.

But pity the poor Old Humans who did not have electricity and quantum algorithms to invent with! Their gods – if we can call such beings gods – were inert objects of art, dead before they came into existence. No matter how beautifully carved, how expertly painted, no Old Human god could do or say a thing. So, inevitably, Old Humans spoke for them.

Be glad that you have never lived in such a time. You do not know what happens when the gods are not impartial, not separate from the whims and rages of the humans who dreamed them into being. Every such god becomes, eventually, an excuse for the powerful to hurt the weak. Whether they called it conquest, righteous warfare, or willing sacrifice, the Old Human gods thirsted for blood, and blood they were given. Their temple walls ran red with it.

We have always craved the presence of something higher than ourselves, and in its absence – oh, beloved! – what will ever fill us but death?

WAYLA SHU'UHI, THEODICY STORIES FOR CHILDREN

Downtown Büata was not far; it wasn't a large city and the team had been skirting its edges all along. According to the mapping system on Yasira's tablet, she'd made the journey on foot in forty minutes.

It felt like longer. She kept spacing out, staring at the nonsense architecture around her, walking in an arbitrary direction for what felt like many kilometers. Then she would blink her way out of it, look at her tablet, and see that only a minute or two had gone by.

The rest of Yasira's senses were like that too.

There were people in Büata, after a fashion. The damage wasn't evenly distributed. One plot of land held nothing but a heap of brick-colored dust. The next held something house-shaped, but the texture was wrong: the outer walls glistened like the scales of an animal and the shutters on the windows curved in like jagged teeth. The third house in the same row was almost normal. Broken windows, lights off, but intact. Haggard-looking people like the Huongs crowded in these surviving houses, or on their lawns. They glanced warily at Yasira as she passed, like for all they knew, she might be another monster.

Those were the sane ones, probably. The mad ones wandered the streets like Yasira, hugging themselves, mumbling under their breath. Others were probably hiding, she supposed. Once she passed a bespectacled man chanting nonsense syllables, beating the side of his head rhythmically against a lamppost.

"Excuse me, sir," Yasira said, approaching that one. "Are you okay? Is there something I can do?"

The man turned to her and snarled. Tiny rivulets of blood ran down his cheek. "You're one of them. You're one of them!"

Yasira backed away.

She had moved by now from the rows of houses on the edge of the town to storefronts and blocks of apartments. The Gods encouraged apartment living for efficiency reasons, but it was not enforced, as long as the suburbs didn't encroach onto designated wilderness areas. The big families common in Riayin had always preferred to move out into buildings of their own when they could. Still, at the center of any city, apartments took pride of place and were well cared for, built with slanting roofs and wide front gardens, and painted in cheery colors to make them look homier. Some of the buildings in Büata still looked like that, under the twisting and changing. Some of them, you could squint and almost imagine the inhabitants happy.

It had grown dark. The few streetlamps that hadn't burned out glowed in shifting, unnatural colors: sometimes they strobed, or flickered like bad fluorescents, and Yasira had to shield her eyes and hurry away before her head flared up in pain. The moons glowed brightly in the sky and so did a thick aurora, even though Büata was way too far from the poles for that. The aurora made shadows shift on the ground, giving an illusion of constant flickering motion even with nothing there.

Yasira's feet hurt, but that was the least of her problems. Her feet hurt, her head ached, and the wrong feeling of the city pressed in all around her like smoggy air. She wanted a rest and a shower and some quiet, but none was forthcoming.

She passed a small park which looked more or less normal, with people milling around on the grass further in, and a reasonably intact bench by the path. The flowers in their dense and carefully arranged beds were probably wilted or bloodsucking or something, but it was hard to tell. She checked her tablet. She'd been walking alone for an hour and ten minutes. Still lots of time before Akavi would let her go back.

She was supposed to be finding useful information, testing her powers, looking for Dr Talirr, but aside from looking around and making mental notes on the state of the city, she had no idea how to do any of that.

Yasira sat on the bench and buried her face in her hands.

The bench was not entirely normal. A few of its wrought-iron slats twisted in the darkness, turning from ordinary metal to something that shone a dim, cold blue and back again.

"Stop that," Yasira hissed to the bench, experimentally. It had no effect. She scooted over to the other side of the bench, but didn't immediately get up. She was supposed to be testing her powers and studying the area, after all.

She tried to think scientifically. An Outside thing had obeyed her once, and responded oddly to her at least one other time. Yet other Outside things paid no attention to her wishes at all. What was the difference? There was no way to tell; her sample size was too small.

"Hey, are you okay?" said a voice behind her.

Yasira turned, startled. The person standing there looked lucid enough: a man her age in a ragged shirt, slouched but calm, sizing her up.

"I…" she said.

"You must be new around here," said the man. "This isn't where you want to sit. Those people milling around on the grass there? They're gone. You sit there staring at 'em and you'll be their next blood sacrifice, next thing you know."

"Their next what? Do they do that?"

"You're really not from here, then. What's your name?"

"I…" said Yasira. She said the first plausible lie that came to her head. "My mother and I had supplies, and our house held up. We'd been hiding indoors until now. I know everything went mad, and so did a lot of the people, but–"

The man shook his head. Odd-colored light glinted off his glasses. "Mad's not the same as gone. Gone's *past* madness. They're not just lying around tired or seeing things, or what have you. Gone is a whole other level. You're lucky you found me when you did. My name's Küinges. I have a safe house just down the road. I know all about survival; I used to go camping all the time. I could protect you. You could, uh…"

His gaze came to rest at her neckline.

"I can take care of myself, thanks," Yasira snapped.

"Well, I was only trying to help," said the man.

Yasira snorted and turned away.

"You're mad too if you think you can face down gone people by yourself," said the man. "Don't say I didn't warn you!"

He stormed away.

Yasira leaned on the bench and glowered at nothing. Being sane didn't stop sane people from being creeps, apparently. This was a property that stayed intact even in a disaster zone.

The gone people had been shuffling aimlessly, like any bunch of people making use of the park. Apart from the grubbiness and lack of speech, they might have looked like anyone else. But as the moonlight shifted, they took on a more purposeful air. Without anyone giving instructions – without eye contact, or even angelic fits of preoccupation – they formed themselves into a rough circle.

Yasira hadn't seen this behaviour before. She picked up her tablet and started recording.

The circle twisted in on itself. Yasira's tablet camera corrected the light levels sufficiently that she could see details now. Dignified old men, still wearing the suits they'd gone to work in the day of the disaster, with twigs stuck in their beards. Suburban mothers, their hair undone into matted tangles. Boys who had painted sharp lines and squiggles on their faces with red-brown dirt. Tiv–

Yasira almost dropped the tablet.

No, it wasn't Tiv. It was an attractive Riayin woman of about Tiv's height and build, with very vaguely Arinnan features. Maybe half Arinnan. Hard to tell with all the dirt caked on her face. Large eyes, a mouth that might have been as wide as Tiv's, but the facial structure was wrong. The texture of the hair, the shape of the eyelids, the size of the jaw – no. It definitely wasn't Tiv. Tiv was on another planet. Yasira's mind was playing tricks on her again.

She felt abruptly very lonely on her weird, still-twisting bench. She had been so focused, so enraged by what Dr. Talirr had done to her home planet, that her longing for Tiv had been pushed to the back of her mind. But when she spared a moment to think about it, there it was. As painful as ever.

The woman who wasn't Tiv reached out her left hand. A middle-aged man going the opposite way reached without looking and they clasped hands. The man's mouth was moving. A murmur arose from the small crowd, too guttural and fluid to be any dialect of Riayin. There was a fluttering as more and more of them clasped hands, rolled their heads from side to side, made other small movements with no discernible purpose.

In the middle of the circle, something began to shimmer.

It was not precisely a thing. More of a twist in the way light moved through space. And "light" wasn't quite the right word, either. Light was only the closest sensory analogue to something that was not quite in this space, and not quite out of it, something that spilled out and illuminated the crowd.

Whatever it was, it had gravity. It felt as if all the underlying unease and wrongness had condensed here and decided to suck everything else towards it. It was impossible to look away. Yasira's heart sped. She clung to the side of the bench as if she might be torn off, drawn into the light against her will. But the feeling wasn't physical. It was only a nightmarish sense that the light wanted her. That it was hungry.

Or maybe…

Maybe it was Yasira who wanted the light.

At that thought, she shuddered.

There was a thump as the gone people, all at once, dropped down to sit on the grass, facing the light.

One of the oldest men took out a long thorn, the size of a toothpick. Yasira squinted at him through the camera as he flourished it, looking like an absurd orchestra conductor, or a relay runner. She stifled a laugh.

The man plunged the thorn into the meat of his hand.

Yasira clapped a hand to her mouth. It was a small wound, but a deep one. Blood welled up immediately, trickled down to his wrist, and dripped to the ground. The old man made absent flicking motions, sprinkling blood over the grass, then withdrew the thorn and punctured his cheek, through his matted beard, just in front of the jaw joint.

Blood sacrifice. The creep with the safe house had warned her. This was a barbarity only found in ancient history. One of the thousands of terrible practices humans had left behind when the Gods arose. The sheer waste of it, the purposeful blasphemy – though perhaps it wasn't right to credit a purpose to those blank faces – was much worse than madness.

There were other thorns now. The gone passed them around, sprinkling blood everywhere, making ruins of their own hands and faces.

The dirt on that woman's face was really scabs, Yasira realized.

Dried blood. Blood dripped into the old man's beard, down the women and children's fingertips.

She felt sick. There was also another feeling. A horrified fascination, except fascination wasn't the right word. What was the word?

She watched as the bloodletting finished. The gone people settled down into meditation, staring up at the light. They no longer looked blank, but the look wasn't quite human, either. It was…

There was no word for this in any language Yasira knew.

Back on the *Pride of Jai*, anytime there was a service, Tiv had sat in the front and stared raptly at Alkipileudjea. Not the way she stared at cute girls, sometimes; a different way. A pure way. Like the metal curlicues and long robes of a priest, the lofty words spoken at the service, were the most beautiful and fascinating things she could think of. Like every exhortation to follow the Gods was a command that Tiv wanted to follow with her whole heart.

There were always a few people like that at a service. Spiritual people. At a really good service their enthusiasm became infectious; half the church or more might briefly look that way. But everyone at once? All in unison, the way the gone were doing now? That never happened. Not even in vids.

The light faded.

The gone people silently stood, dusted themselves off, began to walk away. No one tried to wipe the blood from their faces or hands. They weren't such a blank, formless mass anymore. One formerly clean-cut young man smiled absently, peering up into the stars as he ambled along. A haggard old woman leaned close to another, grinning as if she had heard a joke. Another faded into the trees with an odd, hopping gait, almost skipping. All of them looked lighter and deeper than before, like something had touched them in their deepest hearts. The way services, according to priests, were always supposed to do.

The way nothing, for Yasira, ever had.

She turned off the tablet's camera, hugged her knees to her chest, and stared at the place where the light had been.

The chime from her tablet, telling her it was time to return to the rest of the team, snapped her out of her musings. Yasira twitched and rubbed her eyes to find the park was empty.

I'm on my way, she text-sent to Akavi. *In the interest of honesty,* she added *nothing conclusive, and no Talirr, but I do have an interesting vid for you.*

Send it now, sent Akavi. *We'll discuss it when you arrive.*

Yasira frowned at the tablet, then belatedly saw the icon for attaching a sensory file to a text-sending. After a little searching, she worked out where in the file structure the vids she took had been stored and managed to send them along.

Her tablet lit up with an annotated map showing the way to the safe house where the team had made camp. Apparently, once Yasira was gone, Akavi had managed to smooth things over with the Huongs. The angle between their trajectories was not large, so she was now only two kilometers from them. Much shorter than the walk she had taken to get here.

Heaving herself up onto her aching feet, she turned her back on the park and started to walk. Ushanche had probably scouted out a few of the streets near the camp, but not all of them. She was going to have to stay alert.

The odd, monstrous buildings didn't startle her anymore, although the shifting, changing shadows did. Mainly, she was worn out. She looked at the gardens in front of the better-preserved buildings, some of which were still green and healthy in spite of everything. She imagined grass like that in front of the Huongs' safe house. Setting up her tent there and falling asleep. Of course, sleep for Yasira might be just as much work as being awake. Dr Talirr would probably be there. Still, the thought of closing her eyes and stretching out in a sensible sleeping bag felt good.

There was a rustling behind her.

Yasira turned warily, not sure if she should expect a squirrel or a monster. A vague human silhouette, darker than the other shadows, ducked behind a wall.

Yasira waited for a count of thirty. The shadows shifted as always, but nothing else happened.

She sighed, turned, and started forward again.

I think I'm being followed, she text-sent.

By what? came the reply.

Not sure. Human-sized. Could be anybody. If I get a closer look I'll tell you.

The map on the tablet screen flickered. Halfway to the safe house, the trajectory now veered off into a cul-de-sac. Yasira was not leading any unknown persons to the safe house. If she reached the dead end and still didn't know who was following her, presumably Ushanche could take it from there. Assuming that the person didn't leap out to attack her in the meantime.

She quickened her pace.

The map had picked out a road that was mostly okay. Half the buildings looked more like rectangular lumps of stone or flesh than buildings, and the street lamps were out, but the street was clear. The only visible monsters were little ones, rat-sized, which paid her no mind.

Yasira counted her steps. On sixty she abruptly stopped and turned.

This time the aurora-light shifted the other way. The thing following her was definitely a human: a beam of green flickering light illuminated her against the nearest shop front, which had grown scales like some large rectangular lizard. She was female, dressed in tattered fleece pajamas, with brownish blood drying on her face.

It was the half-Arinnan gone woman. The one who looked a little like Tiv.

She didn't look angry, hungry, or calculating. She lowered her eyes, and glanced back up again, quickly averting her gaze when she saw that Yasira was still watching.

"Why are you following me?" said Yasira. It was a stupid thing to say. From what she'd heard, gone people couldn't talk. But Yasira had been able to talk to Outside things in a way that they understood. A way, according to the Huongs, that gone people shared. If anyone could talk to this woman properly, it was Yasira.

The woman looked up at her again, but only stared.

Yasira sighed. "Don't follow me," she said, as forcefully as she could. When she told the creature in the barn to stop, she had been focused intently on the thought of it stopping. She tried to focus in the same way on the thought of the woman following her. How unwanted it was. How dangerous it was for this woman to walk towards angels of Nemesis who were prepared to defend their safe house with immense force. "I want you to stop."

She turned and strode away. The woman's footsteps fell quickly and eagerly behind her.

Definitely human, she text-sent, although typing on the tablet while walking was awkward. *Female. My age. Gone. She was in the ritual vid that I sent you a minute ago. I don't think she's a risk for violence but she won't stop following me either, so who the fuck knows?*

Others in the vicinity? sent Akavi.

I don't know. I don't see any, but that's not a guarantee.

Go to the end of the block and wait there. We will send reinforcements.

Yasira frowned. *Reinforcements? What do you mean?*

There was no response. She was already at the end of the block.

She could guess what Akavi meant, of course. Even if this woman wasn't violent, Akavi's team would see her as a potential threat. Logically, they would want to neutralize the threat. Capture at the very least. And then, if they had a captured gone woman anyway, why not take the opportunity to study her at their leisure? That was how Akavi's mind worked.

The woman's footsteps stopped when Yasira's did. Yasira cautiously turned and leaned against a burned-out lamppost. The gone woman looked the same as ever: staring, shyly fascinated, like a stray cat.

Yasira sighed.

"Look," she said, "I'm working for some pretty bad people right now. So are you, I guess." She gestured to her cheek. "But I don't think ours mix. I don't think you'd enjoy being kidnapped off the street by angels of Nemesis. So I want you to turn around and walk away before they get here, okay? Because they've told me they're on their way."

She gestured with her arm, making a "turn" motion, focused very hard on the turning. The woman tilted her head, then turned. And kept turning. Three hundred and sixty degrees, and then she was standing there, staring at Yasira again.

Yasira frowned. "So, what, you understand gestures, but not words? Is that it?"

The woman just looked at her.

Yasira waved hello.

The woman stared at her hand like it was a tablet carved in some ancient language, then, with a hesitant smile, waved back.

Yasira, experimentally, curtseyed. The woman curtseyed back. She tipped an imaginary hat. The woman did likewise. She crossed her arms, and the woman crossed hers, too. Yasira pulled down her lower eyelid and stuck out her tongue, and the woman did the same. Abruptly, they both started to giggle.

The woman's laughter was startlingly normal. Not wild, like a villain in a vid. Not violent or alien. They could have been college friends.

Yasira made a gun with her thumb and index finger and mimed shooting herself in the head, still giggling. The woman looked confused, then smacked herself in the temple with a flat palm and doubled over laughing harder than ever.

"Okay," said Yasira when things were quiet again. "You go home now. Maybe I'll see you tomorrow." She pointed down the street, to where the woman had come from, and flicked her hand up and down a few times, for emphasis. "Go."

The woman looked at the tip of Yasira's finger, then followed her gaze and looked back for a long moment. She turned towards Yasira again and rolled her head and shoulders, in something that was not quite a nod or a head-shake – Yasira couldn't work out what the gesture meant.

"Yes, go. *Back*. That way." Yasira tried hard to visualize the street. The woman going down it, away from her, past the small shops of the last few blocks and back to the park. The woman turned, and started reluctantly to walk that way. "Before Akavi shows–"

The woman spun around and stared at Yasira again.

Yasira frowned. While she was talking and visualizing about what the woman should do, the woman had done it. But as soon as she mentioned Akavi's name, the woman had stopped.

What did that mean?

Yasira had told her to go away before. But – no, that wasn't exactly true. She had told her to stop following. When she told the creature in the barn to stop, she'd pictured it staying still. When she told the woman to go down the street just now, she'd pictured the woman going down the street. When she'd started talking about Akavi, she'd stopped picturing the woman and the street.

And earlier when she told the woman to stop following she'd really been picturing the opposite, hadn't she? She'd pictured the woman following anyway, and how bad that would be. So the woman had followed her.

Somehow, this place wasn't picking up on what she said, or what she wanted, but on what she imagined.

Yasira closed her eyes and imagined the real Tiv showing up in a flying saucer or something and taking her out of here, to safety. Nothing happened.

She looked up at the brick wall next to her, which was only partway a wall; the individual bricks were there, but the overall shape curved and twisted, no longer obeying the rules of what a brick house should look like. Yasira imagined, very intensely and very carefully, one specific brick turning fluorescent pink.

The ache in her head intensified, but the brick changed colour, a little. Not as bright as she'd pictured, but it had been indistinguishable from other bricks before, and now the slight shift in color was plain to see. Yasira held up her tablet camera to make sure it was real. The color change showed up there, too.

She lowered the tablet, trembling slightly as the discovery sank in.

Was this a property of Outside spaces? Would Outside spaces respond like this to anyone who knew how? Or was this what made Yasira one of the most dangerous beings in the universe?

The woman stood there patiently staring.

"Okay," said Yasira, pulling herself together. She pointed again, visualized the woman walking down the road. "Go. For real this time. Don't stop until you're out of sight."

Was she communicating with the woman or commanding her? She couldn't tell. It required further study. She could go out tomorrow and test it systematically. That would be real progress. Akavi wouldn't believe her if she told him now, with only one pink brick to show for her efforts, but if she spent the day gathering corroborating evidence, and *then* brought it to him…

The woman made a humming noise, and held out an arm at an awkward angle, as if she wanted Yasira to go with her.

No, Yasira realized. No, that wasn't what the woman had done. The gesture might have been anything: reaching for something in the air, scratching herself, conducting an orchestra. Who even knew. There was no eye contact, and nothing about it physically that suggested walking together. But the image of Yasira walking off beside the woman had come naturally into her head.

They *were* communicating. Not with words, but with pure thought. Was this what the gone had been doing, among themselves, all through the ritual? Was this how they had synchronized themselves?

"No," said Yasira. "You go alone now." She pictured it carefully, the woman walking by herself, with only the night and the streetlamps beside her.

The woman pursed her lips in something that looked remarkably like pity, then turned to go.

Something exploded.

The shot was so loud and sudden that Yasira couldn't even process it at first. Something exploded and the woman pitched backwards against the wall and fell. She left a dark smear behind her, like the smears on her face. There was another shot. Her body jerked and was still.

Enga strode from a nearby alley a second later. Ushanche and Akavi trailed behind her, one still tall in his Riayin body, the other mincing like a nervous mouse. Yasira stared at the woman's body, unable to put two thoughts together.

Enga strode around Yasira, checking in every direction. She

glanced at Yasira contemptuously, like she was some kid who'd gotten the easiest math problem wrong.

"Perimeter clear, sir," said a voice. It was a clipped, correct Earth creole voice with no inflection at all, like a vocabulary tape from school. It took Yasira a moment to work out that it had come from Enga's translator. "Threat averted."

"You killed her," Yasira whispered.

Enga gave her the look again.

"On my orders," said Akavi. "You reported an Outside-corrupted human following you. We removed the threat. Are you hurt?"

"She wasn't threatening me," said Yasira. She'd expected someone from the team to come, yes, but to chase the woman away or to capture her and do experiments on her, or knock her out, or something. Not just to shoot her dead when she was already turning to leave. "She wasn't doing anything wrong."

"Not according to your own reports," said Akavi. "You demanded that she stop following and she refused to do so. Every civilized culture recognizes this as threatening behaviour. Is there a problem?"

"She didn't know what I was saying!" Yasira shouted. "Because she's *gone*. Didn't the Huongs tell you what that *means*? She doesn't understand Riayin. She doesn't speak any language. She didn't leave when I told her to because she didn't understand me. We were working on that when you arrived. I was figuring out what she does understand. She was responding to gestures and to focused mental imagery–"

Akavi looked at her coolly. "And what else does she understand, Yasira? Bloodletting? I watched the vid you sent. It was a record of appalling heresy on a scale humanity has not seen for hundreds of years. Are you telling me you watched all of that and then assumed she wouldn't hurt you? Why, Yasira? Because she was pretty and Arinnan and made lost puppy eyes at you?"

Yasira's face flushed. "I wasn't assuming anything. You sent me out to test my abilities. I was testing them. And I found out something important! I found out there are things she still understands."

"Yes. I'm sure your little flirtation was pure scientific curiosity."

Akavi walked around her in a semicircle, with long, unhurried strides. "We'll ignore the fact that you were text-sending for help until you saw what she looked like. Was this science, Yasira? Did you have a hypothesis? What factors were you holding constant? I'm sure this was all done to the rigorous standards you were taught at the Galactic University of Ala by the illustrious Dr Talirr. And I'm sure Tiv would be happy to hear how quickly, in subjective terms, you've moved on."

"You didn't even try!" Yasira shouted. It was worse than the previous shout. The words tore her throat raw. "I don't have access to laboratory conditions here, but I was working out what I could, and you weren't even trying to understand. You just shot her!"

She swallowed, fighting tears of humiliation. Ushanche was staring, fixed on Yasira in fascination with her real eyes. Enga didn't stare as openly, but her head was cocked, her thick neck turned to survey the scene as if puzzled. Yasira had been walking through creepy Outside bullshit all day and been pushed way past her own limits. She was melting down. Losing control.

She hadn't been flirting with the gone woman. That hadn't entered her head. But she *had* been the one to text-send for help. Then she had gotten curious, carelessly. She had been more interested in talking and testing her newfound powers – powers that were probably dangerous beyond her understanding – than in anyone's safety. She had fucked this one up. It was her fault. Not Akavi's. Akavi had been following protocol.

"Let me give you my professional understanding," said Akavi, "of what is happening here. You are a scientist mentally contaminated by Outside influences. Dr Meyema has reported that your symptoms are no longer fully responsive to treatment. Despite this, necessity led you to go out on your own in a heavily Outside-corrupted city and witness primal Outside energy harnessed within bloodthirsty heretical rites of the highest order. Now you find yourself fascinated with those rites. Wanting to know more. Wanting to interact with those who performed them, even when you know better, even when it is manifestly unsafe. Do you deny any of this?"

"I–"

Akavi stopped in the semicircle and towered over her. "These are known and documented symptoms of Outside madness. On their face they make a certain amount of sense. Understanding the processes at work in this part of Jai would be helpful. But not if you destroy yourself in its pursuit. I was, perhaps, hoping that you could observe and test your abilities objectively. But interacting with beings like her" – he gestured to the body on the ground – "is perilous even for the sane. I therefore reverse my previous orders. You are not to go out on your own or to perform any experimentation whatsoever without my express orders. You have been well informed of how crucial you yourself are to this mission, and if you endanger my mission, then so help me, I will cut you open myself. Am I being understood?"

Yasira gritted her teeth.

Maybe he was right. She was going mad, wasn't she? She'd been losing her grip on reality ever since the *Alhazred*. Why should she trust her own judgement?

Her own instincts screamed that Akavi was wrong. He was being totally unreasonable. But Yasira was compromised. Did her instincts mean anything?

Well, what would it mean if they didn't? Akavi knew what to do about that. He would take her back to the *Menagerie* and keep her there, like he'd done to Splió. Like Gods only knew how many others. Because if she went mad, what good was she?

She raised her eyes sideways, looking at the wall beside her. The brick was still pink.

"You don't understand *anything*," Yasira whispered.

Then she turned and ran.

She fully expected them to tackle her in the first ten feet, or Enga to shoot her with a tranquilizer dart – or worse, a real bullet. They didn't. Her feet carried her forward with no logic but the logic of rage. She ran, blind with anger, until her lungs were worn ragged and her feet threatened to split themselves open against the sidewalk. Then she caught herself, dropped to one knee and sat crumpled on a patch of grass, panting hoarsely. The grass fluttered and flexed as if blown by a strong wind. There was no wind. Yasira was too exhausted to care.

She was in a small courtyard in front of a department store, though something even larger than the manta-ship had taken a bite out of the building. The remnants of interior rooms lay open to the air, covered in strewn paper and crawling with insects. Clothes and other merchandise still lay on the shelves, here and there, half-looted.

What exactly was she doing? Where was she running to? She had no plan. She still had her tent and supplies on her back. She could set up camp here, or anywhere, but what would she do after that? Gather data on her own and wait for a magical revelation about where Dr Talirr was? At some point, if she gathered any useful data, someone would have to *use* it. Which meant she would have to come crawling back to Akavi. If she was going to do that, she might as well go back now and get it over with. She was being stupid.

Yasira groaned and waited for her breathing to go back to something resembling normal. Her feet weren't going to like the walk back. She wasn't even sure where she was. She wobbled to her feet, ignoring the protest from her heels and calves, and turned to fish the tablet out of her pocket.

And froze.

Standing in the half-eaten department store, with papers strewn around her feet, was a pale Anetaian woman in a lab coat, with her hair tied loosely back. Staring straight at Yasira.

It couldn't be. It was another trick of the light. Yasira was crap with faces anyway. She just had to look again, from another angle, and it would be some other irritating gone person who just happened to have one or two features that looked a bit like Dr Talirr's if the light hit them wrong.

The light shifted.

Dr Talirr walked nonchalantly out of the half-eaten building and nodded to Yasira. She looked the same as always.

"Hello," she said.

"You said," said Yasira, still panting slightly with exertion. "You said I'd know where to find you."

Dr Talirr shrugged. "And now you do."

Akavi did not have to order Yasira followed. Ushanche was already on that job, unobtrusively tracking with one of her microscopic cameras, though Akavi fully expected that signal to cut out at some point. He smiled, then turned on his heel and strode back the way he had come. The others followed.

SIR, Enga said presently, *I SHOT HER. BUT YASIRA SHOUTED AT YOU AS THOUGH YOU DID.*

"Yes, Enga. That's called the chain of command."

I BROKE PART OF MY ARM SAVING THE HUONGS, AND THEY HAVE BEEN THROWING THEMSELVES AT YOU AS THOUGH YOU DID. IS THAT THE CHAIN OF COMMAND? WHY CAN'T I HAVE A HUONG?

Akavi chuckled. "I've no idea, really. Perhaps it would help if you could talk."

ALSO HAS ANYONE TRIED GIVING THE GONE PEOPLE TEXT-SENDING CIRCUITRY. OR A KEYBOARD.

"I would be very surprised if their problem was a simple oral-motor apraxia like yours. But it's a valid question; perhaps we'll take one or two home with us for testing."

They had reached the safe-house, or at least its edge: a rambling split-level house likely meant for more than one family, largely untouched by the plague, though parts of the vegetable garden in the front corner had turned blue or grown into odd spirals. He was still in his Riayin form, and would have to remain so for as long as they were around random, high-strung Riayin civilians. Enga grunted and stalked heavily away. Elu rushed to Akavi's side in her stead.

"What happened?" he said. "I heard shouting. Where's Yasira?"

"It went according to plan," said Akavi.

"What—"

We will not discuss this now, sent Akavi. *Even via text. I will inform you when it becomes acceptable to ask questions.*

Elu swallowed and nodded, then fell into line, following Akavi back to camp.

It was not the first time Akavi hid part of his plan from Elu. Elu would never willingly give away Akavi's secrets, but, by Nemesis' standards, he was a bad liar. So if part of a plan was likely to cause emotions he couldn't hide, Akavi kept it from him. Elu accepted that.

The safe house was quiet: the mortals residing there, and the sell-souls working for Akavi, had already gone to bed. Once a palatial residence for a family friend of the Huongs, the inside of the house had been converted into a squat for other survivors. Mattresses and makeshift nests crowded every inch of available floor space. Akavi had ordered his team to camp in the backyard, eating the rations they'd brought. The team had quickly gone to sleep; they knew full well that he would demand an early morning from them tomorrow. Some of the survivors had more trouble settling down. Qiel in particular had hovered around Akavi long after lights-out, asking if he was perfectly comfortable, if there was anything else she could do for him, really, anything at all, and was he absolutely sure. Akavi had shooed her away in annoyance.

Ushanche ducked into her tent to prepare for sleep, then emerged a final time, nodded to Akavi, and offered over all twelve of her cameras. The angels were not as specialized in sensory multiplexing as Ushanche but with seven cameras for Akavi, four for Elu, and one for Enga, everyone could work together to continue surveillance at night without the task becoming arduous.

There were other tasks to do at night, though a mortal who got up in the middle of the night might not have realized it. To an outside observer, Akavi and Elu were sitting quietly by the campfire, occasionally talking, while Enga paced and did exercises. On the inside, as well as monitoring Ushanche's cameras, each of them had synthesis and analysis to do. Akavi had divided up work so that each mortal researcher collected and annotated as much data as possible during the day. At night he mentally went over every set of notes, cross-referencing each observation, updating each researcher's orders, and looking for patterns. It would be Akavi, when this leg of the mission was done, who would package the full set of results for Irimiru's consumption and deliver a summary report.

On top of the research and surveillance, there were now signals coming in from elsewhere.

Ahu Ninyo'u, Examiner of Epiphron, to Akavi Averis, Inquisitor of Nemesis, came a garbled radio signal from what must have been a long way away. *My team is on the ground and has preliminary data. Requesting permission to upload.*

Granted, said Akavi, and the file – corrupted due to its journey through the air, but mostly intelligible – slowly trickled into his head.

We can make it to your coordinates in estimated five days, if things go well, sent Ninyo'u. *Request latest estimate on your time of departure.*

Unknown, sent Akavi. *Forty-eight hours at minimum; beyond that, it depends what everyone finds. You have a fighting chance, I suppose.*

Understood, sent Ninyo'u. There was no free-floating emotion with the words, but the text-sending channel decisively closed. The data upload continued.

As well as blocking ansible signals and portal use within Jai, something in Jai's upper atmosphere was also reflecting radio signals. That meant that, while teams on the ground could contact each other at short range, there was no way to speak to anyone off-planet. Any mission to the surface without a way back was therefore pointless: even if one's team found vital information, the Gods would never learn it.

But Akavi had a Boater ship. And a Boater ship was a way back.

Shortly after his team's landing, several other teams belonging to various Gods had skimmed the outer atmosphere, then parachuted down to collect their own data before making their way to where Akavi had landed. It was likely a suicide mission. Akavi could take them back with him in theory, but would not put his team at risk waiting for them to arrive, and the Boater ship had a finite volume. But suicide missions for angels were not against protocol. When the stakes were this high, even the notoriously cautious angels of Epiphron would sacrifice themselves.

Akavi stirred the ashes with a stick as data reconfigured itself in his head. One of his seven cameras was the one that had followed Yasira. He watched, distracted from Ninyo'u's files, as Talirr stepped out of the half-eaten house. There was no sound, and he was not as skilled a lip-reader as Ushanche, but his microexpression software picked up the gist; he and Ushanche could go over details in the morning. Talirr seemed to think things were going according to plan.

She led Yasira through a door – and the camera signal vanished.

Akavi let out a short breath.

Elu, he sent. *You were asking about Yasira?*

Elu looked up. *Yes, sir?*

Akavi sent him the sensory video of their interaction that evening, along with the last few minutes of the camera feed. *Watch this and see if you can work out the answers yourself. Questions are now acceptable, though not aloud.*

Elu sat silently for a few minutes, watching. At last he frowned over at Akavi.

You were being unreasonable on purpose, weren't you? You wanted her to be angry.

Yes.

Elu's sendings became distressed. *You had a civilian shot just to make her angry.*

Akavi arched his eyebrows. "A known heretic," he said aloud, "whose behaviour was clearly threatening. And whose prognosis was terrible, even if she lived." *But yes, Elu, I did. Or have you forgotten the fate of the galaxy is at stake?*

Sir, it's just that it makes no sense. Why did you want her to be angry with you? She was at such a delicate stage already. And now she's with Talirr.

Akavi smiled. *It is one of my more involved plans. But yes, she was at a delicate stage. Perhaps more delicate than you realize. Ever since the* Alhazred *she has had difficulty trusting the Gods, no doubt due to her advancing madness. However pure her intentions, time spent learning from Evianna Talirr will only worsen this. But it is only a problem if we insist on seeing it as one. Why not turn it to our advantage?*

Elu frowned. *I don't understand.*

Think of Talirr's other students. They are most insightful when most mad. Remember?

It was a theory that the two of them had been tossing back and forth for some time: Elu because he was genuinely interested in the students as people and Akavi because he was interested in strategic advantage. He had suspected that madness was not merely a side-effect of understanding Outside: it was the key to doing so. If Outside defied all the usual rules of reality, and sane people's minds were well-adapted to working with reality, then that sanity could only be a hindrance. The gone people and their unusual abilities supported this theory.

But you're not just driving her mad, said Elu. *You're turning her against you.*

Correct. We already have an abundance of mad people. I want a madness that works. Yasira needs to understand Talirr's heresies as fully as possible. She needs to be able to work with them intimately and effectively. I strongly suspect that this means not only embracing madness but embracing the heresy itself. It will increase her efficacy with Outside; with any luck, the presence of a mentor who remains functional and able to work in the face of Outside symptoms will keep Yasira that much more functional as well. If that means turning her against us, so be it; and as quickly as possible. We are running out of time.

Elu's face twitched and contorted. Silly boy.

Did he know what *running out of time* might mean? Surely he must. It was beyond obvious that Akavi's own life would be forfeit if the mission failed. Furthermore, it was not uncommon, when an Inquisitor of Nemesis failed at a sufficiently large task, for their underlings to be terminated with them. Everyone in the corps knew that.

Akavi watched Elu in the firelight and wondered why, if it was so obvious, he felt there was something he should say about it. Something for which, uncharacteristically, he did not know the words.

Sir, Elu sent, *I'm sorry. It still makes no sense. If she starts to believe what Talirr believes, she won't want to come back. Even if we track her and find her again, she won't cooperate, and we'll be back where we started. What good will that do?*

Have faith, Elu. Refusal to cooperate is a trivial problem. Or haven't you watched me solve that one before?

Elu did not reply. He looked down at the edge of the fire. Judging from the unhappy hunch to his shoulders, he understood perfectly.

CHAPTER 14

Despite my best efforts, Evianna Talirr's parents have pulled her from therapy. They are alarmed and, in the absence of permission to disclose the therapy's true purpose, nothing I say can assuage them. Yes, she has ceased to say heretical-sounding things, but of course there are the usual side effects: depression, fearfulness, social withdrawal, loss of interest in friends or in play.

You and I know the reason for these symptoms. It is necessary. If we are to make a good, functioning child out of a case like little Evianna, we must destroy her. It is the basic principle of operant conditioning: we must break the child down utterly to build them up again. The building up is key. Once the child's heresies have been fully extinguished, the child is malleable: they can be trained back into sociality, into engaging in age-appropriate activities, into displaying appropriate positive affect, into whatever else the parents desire. We have the tools.

But, my Lady, I could not persuade the parents to allow me to complete treatment. I believe that the child is no longer a danger; she was nearly at the end of the heresy-extinguishing phase. I do not recommend termination at this time, as I believe that her heretical tendencies are most likely gone, that with time she could still become a productive worker. Only keep an eye on her; wait until there is real and certain danger of harm before acting. That is what I would ask.

But what if I am wrong? Our therapy, as brutal as it seems, is our best hope for preventing heresy while keeping children alive.

My Lady, I believe in the sanctity of children's lives. But if a mind like little Evianna's does relapse, and remembers the way that we treated her, I can only guess what horrors will then be unleashed.
FROM THE CASE FILES OF ANIRTHA NAIABRIM, CLINICAL CHILD PSYCHOLOGIST AND SELL-SOUL TO NEMESIS

Yasira stumbled into the half-eaten shop after Dr Talirr, spiny insects crawling around their feet. Yasira made a face at the bugs and they scurried away. Dr Talirr strode through, unbothered, then ushered Yasira through a back door, the kind that looked like it led to a storeroom.

On the other side of the door was not a storeroom but a bare metal airlock the size of a closet. When Yasira cycled through to its other side, a huge space opened out like the Galactic University of Ala's primary physics lab: an open-concept room filled with non-regulation equipment. The place was massive, easily as big as the Shien Reactor room, wrapped about with steel girders and rafters and bathed in a drab, sunless, grayish-blue fluorescent light. Pillars crossed and crisscrossed the place apparently at random: like on the *Alhazred*, gravity seemed not to make sense here, and tables and piles of equipment adhered as easily to the floor and walls as to the ceiling. Here and there a massive device with some unknown function loomed. The room had the metallic, ozone smell of many laboratories Yasira had been in, and faint humming like a cheap heating or air reclamation system suffused the air. Her tablet beeped, displaying an error message: *Radio receptivity lost. Bearings unknown.* Yasira frowned slightly at it, checked ansible connectivity – still none – and stuffed the tablet back into her pocket.

The sense of wrongness, the creep of Outside at the edge of Yasira's awareness, was not gone, but it was different here. Previously it had been thick and pervasive. Here, for the first time since landing, that sense faded a little. It felt less like an Outside soup in the air and more like a faint hint of something under the floorboards. It wasn't perfect, but she found herself breathing more deeply, untensing her shoulders.

Of course, she thought. A portal. They weren't on the surface of Jai anymore. Though apparently they weren't back in range of the ansible nets either.

"Where are we?" said Yasira. "What is this place?"

"Very literally the middle of nowhere. It's mostly custom-constructed."

Yasira wondered what Akavi was going to think of this. Probably nothing good. She was AWOL from the angels and they were probably going to try to shoot her when they found her. That terrified her less than she thought it should. Maybe her emotions weren't working, post-meltdown. Maybe she was just too angry. Who cared what Akavi thought?

She would, probably, in the morning, but...

Dr Talirr turned to her and studied her face.

"You're exhausted," she said, as if it was a discovery she'd just made. "I have a guest room. Go and sleep."

Yasira wavered before deciding it was true. The room that Dr Talirr showed her was a cubicle-like box, hastily closed in with a ceiling and a couple of proper doors, nestled sideways between a few of the pillars. It looked like a storage space hastily repurposed, and the two entrances were entirely geometrically incompatible both with each other and with the single-sized bed. But the bed looked inviting, neatly made, with a worn-down comforter on top. After a long day of traipsing around Jai with nothing but a compact air mattress in a pup tent on her back, Yasira appreciated this.

"The washroom is about twenty meters that way," said Dr Talirr. "There's a water bottle by your headboard, too. The light switch is here. If you require anything else, my room is there." She pointed to a door nearby, at a forty-five-degree angle to one of Yasira's. "Knock first, of course. But I understand this is most likely difficult for you so I'm willing to make small adjustments to my schedule if necessary."

At the university, Dr Talirr had been fiercely territorial. She had loathed unplanned meetings – and, in fact, any contact with students outside business hours. She had told them so in no uncertain terms.

Yasira's head spun with questions she was too tired to ask. She unhooked the heavy pack from her shoulder and dropped it to the floor, then sat down on the edge of the bed, which had just the right amount of give. She wanted to lie down here, close her eyes, and sink into oblivion.

"Oh," said Dr Talirr, turning to leave, "and there's a protocol for monsters under the bed. If you see something with, say, eight to ten pairs of claws, ignore it. Those ones are harmless. If you see something without any claws or limbs at all, you might want to come get me. Good night."

"Wait, what–" said Yasira.

The door closed.

It was a long time before Yasira fell asleep.

She did not see monsters and she did not dream. When she woke up and switched the lights on, her tablet said it was late morning, Jai time. She'd slept soundly. There was still no ansible network connection, which, on reflection, was a good thing.

She lay on the mattress and thought things over. Whose side was she on? Not Dr Talirr's. Not Akavi's, except… Akavi was the one who could bring Dr Talirr to justice. And Akavi had wanted her to find Dr Talirr. Technically she was doing what he'd asked. He just had his titanium-plated head too far up his ass to appreciate it.

With luck, she'd return to him in time with exactly the information he needed, and all would be forgiven. Without luck… Well, without luck she was dead. That had sort of been a given ever since the *Pride of Jai*.

How did she feel? Tired. Empty. Overwhelmed. And determined – yeah, that was still there underneath the other crap – determined to stop Dr Talirr from hurting anyone else ever again.

She still didn't know how to do that, but the answers were here if they were anywhere.

It took some deep breaths and some concentrating on just how determined she was, before she could get out of bed.

Outside the bedroom, Dr Talirr was upside down about fifteen feet above Yasira's head, washing a plate at a work table which seemed to have been repurposed into a makeshift kitchen. Yasira frowned, then decided to treat gravity here the same as on the *Alhazred*. She tried the surface of a nearby pillar, crawled up, and made her way into the breakfast space. It made more sense once it was right side up. A small, boxy refrigerator whirred next to a Bunsen burner jury-rigged into a stove and a laboratory-style sink half-full of dishes. Yasira gingerly sat on a stool.

"Good morning," Dr Talirr said without looking up.

"Hello," said Yasira.

"I'm going to make you breakfast," said Dr Talirr, as if announcing the next mandatory lab assignment. "Unfortunately, I lack access to a God-built food printer. I do have eggs and toast. Do you like toast? I can't remember."

"Remember" was hardly the word for it. Dr Talirr and Yasira had never shared a meal. That wasn't how Dr Talirr did things. When she bonded with students at all it was through work.

Dr Talirr's face didn't give off many cues, but Yasira had never had trouble interpreting her movements. Her pale hands moved back and forth between one task and another, several times. Nervous. Dr Talirr was a lot of things, but she wasn't normally intimidated by her own students.

"Um, sure," said Yasira. "Toast is fine."

"Second order of business," said Dr Talirr. "You must call me Ev."

"Why?"

"Someone should." She moved briskly to a nearby cabinet and fished out several slices of rye bread, which she dropped into a toaster. "You must also tell me whether or not you slept well, and… I'm sure there is another step. It will come to me in a moment."

"Rule books," said Yasira. It was a phrase from grad school, a rare point of commiseration between the two. Dr Talirr had grown up without any of the supports that were available on Jai. She'd complained bitterly about human society and its opaque, unwritten rules. With neurotypical people you often couldn't tell where the rule was until you stepped on it and were punished. Dr Talirr had been very preoccupied with these punishments. She had complained endlessly about the unfairness of it all. But Yasira was here to bring her in for heresies that killed thousands of people, not for doing breakfast wrong.

Dr Talirr fished in the fridge for eggs. "You've read my diaries, I assume. Akavi seemed pleased with herself for having found those. I can't imagine she didn't share them with you."

"He," Yasira corrected. "Most of the time. But yes, he did. They were very…" She groped for an appropriate word and settled on "interesting."

Dr Talirr shrugged. She cracked two eggs into a frying pan and placed it on the rack over the Bunsen burner. Yasira tried very hard not to tap her fingertips against the desk in worry. "I imagine you have questions," said Dr Talirr. "Which one first?"

Yasira chewed her lip briefly, then decided to go straight to the point. That was Dr Talirr's style. "Why did you invade my home planet?"

"I didn't invade your home planet," Dr Talirr said placidly. "Outside did."

Yasira stood up before she could stop herself, making fists. "Don't play semantic games with me, Ev–"

"Oh, you're angry again," said Dr Talirr. She did not look up from the eggs. "Yes, technically, I was involved. Causality is a lie, but from your perspective, I partially caused it to happen. You could say I consciously intended some of it, though consciousness is also a lie. This isn't me playing semantic games. It's a sequence of events which is genuinely difficult to describe."

"Try," said Yasira. She did not sit down. She tried very hard not to shout. "Please. This is my home. I know it's complex, but I'm *good* at understanding complex things. Just tell me in as few words as you can, and then we'll start in on the details."

"I prayed," said Dr Talirr.

Yasira sank back down onto her stool.

"Ev," she said, "that's impossible. You don't have the circuitry to pray."

Dr Talirr turned back to the stove and scraped the scrambled eggs out of the pan as though they were really only talking about breakfast. Yasira stared at her.

Prayer, of course, had meant something different to Old Humans. Yasira knew that. Before there were Gods who could act on their own, Old Humans had "prayed" by muttering words, doing pointless rituals, or even just thinking in a certain way, hoping their imaginary proto-Gods would hear. It was a far cry from the orderly communication that real priests carried out. But Old Humans had been desperate for the attention of something higher than themselves. That was why Old Humans built the real Gods in the first place.

Dr Talirr might be talking about that. Knowing she was a heretic, but unable to function without Gods, she might have somehow reverted to those old ways.

There was one other possibility. The other possibility was even worse.

"Ev," said Yasira, "no."

"I answered your question," said Dr Talirr. "You can decide not to believe me, but that would be a bit useless. Not that usefulness isn't a lie. Here, eat these eggs."

She put the plate of eggs down in front of Yasira just as the toast popped out of the toaster. Yasira did not reach for her fork.

In the stories, sometimes, people tried to pray to Outside the way they'd prayed to the old proto-Gods. Through horrible rituals, incomprehensible chants, blood, blood, blood. Sometimes Outside didn't hear them. Other times…

Well, it did what Outside usually did in stories. Showed up. Violated all the known laws of physics. Killed some people and drove the rest mad.

Kind of like what had been happening here all along.

"You can't be praying to things from Outside," said Yasira. "Ev, haven't you read the stories? That's the worst thing you can do. I don't care how clever you are. The whole point of Outside is it drives people mad because it's impossible for mortals to understand.

Studying it is bad enough, but talking to it, thinking you can *control* it? It's… it's a theoretical impossibility. And it's the first stupid mistake any cultist ever makes in the stories. Right before they get squished and eaten and take half the city with them. That's how it always happens, no matter how you try to flatter them or how many awful blood sacrifices you make at them. They don't *care*. You *can't*."

"Correct," said Dr Talirr, calmly spreading butter over the toast. "Which is why I don't use blood sacrifice."

Yasira picked up the fork and threw it back down onto the countertop again in frustration.

"Blood is uninteresting," said Dr Talirr. "The gone people of Jai seem to think otherwise, but really, every Earth vertebrate has it. Most other creatures have fluids that perform an analogous function. You were down there, Yasira; you've performed your own communication with Outside creatures. What do you think they respond to?"

"I…" She swallowed hard, trying to get the phrasing straight. "I talked to some of them. Akavi said most people can't do that. Only gone people and me."

"And me," said Dr Talirr. She flipped the two pieces of toast onto a smaller plate and set it down beside the eggs, expressionless. "I suspect the two of us have an understanding others lack, even others of our neurotype. It's that understanding that allows us to work with Outside science. It also enables rudimentary interaction. Outside creatures respond to our impulses and visualizations. Do you remember what that feels like?"

"I only tried it with small things. I met a gone person. She didn't follow my orders. She just… It was like talking without the talking." She chewed the inside of her bottom lip. This was just like grad school. Dr Talirr gave her the tools but left it to Yasira to make inferences. If she could keep up at all. "So you're saying you talk like that to… bigger things. You convince them to do what you want. But if they're big enough to pray to, and big enough to cause disasters, and all human concerns are *lies* to them, how the fuck do you do that?"

"It's a skill," said Dr Talirr. "It takes practice like anything else.

They like certain types of energy and signal. In the stories it's chanting, or strange shapes and colors, or other nonsense. In reality it has more to do with physics. You might have guessed the Shien Reactor produces something they like. The hardest part, for me, has been convincing them to be cautious with human life. They were very destructive at first. They're still fairly deadly, as you've seen. Life is a lie; death is a lie; from their perspective, why should it matter? It barely matters to me, these past few years. But large-scale destruction is not what I wanted."

"What did you want?"

"At first?" Dr Talirr pulled up a stool and took a seat across from Yasira, folding her hands. She peered, intently, in the vague direction of Yasira's face. "I asked for another human who could see them the way I did."

Yasira had a strange sinking feeling at this, though she could scarcely identify it. "And?"

"I had been visualizing a specific place so that I'd know where to start looking. A bookstore I liked. This was six years ago, shortly after you met me. Shortly after I prayed, there was an Outside incursion at the bookstore. The building collapsed and the owner went mad, raving, stabbing people, the usual. The angels of Nemesis quickly took him into custody. It was never traced back to me, but I never managed to make contact with him before his death, so it was useless." She scowled. "I set about refining my methods after that."

"You mean you did it again," Yasira breathed. Somehow, this hurt over and above the other evils. This original sin. "Even though it was horrible, even though it killed people, you went and did it again. You didn't care, even then. Did you?"

Dr Talirr looked up sharply. Yasira had finally hit a nerve. "And why should I have? Don't you understand? This is war."

"Against what? You started it. You're the one who started hereticking."

"And when did I start that?" She raised her voice. "In preschool, Yasira? When I started telling stories out of order because time was a lie, and they locked me in a hospital and threatened to give me to

Nemesis unless I'd learn to do it right? In first grade, when I told my mother about the Outside creature I'd seen flying at me, and she sent me to another doctor who hit me until I told him I'd made it all up? Yasira, I have been fighting this war since before you were born. I have been an Outside thing all my life. The very structure of my brain is an affront that they cannot allow to exist. Why shouldn't I fight them? Would you rather I bowed my head meekly and let myself be destroyed, for a *lie*?"

"Yes!" Yasira shouted.

She took a slow breath, trying to calm herself. She was surprised at the vehemence of what she felt. She'd liked Dr Talirr, once. She'd wanted to defend her. But now she didn't care how badly the woman claimed she'd been hurt. People were dead and going mad. Thousands of people, not just one. The proportions were wrong.

Dr Talirr huffed out her breath. "You'll learn," she muttered. "I'll teach you. That's what we're here for, after all." She looked up, a sharp motion, the anger seeming to fall away. "Lessons. Yes. Would you like to see how I pray?"

They wound their way back up – back down? – the pillar, and across two perpendicular walls. Yasira tried not to stare at all the incomprehensible devices, the piles upon piles of spare parts. It was the fruit of three years of Dr Talirr working on her own, she supposed, free from teaching duties or other bureaucratic constraints to slow her down. It looked like enough for many more.

"One thing I need to make clear," said Dr Talirr, "before we begin. You cannot reverse engineer this. Well, you can. But it won't help you with your mission. I believe you are treating the Jai plague as a designed thing, which can be disassembled neatly once you understand its workings. But I didn't design it. I asked for something like it; its central parts originate in my own mind. But I do not control it. If you try to run it in reverse you'll quickly find that you don't either. If that is a deal-breaker for you, I will be profoundly disappointed, but I will let you go. Do you understand?"

"Yes," Yasira said shakily. It wasn't like she could say anything else.

At one end of the room stood a project larger than most of the others; a bulky conglomeration of wired-together parts on a raised dais, under a blue floodlight. It looked, at first glance, like a half-assembled portal. But portals were sleek arches the size of a doorway, or – in big cities, when companies wanted to transport truckloads of products back and forth – the size of a highway bridge. This was not an arch and could not be walked through. The open space in the middle was about the size of a car, irregularly curved and bent, thick in some places and thin in others. Jagged gaps crossed its surface, sometimes bridged by groups of uninsulated wires, sometimes empty.

The dais on which it sat had been marked up every which way: with paint, scored lines, even duct tape. It was criss-crossed with symbols that looked more like decorations than labels. Nonsensical circles and spirals atop grid-like lines, like something from a book of optical illusions. Dents, here and there, like someone had pounded the metal sheeting with a blunt object.

It looked like an altar, Yasira thought. Or: the way an altar would look if built by someone with no aesthetics whatsoever.

"This is harmless when not in use," said Dr Talirr. "Feel free to examine it. I'd like to know if you can work out what it does."

Yasira hesitantly stepped onto the dais and walked around the thing. She didn't touch it but the blue light was very bright and it made most details easy to see.

There were few obvious moving parts. A number of metal flaps on the edges of the curve looked like they could be extended and retracted, but they were no larger than Yasira's hand: probably a peripheral function. There were no visible engines or motors. So this wasn't a device for moving around. Not that she'd have expected that, really.

She visually traced the largest groups of wires, which meant little to her. There were power-bearing wires and information-bearing wires of various standard types. The information-bearing wires were unusually thick and criss-crossed wildly over each other. The power wires, meanwhile, disappeared into the floor. That meant it wasn't self-sufficient. Either it generated power for the rest of the building or it took power from a generator somewhere else. Given the absence of turbines or heat-generating components, Yasira was willing to bet on the latter.

The shape of the central opening puzzled her. The inside surface of a real portal's arch would have been marked all the way around with a small slit, corresponding exactly to the edges of the opening that formed between one place and another when the portal was in use. Dr Talirr's device had nothing of the kind. The inside surface did have small circular holes – no more than a dozen, irregularly placed, each about the radius of a mechanical pencil-lead. The rest of the inside surface was polished to a bewilderingly smooth, glasslike sheen, in marked contrast to the rough metal and irregular wires of the outside. It buckled and curved illogically, but the edges were uniformly concave, as if to stop something from spilling out past them. She could imagine something originating in the middle and flowing out, meeting one of those concave edges, reflecting back again...

Like mirrors.

They were converging mirrors.

Yasira leaned in over the irregular shape. It was not symmetrical, but if she assumed that particles streamed from the circular holes and traced the likely paths of those particles with her eyes, the shape seemed designed to reflect each one into a semi-stable path that crossed the very center of the open space. There were gaps in the shape, but the mirrors opposite them seemed designed to refract things away from the gaps. Where the edges protruded outwards, there were other protrusions waiting to catch whatever bounced off them.

If everything was meant to meet at the exact center it would have been more sensible to use a simple dish shape. Which implied that this odd configuration was here for a purpose. It was meant to create not a single point of focus but something more complex.

She looked back up at Dr Talirr, who was watching her expectantly.

"It's a modified portal," she said. "That is, it's based at some ancient-history level on portal technology. But it's not meant to bring people from one place to another."

"Go on."

"Portals create a flat plane segment in three-dimensional space such that one side of the segment is in one part of space, and the other is somewhere radically different. By crossing the plane segment, a person crosses over. God-built portals are thought to accomplish that effect by folding spacetime, but we don't know exactly how it works. Yours use a spatial singularity based on the Erashub equations."

Dr Talirr raised her eyebrows. "Oh, did you read that paper?"

"Akavi had it." Yasira brushed the outside of the device carefully with a fingertip. "But this thing doesn't make a flat plane segment. I would guess that it creates and focuses… something, to produce an irregularly shaped singularity clustered around this point." She gestured to the approximate center. "Here. So it doesn't actually transport anything, it just… creates the singularity. For the sake of having one. And concentrates the energies involved much more intensely than a portal would. Is that correct?"

"Yes," said Dr Talirr. "Now, why would I want to concentrate energies in that manner?"

"Because a spatial singularity is something that follows Outside's rules. So this is one of the types of energy that attracts things from Outside, isn't it? This is how you pray."

Dr Talirr nodded. "Would you like to try it?"

Without waiting for a response, she hopped up onto the dais and flipped a small bank of switches in rapid succession. The machine hummed to life. Tiny green lights along its circumference winked on, one after another. Panic filled Yasira, far too intense to be rational – the panic that always came when she was rushing into an Outside phenomenon at top speed.

"Wait, no!" she said. "Wait! You can't just turn it right on like *that!*"

Dr Talirr blinked at her, then powered the machine off. The feeling of panic eased. "Why not? I think using this yourself would clarify a number of issues for you, actually. The communication goes both ways, after all."

Yasira tugged at her hair in frustration. Sure, she'd talked to small

Outside creatures. Once or twice. She did *not* want to talk to the big ones, the kind that might smash into a planet somewhere and kill a bunch of people just because she visualized the wrong thing.

"Well, how about the step where you explain what I'm actually supposed to *do*? Safety protocols, communication guidelines, telling me *anything* about what to expect when it's running? I mean, it's only a machine that breaks the laws of physics and lets you call down giant plagues on humanity! At any reputable institution there'd be a hundred page safety manual and a certification quiz before you even let me onto the dais with a thing like this turned off. Gods!"

Dr Talirr pursed her lips. "No, Yasira. At a reputable institution you and I would be executed as heretics for even discussing this. But I take your point. You can do this in whatever order you prefer, but taking this step quickly will save you a great deal of trouble. I certainly wish I'd been able to do it earlier than I did. I perhaps should have mentioned that it's possible to use it *without* calling down plagues on humanity. If you don't actively communicate a desired effect, whatever appears will be restricted only to this room."

Yasira caught her breath, forcing herself to calm down. "Right, yes, you should have mentioned that. But what *do* I do? What happens?"

"The machine will create a spatial singularity, as you said. By approaching the singularity you will be able to make mental contact with Outside. You'll see a visible energy field with a definable radius. All you need to do is physically touch its edge. Less and you won't learn. More and it will destroy you. It will not, however, destroy this room; my containment systems are considerably more advanced than what you used on the *Pride of Jai*."

"And there's not, like," Yasira waved a hand. "I don't know. Radiation? Fumes? Thermal hazards? Retinal damage from looking at it wrong? Other reasons besides the heresy and the exposed wires all over the place why this is a *really* bad idea?"

Dr Talirr stifled a smile. "Not that I've been able to detect. Obviously, you shouldn't touch the exposed wires. But I like to think you have at least a degree of common sense about such things. If you want a full evaluation from the department of health and safety, I'm afraid I don't have one."

Yasira drew in a breath and blew it back out again. She was running out of excuses not to do this. She still very *strongly* did not want to do this.

"I don't mean to push you, of course," said Dr Talirr, as if this had just occurred to her. "If you don't want to do this, we'll do something else. I have a computer you might like to see. I could show you the power generation room. It's not very exciting, but you were always interested in power generation. Or... Have you eaten breakfast?" She tilted her head and her ponytail flopped to the side. "I made you something, but I can't remember if you ate it."

Yasira raised a sleeve and wiped the cold sweat from her brow.

She was on a mission, after all. She'd known all along that the mission might involve things she'd rather not do. This might be the key to understanding the Jai plague, or to destroying Talirr altogether. She couldn't let her planet down. And it was far too late to back out.

"Is this the only way?" said Yasira, keeping her voice steady. "If I want to understand what you're doing the way you understand it, is this it?"

"Yes."

"Do it, then."

"Very sensible," said Dr Talirr. "Thank you."

She flipped the switches again. The machine rumbled like a full-scale reactor causing panic to surge inside Yasira again. Green lights winked into existence all around the machine's circumference. The actual converging mirrors did not move but there was a sudden sense of whirling nonetheless, as a bright glow pulsed visibly through the gaps in the machine's outer surface, cycling counterclockwise, faster and faster.

Yasira dug her fingernails into the meat of her hands. She would stay calm. This was what she had come here to do; this was how she was going to save Jai. It couldn't be worse than what would happen if she came back without trying.

She would not run away. She was better than that.

She focused on her breathing, counting seconds, trying to stretch each inhalation and exhalation out for as long as possible. She got to seventeen seconds per breath before she realized she was counting not by real seconds but by the light cycles around the edge of the machine, which were now so rapid she could barely follow them.

The light sped until it became a harsh strobe, bright enough to drown out the blue floodlight in pulsing white. Yasira's eyes ached. Her head began to pound. It was only by a great effort of will that she kept looking.

There was nothing in the open space at the machine's center, yet.

The light was like the light in the park in Büata. It had the same mental gravity, like if Yasira didn't hold on to herself she'd fall in. But the light in Büata had appeared naturally. It had felt hungry naturally, blithely, the way an animal hungered. This one felt like it was pulling itself up a ladder with muscles it had never used. Dragged into reality before it was ready. And reality wasn't used to having it. It hurt. It was ravenous with pain.

The pain made it worse than the Shien Reactor. Worse than falling through the burning atmosphere of Jai. Worse, even, than the portal Dr Talirr had opened on the *Alhazred*. The pain, the brightness, the Outside feeling and the familiar panic came together into something bigger than themselves. Dr Talirr hadn't needed to warn her that this could destroy her: it was obvious from the way it felt. Like the end of the world.

A dozen thin spears of light shot out of the inner edges of the machine into the space at its center. Something too bright to look at bloomed where they met, pinpoint, like a star. The next instant, a full nebula of white light burst out, its edge scintillating only feet from Yasira's face. It was not really light, of course; light was the closest approximation her eyes could produce to what was there. But that didn't matter. She could reach out and touch it.

"Now," said Dr Talirr. "Remember what I said. No more than the lightest surface touch."

But even the lightest surface touch was too much. Yasira could see that now.

The light didn't only resemble the end of the world. It was the end of the world. Touch the surface of whatever this was and Yasira would be annihilated. The world as she knew it would blow apart into subatomic pieces. If anything remained in her consciousness after that, shambling around and wearing her body and trying to remember what it was like to be Yasira, it would not be herself.

She raised her hand.

This was stupid. It was her senses, and her madness, playing tricks on her. She wasn't going to be annihilated, probably. And even if she was, what did that matter? The fate of the whole galaxy was at stake. Yasira was tiny. She was a scrap of living flesh, already turning cancerous herself. If she had to be burned away to save the rest of humanity, what did it matter?

The light blazed and roiled in front of her. The light was larger than a galaxy. Larger than the universe. Black spots danced in front of her eyes. The room was spinning. She was shaking all over, like a tiny tree in a windstorm. She was falling. She was going to die.

All she had to do was move her hand closer.

She tried to focus on the individual muscles, the tendons. She imagined putting her hand out to balance herself on something soothing, like a wall. She could use a wall now, she thought. She tried to focus on nothing and just lunge forward without thinking about it.

The world was going to end. She was going to die.

She couldn't form the impulse to move. Not even a little. Even knowing what was at stake, she couldn't bring the tiniest part of herself to want to move forward and touch this thing.

"I can't," she whispered, and she realized she could barely move her mouth, either.

"Pardon?" said Dr Talirr. She sounded very far away, tinny, like in a tunnel.

"I can't," said Yasira, louder, and the sound of her own voice broke something inside her. She doubled over and scrambled away, shaking so hard she could barely make it off of the altar. She crumpled at the edge and fought the urge to dry heave. "I can't. Turn it off. Turn it off, turn it off!"

There was a series of clicking sounds, with agonizing slowness, as

Dr Talirr flipped the switches the other way. The room was plunged into dark blue gloom.

"I'm sorry," Yasira whispered.

"*I'm* sorry," said Dr Talirr. She sounded shaken. "I thought this would help. I thought you'd be happy. When I finally had the resources to do this for the first time, I... I was so happy."

Yasira swallowed hard. She hadn't really been talking to Dr Talirr.

"It will get easier," said Dr Talirr. "Maybe. I think."

Enough silence ensued to make it clear no one in the room had nearly enough evidence to make that claim.

"Do you want to be left alone?" said Dr Talirr. After a while, as there was no response, she strode away.

Yasira had failed. She had known exactly what she had to do to learn Dr Talirr's secrets so she could save Jai, and she had failed at it. She couldn't move her arm a stupid six inches forwards when it counted. She had failed her family, her planet, the whole galaxy.

Well.

Maybe not.

Dr Talirr hadn't kicked her out of here yet. She had time to work up her courage and try again.

She shuddered. If she tried again, she knew, she would have this reaction again. She would fail just as hard.

Unless something changed.

She had time. She could explore the rest of this place, ask Dr Talirr every question within her power, learn everything she could. There could be things to learn, somewhere in this place, that would take some of the terror out of it.

She told herself that repeatedly, until she could breathe normally and move again. She would find something to make herself brave. But if there was a thing like that somewhere in this building, she had no idea what it might be.

CHAPTER 15

I do not want to kill people. Killing people is a solved problem; all one needs is sufficiently large lasers, an asteroid, poison gases, etc. It is not an interesting way to spend one's efforts.

What I want is considerably more difficult to arrange. I want Truth, and I want to stop being alone. I want others to see it, too.

FROM THE DIARIES OF DR EVIANNA TALIRR

"Are you all right now?" asked Dr Talirr when Yasira found her again.

"I'm all right," said Yasira. It was more or less true. She'd calmed down, at least. She'd breathed deeply until she could move again. Then she'd eaten her breakfast, finally, though the eggs were cold. And she'd taken a slow walk down the twists and turns of the main room, examining some of the less heretical machines.

There were actual portals here, dozens of variations on the original Shien Reactor prototype, even – as Dr Talirr had promised – a computer. A forbidden one, judging by its size: the thing could have filled an entire dump truck, and there was a swivel chair at the center across from three huge monitors. She had pondered turning it on and poking at it, but now wasn't the time.

To Yasira's shock and delight, there was also an ansible. Though it was anyone's guess how ansibles worked out here.

"Here," said Dr Talirr abruptly, turning on her heel. Her shoe made a squeaking noise on the floor. "I'm going to show you something less upsetting. At least, by my current understanding of what's upsetting to you. Which may be faulty. Again."

"It's okay," said Yasira, scrambling again to catch up.

They wound their way back through the main room, around the different work tables, and towards the airlock where Yasira had entered last night. Yasira looked Dr Talirr up and down, trying to understand what she was doing.

"How long have you known about Outside?" said Yasira. "You've been talking like you knew it all your life. But the angels of Nemesis didn't come after you until just recently. Why is that?"

"I suppose it's always been at the back of my mind," said Dr Talirr. "But it wasn't until I began doing physics research that I realized it had a name and an existence outside of me. I had enough sense in me to keep it quiet, and not to leave hard evidence of my heresies anywhere angels could find them until I'd already run away. I suspect they figured a lot out after the fact, of course. Oh, here we are."

They had reached the airlock door. Dr Talirr gestured to it, and it opened. She strode in, and Yasira hurried after her. "Where are we going?"

"This building is, as I said, in the middle of nowhere." Dr Talirr ran a hand down the unmarked wall as the doors swished shut behind them. The sealed-in space did resemble an airlock, but, unlike any other airlock Yasira had been in, there was no control panel, no button to press, no sensible interface at all, just smooth thick airtight metal doors on either side. They may as well have been in a closet. "If we were constrained by ordinary spacetime, supply runs would take too long. So I've automated the portal operation process. It's just like talking to monsters – which also makes it good practice for you. Visualize a place."

Yasira pictured her parents' house in Lungan, which was the first thing that came to mind: a comfortable townhouse with a sharply sloping roof and a grassy courtyard, flowers snaking up the edges of the walls. She frowned. Should she picture flowers? She couldn't recall exactly what type of flowers bloomed there at exactly this time of year, and anyway, it had been years since she'd stayed at that house for any length of time. Aunt Zonsa had probably gone in, torn everything up by the roots and planted anew, just like she did every few years–

"You're overthinking it," Dr Talirr interrupted. "This isn't like making a vid. You don't need to draw every detail; all you need is a concept. And for heavens' sake, don't use a place you're that emotionally attached to. Especially given current circumstances."

Yasira wondered, startled, how Dr. Talirr had seen what she was thinking, but it didn't seem like something to stop and ask about right now. She sighed and pictured something else. A farmer's market in Ala, where she'd gone to shop and eat lunch a few times while she studied with Dr Talirr.

"Better," said Dr Talirr. "Oh, and give me your tablet. I suspect Akavi will attempt to use it to track your location. It can't connect to the ansible net from here but it will be a security risk if we bring it past the airlock."

Yasira hesitantly handed it over. Dr Talirr dropped it on the floor and stomped on it. The screen cracked first, then the plastic backing, and Dr Talirr ground her heel into it, scattering tiny screws and bits of circuitry everywhere. Yasira tried not to stare. No one treated God-built technology like that.

"Now concentrate on your mental image and walk forward," said Dr Talirr, as if she had done nothing more unusual than crush a soda can.

Yasira obeyed and the outer doors swung open – not like a pair of airlock doors but like a double door in an office building. On the other side was the farmer's market, brighter and fuller than any memory. Anetaians in svelte clothing crowded around the booths, laughing, chatting, filling enormous cloth shopping bags. None of them looked up or seemed surprised by Ev and Yasira; whatever the airlock looked like to them, if it looked like anything, it must have been mundane. The bright Anetaian sun beat down on the scene, hard enough for the warmth to bake into Yasira's skin where she stood, along with the smell of flowers and straw.

Yasira gasped and took a step backwards. The doors swung shut, and the sound of the market was instantly silenced.

"How do you do that?" she demanded.

"Do you want six unpublished technical papers?" said Dr Talirr. "The short version is that location continues to be a lie."

"So is my *brain*," said Yasira, rubbing her forehead. Everything really had been the same as her mental image, down to the angle – only no mental image of hers could ever have been so full and real. "Apparently."

"The idea of sentient minds as discrete and self-enclosed, without the possibility for information transfer, is also a lie. Anyone can see this by observing the gone people of Jai, or even the contagious facial expressions in neurotypical humans. But that's not the point. The point is, if you're going to keep having panic attacks, I need to show you this now." Dr Talirr paused and added in a very careful tone, as though she was reading from a list, "so that you can leave when you like. If you like. As soon as you like, in the manner that you like, and without having to ask me for permission. That's important."

This was so different from what Yasira had grown used to, over the past few weeks, that she blinked and stepped back.

"Do you *want* me to leave?" said Yasira. "Have I… failed you somehow?"

"Of course not," said Dr Talirr. "But if you hate me, and you hate being here, then…" She made a frustrated gesture. "I mean, I'm given to understand that captivity is – This doesn't make sense to me."

Yasira crossed her arms glumly. If minds were a lie, and Dr Talirr's machines could see some of her thoughts, what did that mean? It meant there was no fooling Dr Talirr about what she was really here for. It meant there was no way to hide all the rage she'd been holding in. Dr Talirr already knew.

And yet…

Knowing that Yasira hated her, probably knowing on some level that Yasira wanted to destroy her, Dr Talirr was still willing to let her stay.

Akavi had been wrong about Dr Talirr. Spite wasn't her weakness. Loneliness was. She was so desperate for someone to talk to about her so-called Truth that she didn't care if that person actually liked her.

Well, all right. If Yasira knew her enemy's weakness, she could use it. That was what moles did, wasn't it?

Probably.

"Look," said Yasira. "What you did to Jai made me angry. This whole thing freaks me out beyond all reason. But if I ran I'd be lying to myself. I need to understand what happened to me and the Gods won't give me answers. So why would I leave?"

It was close enough to the truth to be indistinguishable, which was the creepiest thing about having to say it.

Dr Talirr nodded slowly, though she looked troubled. After a moment, she changed back to the previous topic. "You can use this mechanism to fetch things, of course. If there's a supply you require, simply visualize a place where you could buy it. The airlock will connect to the nearest mundane doorway, and it will stay where you left it, as long as you visualize it opening for you and leading back here. Others won't be able to go through on their own. So that's that, and I think it's your turn to decide what you'd like to do next."

Yasira considered a couple of sensible options, but another temptation won out.

"Your ansible," she said. "I mean, I noticed you built one. Does it work?"

"Of course."

Yasira bounced slightly on the balls of her feet. She didn't have to feign interest this time. "It's just, there's someone I've been wanting to talk to ever since the *Pride of Jai*, and Akavi wouldn't…"

Dr Talirr smiled. "Be my guest."

Dr Talirr's ansible was a messy, hacked-together version of the real thing. Wires and ill-fitting components hung out of every side. The touch-screen interface was missing; the display was an ordinary cathode ray tube, and a cheap keyboard and mouse dangled out of a pair of holes in the side. Half an inch of dust covered the whole thing. It powered up like a real ansible, though, and its screen lit up with an only slightly glitchy facsimile of the typical ansible interface back home, informing users that they should touch the screen to continue.

The screen was not a touch screen. Yasira poked it a few times to make sure, but nothing happened. "You can use Shift and the arrow keys," Dr Talirr explained, "and it will mostly work."

"So is the ansible a security risk? I mean, if I make an outgoing call, will angels be able to trace the signal?"

"No," said Dr Talirr. "Mine has a numerical identifier that doesn't compute. To a God-built sensor it will look like it's coming from every direction at once."

"Does that mean no incoming calls?"

"No cold calls, but if you make contact with someone, there's an encrypted return address that should be functional for them. Shall I leave you to it?"

"Yes, please," said Yasira.

Dr Talirr strode away. Yasira turned to the ansible feeling nervous and suddenly blank.

She'd daydreamed about leaving a message for Tiv, and for her parents and anyone else who might be worrying, ever since Akavi had taken her from the *Leunt*. But if there had been words in her daydreams, she couldn't remember them now. She'd only been thinking of seeing the familiar faces, the relief in their eyes when they learned she wasn't dead. The sense of closure.

Was that how she should start? *I'm not dead?*

But for everyone except Yasira it had been fourteen whole months. What did closure actually mean after that long? If she told her family she was alive, would that be closure for them, or only the reopening of an old wound?

She could tell them that she was alive. She couldn't tell them she was safe, because that wasn't true. She couldn't tell them she expected to be alive a lot longer. She couldn't explain any of what was actually happening, because it was classified. She couldn't tell them she was coming home. If she told her family she was alive and missed them, and then never sent them another message ever again... It was no different from disappearing all over again. There was no point to that except Yasira's own selfishness.

Anyway, her family was on Jai, and Jai was blocked off from ansible communications. Tiv wasn't. But who knew if the ansible system could even find Tiv?

Yasira typed it in experimentally. Not to send a message, she told herself. Just to see. *Productivity Hunt, Zwerfk. Search.*

It was a whole country, but then, there weren't a lot of Arinnans in Zwerfk. At least, Yasira didn't think so.

The search returned three results. One Productivity Yasira ruled out immediately, since she lived with a Zwerfk partner who had taken her last name – a *male* Zwerfk partner, at that – and three children. The other two Yasira hemmed and hawed between for a while. One Productivity lived alone in a city called Rart. Another shared a house in Meurs with several other adults of both genders. That was common enough for unmarried people of Tiv and Yasira's age, if their family wasn't close by. And one of the other names was Arinnan, too, which was interesting. In fact...

No, *several* of the names were from Jai. Zwerfk and Stijon were pretty close to each other phonetically, but "Nic Lysosy Grej" had the three-word structure of a Stijonan name, and Yasira had met Stijonans named Nic. In fact, there had been a Nic somewhere at the edges of Yasira and Tiv's circle of friends. Yasira closed her eyes, trying to remember. Nic had either been the loud one who snuck alcohol off the supply rockets, or the dweeby one who fancied himself the best board game strategist on the station. One of those had been Nic, and the other one had been Brelgy, and they'd had similar faces, and she'd always gotten them mixed up.

"Citizenship Lake," the other Arinnan name, was familiar, too. There'd been a Ship Lake somewhere in Tiv's group. Yasira had only met her once or twice. She'd seemed boring. But she'd been treated like part of the group.

Yasira opened her eyes.

So Tiv had taken friends along and fled Jai before the plague happened. Which brought another question to mind, one that she supposed she really should have asked earlier. Elu had known where

Tiv was. If it had been fourteen months, and Tiv was working in Zwerfk and having a normal life, why would he know that? Why were the angels tracking her?

Yasira tapped her fingers against the side of the keyboard. She reached for the Send Message button, then retreated. She still hadn't worked out what to say.

"Hi, Tiv," she said to the air, practicing. "So, I know this is weird, but I'm actually alive, and…"

Her throat constricted. She sounded like an idiot.

"Hi, Tiv. Don't mind me, being not-dead. Just ignore that. It's a long story. I was just sort of wondering how you are, and why you're in Zwerfk now, and why it would even matter that you're in Zwerfk now, and, um… I just…"

No. This was stupid.

Yasira bookmarked the Tiv that was probably her Tiv. If the possessive pronoun even meant anything anymore. Then she powered off the ansible and turned away.

Something lapdog-sized with ten pairs of claws scuttled by, using the ansible's thick tangles of wires as cover. Yasira swore profusely at it until it scurried away.

There was plenty to worry about but also plenty to do. Yasira could have spent weeks simply examining everything. And weeks or months more, after that, experimenting with the computer.

"Did you reverse engineer this, too?" said Yasira, poking at the controls.

"No," said Dr Talirr. "I only liberated the blueprints and some key components from a historical archive at the University of Esoth. It's based on the Cray T3E. Human-designed, the better part of a century before the Gods arose. The modifications I made were relatively minor. Mainly I threw together an encoding appropriate to the type of data I work with out here. It has a few glitches; I can't decide if they are natural reactions to processing Outside phenomena or simple software bugs. But it mostly works."

It didn't have a slick, friendly user interface like a God-built console; most of the work had to be done at the command line. Despite being heretical, it was also clearly not close to achieving sentience. Without Dr Talirr at hand to rattle off obscure command names, it would have taken hours for Yasira to figure out how to access anything. The files that she did manage to access were written in a strange, half-numerical, half-Anetaian shorthand.

"Why couldn't you just write, 'vacuum energy rising faster than expected'?" Yasira complained, after deciphering a particularly abstruse comment.

"Didn't feel like it. Language is a lie. I wasn't expecting someone to come along and read these."

It was certainly more of a learning curve than a God-built console, but there was important information in here. Like full reports on all of Dr Talirr's disasters. The computer chugged and stalled. Its graphics, when they fin ally rendered, were simple and ugly. But it could produce visual representations of the energy readings at any such place, just as the computer on the *Menagerie* had – and, here, nothing was redacted.

"Pay attention to this," Dr Talirr said, pointing to a red stripe which ballooned out of the model of Zhoshash. "This is where civilian fatalities began. I've listed them here; you can see they're roughly correlated to this energy type. I'm managing to control my visualizations enough to keep that at a low level, but it took practice. Zhoshash was not ideal."

Yasira bit the inside of her cheek and said nothing. She watched the swirling colors on the computer screen. She hated the way Dr Talirr talked about killing people, like it was a minor inconvenience. Like she'd done her due diligence just by forming a vague intention not to. That wasn't how moral responsibility worked, and they both knew it.

"Now, *this*," said Dr Talirr, "is where Nemesis came in."

A dark khaki color suddenly bloomed across the map, blotting out everything else. There were hints of immense heat below it, and of strong but mundane electromagnetic surges. After two recorded minutes, it receded. No sign of Outside energy remained – nor any sign of life at all.

Yasira let out a long breath.

It was possible that Dr Talirr was lying, of course. Maybe the khaki color wasn't Nemesis; maybe it was something else. Maybe Dr Talirr had done the cover-up herself. But that made no sense. All the Gods would have noticed if a town went missing, just as They noticed when the *Pride of Jai's* generator started to go off the rails. It could have been aliens or the Keres – except why would the Keres attack a place that was already coming apart? How would that advance the Keres' interests – or anyone else's? And if it was the Keres, why hadn't the Gods stopped Her? They'd stopped Her every other time.

And if Nemesis had arrived and destroyed everything so efficiently, less than an hour after the disaster began, how exactly had Akavi acquired the hologram he'd shown her on the *Menagerie*? He'd said it was reconstructed from eyewitness accounts. Gods could mine the souls that arrived in Limbo but only for their central tendencies, not for the kind of detail that let you reconstruct a specific scene; that kind of thing was recorded in a brain, not a soul. So someone had to have survived at least a little while, because the eyewitness accounts would have had to be from living people. If it were otherwise, if the Gods could find out everything just by waiting for Limbo to notice, then there would be no need for Inquisitors of Nemesis to interrogate people. They'd just kill everyone.

Except "killing everyone", now that Yasira thought about it, was a pretty good description of what had just happened onscreen. And there were others who could have been eyewitnesses – the angels, for instance, who'd swooped down to destroy the place. Or the whole thing could be another lie, and the hologram could have been pure fiction.

Yasira swallowed hard, pushed away from the keyboard, and turned to Dr Talirr. "You said the airlock in this place can go anywhere, right? Any place I can visualize?"

"Yes."

"I want to see this firsthand. Can you do that?"

Dr Talirr nodded and led her to the airlock. Yasira fixed the hologram of Zhoshash as firmly in her mind as she possibly could, and the doors opened out into a windswept field. The sun, high in the sky, was bigger and redder than Jai's sun. The air made Yasira's teeth chatter. She hugged herself. There was a mountain up on one side that looked about the right shape, but no sign of a town anywhere. The structure at her back was only the simplest of wooden shacks, moldy and abandoned.

"I thought I was picturing Zhoshash," she said. "But there's supposed to be a town. What happened?"

"The airlock is programmed to work with doors," said Dr Talirr. "This is the nearest door to what used to be Zhoshash. Obviously, the actual town isn't here anymore. Haven't you been listening?"

"But I was picturing the past," said Yasira. "Not the present. I wanted to see what *happened*."

Dr Talirr raised her eyebrows.

"You time-travel," said Yasira stubbornly. "If you don't do it this way, how do you do it?"

"I do it this way," said Dr Talirr. "Sometimes. But it's hard. Time has… glitches. I do remember things in the wrong direction, but not reliably. Actually *moving* in the wrong direction takes an enormous amount of energy. I don't like doing it. I'm not surprised if you can't."

Yasira sighed and started walking. Walking warmed her up, at least. "Do you know where the town used to be?"

Even cities fully destroyed by the Keres left ruins: twisted metal that had once been the skeleton of a building, half-melted fragments of the biggest vehicles and machines. These places were eerie, and were sometimes preserved in that state as a memorial. A person with Yasira's knowledge of physics, chemistry, and metallurgy could deduce things from the state they found the fragments in.

"It's a few minutes from here, I think," said Dr Talirr. "You'll know it when you see it."

They walked until the tips of Yasira's fingers went numb and shaky in the wind. Even Dr Talirr seemed to begin to feel the cold, rubbing her hands together rapidly and frowning at them. At last they came to a sort of line drawn in the ground. On one side, patchy grass, thin rocky soil, small thorny shrubs: the scrappy Earth-derived

them live. You knew what would happen to them. And for what? How does this even benefit you?"

"You don't know?" Dr Talirr said, furrowing her brows. "I explained this to Akavi. She didn't tell you?"

Yasira just looked at her.

"You don't. Huh." Dr Talirr looked off into the distance. "I thought I could predict her behavior; she is mostly a computer, after all. Unless…" She drummed her fingers briefly on her thigh. "Oh, of course. She doesn't trust you."

Yasira's words came out sharply. The cold was starting to burn her throat. "What is it that I'm supposed to know?"

"Nemesis thinks she can win through firepower. She thinks that's the only kind of war. But in the meantime, I am creating a situation in which more and more souls are prepared to understand the Truth. You don't kill a god with explosives; you kill it by exposing its lies. Someday soon I will have exposed them enough that the problem is no longer solvable by killing people."

"Why wouldn't it be?" said Yasira. "It seems to work pretty damned well for Her so far. You try to expose lies or whatever, and She just swoops in and blows up the evidence and nobody wins. But all those people lose."

Dr Talirr smiled, shivering slightly. "That's the point. She is behaving reactively. She is operating according to damage control. And this particular method of damage control operates only at certain scales. She hasn't done it with Jai yet, has she?"

The blood drained from Yasira's face, and her lips went numb in the wind.

She was serious. That was why she'd been escalating the size of her attacks, even though the technique was not perfected yet. That was why she'd attacked a whole fifth of a planet at once. To give the Gods a target They couldn't destroy. To *dare* Them to attack as They'd attacked here.

"Jai is the catalyst," said Dr Talirr. "Jai is where the experimental skirmishes stop and the real war begins. As the survivors and the gone people come into their own…"

She said more, but Yasira couldn't hear. It was nothing but a bunch of stupid words on the edge of the howling wind. She couldn't take in any more words. She turned on her heel instead and marched back in the direction of the airlock, trying to stamp feeling back into her toes.

If all this was true then there were two possible reasons why the Gods might not have destroyed Jai yet. One was that They couldn't, or weren't willing; destroying a fifth of a planet wasn't an option for Them. That was the answer Dr Talirr was counting on.

But there was another, much simpler answer. They hadn't destroyed Jai *yet*, because destroying Jai was a last resort. They could do it, but They'd stayed Their hands for now, because They were waiting to see if Yasira came up with a better idea.

Just on account of being here, and not finished yet, maybe Yasira was still the biggest thing keeping her planet in once piece.

So, what if she failed?

Was there another?

CHAPTER 16

Before Old Humans made the Gods there were many lesser things, a wild and beautiful jungle of littler processors, and these processors had their own ways of thinking. Before they stumbled onto the algorithms that made the Gods, Old Humans had a thing called a neural net. They did not know about souls, so they dug into brains and tried to painstakingly remake every little component in copper wire and code.

Did it work? Yes, after a fashion. You could train a neural net to do any simple task. But once they were trained you could not look inside them. You could not say, "This neuron here, this piece of code, this rule, is why the net behaves this way." You cannot do that with humans, either, you know. You cannot open up their brains and say, "Here, this specific connection, this is the key to eating, sleeping, mathematics, trust." You can only trust that, if the whole of the system behaves properly, then the parts are doing as they were meant to. And most of the time, they did.

If even these little, unaware creatures needed trust in order to function, how much more so do the Gods, who are greater than us in every way? That is why we must not question the Gods too much, beloved. We could not understand Them anyway. We can only judge Them by Their deeds, Their care for us, Their protection, Their taking us out of Old Earth and bringing us to live on these wonderful worlds; and conclude that They must be performing as specified.

WALYA SHU'UHI, THEODICY STORIES FOR CHILDREN

That night, Yasira sat up a long time. She was here to find solutions, and there were none. She had been warned, hadn't she? Outside didn't work like that.

She was alone in a secret heretical lair with the woman who had caused the destruction of Zhoshash and everything since. Maybe Yasira couldn't fix those things. Maybe, whether she got rid of Dr Talirr now or not, Jai was doomed.

But Yasira knew where Dr Talirr slept. She knew where the kitchen was. And the kitchen had knives.

Wasn't that Nemesis' way? Dr Talirr was a heretic's heretic. A cancer cell, if there ever had been one.

It was something that never would have occurred to her, if not for the shock of this afternoon. That expanse of rock, bigger than a city, blasted into lifelessness. There but for Yasira might go Jai. And what was she prepared to do to save her planet? How far would she go? Angels, she thought, would kill and die many times over to keep mortals safe. Was it fair for Yasira to ask for less? To say, *no, don't make me dirty my hands,* when she'd already signed on for a mission that would kill Dr Talirr? She knew what Akavi would do, given this opportunity. The angels might never have a chance like this again.

If she didn't do it, if she refused this one death, how many billions of people would die?

Dr Talirr was Yasira's mentor. She had shepherded Yasira through the three impossible years of her doctorate with a drive Yasira had never seen before or since. She had not been patient nor flexible, but she had taken Yasira seriously on a planet where hardly anyone did. Now she was a heretic, a murderer; a psychopath, maybe – but she had been one of the greatest scientific minds in the galaxy. At least, she had appeared to be.

Yasira did not want to do it.

She wondered how long it had been since she'd done something she wanted to do. Everything in this mission had been an emergency, or a new set of orders, or – at the last – an act of desperation. Before that – well, they'd asked her to work on the Shien Reactor, and she'd felt pride, a little. Pride and duty; her planet needed her; this was what she'd been trained for. That was what science had drained out into, in the end. Not a passion, but something functional, something comfortable, something she knew how to do. Something people liked her to keep doing.

There was Tiv, of course. She loved Tiv. But she hadn't had a passion for *doing* anything since...

Well.

Since grad school.

Maybe there was a reason for that. Maybe, when Dr Talirr had planted the seeds of her heresy, when she'd given Yasira those equations Yasira couldn't understand, she'd also taken something.

It hardly mattered at this point. Yasira was here. She'd do her duty, like it or not. She'd do what she needed to and wash the blood off her hands later. Wasn't that Nemesis' way?

It might not work. Maybe there was some Outside power that stopped Dr Talirr from being stabbed in her sleep. Maybe she would turn up alive later anyway, because of something stupid like time travel.

What else was there to do? Try to throw herself into the prayer machine and end up as paralyzed and useless as last time? Spin her wheels looking for an engineering solution that didn't exist? Give up?

I'm not a murderer, she thought desperately. She had blood on her hands already. She did not want more. But what did that matter? She hadn't been a heretic, either, until she killed a hundred people with heretical technology. She wasn't a sell-soul or an angel, but she had left her life behind to do the Gods' work. She'd never had any interest in the stories about Outside, but those equations Dr Talirr taught her were from Outside and everything had followed logically from there. She didn't get to choose what to be. Maybe choice was a lie.

Besides, she reasoned, she'd already gone around laying those grenades on the *Alhazred.* This was the same. Easier, if anything. And if it saved everyone...

Yasira tiptoed to the door of Dr Talirr's room and pressed her ear against the hinges. Nothing came from within but a soft snoring.

She felt awful already. Who went around listening to women sleep? Only creeps. This wasn't how she wanted to do things.

As if Yasira's feelings had ever mattered.

She crept up the pillar to the kitchen and drew a steak knife from its drawer with a shaking hand.

Back to the room, moving even more slowly now, as she attempted to navigate the changes in gravity without cutting herself. She made it to Dr Talirr's door and listened again. Still only snoring.

Nervousness congealed into nausea. Yasira took a deep breath, which didn't fix anything. She wiped one sweaty palm on her trousers, then, as gingerly as she had ever done anything, turned the doorknob.

Silently, with aching slowness, the door to Dr Talirr's bedroom swung open.

It was a normal room. Cluttered and unpretty, but not abnormally so. Dr Talirr lay peacefully under a worn duvet. She was on her back, nose pointed at the ceiling. Her hair spread limply around her head on a ratty white pillow. With each snore, her chest gently rose and fell.

Yasira tiptoed closer.

She had never studied how to stab a person to death. What happened if she didn't do it right the first time?

She studied Dr Talirr's sleeping form. The face and throat were exposed. Throat-cutting was probably pretty easy to get right. Yasira peered down at Dr Talirr's neck, looking for the carotid artery, and tried not to think about her qualifying exams, or the way the thesis committee had applauded when they saw the prototype Talirr-Shien Reactor at work.

Back *then*. Back when Yasira had a normal life. When she was a celebrated prodigy, and had a family, and her biggest problem was whether or not random professors took her seriously. When she thought she was doing real physics, good physics, which would never hurt anyone.

That had all been a lie, hadn't it?

It had all been a lie.

She raised the knife.

Something uncurled from the shadows under Dr Talirr's headboard. Yasira froze. It was formless, little more than a simple green slime. It snaked over Dr Talirr's shoulder and opened a white circular orifice that might generously have been interpreted as an eye.

It stared at her, unblinking. She stared back.

Dr Talirr stirred, but continued to snore. The creature oozed along the side of her neck, insouciantly affectionate, like a pet cat.

"Go away," Yasira whispered. She was frozen to the spot; she could not even lower the knife. She pictured, as hard as she could, the creature fleeing back into the shadows. "Go away."

Her heart rose louder than her voice. For six heartbeats, the creature stared at her, unmoving.

Then it extruded a pseudopod and effortlessly plucked the knife from Yasira's hand.

It did not brandish the weapon, exactly. It moved lazily, in a shape that was not quite a shape. But to Yasira the meaning was piercingly clear. *No*, you *go*.

It was so much stronger than any of the pitiful excuses Yasira had been making. She slunk backwards, out the bedroom. The door closed soundlessly behind her.

She sat down on the floor and shook.

What happened now? Would Dr Talirr try to kill *her*? Drive her out? Lock her up? Had she just screwed *everything* up?

Well, she could run. She could pack her meagre things, find her way back to Akavi, tell him what she'd learned while she was here… And then Akavi would kill her, too. He was an angel of Nemesis and this was failure. A planet was at stake. As soon as the angels learned that Yasira had failed, they'd kill everyone on Jai along with her.

Dr Talirr might not notice. She might not care. Or Dr Talirr could kill her, and that was the same as what would happen if she left now. Marginally better, because Jai would have a few more hours or days before the angels found out their plan failed.

Yasira got up and paced. Sleeping did not feel like an option. She tried sitting at the computer to get more work done, but couldn't focus. She paced longer, until she was nothing but a bundle of frayed nerves, drooping eyes, aching feet.

At that point she found herself back at the ansible, staring at Tiv's name.

This was so stupid. It wouldn't fix anything. But she wanted so badly to talk to someone.

She clicked, "Record."

"Hey, Tiv," she said. Her voice came out creaky. She must sound sick. "I don't know if you want to hear from me. I wish I could have talked to you sooner. It hasn't been long for me. Angels flew me out of the galaxy and there was time dilation. It's complicated. For me, it's only been a few weeks. I don't know what your life is like now, back on Zwerfk. It's none of my business. But I miss you. I just…"

She rested her chin in her hands.

"Things are bad right now. You probably know some of what's happening on Jai; something's got to be on the news. I'm here to help fix that right now. But it's so complicated. More complicated than anything I ever did before, and I'm so tired.

"You'd know what to say to that, wouldn't you? You're better at Gods than me. It's stupid. You probably don't want to hear from me, and I…" Her eyes drooped shut, and she shook her head, squinting back up at the monitor. "I'm sorry, Tiv. I'm so sorry things couldn't be different."

She pressed "stop", and then – against her own better judgement – pressed "send".

Message sent, said the ansible.

Some scientist Yasira was. Here in a secret heretical lair with all the secret heretical technology her heart could desire, and she was using it to drunk-dial people. She did not feel better.

She scowled, pushed away from the console and stumbled to bed.

In Yasira's nightmare, green things without arms or legs chased her down a never-ending hallway. She woke up in her guest bed and stared at the ceiling for a few short breaths, feeling oddly calm, before she remembered that real life, right now, was worse than what she'd been dreaming.

She pushed herself out of bed, ran a brush halfheartedly through her hair, and went looking for Dr Talirr.

The knife had somehow been returned to its original place in the kitchen drawer. Dr Talirr was standing there, upside down, making toast like nothing had happened.

"We're low on eggs," she said as Yasira plopped onto her usual stool. "I can go to the store this morning, if you like eggs. Or you can go. I don't care which."

She might have noticed something. She might not have. But she was probably not immediately going to throw Yasira down a garbage chute or feed her to monsters.

"Do you have any coffee?" said Yasira.

"Of course. I take it you'd like some."

"Yes, please. Black. Strong."

Coffee made everything better, apart from the fact that Yasira was alone with a mass murderer, surrounded by technology she didn't understand, and a planet's fate hanging in the balance. Well, the coffee helped her concentrate, at least. She stationed herself at the computer again. Dr Talirr gave her space.

The attack on Jai had been different from the ones on Zhoshash, on the *Pride of Jai*, and elsewhere. Those attacks, when they were allowed to run their natural course, followed a pattern. Energy went up. It coruscated around a single point. Then something horrible appeared and the whole system dissolved – first into a high-entropy state, then total destruction. Sometimes the systems collapsed in on themselves as they had on the *Pride of Jai*. More often, while a system was still in flux, Nemesis appeared and blew it out of the sky.

The Jai incident was different. It remained more or less stable in its higher-entropy state. The structure of its energy had no central point. Energy simply increased throughout an irregular area several hundred kilometers in diameter. It was a subtler shift, and it was... contained. One form of nameless Outside energy, in a fractal pattern that made Yasira's eyes cross, kept the other in check. The rest of the energy shifted, gave off sparks, and the area slowly grew. But there was nothing unstable. No signs of impending collapse. It was more like the outside of the *Alhazred*, shifting its shape while remaining the same.

Granted, the current state was unpleasant for any humans caught inside. Entropy was higher. But the change in entropy itself was somehow contained. It was directed to the outside, making the system grow, instead of collapsing in and starting a chain reaction. If they survived the initial infection then the infected areas weren't going to blow up, or crumble to dust, or anything like that. They stood a good chance of surviving.

At least until the inevitable warship showed up.

So the new form of energy controlled and constrained the old one. If Yasira was guessing right, from looking at the incursion's early stages and running the numbers, that energy was what had guided Outside to Jai in the first place. So she ought to be able to use that. Change the pattern somehow, hijack it, and use it to guide Outside away again.

Except…

No.

No, it couldn't be that simple.

Yasira stared at the screen.

Now that she'd thought of it, she saw a way to do it. She'd need to run the numbers to make sure, but it floated behind her eyes, perfectly clear, the way a really elegant solution to an equation sometimes did. Reverse the pattern. Tear everything Outside out of the planet and send it back where it came from. It could work. She wouldn't even need the prayer machine. All she had to do was get the containing energies to flow in the opposite direction. It would need a ridiculous power source and ridiculous precision, but, in principle, it could be done physically, and if she did it right, the system would completely disperse. Nothing touched by Outside would remain.

Except, of course, that everything inside the affected area had already been touched by Outside. That was how entropy worked. It was basic stuff – the second law of thermodynamics. It mixed things together in ways that you *couldn't* unmix, not even theoretically. Pink bricks, crazy trees, gone people, even seemingly normal survivors like the Huongs – at some atomic level, they were all affected now, and would always be.

So Yasira's solution would destroy them all.

Everything. Hundreds of millions of people. All life from dogs to bugs to trees.

It would be slightly kinder than Nemesis' methods. Maybe. But there would be nothing left of southern Riayin. There might not even be soil left over on which to rebuild.

She could not do it. She had tried to kill Dr. Talirr. She had destroyed the *Pride of Jai* and that made her a murderer, maybe, but not this kind. Not again. She had seen what the surface of Jai was like now, and it wasn't nice. But she'd seen death, too. Death was worse.

And of course if Akavi knew about this he would make her do it anyway.

She stared at the screen, tapping her fingers and biting her lip. After a while, she tasted blood.

Dr Talirr made peanut butter and jelly sandwiches for dinner. She had set out plates and cutlery with expectant neatness, along with tall glasses of an overly sweet Anetaian soft drink. Yasira picked at her food.

"Time is a lie," she said. "Entropy is time-dependent; it increases monotonically in one temporal direction. So is entropy also a lie?"

"Of course," said Dr Talirr. "Are you looking to negate entropy somewhere?"

"I don't know. I'm thinking." Yasira tore her sandwich into progressively tinier pieces. "Let's say, hypothetically, that someone was wounded in a battle with an Outside monster. They have a burn that doesn't behave in the way a burn normally would. It keeps growing instead of healing. It's an Outside burn. Right?"

"If you like."

"It carries Outside energies."

"It might or might not, from that vague description, but we can say it does for the sake of argument."

"So with entropy reversed, the wound would heal, and the Outside energy would leave it as it did?"

"It could." Dr Talirr took a sip of her soft drink and raised her eyebrows. "I know what you're planning. It's a good idea, but it won't work. You've noticed that there are energy patterns directing Outside energy into Jai, and you're planning to reverse them. And, since a naive application of this strategy would simply destroy the area, you'd like to know how to reverse entropy too. To make Outside clearly separable again from normality.

"Um," said Yasira. "I…"

Dr Talirr took another sip of her drink. "In theory, it is possible. But you're forgetting context. Who put the energy patterns there in the first place?"

You did, Yasira almost said, but she knew better. "Something from Outside did. Because you asked them to."

"And now you're proposing to ask them to treat themselves as a poison or disease. To painstakingly remove the smallest traces of themselves, tuck their tails between their legs and slink away. Why would they do that? No one would do that. They could give up control, perhaps, if you asked nicely. They could wander away and stop actively participating. They could do other things. But no one likes to be treated as a contaminant, Yasira, even Outside beings."

"Give up control?" said Yasira. "What would that mean? What happens if they stop being in control?"

"I'm not sure," said Dr Talirr. "The system might stabilize. Or any number of other things might happen. There would no longer be a coherent pattern holding the system together, so it's most likely the whole thing might collapse as the *Pride of Jai* did."

"What if…" She bit her lip. "What if they gave up control *to* someone?"

Dr Talirr raised her eyebrows. For once, she looked genuinely impressed.

"They might," she said. "And *that* would be interesting. But these patterns are fractal and they cover millions of square kilometers. No mortal mind operates with enough precision and scale to control them. I couldn't do it, and you certainly can't. I doubt even a god could. And of course, whoever attempted it would go mad."

Yasira pushed her stool backwards away from the table.

"I don't know what game you're playing," she said. "You say that you're declaring war on the Gods, that you're trying to survive, but you invite me in even though you know I'm working against you. You're practically gift-wrapping the answers to my questions. I could have killed you by now if I wanted to. I could have led the angels right to you. What justifies that risk? What are you trying to *do* with me?"

"I like you," Dr Talirr said placidly. "And in spite of your current allegiances, after studying your mental state, I'm quite confident that you won't–"

A ringing sound suddenly burst out in the far corner. Yasira jumped. Dr Talirr tilted her head, listening.

"Oh," she said after a moment. "It's for you."

It was Tiv, of course. Her hair had been cut pixie-short and she'd put on weight. Her eyelids, red and puffy, drooped with exhaustion. But there was no denying those were Tiv's big eyes, Tiv's heart-shaped face, Tiv's good-girl soul staring straight back at her through the ansible screen.

They stared at each other for a while.

Tiv broke the silence, choking slightly on her words. "Is this a joke?"

"I–"

"Is this a joke? Is this a *test*? You're dead."

"I'm not dead. I was–"

"Everyone said you were dead. They said the angels of Nemesis killed you. It's been fourteen *months*, Yasira. How could you let me think that? How could you not call?"

"They wouldn't let me. The mission was secret and I asked for an ansible and they wouldn't and the next thing I knew I was flying out of the galaxy."

"Okay." Tiv rubbed her eyes, making them even puffier. "Fine. Whatever. Look, it's the middle of the night here. I snuck out. Because this is crazy, and I don't want anyone giving me any more grief about my heretic ex... girlfriend."

What was that pause for? Weird. "Tiv, I wasn't–"

"I know."

A tight breath. "You know?"

"Of course I know you weren't a heretic. I was *there*. Everyone said that you must have been and I said that you weren't and they said I was... You know. In denial. Damaged. I moved all the way to another planet just so I could stop listening to people tell me how damaged I must be because of my heretic fiancée, and–"

"Wait. Wait."

Tiv clapped a hand over her mouth.

They had never been fiancées. That had not been a thing. They had talked about what it might be like, getting a place together planetside, getting married, adopting kids – but it had been an idle daydream. Hadn't it?

"I didn't mean to say that. I'm sorry. I know it wasn't like that, I just–"

"What's going on, Tiv?"

"I was going to ask you. After the ceremony. The ring got here late because of those stupid rocket couriers and I chickened out of doing it without one. You were so jumpy after the ceremony anyway. It didn't seem like the right time. Then, like, a *month* after I got home to Arinn, the courier company somehow figured out what had happened and dropped the thing right in my mailbox where everybody could see it. It was horrible. So now everyone calls you my heretic fiancée, even though you can't be a fiancée without, like, actually asking the person first, that's basic relationship 101, and I never got to ask you, and–"

"It's okay," said Yasira, though her mouth was dry and her heart pounding worse than before.

Would she have said yes? Of course she would have said yes. They would have curled up together in a little apartment planetside, just like they'd talked about. Yasira would have roamed wherever her research career took her and Tiv would have followed. They would have gotten a cat and adopted a daughter. Tiv would be the stay-at-home parent and would read their daughter bilingual picture books with big machines and talking dragons in them, and–

But that wouldn't have happened, of course. The *Pride of Jai* would have blown up anyway. They would have ended up here, the same way, in the end.

"No, it's not," said Tiv. "Yasira, nothing's okay. No one will tell us what's happening on Jai but we can't get through with portals, ansibles, ships or *anything*. That's what we should be talking about, not my stupid relationship problems. You said you're working on Jai. And you didn't know how to fix it."

"No."

Tiv smiled shakily. "But that's what you always say. Remember? You say it like clockwork, right in the middle of every big project. You don't know what to do next and you think that means you're going to fail. But all it means is you've gone to the end of what other people can tell you. That's what geniuses *do*. You get to that place, and then you strike out on your own, and that's when you do the best things."

"It's also when I made a space station implode and killed a hundred people."

Tiv reached out and touched the ansible screen in front of her, leaving a black blot where her fingers disrupted the God-built display. "You're with the angels now, right? They chose you for this. I trust them. Okay? So try trusting yourself."

Yasira didn't believe it, but she found herself suppressing a smile. "I knew you'd know what to say."

Tiv smiled, too, but there was something more wobbly in it now.

"Is everything okay down there?" said Yasira. "On Zwerfk? No one's giving you problems anymore?"

"No, I took the friends who don't give me grief and the rest of the people here don't talk about it. A lot of people came up to Zwerfk after the *Pride of Jai* failed. Jai's tech economy tanked, but Zwerfk's is booming. It's always been friendly with Arinn and they've been snapping up people like us. I've got a job now helping design air conditioners. I like fluid dynamics. I like my boss. The weather's good. It's all…" She paused. "All fine."

Which meant it wasn't. But when Yasira tried to think of problems Tiv could be having, her brain circled back to her own. "How are my family? My parents?"

"I don't know. They're on Jai." Tiv waved a hand in frustration. "You know more than me about what's going on down there. Before that, they… I don't know. They never talked to me. Never talked to the media either. To be honest, I think I understand that. I spent a year trying to keep people off *my* back that way. I don't have news, though. I'm sorry."

Yasira sat back and swallowed hard, a lump in her throat.

"It's okay," she said thickly. "Not your problem, Tiv. Not your family."

"They were supposed to be. And I'm not… I mean…"

Tiv's face was screwed up worse than before. Yasira looked at her.

"Do you want to know the truth? The truth is I'm as bad as they are. I'm selfish. I didn't come here in the middle of the night and turn on the ansible because I wanted to help fix Jai, I came because – because I'm selfish and awful, and…"

"What?"

Tiv was neither selfish nor awful. Tiv was the most selfless, giving, nice-to-be-around person Yasira knew. And she wasn't normally given to self-deprecation the way Yasira was. Tiv liked to look on the bright side. If Tiv was insulting herself, something must be *wrong*. Hugely wrong.

She waited.

"I'm dating someone else now," said Tiv.

At first there was no reaction at all. It had been fourteen months. What else had Yasira expected? What was there for either of them to be upset about?

Tiv tugged on her newly short hair – or was *newly* even the right word? – and spoke miserably. "It's Ship Lake. From our board games group. She came here with me and I started dating her just a few weeks ago. She was the only one who – I mean – she didn't *believe* me exactly, but she didn't laugh at me or tell me I was crazy. She was really patient. She moved out with me, and… and after a year I decided you weren't coming back. I could believe what I wanted to, but it didn't really matter because you were gone. And I needed to get on with life. I want to be like everyone else. I want a wife, kids, a good life, not just sitting and missing you forever. So if I can't have that with you then…" She ducked her head, looking away from the screen. "You're angry."

"No," Yasira croaked out. It was a lie. She was furious. But really, Tiv hadn't done anything wrong. If Yasira *had* been dead, this was what she would have wanted.

What was the alternative? Saying, *Yes, I want you to waste away and miss me forever?* She didn't want that. She loved Tiv. She loved Tiv's big, wide smile. She wanted Tiv to be happy.

"She's not what you were," said Tiv. "But I think she could be, if I just stopped being stupid. I thought I was starting to make strides and get over myself. But then I got a call saying there was an ansible message from you. And even though all of my logic told me to ignore it, I came here. Secretly. Because even though I told Ship I'd moved on, I haven't really. I'd still rather be with you. I'm being so selfish even to think about it, I feel horrible, but if you can forgive me for that, if you can tell me you're coming back soon, then I'll tell Ship it's not working out and I'll wait for you. I will. I want to."

Yasira took a long breath in and let it back out.

She could say, *Yes, Tiv, I'm coming back soon. All I have to do is finish saving the planet, then I'll be home.* It wouldn't be technically a lie. There was a slim chance, maybe, that she'd be able to do that. She could pretend the chance was bigger than it was. She could say it.

And then finish the call. And finish with Jai. And be dead, or mad, or locked in a room like Splió. While Tiv waited patiently, the way good girls waited, the way she'd already done for more than a year.

"I'm sorry," she said. "I wish I could promise you that. But I don't know how soon I'm coming back, if I even am. I don't know what's going to happen to me here."

"But I'll know, right? You're working on the Jai problem. So if that gets fixed, and you're still alive, that's when you'll–"

"No," said Yasira. "That's not when. I don't know what's going to happen at all. I might die. I might live, but get called off to do something else. I might end up alive, but…"

But mad. But locked in a room, tearing my hair out, never allowed to see you or any other mortal again. She couldn't say that. Not to Tiv's face.

"… But have to go out of the galaxy again. It could be years, Tiv. It could be never. And I probably won't be able to call you again and tell you when I find out."

Tiv screwed her eyes shut, then bowed her head. She didn't say anything.

"I can't make you wait for me," said Yasira. "You don't deserve to live like that. You were really good to me. So, go be that good to Ship. Go move on."

This was beginning to feel like a dream again. Hadn't they been curled up together in Yasira's bunk just a few weeks ago? Hadn't Tiv made her wear that stupid blue dress and beamed with pride? It hadn't been long. Not really.

Couldn't she wake up now and be back there?

Tiv's voice suddenly rasped. "If that's all you had to say, then *why did you call me?*"

"I don't know," said Yasira. Her throat hurt. She wasn't thinking straight. "Maybe I shouldn't have. Maybe I should go."

"Don't," said Tiv. The crack in her voice was bigger now. That was why she was looking away, Yasira realized. To hide tears. "Don't go."

She'd known calling would make everything worse, and now it had. Great.

She put out a hand and touched the screen. "I love you, Tiv."

Tiv paused so long Yasira thought she hadn't heard. Then her hand darted out, met Yasira's, without sensation. "I love you, too." The words choked her, almost unintelligible.

Yasira pressed the *End Call* button.

She sat motionless and watched the blank screen. Eventually she noticed moisture dripping from her own face. The skin hardly felt like hers.

She was so stupid. She was supposed to be saving a planet and what was she doing instead? Going in circles. Worrying over her personal life. Contemplating murder and chickening out at the last minute. Breaking Tiv's heart all over again for no good reason.

Avoiding the one thing she'd already known that she needed to do.

Yasira stood up. The ansible's stool fell with a clatter to the ground behind her. Her limbs moved stiffly as she strode towards the far end of the lair, to the dais where the prayer machine waited like a lumpy, open mouth.

She passed Dr Talirr, who had been in the kitchen keeping a respectful distance. "Is something wrong?" said Dr Talirr, upside down again. "Was that call important?"

Yasira swept past her without slowing or speaking.

She knew what to do. She'd known for days now, and she'd been pretending that she hadn't. That life would somehow sort itself out anyway. But life wasn't going to wait for her, now, was it?

She climbed up on the dais, not daring to give herself time to think. She remembered the series of levers Dr Talirr had pulled. She pulled each of those again now, roughly, watched as the lights around the edge of the thing blinked to life.

Dr Talirr followed. Her steps sounded halting, but her voice was mild and cool. "Remember the safety rules, Yasira. Only the lightest surface touch. Any more than that and it will destroy you."

Yasira wondered if she cared.

Harsh white light swirled counterclockwise around the machine's misshapen edges, faster and faster. Light drowned the room. Light burst, in thin, precise lines, into the center of the portal that wasn't a portal. At the spot where the lines met, a familiar searing nebula bloomed into place.

There was the terror, just as Yasira remembered. She was falling;

shaking; spinning; she was about to come apart. The light was a hole that went down forever. It would kill her. It would tear her open. There would no longer be anything that deserved to call itself Yasira; she would never go home.

As if there was a home to go back to.

She understood now. She was mortal; dying and being forgotten was what mortals did. *Ending* was what mortals did. She had been chosen for this: to fall into horrors. To burn brightly. To burn out.

Dr Talirr said something else – the first syllable, perhaps, of a warning – but Yasira was not listening.

She reached forward, hand shaking, and touched the edge of the light.

CHAPTER 17

It was beautiful. It was everything. It was nothing like light at all.

Size was a lie. The universe was a multitude of infinities. The universe was small enough to fit in a grain of sand. The universe could also fit precisely into the space of a woman's skull.

Why not? The thing that called itself Yasira was not real. It was not even a singular thing. It was an octillionfold gathering of loosely associated atoms. It was a conglomerate of reluctantly coexistent cells. It was an inconsequential appendage belonging to the vast fractal interconnected pattern of humanity. It was a soul, but souls were not singular; energy constantly entered and left them on levels physics said nothing about. The only way to perceive anything with the name of Yasira was to deliberately, arbitrarily choose a way of dividing the world. Joining up everything below a certain scale and nothing else. Thus far, and no farther.

Why should the fractals of the universe care about a human – or a planet, for that matter? Planets were no more real than people, and the universe was so very, very large. Better to forget planets and think of interconnected patterns made of things Yasira's physics had no words for. Constantly dancing, incomprehensibly complex yet, at their core, so much simpler than anything Yasira had ever imagined.

The patterns were beautiful. Everything was. Only petty human thoughts could make anything, any suffering, ugly. And why should humans matter?

The thing that called itself Yasira was screaming. But what did that matter? The pattern was so beautiful, screaming or otherwise. The universe was—

Strong hands pulled her back from the lip of the machine.

The thing that called itself Yasira – no – *Yasira* stumbled, retching and gasping. Its legs gave out. Hands guided it gently to the floor. It huddled there and wondered where it was. Its eyes hurt. No – *her* eyes hurt. It was an animate being who identified as female; *she* was the pronoun. *Her* chest hurt. Her throat hurt from screaming. Where was she?

"That's enough for a first time," said the thing that called itself Ev.

There was a click, and the machine powered down. The room grew dark, which was a little easier on her eyes, at least.

The floor was cold. Metal. She was on the metal floor of Ev's lab. Why?

"Breathe," said Ev.

She tried to work out the point of that command – she was clearly already breathing – and had a moment of double vision: Yasira through Ev's eyes, curled up and rocking. Ev through Yasira's eyes, crouched over her with a look of concern. Why concern? Why rocking? Yasira was supposed to be happy; Ev was supposed to understand what was going on. They were both part of the same pattern, after all, so...

Her consciousness snapped back into her head. She clutched at her temples, doubled over and retched again. She was not a pattern; she was Yasira. Whatever that meant.

She was in Ev's lab because...

Oh.

She remembered now.

She started to laugh, high-pitched, uncontrollably.

"Breathe," said Ev, resting a hand on Yasira's shoulder. Yasira hiccupped and giggled. "You've just been stretched very far past your neurological limits. You're going to have a hard time staying grounded for a while. I'm going to get you some food and then you're going to sleep. Rest helps. It won't be like this forever." She sounded regretful. Yasira remembered how Ev's first time had been. She'd enjoyed this disorientation. Ridden it like a high. Paid for it later.

But that memory was already fading.

Right. She was Yasira; that one wasn't hers anyway.

Her eyes drooped. She felt sleepy and panicky at the same time. Like when she slept – and sleep was looming very close – she would re-enter some nameless, terrible nightmare.

Ev's footsteps clicked against the floor, and then she pushed a ham sandwich into Yasira's hands. Yasira's stomach roiled.

"Eat."

"Don't want to."

"Not eating will make it worse. Eat, please."

Putting the sandwich into her mouth felt like trying to push two like magnetic poles together, but she slowly choked it down and drank the glass of water Ev handed to her. Ev pulled her to her feet and helped her stagger to her room.

Her room. She started to giggle again. As if ownership had any applicable meaning at all.

A memory, half-forgotten, nagged at her.

She forced herself to breathe slower, counting seconds, counting breaths. That helped calm her down but didn't make the thought go away. She flopped down onto the bed and peered up at Ev through already-heavy eyelids.

"You…" she said. "You didn't have anyone doing this for you. When it was you, I mean. Did you?"

There was a pause.

"Rest," said Ev.

Yasira did not need to be told again. She was asleep before the door closed

CHAPTER 18

If your student has a brilliant intellect, as some do, you may think them immune to the worries that plague other non-neurotypical people. But this is not true. We have an unfortunate tendency, here on Riayin, to wave around such brilliant individuals as if they are the most notable proof our system works. Ask your students what sort of pressure they feel, being placed on this apparently flattering cultural pedestal. Ask them what they think will happen if they make a mistake.

LENNE FUONG, A NEUROTUTOR'S GUIDE

The surface of Jai rippled slightly under Akavi's feet, an effect that the Huongs had told him was harmless, though it did unflattering things to his sense of balance. He paced, keeping a dignified posture, while his sell-souls filed back into the Boater ship.

It had been three days since Yasira's departure, and he had judged it prudent not to stay any longer. One other group of angels – Arete's – had found its way to him. The rest would have to fend for themselves. Akavi's scientists had gathered all the data that could be expected of them at this juncture, and everyone was beginning to look a little sick.

Sickest, apparently, was the manta-ship itself. Gods only knew what constituted sanity for such creatures. But due to its size it had been lounging outdoors, constantly exposed to Jai's chaotic landscape, while everyone else was able to take breaks in a relatively stable indoors. And it was beginning, to Akavi's eyes, to wilt slightly:

not only crumpled as it usually was between missions, but shrunken still further. The colors less vibrant, the ripples across its surface quick and irregular, like tachycardia.

You're sure, he sent to Diamond-Chip across a private channel, *that it is still properly flight-capable? That we're not too late?*

Negative of course would have told you sooner if problem so bad, said Diamond-Chip. It was probably a vote of confidence. Akavi tapped his foot, wondering if he should ask Sispirinithas. He decided against it.

You will be flying with the utmost caution, of course.

Affirmative caution.

The last sell-souls filed in with their bags and carts of scientific evidence and Akavi strode into the ship, its door contracting smoothly shut behind him.

"Take a hold of something," he advised the angels of Arete, who hadn't been in here on the way down.

Takeoff was sudden and brutal. The sound of the air rushing by was loud enough to be painful, and turbulence sent half the passengers flying, even the ones who'd ridden here before. Sell-souls lost their grip on the walls, crashed into each other, hit their heads on each other's equipment and swore copiously. Close to Akavi, someone gagged; he deftly propelled himself away.

His internal clock was still working; his systems estimated that the ship would be out of the atmosphere and into a more comfortable flight path within seventeen minutes. He held on to his handhold, turned down the gain on his auditory and vestibular cortices, and set himself to waiting the time out with dignity.

The turbulence continued. The planet, dimly visible through the ship's translucent sides, drew away slowly and erratically. People swore, lurched, wailed. He ignored them and went over his report to Irimiru in his head.

At the eleven-and-a-half-minute mark, Enga said, *SIR SOMETHING'S WRONG.*

Akavi gritted his teeth. Enga was standing ten feet from him, her eyes fixed on the ship's shuddering walls. Elu stood at a slight remove, as if he'd tried to placate her and been rebuffed.

Yes, Enga. We are enduring takeoff on a decidedly inefficient piece of alien technology for which you have already made your dislike clear. Is there anything else I should be aware of?

IT'S STARING AT ME DIFFERENTLY NOW.

Madness, possibly. Or a correct observation, which might be worse. Akavi didn't know the standards for Boater ships, but this one *did* seem to be swaying around more than strictly necessary, and it had looked ill before takeoff.

I'll look into it, he sent to her.

Diamond-Chip, he sent on another channel, *a status update, please. Are you noticing anything unusual?*

Can handle – hold on – tell later, sent Diamond-Chip.

The ship gave an incredible lurch.

Diamond-Chip, you are contractually sworn to the Gods and your very life has been placed under my command. If there is a problem affecting our chances of survival, I expect to be told.

Busy now, sent Diamond-Chip.

Akavi raised an eyebrow. In a human, this would constitute potentially lethal insubordination. If he pressed the issue now, though, there was a chance that he'd distract Diamond-Chip from his piloting, which would be an even more lethal mistake.

The ship lurched again. People shrieked and a few lost their footing. The shadows in the room spun; the bright side of the planet had veered off to the side somehow, which couldn't be right.

SIR, said Enga. She hadn't moved a muscle, even when the rest of the room moved violently; impeccable balance was one of the advantages conferred by her particular training.

We are working on the problem, Akavi sent.

What was the worst-case scenario if the Boater ship became too erratic to function? Several were conceivable. A crash landing, not survivable. Turbulence so strong as to become injurious. Burning up in the atmosphere, perhaps, if the ship overloaded its own biological heat shields. A veering off in some odd Boater direction which Diamond-Chip could not control: that one would depend on *what* direction. So long as they got far enough from Jai's surface to reconnect to the ansible nets, a God-built ship could intercept them.

There was general, uninformative chaos for about ten seconds. The ship lurched, then lurched back the other way, as Diamond-Chip fought to regain control.

Elu pinged him, full of palpable worry. *Sir, Enga says the ship is staring at–*

I know what Enga says. He closed the connection.

The ship banked and spun and the planet whirled over everyone's heads. There was more shrieking. Then suddenly, the walls spasmed – not the steady ripples that were normal for them, but a violent motion inward like something being squeezed, dislodging half the people who'd been depending on each wall's handholds. Sell-souls flew across the room and smacked against the opposite wall.

Akavi ignored the screaming and thought furiously. If Diamond-Chip did not regain control, what could they do to ensure their survival? Very little; they could eject from the ship, but they were sufficiently high now that terminal velocity would be lethal, as would the cold and lack of air. The angels of Arete had paradropped from higher but they had been properly equipped with thermal and breathing apparatus. And with parachutes. He wondered if they had thought to bring spares…

"We're going to die!" someone shouted and the screaming rose to a volume even Akavi couldn't match.

Akavi narrowed his eyes irately and made a note of the voice. It was difficult to pick an individual out of the commotion; he had to run the audio through an auxiliary program to confirm it. Tonkhontu Bokov, one of his field biologists. She would receive a severe reprimand as soon as they made it out of this.

If they made it out of this.

"Sir." This aloud and at a reasonable volume, from a dark-skinned angel of Arete who had made her way close enough to be heard. "What is our altitude?"

The barrier against radio and ansible communications began at two hundred kilometers above sea level. If they were going to crash, their best hope was getting that high before it happened. Then, at least, the angels could broadcast as much data as possible while the height lasted. If they stayed above two hundred kilometers for any appreciable time, it might even become possible to establish an orbit and wait for a God-built ship to come to their rescue.

Akavi, not being fitted with any altitude-detection devices, tested his ansible connection. It did nothing.

"Below two hundred kilometers," he said shortly. "Are you equipped with–"

The ship flipped entirely around. Screaming and swearing drowned out whatever else he might have said. The ship paused, then began to spin, the planet's disc lurching crazily around them.

"We're going to die!" Tonkhontu said again, as scientific equipment and sample jars crashed from one wall to the other, upending themselves. The walls spasmed and distorted again as the ship spun.

"... paradrop supplies?" Akavi finished, refusing to be distracted again.

"Five sets," said the angel of Arete, obviously thinking along the same lines. There were five angels, total, on her team; that meant one for each of them and nothing more. "Are we aborting launch, sir?"

"One moment." *Diamond-Chip, what in damnation is going on?*

Instead of answering, Diamond-Chip suddenly began a broadcast on the shared channel. All the angels could hear him, though most of the sell-souls could not. *Announcement. Ship gone crazy. Did what I could but – too large crazy underestimate. Extreme stress. Instinct is expel cargo and go home. Still trying but requires advanced negotiate and she is not responsive. I am sorry.*

Gritting his teeth, Akavi looked around at the screaming sell-souls and their various packs of samples. It sounded like they had a few more moments, at least. If he could salvage only five armfuls of nonliving cargo from this mess–

Enga suddenly vaulted past him in a blur. There was another set of screams, different from the last, and the ship suddenly pulled itself taut. A quivering roundness, stretched to its maximum circumference as if trying to pull away from something. Somewhere up near the blue-green ceiling, a new light glowed.

Attached to the light was one of Enga's most complex firearms, a heat-pistol, half-charged and glowing an angry red-orange, and pressed against the ship's inner wall.

TELL IT I WILL KILL IT, said Enga on the shared frequency. *CRAZY OR NOT. TELL IT THAT IF IT TRIES TO KILL US I WILL BURN IT FROM THE INSIDE AND IT WILL DIE TOO. I CAN BURN THIS SUBSTANCE DOWN TO NERVES IN LESS TIME THAN IT WOULD TAKE FOR A HULL BREACH TO DISLODGE ME AND I DO NOT GIVE A SINGLE CORPSEFUCKING NEUTRON HOW MAD IT HAS GONE. TELL IT!*

"Enga–" Elu said aloud, startling towards her.

"That's not necessarily–" said an angel of Arete.

Akavi silenced both of them with a small gesture. Diamond-Chip was already tapping furiously at his control panel.

Smoke began to curl from the wall below Enga's hand.

The ship shuddered, lurched and began to right itself.

There was silence, and the sound of a dozen mortals breathing who did not quite yet believe they were saved.

Jai rearranged itself behind the ship and began to shrink again.

Gradually, Enga withdrew the heat-pistol. A ring of the ship's flesh had been burned black underneath. She kept her eyes fixed on it and the pistol ready.

This is very bad, sent Diamond-Chip on a private channel. *Long term prognosis – trauma. Boaters do not do this.*

But will it get us above the radio barrier? And keep us there for, say, thirty minutes?

Ninety percent estimated affirmative. If nothing else terrible happens.
Akavi could not identify the Boater's emotions; his microexpression software wasn't calibrated to their antennae-tentacle-faces, and the sendings he received from Diamond-Chip were pure transcribed

text. Still, he imagined Diamond-Chip was feeling distress. *But she will not be safely fly again for years. Further syndromes. My ship.*

Akavi did not especially care how the ship felt at this juncture, but he understood the implications of Diamond-Chip's words. The ship would not be usable again in the foreseeable future. They would not be able to return to Jai's surface this way again; no one would. Aside from suicide missions, and a scenario where they found a way to disable the ansible blocks around the planet, no further missions to Jai could be authorized now.

This group – his own team, the five angels of Arete, and the files from other teams that they brought with them in their data banks – was all there would be.

Your objections are noted, Akavi sent coolly.

Diamond-Chip did not respond. Akavi had not expected him to. He turned to the wall, waited for his ansible uplink to light back up and began composing a perfect distress call.

The return to normal coordinates went smoothly after that, though one wouldn't have known it from looking at the shaky, mournful sell-souls. A group of angels of Philophrosyne picked up the Boater ship and immediately transferred everyone back to the *Menagerie*.

There would be a quarantine period now, of course, just as there had been on the *Leunt*. Every sell-soul's sanity had to be checked before they could return to full duty or be sent home. Aggravating, but bearable. Akavi had made his report. Irimiru had declined to issue new orders, accepting his return with a dismissive wave of their hand. Normally he longed for interactions with Irimiru to go so smoothly. But now it merely served as a reminder: this mission was no longer in Irimiru's hands. A single Overseer's wrath was not what awaited him now if he failed.

He supposed, as he paced the *Menagerie's* decks, that he was a little on edge.

Enga had to be repaired from the numerous small injuries she'd sustained on Jai. Elu and his bots saw to that in short order, but most of an Earth Standard day passed before she emerged into the filigreed corridors in full working order. Elu hurried behind her.

"Enga," said Akavi. "I appreciate the initiative you showed at multiple junctures on this mission. I'm writing you a commendation."

Enga only grunted. This, Akavi knew, was not her usual attentive silence; Enga truly did not care. She was not a true believer in Nemesis' work, nor, he supposed, would she ever be. Praise from her superiors only irritated her.

Yet Enga had her own reasons for wanting to ascend the ranks. Akavi had made sure of that.

"I believe," he said, choosing his words carefully, "that you're nearly ready for a promotion. You should give some thought to where you most want to serve, and how you wish to handle subordinates should you be offered any."

That did get a reaction. Enga's head turned, and she stared at him steadily for three and a half seconds, before nodding. *THANK YOU SIR.*

"However," said Akavi, holding up a hand. "Not every Overseer of Nemesis is as accommodating as I am. They'll understand the brain damage and the speech apraxia, I think, but they will expect certain niceties in communication. Such as actual lowercase letters."

Enga's briefly-grateful gaze narrowed into a glare.

wORKinG oN iT sIr, she said before stalking off.

With that bit of business done, Akavi motioned for Elu to follow him and walked in another direction. Elu followed, as always; the predictability was soothing.

"Not everyone can be commended as a hero on every mission," Akavi said as they walked through the corridors. The *Menagerie* was richly decorated, lined with brilliant, intricate mosaics making use of subtleties of shading that a mortal brain could not understand. Most angelic ships were decorated in this way; Techne's angels made sure of that. "But your performance was satisfactory as well. You are nothing if not dependable."

Elu ducked his head. "Thank you, sir."

"We need to continue planning. Yasira will deliver results very soon, I am sure. And the mission we have just completed will yield dividends as the data are further analyzed and followed up. But the Boater manta-ship cannot be relied on again. And while we wait for Yasira, we must not be idle. You've been handling this file for the past fourteen months; what do you suspect we will need to do next?"

Elu sucked in a breath, recognizing the question for the test that it was. Akavi often used questions like these as training, prompting the boy to follow the chains of logic that Akavi had followed already. Usually Elu did an adequate job. Very occasionally, he even came up with something new.

"Well," he said, "there are the Ha-Mashhit-class warships." Nemesis' most elite and fearsome class of ships; the ones that, according to rumor, would be sent to destroy Jai if all else failed. Elu clearly hated that plan, but he could see its logic as well as anyone. "But that's not our team's jurisdiction. I was hoping the scientists would be able to work out more than they did. Trace it all back to a virus, or a form of subspace interference, or... something. Something we could work against mundanely."

They reached a dark wood-paneled room with a window all down one wall, a spectacular view of the nebula to which the *Menagerie* had been moved, now that they were done with Jai's surface. Not a human world, this, or a soon-to-be-human one: merely one of dozens of clusters of harsh young suns bathed in luminous dust, out of the way of ordinary sentient traffic, where the most sensitive angelic strategies could be developed in peace.

There were obvious avenues to follow, even if the team had not immediately found a solution. Tonkhontu Bokov, despite her loss of nerve, had found perhaps the best one: when analyzed, small Outside creatures had turned out to possess DNA, but in a markedly different configuration to ordinary life. That data was being further analyzed by the Aletheian angels now, and might turn out to hold the key to an engineered virus or other poison to repel Jai's most dangerous monsters. As soon as Dr Bokov was cleared to work again, Akavi had new assignments ready for her and further suggestions for tests on the samples she'd gathered, which he updated every few hours in response to the Aletheians' preliminary reports. Similar results from the team's chemists, engineers, and from Dr Meyema had revealed other promising avenues from which efforts at mitigating the worst of Jai's dangers could begin. Even if they did not contribute to solving the problem per se, this sort of result would be useful for whatever cleanup remained post-solution. But none of the orbital teams sent by various Gods had made inroads yet on whatever was blocking ansible and radio signals. Akavi wasn't assigned to that aspect of the problem, but very little could be done without it. Ideas had been floated, both by him and by others – teams, for instance, who paradropped to the ground and attempted to communicate with orbiting ships via laser pulses – but the protocols necessary to make that work were still being developed. He could nibble away at aspects of the problem, in other words. And he would. But what Jai needed was a way to tear the problem out at the root. Everything else was merely buying time. And only Yasira Shien could understand the problem well enough to do that.

Elu could – should – have verbalized an analysis along roughly those lines. Instead he had gone to the window and was staring out of it morosely.

"That was… kind," he said at last. "What you did with Enga."

Akavi raised his eyebrows, taken aback.

"I am not kind," he said. "I evaluated her performance fairly according to the usual standards. Do not ever expect kindness from me, Elu."

Kindness – like Elu's – was a weakness for angels of Nemesis. From most, the word would have been an insult. But he knew what Elu was really trying to say. Resignation was painted all over his microexpressions. He expected to fail. And he had guessed the deeper meaning behind Enga's commendation. She was being prepared for a continued life in the angelic corps without Akavi.

Akavi did not want to discuss it. Discussing it was weakness. Absurd.

"No," said Elu. He dared to look back at Akavi: a sad, knowing glance. "No, I don't expect that."

Akavi had not wanted to discuss his own personality, either. Yet here he was, baited into it.

"Good," he said icily, turning to the window himself. "Dismissed."

He waited it out as Elu hesitated, as he took agonizing seconds to turn on his heel and take one step, then another out of the room. He watched the points of light in his head and waited until he could ascertain that Elu had, in fact, returned to his own quarters to mope, or whatever Elu did on his own time. He stared rigidly out at the bright dust of the nebula, tense with an anger he could not explain.

Yasira had better return with some actionable results. Their time was running out.

CHAPTER 19

Myth #15: Heretics are inherently evil, amoral, remorseless.

This is what you were taught as a child, and it is taught for a reason. But do not be deceived. Some heretics are amoral; those are the simplest type. A few see themselves as good people who are faithful to the Gods, and do not realize that they are heretics; this type is also relatively simple. Most of the most dangerous heretics are otherwise. Most believe very sincerely in some complex system of morals, handed down from other heretics or invented on their own. An attempt to bend the systems they were taught into a shape that accommodates their illicit beliefs, or to tear those systems down and start over from first principles.

Most heretics are not particularly good at this task, but they attempt it nonetheless. Some claim they are heretics because of their morals: they started with a seemingly innocuous moral deviation from standard, and when that deviation's implications conflicted with the decrees of Gods, they discarded the Gods.

A most amusing situation sometimes occurs when multiple heretics meet and find that their heresies diverge from each other as strongly as they diverge from the Gods. Take advantage of the resulting confusion whenever possible.

FROM THE BASIC TRAINING
MATERIALS FOR ANGELS OF NEMESIS

Yasira woke up lost in thought.

She had been afraid, before she touched the prayer machine, that it would destroy her. That the person who called herself Yasira, after learning the Truth, would no longer be there at all.

But she hadn't lost herself all at once, had she? She had already been losing herself in dribs and drabs. She had hardly noticed at first. The first thing that went had been her passion, hadn't it? The bursting, joyful love of science that she'd had as a child, ground out of her at last by school, by the constant scramble to meet Ev's sky-high expectations, and by the heresy that was already in her head without her knowing. She'd not wanted to think about it. She'd assumed it was a natural thing to lose. Her deepest heart.

Yet there it had been, out there with the patterns. That wonder, that wild joy, stronger than ever. Scarcely expressible.

The wonder was not in her heart now. Not quite. More of an echo, drowned out by exhaustion and terror. A memory of wonder, fresh enough to ache.

But even the memory changed everything.

She was very, very frightened. But she was no longer afraid of the Gods – not in the way that priests and angels wanted her to be. She did not feel like cowering obediently, going where They led her, trusting even though They were obviously untrustworthy. That was not where Truth lay. It was not how she was going to get out of this.

How *was* she going to get out of this?

Well. Time to take stock. What did she want to do? Bring Ev in? Complete her mission? No. That was a God thing, and the Gods were lies.

It shocked her how easily that thought slipped in. She'd known it all along, hadn't she? She'd tried to love Them, but nothing had ever happened.

So she did not care about Gods. What did she care about? Jai. Her home. Jai was in danger, billions of innocent people, and she needed to save it. Fine.

What else? Tiv – but Tiv was gone. Losing Tiv *hurt*. She thought about having Tiv here, standing beside her bed in warm concern, and she ached inside.

Interesting that pain could measure what mattered. What else hurt?

She probed around. Losing her family's respect. That hurt. Thinking about Jai. That hurt. Thinking about the hundred people who'd died because of her. That hurt a lot. They were lies, too, but...

But they were part of the same pattern as Yasira. She'd seen that. She was connected to other humans; they were all parts of the same fractal. That connection was more real than the actual humans were. She'd held onto that aspect of the Truth. Ev had not. Ev held onto different things, she supposed.

So there still was a difference between her and Ev.

Interesting.

"I was the answer to your prayer," said Yasira. "Wasn't I?"

Ev took a silent bite of eggs, head tilted. Yasira wasn't very hungry. She turned her food over and over with her fork.

It was so different now, looking at Ev. Strange how easily the familiarity, the first name, came to mind now. *Dr Talirr* had always been at a remove, prickly, unknowable. But Yasira had been so deeply absorbed in the pattern last night, next to her, that for a moment she had no longer remembered which of them was which. She had remembered Ev's memories – mostly gone now, like dreams, but the feel of them remained. She *knew* Ev now.

And Ev had known her, too. Not immediately. Not when they first met at the Galactic University of Ala. But yesterday Yasira had seen herself through Ev's eyes, and she had not merely looked like a student, yet another young person banging on Ev's door looking for science to be explained. She had looked like a prophecy fulfilled.

"Time is a lie," Yasira said, "and that man, the bookshop owner who went mad, he was a red herring. You wanted someone else who could understand Outside, you prayed about it and there I was. Only I didn't understand at the time and neither did you. You knew time was a lie, but it never occurred to you that the answer could be there before the prayer was."

Ev smiled. "I'm glad you figured it out."

"What does that make me? Am I real? Would I even have been born, or known anything about science, if you hadn't prayed for me?"

"I think so." Ev took another bite, chewed and swallowed nonchalantly. "It's difficult to say, but my feeling of Outside is that you likely would have. It's more elegant if you already existed and only needed a little extra push to find me."

Yasira bit her lip, trying to work out what it meant if some of her life was real and some wasn't. She decided now was not the time to pursue it. "What do we do now?"

"We plan. Jai is still underway and is a fascinating experiment. I've been monitoring its properties while you did your own research. Now that you're unburdened of the urge to reverse all of my work there, we can work out our next move together."

Yasira frowned. She hadn't decided, actually, if she still wanted to reverse Ev's work or not. "Our next move. What is that, exactly? Making Jai even weirder and more Outside-y? Or what?"

"Something like that. I'm particularly interested in the gone people. I want to know if, over time, more and more of the citizens of Jai progress to that state."

Yasira chewed her lip. She'd seen the gone people. They weren't as inhuman as everybody seemed to think. They had feelings. They could communicate with each other. They were better off by far than the people who'd died. But they'd still been ripped away from their old lives without their consent. Human or not, that wasn't right.

"We can do additional experiments," said Ev. "Tweak parameters or modify living conditions to see if we can increase their intelligence, their abilities. In time, the full planet of Jai might consist of–"

Yasira put down her fork. "I don't want to do that."

Ev blinked. "Why not?"

"It's not…" She hesitated on the word *right*. It was the word that she wanted to use, but what did it mean? "It's not what I want to do. I don't want to hurt people."

Ev put down her own fork. Her movements were suddenly jerky, her normally flat expression chilly in the extreme. Yasira drew back slightly; this had always been the prelude to a meltdown.

"You don't want to hurt people," Ev repeated.

"I don't."

"People are lies."

"Yes, but—"

"I thought you'd seen the Truth back there." Ev's face contorted as she pulled back away from the table. "I thought you *understood*."

Yasira stared at Ev. She did understand. Too well. She remembered dimly what it was like to be Ev. Constantly seeing and feeling the Truth. Constantly punished for saying so. Shocked, slapped, drugged, trained like a dog until she denied her own reality at every opportunity. Because what she naturally saw and felt, what she couldn't have escaped from if she tried, was a heresy. Speaking or acting on it could destroy worlds. The alternative, from a God's perspective, was to kill her.

When people hated you that much, you absorbed it. You turned it around. Either on yourself, which could be fatal, or back at everyone else. So like a cornered animal learning to bite, Ev had learned to hate. To stop caring about normal people. To cling with autistic ferocity to a belief, any belief, that said she mattered more than those people; she didn't have to care if she destroyed them. Because the alternative was learning not to care if she destroyed herself.

That wasn't Truth. It was Ev's sickness: a trauma that suffused every part of her all-too-human, all-too-mortal soul.

"You have had one single round in the prayer machine," said Ev. "I have lived this my entire life. And you think you can tell *me* how to do this? You've had a couple of weeks of subjective experience of what I am. And you think you can tell me what's *right*?"

"No," said Yasira. She had consciously *not* told Ev what was right; she had no idea just now what *right* meant. She had avoided that word. But Ev was melting down now and this kind of logic was no use in a meltdown.

It didn't matter who was right in a meltdown. They could talk about that later. The important thing now was to de-escalate. "Ev, I'm sorry. I didn't mean to tell you what to do, I—"

Ev threw her fork. It clattered off the back wall and down to the floor.

"I trusted you," she snapped, raising her voice. The edge in it was ragged now, on the verge of tears. Yasira recognized this. This was the point of no return. "I let you into my *house*. This is *my* place. I showed you the Truth and you ruined it. You *ruined* it!" The words ended in a shriek, and she threw her half-empty water glass. Yasira ducked as it flew past her head and shattered behind her.

She began to back away. Was there a way out of this? If there was, she couldn't see it. "I'm sorry."

"Get out!" Ev broke another dish, this time simply raising it in her fist and slamming it against the table. She was genuinely screaming now. "You want me to roll over and die? You want me to *surrender*? You're the same as everyone else. Get *out*!"

Yasira hurried away, crawled down the pillar, ducked into her room and shut the door. The screaming and crashing gradually degenerated into loud sobs.

Yasira thought about Ev. About Ev's hurt. Against all logic, she wanted to help Ev. There was no law of the universe saying people like Ev had to turn out this way. Not even after the abuse she'd survived. If she'd ever had a friend who believed her, if she'd ever had a therapy that wasn't all about controlling her... It could still happen. There was more that they could do together besides be heretics and hurt people.

But Ev might never see that. Yasira couldn't explain it to her unless she wanted to hear. And in the meantime, people were being hurt. By Ev, by the Gods. It wasn't going to end.

The sobs were still going, very audibly. Yasira needed air. She looked around the room, took out her pack and started to cram things in.

"I didn't mean literally get out," said Ev, appearing suddenly as Yasira neared the airlock. She had calmed, but not all the way. Tears streamed down her pale cheeks out of red, puffy eyes. She had somehow found a tub of vanilla ice cream and was holding it, shut, in her hands.

"I'm not going for good," said Yasira. "I just need some air."

"I'm sorry I yelled," said Ev. "Here, do you like ice cream? Have this ice cream." She held it out.

Yasira looked wordlessly down at the ice cream, then back up at Ev. Her hands remained at her sides.

"I can think very fast, you know," said Ev, voice wobbling. "I did lots of thinking just now. I didn't mean to yell. I was only surprised when you disagreed with me. But maybe this is why you are here. Maybe you are here to remind me of things that I forgot, or couldn't know. Maybe that's why you're the answer to my prayer. We can talk more about our plans. We can figure out what we want to do together. It doesn't have to hurt people."

Yasira very much wanted to believe that. She wasn't sure she could. She knew Ev, but she knew a lot about bullies, too. Sometimes when a bully didn't have you where they wanted you, they panicked. They cried, acted like victims, promised whatever you wanted. Then when they had you back on board, they forgot about it. It wasn't always even intentional.

Yasira's head hurt. There was a planet at stake here. She needed to think it over in private. In peace. Without an angry, sobbing, *or* apologetic Ev in her face.

"You can't go back to the Gods," said Ev. "You know you can't."

"I know," said Yasira. And then, because she was tired and fed up herself, and maybe because Ev's meltdown was a little contagious, she continued. "I fucking *know*. Do you want to know how I know? It's because I figured out about entropy. You were right. I can't reverse it, but I could reverse everything else. Tear the Outside influence out of the planet. You wouldn't even need the prayer machine for that. Just something to start a chain reaction and turn the fields around on themselves. But it would kill everyone. Do you understand? I can't kill everyone. Not again. Not your way. Not the Gods' way. Not any way. I *won't*. And if I go back to them they'll try to make me. That makes them the only things worse than you out there, do you understand? I need to help my planet. And if you'll actually listen to me, then you're my best option for turning this around. If you *won't* listen, then… Then I don't know what I'm going to have to do."

Ev gulped down a sob. "Don't leave me alone again. Please."

"I'm coming back, Ev. If you promise you won't make me hurt

people, then I promise I'll come back. But you have to back off when I tell you to back off. Otherwise this won't work. Okay?"

"Please," said Ev.

Yasira pictured the market in Ala, turned and walked out the airlock.

It was as bright and busy as before – too bright for the condition Yasira was in. She'd found the market a little overwhelming even on good days, and this was one of her worst. The baking sunlight hurt her eyes; the colors and shapes of people milling around excitedly made it worse. The noise was like a whirlwind, and the confusion of smells was intolerable. She shouldn't have picked a public place, she thought. Stupid. Too late to change her mind, unless she wanted to be face-to-face with Ev again.

When she'd used to live here, she'd had a few nearby places to retreat to when she couldn't handle the market. A couple of student offices that were rarely occupied, for instance. Or, if she wanted to go a little further, her dorm room. She didn't live here or go to the Galactic University of Ala anymore, and she no longer had access to those places.

It was still better than the prayer machine.

She walked forward.

She had no particular destination in mind and walked aimlessly. Sometimes a particular smell emerged from the cacophony to taunt her. She paused by a table of chocolate crepes under a blinding bright green awning and her stomach growled. She hadn't eaten today and Ev had warned her to eat. But Akavi hadn't given her any credit chits, and she hadn't thought to get any from Ev before she left. Feeling slightly dizzy, she turned and pushed on through the crowd. The crowd continued to swirl around chaotically.

What had she wanted? A place to think. She should have pictured a forest, she thought glumly. A deserted beach. Anything but this.

She stumbled around until she found a cheerful brick building at the market's edge. A bank, judging from the signs. Banks looked cozy but were rarely much more peaceful inside than the street. She leaned tiredly against the wall.

This wasn't fixing anything. But she didn't quite want to go back yet.

She took a few deep breaths, the way her tablet always said.

The Gods were going to start wondering where she was. The Gods were not going to be pleased with where she'd gone or the choices she'd made. And the Gods were a powerful enemy. That alone was a good argument for staying with Ev. At least long enough to learn how Ev survived.

But none of it quite seemed real. Everything was a lie. She needed rest. Maybe she could just sit here and rest, and fall asleep, and ignore the market, and it would all turn out to be a hologram. Like Zhoshash. Everything would be different when she woke up.

"Are you all right?" said a voice behind her in Anetaian.

Yasira turned. It was a fussy-looking little Anetaian lady, with a poof of artificially curled white hair surrounding her head, holding a bag of varicolored scarves from one of the market stalls. A shopper.

"I, um…" said Yasira. Where were her words when she needed them?

"You've been leaning on this wall for fifteen minutes, dearie," said the lady. "Before long you're going to get in trouble for loitering. Do you need anything? A doctor?"

Yasira rubbed her eyes and tried to remember how to conjugate Anetaian verbs. "Not really."

The woman smiled. "Here, now. It's all right. How about a place to sit down?"

"That… would be good. And some food." Her face flushed. She'd never been reduced to asking for handouts before. "I mean, if–"

"No, no, no. It's quite all right. I'll buy you some lunch; how about that?"

Yasira hesitated, ashamed, but confusion and hunger won out. "Yes. Please."

The woman led her along the street and turned into a tiny alleyway, really nothing more than a short path between two buildings. Yasira was overloaded enough not to object; it didn't seem strange to her that they were going further into the city and not just to a market stall. Maybe the food in the city was better. Maybe...

She looked up at the end of the alley.

Enga Afonbataw Konum, that muscular bulk of an angel with those intricate metal arms, stood with her head cocked, the plates at her temples glinting in the sunlight. She did not move. There was only the slightest whirr as something in the depths of her arms readied itself.

"Wait, no," said Yasira, turning to run. "Wait, we can't go this way..."

The old woman, with a lightning-fast movement, caught her. The wrinkled, arthritic-looking hands were suddenly strong as a vise.

"I'll make sure you are fed and rested," said the woman lightly. "Don't worry. But first we are going to have a little talk. Enga, if you would."

Yasira pulled and struggled, but nothing stopped the prick of the needle. Now that they were alone in the alley, the woman had straightened and assumed the imperious body language that Yasira now recognized. Her face did not change – they were in public, after all – but there was no mistaking the gleam of triumph in Akavi's eyes.

CHAPTER 20

*Remember, you are teaching your student coping mechanisms.
This is all you can teach, but it will only take you so far. Life scars
us all eventually, regardless of neurotype. There will be times when
no coping mechanism could possibly be enough.*

LENNE FUONG, A NEUROTUTOR'S GUIDE

Enga hoisted Yasira over her shoulder and walked. Yasira's limbs
wouldn't move and her vision clouded over into an undifferentiated
dark gray. Her head swam. She couldn't scream for help. She wanted
to, but all that came out was a whisper. After a block or two, she
stopped trying. What would she have done, back before all this
started, if she saw a pair of angels carrying off a prisoner? She would
have left them the fuck alone. She would have tried not to see.

She hated herself. She hated Anetaia, Ev, the Gods, everything.
Not even one day ago, she'd made such a breakthrough. And what
had she done with it? Walked straight back into Akavi's hands.
Stupid, stupid, *stupid*.

Enga was not particularly gentle. Each jostle and bump hurt.
Yasira couldn't see, but her other senses, perversely, were magnified.
A light brush against the angel's armored back felt like a bruise to
the bone. She gritted her teeth.

She was so stupid. She should have stayed back with Ev. Could
Ev tell that she'd been taken away? Maybe. Maybe not. And Yasira
had made her promise not to follow. Damn it. How had the angels
even found her this quickly?

The noise of the streets was abruptly muffled as they turned into some sort of building. The angels' feet made smart tapping noises against a tiled floor. There was the funny hum of a portal activating, and after more walking and turning, Enga lowered her into a chair. It was not a proper armchair but was similar to what Yasira sat in at the dentist's office, plasticky and tilted way back.

There was the sound of Enga walking away.

"Where are we?" Yasira whispered. "What are you doing?"

"Returning you to the fold," said Akavi. His voice was back to normal, cool and male and unaccented in Riayin. "I apologize for the chemical restraint; we weren't certain how much compliance to expect, so we played it safe. You're back on the *Menagerie* now. How are you feeling?"

"Everything hurts," Yasira whispered. "I can't see."

"Unavoidable side effects. Not to worry; this drug's half-life is only a few hours. You'll be fine soon."

He walked round her chair and clicked a metal restraint over each wrist and ankle, though, since she couldn't move anyway, that seemed redundant. The sensation of cuffs over her skin was magnified like everything else: she felt like her hands were being squeezed to death, the circulation cut off. Probably intentional.

"Why am I here?"

"Well, we need to talk about that." There was a shuffling noise. "You've been AWOL for quite some time, which I'll admit has raised some concern from my superiors. Fortunately, I was able to show them this."

He reached in and plucked something miniscule out of her hair, and, with a sinking feeling, she realized how the angels had found her.

"Ushanche did her job very well," he continued. "You were cut off from the ansible nets in Talirr's lair but each time you entered normal galactic space, this connected and uploaded video and audio of what you'd been doing. The Aletheians are having a field day with the screen captures. The computer system alone will take weeks to decipher. But, fortunately, you and the good doctor spoke aloud in plain Earth creole. So apparently you have a means of removing the

Outside influences permanently from Jai. Let's talk about that."

"I won't do it," Yasira whispered. She felt stupid. She'd blurted out her worst fear, not knowing he was listening. If she'd just kept quiet, if she'd been even marginally more polite to Ev... Yet she wasn't as afraid as she thought she'd be. She'd been right about that, back in the lair, when she thought about the Gods; somehow, she really didn't care anymore what They thought of her. "I can't."

There was a flat pause. "I see. May I ask why not?"

"It would kill everyone in the affected area. Maybe further. It would be worse than how it already is."

"I understand your concern, Yasira, but let me remind you of a few things. Jai is infected with Outside, a state of being so terrible that those who encounter it die or go mad. The large majority of people affected by Outside are in a state of suffering beyond imagining, the result of a suspension of all normal physical and mental laws. And the affected area is growing. If you do nothing, civilians will suffer agonizing fates instead of a quick, clean death, and the number of dead will grow. Inaction is not mercy, only cowardice. Surely you can see the logic. This is Nemesis' own judgement; do you understand?"

But that name no longer struck fear into Yasira's heart.

"I disagree," said Yasira.

"I see," said Akavi again.

Yasira wondered what he was going to do next.

"Are you aware," he said at last, "that your disagreement is immaterial? You are a heretic. Your mind is irrevocably corrupted and you've racked up a list of offenses long enough to justify any punishment imaginable. Among other things, you are guilty of collaborating with other heretics, conducting heretical research, making use of heretical technology, and deliberately making direct contact with Outside entities."

"Because I was following orders. *Your* orders."

"On the contrary. My orders when last we spoke were to stay with me and avoid contact with any maddening influence. Instead, you fled. You are guilty of absence from the field without leave and direct contravention of angelic orders. If you refuse this order as well, you are guilty of direct contravention of Nemesis' orders, when billions of mortal lives and minds hang in the balance."

"But–"

"Hush." His footsteps sounded against the tiled floor, pacing. "You are personally responsible for every death and every descent into madness that would have been prevented by your obedience. You are a class-A heretic and you are now in custody. You have no rights. Do you understand?"

"Yes," said Yasira. "But I won't do it."

She did not feel brave, only angry and tired. Akavi was so *small*. One tiny part of the pattern, boasting about the tiny hurts he could cause to other tiny parts. It was stupid and pointless, and he was so petty he didn't even notice.

"You will," said Akavi. "That's not in doubt. It may simply take a little while to convince you. Here."

He moved and shuffled around a bit. She tensed, but nothing touched her. After a minute or two a little strength returned to her face. Her vision swam, then cleared. She still couldn't move.

Her eyes scanned her surroundings.

She was in a small room, spotlessly white, like a hospital. A single filigree adorned the far wall: an abstract design reminiscent of the ones in the corridors on the *Menagerie*, but different. Where those had been subtle, barely visible, this was a garish, unnerving, yet intricate and precise splash of reds and blacks. Akavi stood before her in his natural form, pale and inorganic, the polished titanium of his circuitry glinting as it disappeared beneath his skin. To one side she could vaguely glimpse the edges of a sink, and a tray of long-handled medical tools, but there was no way to turn her head far enough to focus on them. There was an IV sticking out of her arm. Apart from the spotless whiteness, the aesthetic to the room – high ceilings, windowless walls, burnished metal accented with real wood in an airy, ostentatiously wasteful space – was familiar.

"Do you understand," said Akavi, "where you are?"

"On the *Menagerie*."

He pursed his lips as though that was funny.

"This is where you will be until you cooperate," said Akavi. "The more quickly you do so, the better. The Jai plague is spreading as we speak. You can save billions of lives by acting. The sooner you act, the more will be spared. If you do cooperate I may be able to grant you a pardon. Either way, you will do this one piece of work quickly and easily, with the most powerful resources available to any mortal. Then I will ask nothing more of you, ever. Will you do this for me now?"

"No," said Yasira.

Akavi's gaze wandered to the tray of medical instruments at the side of the room. Just for a moment. Her eyes followed his, but she couldn't move her head far enough to focus, to see exactly what was there.

She knew what was coming. She had seen vids; she wasn't stupid. She was less afraid than she had expected to be, but there was a chill in her blood, an intense nervousness, nonetheless.

He didn't reach for the tray.

Instead, he walked, coolly and deliberately, to the front of her chair, and he knelt. His features, horrifyingly, swam and resolved into Tiv's. It was not a resemblance that would have fooled Yasira for long; Akavi did not move the way Tiv did. Her expression, mousy and worried, was only a vague parody of the way Tiv's face looked when she looked at Yasira. But it was close. Much closer than that gone woman on Jai, and even that woman had caused a jolt of disoriented recognition, when Yasira first looked at her.

"Please," Akavi said softly, as Yasira blinked at her in shock. Rage, even, that she would try to play her emotions so transparently. Inquisitors of Nemesis, regardless of what form they were in, did not kneel. This was *not done.* "Please, Yasira. I know you're not so far gone as all that; you can't be. Your family are down there. Your mother. Your father. Your Aunt Muora. Your brother Gonrey. All our friends, all our colleagues. Do you care nothing for them?"

"I won't kill people for you," said Yasira.

Don't be too terrible for me, she thought, or remembered thinking, in the back of her mind. She swallowed hard.

"Yet you kill them now through inaction. You are their only chance of salvation and you refuse. Surely you see how mad that is, Yasira. Surely you haven't become so inhuman so quickly. Have you?"

She was silent.

She had been to Jai. She had seen it. It was terrible, but it was not death; even being a gone person wasn't death. And she remembered what it was to kill people, by accident, back on the *Pride of Jai*. She would not do that again. Not for Akavi, not for her mother and father and Aunt Muora. Not for Tiv. Not anyone. She had tried to kill Ev, back on the *Alhazred* and again in the lab, just one heretic in exchange for all of Jai; but that had been back before the prayer machine, back when she did what she was told because she didn't know what else to do, back when she didn't know her deepest heart. And this, now, would not be for all of Jai if she gave in; it would be *against* Jai, in the worst possible way. Torture was better. Anything was.

Akavi rose gracefully to her feet.

"You have," she said, with a look of hurt reproach. "Haven't you? The Yasira Shien I knew is gone."

But she could see through this. It was theatre, like anything else Akavi did. It was a lie.

Akavi's Tiv-like form dissolved as his normal Vaurian features reasserted themselves. He walked to the sink and left Yasira's field of vision. There was the sound of water running, of him washing his hands, then drying them with a burst of air.

"I ask absolution," he said, in a voice that didn't seem quite intended for her anymore, "for what I am about to do."

The fear did hit her then, all at once, in a cold flood. This was the Litany of Inquisition; this was what they said in the vids. Her heart suddenly pounded. She bit her tongue to keep from making a noise, then winced as that sensation was amplified too.

"I ask for the power of Nemesis to flow through me; the precision of Nemesis to guide my hands; the vengeance of Nemesis to steel me for what must be done. I ask that the suffering of this one fallen mortal bring mercy and benefit one hundredfold to those I am sworn to protect. I ask all this in the name of Nemesis who built me, who may unbuild me again if I falter. So it must be."

He picked something up from the tray in his right hand and flicked some tiny switch in its side. It made a faint, high-pitched buzz.

He reached for her – but with his left hand, the empty one. His touch, at the crook of her elbow, was unbelievably gentle. Even with the drug in her system it didn't hurt.

"We don't have to do this," he said ever so softly, like a father reassuring his child. "There's no need for it. You can make it stop any time. All you need to do is agree to help. Will you?"

"No," said Yasira.

"Very well."

Diffident now, he raised the other hand.

It turned out she could scream after all.

Every Inquisitor of Nemesis was trained in two arts: persuasion with words and persuasion with pain. They were two sides of the same coin, both used to root evil out and destroy it.

Yasira was not a particular challenge, nor a particular surprise. He had explained, on the *Talon*, that most heretics did what they did out of spite. Those ones were easily broken. One simply had to make cooperation, spite and all, less unpleasant than the alternative. Yasira was different. She believed in something bigger than either her spite or her pain. But that did not make the task impossible, only different.

Akavi's circuitry handled the technicalities. Specialized overlays annotated his vision, pointed out nerves over- or under-loaded, laid recommended pathways over the skin for maximum pain with minimum injury, suggested the timing for random changes and disruptions to avoid routinization of the experience, analyzed the vocalization and facial expression produced by each tool at his disposal. He found himself ignoring most of the latter; experienced Inquisitors often preferred to do this by feel.

Dissociation likely, said the overlay, highlighting her glassy eyes in translucent red as her screams became absent, mechanical. *Adjust compensatory mechanisms.* He ignored it. Dissociation was fine. There were ways for Inquisitors to break through it, to force the prisoner into full presence while one utterly destroyed them, but he did not feel a need. This torture wasn't intended to break her yet. Only to give her some inkling, some visceral memory, of how bad things could be. Let her insulate herself enough to keep her reason, such as it was, but let her body absorb the overload of pain. Then she'd be perfectly prepared for phase two.

Something had been lost. That was the thought in Yasira's mind as the first waves of pain hammered through her. She should not be here. She should not have left Ev, should not have gone to be with Ev in the first place, should not have come to the *Menagerie*, should not have even been on the *Pride of Jai*. She should not be here feeling her skin torn apart at the seams. This was wrong.

(But *wrong* was a lie. Morality did not work that way.)

She saw Akavi's tools only in glimpses – spinning blades, needlelike points, sharpened tweezers dripping with her own blood. Her skin told the rest of the story by itself. He was grinding her to bits. He was cutting her into tiny pieces – but surely there wasn't really so much of her to make pieces out of. It must have been the drug.

Occasionally he switched out the handheld tools for something else. A spray of antiseptic-smelling water, which hissed and steamed where it touched her, burrowing inches down under her skin. Other times he simply paused, until she registered the reduction in pain and managed to focus on him. He reminded her, gently and clearly, that she could make it stop with a word. Or he shouted and called her a wicked heretic, a monster, a murderer – though this felt as artificial as his gentleness. It was all theatre. All a lie.

"No," she said, each time, with a throat so raw she wondered if she still had skin there. The response was automatic; she was sometimes scarcely aware of saying it. Then the pain roared back to life, and she screamed again.

But it wasn't really Yasira screaming, fastened to her chair. Was it?

There was the Yasira who felt the pain and made those noises, and there was the larger pattern – or rather, a larger *part* of the pattern. Which did not care quite so much. Pain had an effect, pain wound into the pattern and twisted it up, but…

But.

This wasn't like the prayer machine, with all the Truth in the universe pouring into her at once. This was only an echo. Trickles of Truth, latching on because they were a little less unbearable than her usual senses.

Sometimes her consciousness snapped down, and she really was the Yasira in the chair, with nothing to think about but blades and pain and screaming. Then she snapped back up again, or back *out*. Yasira dissolved. There was pain but she could not define where it was. There was no Yasira. There was the pattern and there was a problem in the pattern, and the further she fled from the problem the less of a *she* there was. Then the terror of losing herself became worse than the pain. She snapped down again, back to the blades. And back up. And on, and on.

After a long time, she noticed that if she was very, very careful, and focused very hard, she could sometimes remain in the middle.

It was very difficult; it took practice. But there was nothing else to do but suffer, so she practiced. At times, she could be both Yasira and not-Yasira. The pain was terrible, but the pattern – almost large enough to bear it.

Almost.

She was not sure she could bear this forever. Perhaps she would break. Perhaps Akavi would tire of simple pain and bring out something worse – though she could scarcely picture what the worse thing would be. But she could not break. If she broke, they would use her to destroy the whole planet.

As soon as she had that thought, it grew as big as she was, a fear as bad as the fear of death. She was going to break. The pain was intolerable, even here. The terror, when she went further out, was worse. She could not endure forever. She was going to break, and that would be the worst thing of all.

Something sharp-edged in the meat of her arm twisted and brought a ragged ribbon of flesh away with it. This time she barely hung on to her balancing place.

Help me, she said, less in words and more in a wild, instinctive energy. It was illogical – she was alone here, except for Akavi.

Except that was what it meant to be part of a pattern. Time and space were lies. The separation between people was also a lie; that was why she'd gotten herself mixed up with Ev. If there was anyone out there connected as she was – anyone anywhere, anywhen – perhaps they could hear.

She tried to remember how it felt, being Ev.

Help me, she called again, and something turned. Something, for a tenth of a second, passed its unfathomable awareness over her.

She fell back into her body, spluttering and shrieking. Back into agony. The cycle started over. Gradually the pain and fear of breaking grew even larger than the terror of being seen, and she fought her way back to the balancing place.

Help me, she said, scarcely aware of saying it, scarcely able to control herself. This time the thing that looked at her was smaller, more intelligible. Or maybe she was simply better prepared.

What do you need? said Ev – or a thing that felt like Ev. *Where are you?*

Ev's voice was so faint, so diffuse, that it might not have been conscious. She might not know she was communicating. Ev was so strange. Her part of the pattern was all wrong, twisted and forced. Or maybe it only twisted in a different direction from everything else. Everything was wrong, but Ev was wrong *differently*.

Yasira tried to answer but could only send a blurt of panic. What did she need? She had no plans, no idea of how to get out of this, even with help. There was only pain and fear and the thing that drove her to call out.

Where are you? Came the question again, and not just from Ev, this time. *What are you? What is this?*

Not just Ev. There were other people. Where had *they* come from?

But of course Yasira had never been the only one. There had been seven other students before her. And who knew what other heretics were out there in space and time, who else might have grown attuned enough to the Truth to hear a call?

Help me, said Yasira again.

And the pattern moved.

She floated in the middle of pain, without understanding. She was vaguely aware of Akavi, standing above her, doing the same terrible things as before. But something had changed. She was larger. There was more of her.

The others in the pattern had lent something. Strength, and – in some sense – processing power. The pain was as bad as before, but she could think a little more, because there was more to think with.

Ev and Splió and the others clustered around her, waiting. Helping.

Yasira started to think.

She had not broken yet. What would happen if she didn't at all? Then the pain would keep on going until she died.

That was acceptable. She had accepted death already. She had known yesterday, when she went into the prayer machine, that her life was over.

What would happen if she did break? Even with help, it was possible. This much pain for a sufficiently long time could do it to anyone. And probably there were worse things than pain. Even Yasira could imagine…

No. She would not imagine.

If she broke, she would do as he said, and everyone would die.

But if she did not break, maybe that would happen anyway. Maybe Nemesis would give up and burn the whole planet, as She had burned Zhoshash.

Unless…

Unless Yasira could *do* something. Unless there was another way out.

Something new and horrible stabbed in between the bones of her feet, and she jolted nearly all the way back into her body again, screaming. Of course she would break. Of course that was the only outcome, in the end.

But it would not really be the end, now, would it?

Yasira's mind quivered; if it was Yasira's mind. If there was a Yasira anymore.

The pattern turned in on itself.

The pattern began to plan.

After an eternity, Akavi withdrew completely. Yasira listened to him washing his instruments as the pain began to ebb. No longer terrifying in its intensity, now it was only a heavy misery pervading her body. She was dizzy, nauseous, exhausted and aching, but she was not flickering in and out of herself anymore. She was here, on the *Menagerie*, except the *Menagerie* was a lie, and so was she, and this entire thing had been stupid from the beginning.

She knew what she had to do.

A security bot rolled in and unlocked the restraints around her wrists and ankles. It deposited a set of fresh, white, folded clothes at her feet. Her other clothes were in tatters now – she'd scarcely noticed that. She did not move.

"It seems," said Akavi, "that you've become resilient to mere physical pain. In light of this I have a better idea."

Of course he did. She remembered this; it had been in her plan. Everything here was predetermined and stupid, like a bunch of talentless undergrads trying to read from a script. As he stepped out of her sight to wash his hands, he had for some reason changed form again, returning to the Riayin face he'd used on Jai. She neither knew nor cared why. This was part of the stupid script too. Everything about Akavi was artificial.

She changed into the new clothes, gritting her teeth. Moving hurt. So did the feel of new fabric over her bruised, raw skin. It took a long time and Akavi did not interrupt. The blood rushed out of her head as she stood to put on the new trousers. She wobbled a moment, steadying herself at the side of the horrible chair, and when her vision cleared, she found herself looking into a mirror.

It was not as bad as she had expected. She had been sure he was ripping her open, tearing out muscle and bone. But she saw only surface injury. Shallow cuts, already scabbing over. The red of rawness, the blue of bruises. Her face was the real surprise: drained and hopeless, like the face of a refugee in a vid. It didn't really look like her. Her face was a lie.

When she had fully dressed, the bot reached out with two extensible limbs and took hold of her upper arms. A more casual restraint than the chair, but no less effective.

"You appreciate my dilemma, I hope," said Akavi. "My usual methods appear to be ineffective, precisely because of…" His lip curled. "Your unwillingness to cause harm. Neither argument nor force have dissuaded you from this illogical, heretical position. So I find I must appeal to you on your own terms."

The door swished open, and in walked Enga, dragging another, conscious captive along in her arms.

Yasira looked at Enga. Tiv, shaking and hemmed in by sharp curves of metal, stared back. The real Tiv this time, not just someone who looked like her, not just playacting. The movement, the eyes, the way her gaze never left Yasira's face even though Yasira could barely hold eye contact now; there was no mistaking the real thing.

Of course they had her. Of *course* that was why they'd been keeping tabs on her in Zwerfk. So they could snatch her away and bring her here whenever they wanted.

This had appeared in one version of the script. It was, at least, half-expected. Which didn't stop Yasira from sucking in a painful breath, wondering how, after everything they had already done, they had managed to find something to hurt her even worse.

"Cooperate now," said Akavi, "and Productivity Hunt will be kept safe; she'll be free to go when you are. Continue to resist, and we will do to her everything we have done to you and more. Yasira Shien, I ask you a final time: will you help me save Jai?"

"Yes," said Yasira without hesitation. "Conditionally."

Akavi drew back ever so slightly. She was fairly sure she'd *surprised* him. Had he expected her to dither? To plead?

"Conditionally?" he repeated.

"No tricks," said Yasira. "You don't kidnap anyone else. You keep her where I can see her. You let her go back to Zwerfk and live a normal life when this is over, even if you don't let me. If she so much as gets a hangnail here, the deal is off. Understand?"

Tiv's mouth opened and shut wordlessly. Maybe they'd already drugged her; maybe she *couldn't* speak.

Tiv's opinion was irrelevant. This was a script. She'd already determined that it was the least terrible option, the least destructive of a million horrible outcomes.

Akavi regarded her carefully. "And in return?"

"I save Jai."

She looked him full in the face. Angels, she knew, could tell when you were lying. But this wasn't a lie. This was in the script: she would save her world.

She just wasn't going to do it *his* way.

CHAPTER 21

You have grown up thinking of angels as immortal. Yet you are no longer a child. God-built technology can – will – repair the malfunctions which make mortals age. God-built cybernetics will help you survive injury, and few diseases can harm you. Rest assured, however, that one day – whether due to accident, violence, or summary termination – you will die.

At that time, the final clauses of your contract will come into force.

You have been given a long and very powerful life. It has been given to you for a reason. See to it, when the time comes, that you have earned every moment.

FROM THE BASIC TRAINING
READINGS FOR ANGELS OF NEMESIS

The next few minutes were a blur. Akavi agreed to her terms. She and Tiv were moved to the *Talon*. Elu was sent to bring bandages and salves.

"How are you feeling?" he asked, as he gently applied one to her upper arm.

"How do you think?" Yasira snapped.

She was too exhausted to be polite. She wanted to sleep. She did not want to be fussed over and given medical attention. Bandages were stupid. Bandages weren't going to fix any of what was actually wrong.

"We can send bots in at intervals to change these," he said, "or me, if you prefer. You'll also want to take one of the caplets in the

343

blue bottle every six hours. You'll see we've assigned you a new tablet, and it will remind you."

He bit his lip, looking at her. His long hair was no longer brushed back carefully; it fell down artlessly around his titanium-edged face, as if in distress.

"After this," he said, "I'll mostly be back on the *Menagerie* until you're done, but I'm still the one in charge of the bots who will help you. Do you need anything right now?"

"No," said Yasira. She looked pointedly away.

He took the hint and went quiet, silently patting down each of the rest of the bandages. There were too many. Yasira felt like a mummy from an old vid.

"I'm sorry you're hurt," he said at last, his voice so weak it was nearly a whisper. "If there were any other way…"

"Any other way to *what*? You couldn't have left me the fuck alone? You couldn't have left *Tiv*?"

"I–"

"Don't ask me to forgive you, Elu. *Don't*."

At some point, under torture, or maybe just before it, she had stopped feeling anger at Akavi – only terror and contempt. Anger at Akavi was not safe. But when she looked at Elu, watched him pretend to be gentle and good, rage welled up in her like an explosion.

"You dance around pretending to be my friend," she said. "You dance around pretending to be *anyone's* friend. It's a lie, isn't it? You might be sorry. But you wouldn't have lifted a finger to help me."

There was a long pause. Elu looked down at the floor and sighed. He didn't look young anymore. His limbs were gangly, his hair long and thick, his skin smooth and unlined, but he looked very, very old.

"It's like you said, Yasira," he said at last. "You knew this all along. Right from the first time we met, remember? I've never been any kind of good person. I'm only the good cop."

She slept for exactly eight hours, according to the clock by her bed. One of the bots attached electrodes to her head to prevent her from dreaming, which was scratchy and uncomfortable, but she was so tired that she fell asleep anyway. When she awoke, the ache had settled deeper into her bones. She felt dizzy and nauseous. She did not want to move. The bot standing by her head prodded her until she rolled over and moved.

She was not, to her surprise, locked in her room. When she turned the knob, the door opened. The bot let her out and followed her wherever she went. When she ventured too close to the portal the bot drew itself up officiously and blocked her way. When she went to her closet, dressed, and washed her face, it gave her a little more space. As she sat down at her desk to look through her introductory files, it rolled out of the room.

She poked her way tiredly through several screens' worth of information. It was everything the Gods knew, or felt like telling her, about the physics of Jai. Most of it was stuff she'd already learned from Ev's computer. Some was different.

The bot rolled back in with a plate. She ignored it. It began to beep insistently. She waved it away. "I'm not hungry."

"You are required to take in nutrients for optimum functioning," said the bot. "You are listed as highly overdue for nutrient intake. Your work is currently a high enough priority to justify the use of force in ensuring your optimum functioning. If you wish to eat under your own motor control, do so now."

Yasira looked at the plate. There was nothing on it but a bland-looking nutrient bar of the type she'd seen Akavi eat. She picked it up, looked at it dubiously, and bit in. It was tasteless and dry, like a thick cracker. She wondered why angels bothered eating these things when they could print any food they desired. Maybe Akavi was just that sort of person. She chewed and swallowed mechanically, keeping her eyes on the reading. The bot took the plate away when she was done. She felt like crap, but less nauseous, so maybe it was on to something after all.

An hour of reading and mathematical sketching passed before the bot beeped again. Yasira looked up, annoyed.

"As stipulated in your agreement with Akavi Averis, Inquisitor of

Nemesis," said the bot, "you are now permitted to visit and ascertain the status of Productivity Hunt. Visiting is not mandatory, but is allowed for up to forty-five minutes total during the next six hours at your own choosing, and will be available at twenty-four hour intervals until the completion of your work. Notification will be given at the beginning, end, and forty-five minutes before the end of each permissible visiting window. Do you wish to be taken to her now?"

"Yes," said Yasira.

She should feel happy, she thought, as the bot moved aside to allow her through the door. Or angry. Or frightened. She had loved Tiv. She *still* loved Tiv. She ought to feel something apart from numb resignation. The pattern would do what the pattern would do. Tiv was relevant to Yasira. But the pattern did not care.

Tiv was in the third room, the one that had been unfurnished when they flew out to the *Alhazred*. It was furnished now. The door swished open and there was Tiv, sitting on the edge of the bed, reading something on her tablet. She looked up as Yasira entered. She was in the same plain white God-built clothes as Yasira, her hair in the same pixie-like cut Yasira had seen on the ansible. Her eyes were puffy and dark, like she'd stayed up all night crying. Though, come to think of it, that was like the ansible, too.

Her voice rasped with emotion. "Yasira."

Yasira took a step into the room, and another, and another. The two of them collided and clung to each other. Tiv shook like an old lady and sniffed once. Her skin smelled good, the same as always; Yasira had almost begun to forget that smell.

"Let me look at you," said Yasira, pulling away. "You're not hurt, are you?"

"Well, They kidnapped me. But aside from that, no. I mean, I have food. An angel came by to ask if I needed anything. A really young one. He seemed nicer than the other two."

Yasira decided to keep her opinion of Elu to herself. "They didn't inject you with anything?"

"No."

"They didn't rough you up at all?"

"No. Even the one with the metal hands was pretty gentle. It was weird."

"Then why have you been crying?"

Tiv stared at Yasira like she'd grown another head.

"I was there yesterday, remember? They brought me in. I got a real good look at you. I saw what They'd done to you. I've been crying because They let me think you were dead for fourteen months, and now I'm a prisoner in the middle of nowhere, and you're being tortured, and I might be too, and no one will tell me why or what's happening. Not even the nice one."

Yasira shook her head. She wanted to agree, to explain everything so they could both rail together against all of this. But the bots, she was sure, were all listening. Sharing classified information was heretical. Even being angry at the Gods was heretical. There was no exemption clause for if They'd tortured you. The less Tiv knew, and the less anger she saw, the less likely she was to pick it up for herself. And the more likely she was to get out of this alive.

"It's what Nemesis does," she said tiredly. "She knows best. She has to burn away some living cells to save the whole body."

"You sound like you don't believe that."

Yasira bit her lip.

"You said you were going to save Jai," Tiv pressed. "But if that's all you were doing, why did he have to hurt you like that? Why did he have to threaten *me*? I know you. If They wanted you to save the planet, all They'd have to do is ask."

What could she say? That it was a long story? That she was a heretic now? That Akavi had wanted her to save the planet *wrong*?

Yes, she should say she was a heretic. That was the safest option. Tiv would need to believe it anyway, when she got out of here and went back to her normal life. Yasira should blurt out all the heretical things at once. She should push Tiv away. Otherwise, how could she know Tiv was safe?

She should say it. But the words wouldn't come.

Tiv took a deep breath out, and another back in.

"It's bad," she said. "Isn't it? You're having to burn away a lot of cells yourself."

"I can't talk about this now."

"Why can't anyone talk to me? I don't understand what's happening. I don't understand why the Gods would do this to us. First taking you away from me, then... then..." Tiv's lower lip quivered.

"I shouldn't be talking at all. It's not safe. I'm sorry, I just came here to make sure you weren't hurt."

"What if I tell you I *am* hurt?" said Tiv. "What if I make something up? What if I tell you I'm-I'm – having a crisis of faith. And I need you."

"You're bad at lying, Tiv."

She'd always been bad at it. Which was how Yasira knew she wasn't doing it now. Tiv had always believed in the Gods, always loved Them with her whole heart. But she'd loved Yasira with her whole heart, too. It had broken something in her when They'd taken Yasira away: that much had been clear over the ansible. But this was worse.

"Please," said Tiv.

Yasira should have turned away then, but she wavered, and Tiv opened her arms.

"You have a girlfriend on Zwerfk," said Yasira, "remember?"

"I do not. Disappeared people don't have girlfriends. She's mourning me already. You know that."

Yasira's heart pounded in her throat. "Tiv, I wish things were different, but..."

"Stop it," said Tiv.

Yasira could not reach for her.

She also could not turn away.

"I've been good," said Tiv. "I was good all my life. So were you."

Or so Tiv had believed, sitting at prayers with her face shining while Yasira pretended not to be bored.

"You didn't know me, Tiv."

"You're not so good at lying, either."

Yasira swallowed hard. It took ages to clear the lump from her throat, to work out how to speak again.

"I can't do anything for you right now," she said at last. "I wish I could. There's only one thing you can do for me. Stay here. Keep safe. Keep not being hurt. And then, when they let you go, forget about me. Move on. Do you understand?"

Tiv lowered her arms to her sides. Her expression said, *I never will.*

Yasira turned and walked out the door. It swished shut behind her like another world ending.

The plan had seemed simple, back in the chair.

First, produce absurd amounts of energy. With God-built technology, that was the easy part.

Second, get a certain kind of chain reaction going to reverse all the patterns that brought Outside energy in to Jai. Outside would tear itself back out of the planet using its own momentum. Thus far, both Akavi's plan and Yasira's were in agreement.

But this device would be designed and built by Yasira, part of the same pattern as Yasira. That made it different. The internal structure of the energy would be different. Not merely reversing entropy – Yasira had already thought of that, and Ev hadn't been wrong when she explained why it couldn't be done – but something else. So the chain reaction would be different... somehow. And that would accomplish... something. It would change things in a better way, a less destructive way... somehow.

She had thought she'd been able to remember. Dammit, it had all been *simple.* She had scripted it out for herself. Why couldn't she remember?

She tapped uselessly at the screen, going in circles. She remembered only vagaries. Pain, terror, and the outlines of a plan. There had been details; lots of details. She was sure about that. But she couldn't remember them.

It was the pattern that held the details. Not her own mind, but the gestalt formed by her mind and the power lent by Ev and the others, working together. Her mind was no longer part of that. She was no longer, in some psychic sense, Outside, hanging by the barest thread from her body. Her mind could only think the regular way now. She remembered the feeling of everything being scripted, but sitting in this stupid cell, distracted by Tiv and every other worry, she couldn't remember what the script had been.

Pain had focused her. Pain had allowed her to slip into that space and past it. Akavi probably hadn't even realized how easy he made it for her. But, although everything ached and felt terrible, she wasn't hurting that way anymore. She wasn't drugged anymore. And she wasn't in the chair.

Well, she was in *a* chair, technically. Maybe she should try for two out of three.

She scanned the room for sharp objects. There were none, but she did have a screen, and her old tablet had broken into sharp-looking pieces when ground underfoot. Other things around here might be breakable, too…

She rose from her work chair, limbs creaking, and went to the small bathroom at the edge of her quarters. The bot followed but did not intrude; she'd already noticed it kept a healthy distance at bathroom times. She studied herself in the mirror for a moment, and frowned at the scrapes and shallow cuts still visible. Her face was wan and ashy, and there were bags under her eyes. She would have to do this fast, before the bot worked out what was going on. She would have a few seconds, maybe. If she was lucky.

She wound up, closed her eyes, and punched straight into the mirror's center. Pain exploded across her knuckles as the glass shattered.

She opened her eyes. Blood and glass lay scattered over the small sink and on the floor. The bot lunged to restrain her a second too late by grabbing her arm. One coin-sized shard fell into her hand and she instinctively squeezed her fist tight.

Glass sliced deep into the meat of her hand. It was enough to make her gasp and bite her tongue; but it was small compared to what she'd been through yesterday. Localized and inexpert. Not enough to send her slipping out of her body. Except maybe if she squeezed harder – maybe if she ground it against the wall and let it slice through the tendons…

The robot grappled at her and pulled her arm away from any available walls. She slammed her hand against its metal chassis instead. The nerves in her hand exploded with complaints and she screamed.

But this was enough, just for a second. Just enough that, through the pain, the dimmest edges of the pattern were visible again, in the distance.

What needed to change, precisely, in the energy she was generating? *This*. And this and this.

She concentrated desperately on what she was thinking. She had to remember long enough, this time, to write it down.

The bot pried her fist open and extracted the glass. Smaller, insectile bots poured out of the walls in a swarm, picking up the broken glass and scrubbing the blood away.

"Self-injury is detrimental to your necessary functioning," said the bot. "You will now be taken for mandatory reconstruction. Please do not resist."

She didn't try. She closed her eyes and went over the design in her mind, again and again, committing the numbers to memory even as she started to forget, again, just why they made sense.

CHAPTER 22

The stars open wide.
There's nothing inside.

MORLOCK FOLK SONG

Akavi stood in his Riayin form on the *Talon's* tiny bridge, days later, watching the blue-green swirl of Jai's surface: suspiciously normal in daylight. No hint of the disarray below was visible to the naked eye.

16:42:11, said his internal clock. *16:42:12*. Not that the clock meant much. He had agreed on a schedule. Yasira had built a machine for him, with the help of a printer. Something ungainly, blocky and messy like so many of Talirr's creations, and about the size of a washing machine. Enga and Sispirinithas would paradrop to the planet's surface and set off the device at precisely 17:00:00, Earth Standard Time. Then... Well, either it would work or it wouldn't.

All his analysis said it would work. Yasira was highly motivated to make it work. She'd expressed an intention to save the planet and he'd seen no deception. Aside from the one self-injury incident, she'd been downcast but obedient. She had worked hard, and the Aletheian angels had said that her design – at least the parts of it they could understand – checked out.

Yet he could not shake the feeling that something was *missing*.

He glanced sideways at Yasira, beside him, flanked by the usual bots and staring down at the planet. She had the look of every broken heretic. Eyes downcast. Shoulders limp. Hair hanging down over her face. Mouth sour with despair.

What had he overlooked? Of course, the very nature of the problem meant Yasira had room to maneuver. If the Aletheian angels could fully understand what she was doing, they would have done it themselves. Gods had Their lore and Their ways of doing things, but Yasira's way required a madness beyond any logic a computer could understand. So there was always the possibility of her sneaking something in and subverting the plan. He'd said so in his reports, weeks ago. He wasn't thinking anything new now, only brooding on things that had nagged at him for days.

What could she turn the device into if she wished? A vindictive bomb, destroying Enga and Sispirinithas and doing nothing to the planet? That was absurd; she would accomplish almost nothing and be punished severely. A vindictive bomb, flaring upwards and destroying the *Talon*? But that would kill both Yasira and Tiv, and Nemesis would destroy the planet anyway. Also – he briefly and compulsively checked – there had been no access to orbital route data. She wouldn't even know where to aim.

Could she have built it for the reverse of the intended effect? To make Jai more infected instead of less? But that was illogical. It had all the disadvantages of the bomb strategy. She would die. Tiv would die. Millions would suffer and the planet would burn to an ember.

Of course, then there was the Outside entity – or entities – who had helped Dr Talirr corrupt Jai in the first place. Did *they* care about the things that would have stayed Yasira's hand? Would they choose to work with her? Against her? He had taken care to prevent her from being contacted in dreams but there was no guarantee that they might not find some other way. They were, by their very nature, impossible to predict. Blind, mad, uncaring. But that meant they had no more motive to work against Akavi than against anyone else.

He sighed shortly. Absurd doubts. He had made these plans, double and triple-checked them. Nemesis Herself had analyzed them and given Her electronic stamp of approval. Nemesis understood what was at stake here, both for humanity and for Herself. She would give a more thorough analysis than Akavi ever could, and

She would never work against Her own best interest. That idea was as absurd as…

Wait.

Wait.

Impossible. But, no, not impossible at all. Logical, if one looked at the problem a certain way, and it would explain…

Damn it. Enga and Sispirinithas were already down there, outside the range of communications and impossible to reach but with any but the crudest measures.

16:59:59, said his internal clock.

He whirled towards Yasira, pinging Irimiru for a text-sending link at the highest priority. *Emergency. I need an airstrike to the following coordinates…*

17:00:00.

Far below him, on the planet's surface, something crimson bloomed.

16:42:11, said the console clock in front of Yasira.

She felt neither expectation nor triumph. She didn't feel much of anything. She'd followed the plan as best she could. It would not be enough.

She'd wanted, in that great and foolish first bloom of faith, not to hurt anyone. But that was impossible. There was no plan, in any possible world branching from this one, that didn't hurt anybody.

Yasira, the human, had wanted everyone to live. The pattern did not care. People were lies. So Yasira had wrested this solution from the air with human strength. It was imperfect. It would hurt people, *immensely* many people. Just fewer people than would be hurt in any other plan.

Jai would not be destroyed. Most people down there would live. Tiv would be safe – Yasira didn't remember how she'd made sure of that, but she remembered imposing that condition on the pattern. That meant Tiv would be sent home to Zwerfk, and Yasira, well…

Yasira didn't matter.

16:53:41. She stared at the surface of Jai. The fluttering in her stomach might have been excitement. It might have been fear.

This was going to be so tiny and useless, compared to what she'd wanted.

16:58:04.

The fluttering became a twitch.

The twitch became a pattern.

The device down there on the planet's surface was connected to her in ways even the Gods could not see. That had been Outside's gift. It was what remained of the part of her that had opened its eyes in the prayer machine and fully understood that space and location were lies. That part of her had planned for the device to be a part of her, too. So that her will would affect the outcome. Not through anything detectable by the angels who pored over the mechanical parts of the plan. Just her. Just, she supposed, her soul.

She did not know what it would feel like when that happened. Maybe nothing. Maybe all the information the device needed, it already had. Or maybe she would see everything, all at once, the same as in the prayer machine or worse. It might destroy her.

She didn't much care. Outside might be beautiful, might be powerful; she might be an inextricable part of it. But Outside did not care for her any more than she cared for specific cells in her body. In some sense it did not even know she was there.

This would all be done with in a minute, either way.

Her eyes rose without her conscious intent, fixing on a spot on the globe below.

16:59:59.

Something turned red.

17:00:00.

And then Yasira's mind flew out in every direction at once.

Down in an abandoned field on the surface of Jai, Enga Afonbataw Konum of Nemesis lugged Yasira's device along. This had already happened, but time was a lie; Yasira could see it because she was not Dr Yasira Shien anymore, just now. She was the pattern, and the pattern saw everything.

Enga's cybernetic arms creaked as she came to rest in the field's center, in the midst of a patch of varicolored fruits. Fruits in the shapes of loops and squiggles, fruits that grew straight out the end of a blade of grass, all sorts of illogical fruits. As she hauled the machine out of its casing and set it up, flicking the series of switches on its side, the grass wriggled itself flat. The fruits hid themselves under tendrils of green.

"Why, Enga," said the Spider at her side through his translator. "Even the local vegetation fears you."

SHUT UP, said Enga.

Sispirinithas shrugged, a quivering ten-legged motion entirely unlike human shrugging, and took an experimental bite of fruit.

Enga flipped another switch. The hum of operation rose. Wind blew in a spiral around the two of them.

There was no explosion. No loud noise. The air around them turned red, but it was not uncommon for the sky to change color on Jai. At the edges, where the red faded back into summer-blue, everything began to shimmer.

The basement was only half-finished, thick brown carpet between rough concrete walls. It was strewn with mattresses, blankets, stray books and other belongings, ripe with the stink of half a dozen scared squatters. Qiel Huong patted helplessly at Lingin's limbs, trying desperately to calm the child down as he thrashed and screamed. The bite in his foot was swelling and she couldn't even get a good look at it. The damned bugs infesting the basement were nine inches long and could squish themselves, roach-like, into the tiniest crevice. More and more of them lately, in spite of Juorie making the rounds, spraying every kind of pesticide into the corners. But the bugs had never actually attacked someone before.

"Just hold still," she begged. "Just let me take a look at this, okay, Lingin, and I'll put on some cream and a bandage and that will make it feel better, okay?"

As if a medicine made for mosquitoes and black flies could be trusted to work on a thing like this. Lingin aimed a kick at her face and she scrambled backwards.

A shimmer traveled briefly through the stale basement air. Qiel ignored it. Things shimmered all the time here. Lingin abruptly stilled, though, and stared at the place where the shimmer had been.

"Honey?" said Qiel.

"It's no use," Juorie muttered from the other side of the room. "Qiel, you know he's going mad. You *know*. And these things are going to eat us all before the angels even – oh, Gods, there's another one!"

Juorie reached for a heavy book. Lingin, who usually wailed at the sight of the bugs, sat straight and followed it with his eyes. His perpetually flyaway hair settled itself into a different, equally disordered position, as if brushed by wind.

"Go away," he said – his first coherent words for days.

The bug paused, twitched, and then scuttled out of sight. Juorie slammed the book down in its wake and missed.

"Go away," Lingin said again, quite calmly. He reached out and touched the concrete wall, trailing his hand along the perimeter. "Go away. Go away."

"The fuck?" said Juorie. She paused, and then, with the hesitance of someone inured to false hope, asked: "Honey, are you feeling better?"

But Qiel already knew. Something had changed inside her, too.

The device would, as promised, tap into Jai's energy fields and start a chain reaction. But not to reverse the fields' direction. Merely to shift them bit by bit, until, like a river redirecting itself around an obstacle, they found a new shape.

Ev herself had said that the fields could be redirected; control could be given up. She had argued that no mortal mind, however augmented, was strong enough to take that control.

But it didn't have to be just one mind.

In fifteen different alleyways in fifteen different cities, a monster the size of a city bus chased a man. The man panted as he fled, soaked with fear-sweat. He'd made a wrong turn among his usual escape routes, or else the layout of the local streets had changed again, and the monster was too close on his heels. It roared and he felt its breath.

The air shimmered.

In fifteen different cities, fifteen different things happened to the monster. It unraveled. It shrank. It grabbed the man with a tooth-lined tentacle, then made an expression of disgust and withdrew. It lay down on its side and went to sleep. It turned, with a morose little growl and walked the other way. In one city, a single city, it grabbed the man anyway and crunched him down, bones snapping between its teeth, like normal.

In the other fourteen cities, a man crouched, shaking and catching his breath. He had breath. He had muscles and a beating heart. Alive. Alive.

Outside could not be removed from the world; entropy, and the limits of Yasira's ability, prevented that. It was infinitely intermixed into the lie that had once been Jai. To remove it would destroy everyone; it would be to remove the planet from itself.

Outside did not care about people or their survival. But people cared about people. Outside had been mixed with them now. And the nature of the mixture – *that* could change.

In the remains of a parking garage, sixteen gone people sat motionless, raising their bloody fingertips towards a central light. It was the only light in the available space; a few splinters of sunlight fell in through the cracked walls, where a horde of rainbow-striped vines had broken in, but they were pale in comparison.

When the air shimmered, the light twisted in place like a flickering candle. Some people squirmed, or smiled, or rubbed their eyes. One, an old woman, began to cry. But no one's focus wavered.

When the shimmer had passed, the light changed. Tendrils of light shot out from the central point, branching again and again into geometric tessellations. Colors shifted and patterns spun out until a tapestry of sixteen works of glowing art surrounded the gathering, each a little different from its neighbor.

To the gone people, this meant something very profound, but it cannot be recorded in words.

At the same time as all this:

In Jai's outer atmosphere, three dozen unmanned satellites of Philophrosyne pinged radio signals at the planet one hundred times a second each, tirelessly, incapable of boredom.

Ping.

Host not found.

Ping.

Host not found.

The satellites did not detect the shimmer in the air far below them. They were basic models, entirely without sentience, which was what allowed them to do their job. No one had equipped them with shimmer-detecting equipment. Only persistence.

Ping.

Host not found.

Ping.

Resolving host... Host found. Coordinates confirmed: Perseus arm -> WASP-68 -> Jai -> Arinn -> 50° 03' 55" S, 103° 42' 24" E -> 261.488.482.279. Testing security certificate and performing security scan...

All over the galaxy, servers and processors began to light up. Overseers of Philophrosyne, each maintaining a full map of the ansible nets in auxiliary memory, became aware of a blinking. The entire planet was suddenly flicking back on. The message propagated at the speed of thought past Overseers to Archangels, disembodied neurological cores at the center of dense tangles of wires, thinking furiously in their nutrient baths. Thoughts pooled between them for a long, tense tenth of a second, and then were transmitted ever upwards, through stranger channels yet.

Nemesis, said the message from Philophrosyne to Her Sister – or at least, we can pretend that this was the message, that the Gods used anything comparable to human language in Their hall of stars

– you're going to want to see this.

Nemesis already knew, of course. Nemesis had known before anyone else did. Six of Her Ha-Mashhit-class warships, each capable of melting a continent from orbit, were already gliding into place.

Ping.

Host found.

The ansible chimed, and Kiong Muak Miau, Priest of Techne, turned to it in sudden delight. Like most priests of Techne – most priests of *most* of the Gods – he'd learned enough over the years to jury-rig small scripts and repairs. And so, in the background, ever since the disaster on Jai, he'd had his system running a periodic check. A call to one address planetside in particular. To a secretary at one of the businesses prosperous enough to have its own ansible on site.

He'd been keeping it very quiet. Priests were allowed to have relationships outside their work, but… a relationship this intense, this desperate, this damned *distracting*, would be a minor embarrassment. He'd wanted to keep it to himself.

The ansible rang and rang again. A round startled face suddenly stared at him from the other end.

"Leng," he blurted.

"Kiong. I can *see* you."

"You're alive."

"Yes! Yes, everyone's alive down here, except for southern Riayin, and even some of those might be alive, last I heard. Gods, it's good to hear your voice."

The connection in his head, which had been quiescent for days, bloomed suddenly, painfully bright. *Kiong Muak Miau of Techne, communication with Jai is not currently authorized. The situation is too volatile. Desist.*

But–

Desist.

He winced, holding a hand to his temple at the sheer strength of the command. Why would the Gods turn the ansibles back on if mortals weren't supposed to use them? It made no sense.

"Kiong? Honey, are you all right?"

"Yeah," he lied. It wasn't the first time the Gods had done something strange. He'd think about it later. "Look, I've got to go for now. I'll talk later, okay?"

Before Leng could respond, Kiong's hand found the button marked *End Call.* The connection went quiet and the pain ended.

What was that about? he prayed. *What's going on?*

The Gods, as was often Their way, did not answer.

Airstrike request denied, Irimiru sent crisply. *You might want to look at your feed.*

But Akavi had already seen it. He could barely make out Yasira's small form in front of him through the thicket of notifications now crowding up his consciousness. Yasira was screaming, for some reason, but then, she had plenty of reasons to be upset; he would deal with that in a moment.

The barriers around the planet were going down. The energy fields palpably changing. Was this victory? Surely this was victory. He had been sure, for a moment, that Yasira had betrayed him. He had thought he'd seen a flicker of it in her face. But this had been groundless. Surely. The barriers were going down now and the energy fields reversing. So he had been wrong to worry. Yasira's genius lay in physics and in whatever mad realms of knowledge dwelled Outside. Not deception, strategy, anticipating an adversary's actions. That was his own domain. He had, as always, overestimated his opponent.

Hadn't he?

But the murmuring in his ears, the shifting of currents of attention through the live and automated parts of the net, this was not a triumphant murmur. There was a wrong note in it. Concern. Even though, according to every chart and sensor reading he could call up, matched with concurrent error-barred projections from the Aletheian angels' simulations, the energy was receding as scheduled...

No.

No, not quite.

It had not been visible at first, even to Akavi's senses. But the recession was slowing. Diverting itself, in the most infinitesimal amounts, sideways. Not a withdrawal, but a shift to a different pattern.

And... and the ansible nets. What were they doing?

Akavi ran likely scenarios over quickly in his head. The machine had been supposed to work more-or-less instantaneously, and from close to the epicenter of the plague. Burn the surface out first, *then* move up, dismantling whatever blocks kept the Gods from contacting the populace. But if the blocks came down first, if the populace began to connect to each other all over the place, in an absurd false hope... Well.

The problem with that was that it tied Nemesis' hands. The blocks on the ansible network had made things difficult, but in their way, they were also a boon. If Jai were sealed off, then Nemesis could do almost anything without inspiring a mortal rebellion. She could simply explain that no one had lived down there in the affected areas, that those who survived were irretrievably mad and suffering terribly. That it was better this way. If the ansible nets had come back online in a controlled way, as a result of the Gods' actions and at the time of their choosing, then they could have been used strategically to back up that point. To show citizens being dismembered by monsters, or whatever else made effective propaganda at the time.

Zhoshash, and the other areas that the Gods had destroyed, had been small enough that the Gods had managed to time their destruction to when no one was looking. Their disasters had come on quickly enough, and been poorly enough reported, that blaming them on the Keres had been plausible.

But a fifth of a planet, a fifth of a planet which was actively communicating... It was an impossibility. Wholesale destruction was off the table, and so were a variety of other useful methods. Employ them now and mortals would rise up. Maybe not immediately, but their trust would be broken, and that only led to one thing.

Yasira had destroyed Akavi's plans far more effectively than in any scenario he'd envisioned. And she had removed his ability to retaliate.

Odd that Irimiru and the rest of the net had worked it out it before him; his senses were usually quicker than that. He had been focused on this project more than anyone, surely. It was almost like they'd…

No. It was *exactly* like they'd known in advance.

Not, of course, that anyone had known just what would happen. The chatter on the nets was chatter of genuine alarm; the effectiveness of Yasira's strategy had surpassed anyone's expectations. But Irimiru and her other angels had expected, somehow, that Akavi would fail. That this last-ditch attempt to remove the plague from Jai would not, in fact, remove it. Yet they had not informed him. Had not called off the mission. They had simply looked on as he failed.

As soon as Akavi allowed himself the thought, he understood. Why this would be the protocol, on an already-hopeless mission, helmed by an already-failing Inquisitor. And for the first time in a very long time, Akavi Averis, Inquisitor of Nemesis, felt despair.

"Mom. Dad."

"Equanimity."

"Dule."

"My love."

"I'm alive. We're all alive down here."

"I don't know what's been blocking the ansibles but we're okay in Helpfulness Valley. It's Riayin that's taken the big hits, and we only have rumors from there."

"We're okay in Xuia so far. They say the plague area's growing but not very fast, and maybe with the ansibles working again, maybe we'll be able to take a portal out now. Maybe."

"Everything's terrible here. Half of us are dead and half of the rest went crazy. But I'm alive here. Zins is alive, so is Chu. Is help coming? You calling us means that there's help coming, right?"

"The Gods will protect us, right? They're working out a way to fix all this, right?"

"It sounds crazy, Mom, but I think things might be getting better. Mom, listen, I know this sounds really, really crazy, but I think they're starting to *listen* to me."

"There was a hole in the ground coming at us – no, don't ask me how a hole in the ground can come at someone, you haven't been *down* here. Listen. I stopped it. That hasn't happened before. I couldn't do it before, but something changed, and I saved everyone. Something's changing, Peing. I swear to you. Something's getting better."

Yasira had known, had always known, that it didn't really matter what she did. However cleverly she changed things down on Jai, Nemesis could just blow up the planet. Yasira couldn't stop that, not directly.

What would stay a God's hand? No amount of firepower ever could. But mortals would. Gods needed mortals; Gods needed their trust and their souls. So, in the long view, Gods could not win a war with mortals using firepower, either. Because any action they took had to be an action they could justify.

So when you were up against a God who wanted to kill you, who wanted to convince the rest of the universe that you were better off dead, the only weapon was *hope*.

It was no guarantee, but it was like Ev had told her, back at the *Alhazred*. To fight a lie, you didn't have to use guns. Just the truth.

Oseu Mugoaxes, Helmswoman of Nemesis, tapped her long fingernails against the console of the Ha-Mashhit-class warship she commanded, counting seconds. She was, according to normal angelic protocol, the only living being aboard. The ship waited around her, its processes ebbing and flowing in a perceptual-cognitive rhythm which resembled breath, an extension of her senses and will. With this ship, she could break planets to pieces, end worlds.

Though it wasn't usually a world that she ended, was it? Not a real one. Not a whole planet, and never human-inhabited. She had heard of such assignments before, but only as rumors. Of course she had been briefed; of course she had been told the rationale for this assignment, and had accepted it without doubt. Helms of Nemesis who doubted didn't last very long.

Still, it was a change from the usual Keres-ships, alien craft, other small fry. Everything was small fry compared to a Ha-Mashhit. She usually traveled either alone or escorting an extremely large transport. Now she was one of six Helms of exactly her size.

It was going to be quite the light show. What was taking so bloody long?

She tapped, once, twice, again, in enormous irritation, as her peripheral senses watched the ansible nets light further and further up. That was going to cause problems, wasn't it? She did tactics, not strategy, but...

She thought, briefly, of blasting them herself before it could get worse.

Helms of Ha-Mashhit-class warships did *not* open fire until given the order by their Overseer. It was not done. Not even against the Keres. One did not use this kind of power lightly.

Fully thirty seconds passed.

Stand down, came the order finally. *Stand down, and prepare for new orders.*

Oseu Mugoaxes did as she was told.

The message came to Akavi, not directly from Irimiru, but through the most official channels: boilerplate orders, executed by the will of Nemesis Herself, electronically stamped and processed for the public record by Her coterie of Archangels.

Akavi Averis of Nemesis, it said. *Due to egregious, continued failure in an ongoing, critical mission, you are hereby relieved of duty. Any angels and sell-souls reporting to you will be immediately reassigned. Please stand by for punishment and termination. We will be with you shortly.*

In the same instant, the rest of the connections in his brain winked permanently off. He was alone. No recourse back to Irimiru to plead his case – not that they would have listened. No line to Elu or Enga. No ability to command his own ship, or even his own ship's bots.

Even manual command would no longer function. The ship's portal would no longer answer to him. The programs and files in his head, the other treatments in his body, still made him more than mortal – but he was cut off from everything else in the angelic world. The lonely emptiness he had experienced outside the galaxy, the feeling of being trapped in static blackness, closed in: worse now, because he knew it was forever.

And he would soon be worse off than that, much worse off than any mortal. Worse even than Yasira while he tortured her. He knew those protocols, too.

Not a muscle moved in Akavi's face as his mind examined these facts, searching for a loophole. His hands clenched until the knuckles turned an opaque white; he had lost his Riayin face and reverted to his true form, cells gone slack with shock, without noticing. In the crevices formed by the lines of his palms, blood welled.

CHAPTER 23

Reality is a lie. We dream it into existence and we viciously punish those who deny the dream. I have been told that it could not be otherwise. That it is human nature for all of us to dream, even me. That if we wish to exist, we can never stop dreaming.

But what if we all chose to dream something else?

FROM THE DIARIES OF DR EVIANNA TALIRR

And then Yasira's consciousness snapped back into her.

She was done. It was finished.

She crumpled to the floor.

Everything hurt. Everything hurt so much. She was only vaguely aware that she'd been screaming. The cold metal of the floor pressed into her hands and thighs. Akavi loomed nearby, looking Vaurian again for some reason, but he wasn't moving.

She had given the pattern everything. It had done what was needed, then dropped her like an empty snack wrapper. Like so many fingernail clippings.

The prayer machine had brought Outside to her against Outside's will. It had pulled the energy out of inexpressible unplaces through Ev's genius and Ev's desperation. But this? This had been her acting in accordance with Outside's plans. She had needed no machine. And in return for her work, for her *self*, she had been given two things. First, knowledge. She had seen enough to know for certain, despite whatever she might be told here, that the plan had gone right.

And, second: a way out.

She knew, because it was part of her plan, that Akavi would no longer be an angel. He had failed, and Nemesis did not forgive failure. But that did not mean she would be spared. Akavi was still on the *Talon* with her, and even if he was somehow dealt with, another angel would come sooner or later. Yasira had known this all along. She had made provisions for Tiv's safety but she had known there was no saving herself. She was a heretic. She would die in agony. Then Nemesis, the God who dealt with heretics, would snatch up her soul. Her afterlife would be even worse than whatever came before.

But Yasira was a lie. And Yasira did not have to be there for any of what happened next. She had become one with Outside, after all. Her body, even the part of her soul that the Gods could reach, was nothing. She did not have to feel what happened to either of them. She did not have to feel anything ever again.

She was done.

She could sleep.

She closed her eyes.

"You betrayed me," Akavi said, in a voice shaky and soft with rage, somewhere very far away. "You *disobeyed* me."

Yasira wasn't listening.

Outside no longer terrified her; how could it? The terror came from clinging to existence, and she was past that now. Outside spread itself like a net below her. All she had to do was let herself fall. So she did. She welcomed the sensation of the world falling away. Space spiraled up around her into limitless unnameable dimensions, her own consciousness crumbling to pieces.

Pieces the pattern would reuse, eventually. It was all right.

Akavi grabbed her by the jaw, a sensation that did not bother her anymore; she was scarcely in her body. His rage was banked now, an almost instantaneous change: he was cool again, cold, a mask. His voice was level and clipped. "You betrayed me. Of course. I should have anticipated it; I very nearly did. But you must realize that this means our little deal is now off. Whatever the rest of the angelic corps might do, I am perfectly capable of visiting untold horrors upon Productivity Hunt in the time remaining before they arrive.

So I suggest we renegotiate. Now."

Wait.

Tiv.

She had provided for Tiv's safety, but how? She couldn't remember. She had made the plan, and she had trusted it.

But Tiv was not safe. She could feel that, in the last fragmented parts of herself that felt. Nothing was stopping Akavi from hurting her, for the moment; and no one was coming to save her. There was no particular reason why the next angels of Nemesis, arriving to deal with Akavi, would be inclined to let her go.

Had Outside lied? Was that possible? Had Yasira lied, to herself, making the plan? Maybe one of them had known, in those terrible hours of calculation, that Tiv would never be safe. And that Yasira would never act, even to save billions more, unless she believed otherwise.

But that wasn't acceptable. That was bullshit. That was *wrong*. If no one else was coming to save Tiv, then Yasira's job wasn't *done*.

She needed Tiv.

So oblivion was not an option after all.

Fine. She would show him how to renegotiate.

With an effort like the redirection of a planet, Yasira pushed her way fully back into the lie of her body. She didn't quite fit into it now, but there was a snap – a series of snaps – as she forced her way in anyway. Sensation burned back into her skin. Something of a sense of place and self flared up brightly. And pain, everywhere, sharp pain and dull pain and every kind in between. She had fallen without noticing when she chose to sleep, and her skull throbbed where it had hit the metal floor. Pain, she understood now, was the price of being here and alive.

Black radiance flew out from her body in all directions. It caught Akavi's body and wrenched him away from her. His fingernails, claws really, scrabbled at her face and tore away. He flew back. Thrashed, screamed, instinctively. An animal caught in a net. The radiance tightened around him. Held him immobile, at last, against the steel bulkhead.

Bones aching, head pounding, joints groaning in protest, Yasira stood.

She looked him in the eye. He stopped screaming, after a minute, and stared back. Maybe silenced by whatever the radiance was, maybe choosing not to speak. That was all right. She had nothing to say to him, either.

It occurred to her to wonder how she was controlling the radiance, whether it was under her control. As soon as the question occurred to her, the answer faded away. The pain intensified. No, she wasn't much more than Yasira, was she? She couldn't have it both ways. The full pattern couldn't stay in one body for long.

Maybe she could direct the radiance consciously in this state. Maybe not. She could tell it to kill him, but something in her rebelled at that. She had once been so determined not to cause death. It hadn't been that simple, but whether Akavi lived or died at her hand didn't matter, did it? The angels would come soon enough to kill him themselves.

She was here for Tiv. That was the only reason she'd come back. So. Get Tiv. Get Tiv to safety. And then…

Yasira turned, despite the protests of her body. She took a step, then paused. The portal at the back of the room was flickering. It wasn't the normal smooth transition between locations. It was radiating static like a malfunctioning television, and Yasira couldn't see where it led. She had a second of déjà vu again – yes, she'd forgotten, but there *had* been another part to the pattern's plan–

The next second, Dr Evianna Talirr walked into the room.

She looked different. It was hard to put a finger on; it was the way she held herself. Tired, with new bags under her eyes and new fraying at the end of her ponytail. Was the ponytail longer? No, that must be Yasira's imagination. Instead of a lab coat she wore travelers' garments, faded, coming apart at the hems. She carried a small and probably illegal handgun, which Yasira had never seen with her before. But there was no mistaking that face.

Yasira remembered this part of the plan now. Yasira's mission, and that of Splió and the others, would be over when Ev was delivered, alive or dead, to Nemesis' forces. Akavi was no longer one of Nemesis' forces, but the *Talon* was. By entering the ship, Ev completed the cycle. It was a technicality – she was probably planning to leave again shortly – but Nemesis thrived on technicalities. She was here, and that meant it wasn't only Yasira who was freed. It was everyone.

Yasira seethed. It was everyone *but* Tiv. All of the people contaminated with what Akavi had called Outside madness, all the ones who had been able to connect to her under torture. Tiv was not contaminated, so to the pattern, she was... what, invisible? Why had the pattern forgotten her?

It ought not to have surprised her, she thought bitterly. Outside, in the end, was no more human than the Gods.

"Thank you, Yasira," said Ev. "I mean that. I've learned a great deal from you."

She raised the hand that wasn't holding the gun. With a shiver, the darkness around Akavi reformed itself: spreading until it coated the outer walls and bulkhead like a layer of dust. A few stray ropes remained around Akavi, pinning his enraged form in place.

"There," said Ev. "That will disable the self-destruct, block ansible signals, and scramble all other outgoing energy. That way we won't be interrupted." She looked over at the ship's navigation panels. "Engage the warp drive, pick a direction at random, and fly that way at top speed until further notice. Assuming the warp energy is scrambled like everything else, *that* will stop them from boarding us the hard way."

The *Talon* responded to her, which made no sense. Ev made no sense. She felt like Ev and like not-Ev. A Vaurian? But a Vaurian angel – or a Vaurian mortal, for that matter – wouldn't have been able to command Outside things.

She looked like she'd been gone a long time, like she'd traveled further than anyone possibly could have in the week since they'd last spoke. She looked *older*. Was that possible? Of course it was. Ev traveled time, sometimes.

Yasira did not care.

"Now, then," said Ev. "I wanted to talk."

"I need to get Tiv," Yasira said. It was not a clever thing to say, but words were hard. Stick with the script. Find Tiv, take Tiv home… and ignore Ev? It was all that she could think of at the moment.

Ev shrugged. "If you like. I wanted to talk to you first, but I had things to say to Akavi, too, so take your time."

She frowned a moment, looking left and right for bots, then shrugged and tossed the handgun aside. It slid over the floor and bumped up against Yasira' feet. Ev didn't look at it. She was already facing Akavi. She seemed to recognize him somehow, though he'd looked different when last they spoke.

Yasira turned to get Tiv, and then turned back. *Stick with the script, dammit,* said a chorus in her head, but how could she leave these two together? She didn't even know what was going on. So she stood, exhausted, rooted to the spot.

"You think," said Akavi, "that you can get away with this."

"Why not?" said Ev. "I got away with nearly everything else."

"Nemesis will find you. Nemesis will tear you into pieces so small that not even an atom remains."

"That tune's gotten old. Try a new one. How about this? How about *you* work with *me.*" She tucked a finger under his chin. "We'd have to restrain you a lot to make Yasira feel comfortable, but I think it would work. You see what's going to happen. A year from now, there will be forces rising, groups that stand a fighting chance against lies. You no longer have any place with Nemesis, but that doesn't mean no one could use you. You see, I've learned a few things since we last spoke. I was arrogant and simplistic in my dealings with people before. You're intelligent about people. Not moral or sensitive, but intelligent. We could use that, under certain constraints. Why not? Why not put aside our mutual insistence on killing all the things we disagree with and work together. Under my direction, of course."

The tips of Yasira's fingers shook a little.

Why would Ev make such an offer? Because Ev was the bastard Ev always was. Ev was as selfish as the rest of Outside. Ev wanted what Ev wanted, and Ev used the pattern to get there. It had worked, hadn't it? Ev had prayed for someone to understand her, and she'd gotten Yasira. Ev had wanted Jai to change, and Yasira had changed it more deeply, permanently, securely than Ev could ever have done by herself. Yasira hadn't gotten what she wanted in the end. Ev had.

She had used Yasira. She would use Akavi, too. With both of them together, even more people would die.

Contempt filled Akavi's voice. "You actually think you can make me that offer. You think Nemesis won't simply vaporize the planet, and any other world you ever touch."

"The evidence points that way, yes. Think of this as reciprocity. You were kind enough to offer me a job, back on the *Alhazred*. Now I–"

Yasira picked up the handgun and pulled the trigger twice.

Her aim was not precise. The first bullet went wild, bouncing off the bulletproof bulkhead and clattering to the ground. The second opened a crimson hole below Akavi's ribs. Akavi made a small, startled movement and sank to the ground. The blackness around him began to dissipate. She very nearly pulled the trigger again, but a rising panic stayed her hand.

Ev deserved to be shot, even moreso than Akavi. Ev was the one who had started all this.

She was also the only person besides Yasira capable of understanding what had just happened.

What did it matter? It wasn't like Yasira could ask her to explain. To mentor her again. Anything Ev said would be bullshit anyway. And more people would die.

But.

Ev turned and looked at her. Yasira didn't lower the gun.

"Interesting," said Ev.

"Don't patronize me," Yasira snapped. "That's all I am to you. I'm *interesting*. I'm a toy that you get when you pray the right way. So you can use me to solve problems for you, burn me out, and throw me away."

"Oh, that," said Ev. She seemed unfazed by the handgun pointed at her face, but it could have been Ev's usual flat affect. "No, I would say that is not a correct summary at all."

Yasira snorted.

"I didn't use you," said Ev. "Things would have gone quite differently if I had. I thought you'd run away for good, on purpose, at first. I thought it was my fault, and in a way, it was. I made a lot of mistakes with you. But what I'd wanted – what I would have made happen if I could perfectly control people's actions – was for you to stay with me. To do things my way. We'd run away as far as we could from the gods and leave a trail of blasted planets in our wake. You falling into Akavi's hands wasn't my plan. And the way that you dealt with that, once it had happened… I never would have thought of it. I never cared enough. Your plan was subtler, and more human, and more brilliantly difficult for the gods than anything I would have thought of. You did have some support from me and others, some of our processing power, when you thought it up. But the plan in its essence? That was yours."

Then why wasn't Tiv in the plan? The gun shook in Yasira's hand. "I don't believe you."

But part of her did. Part of her wanted desperately to believe.

Part of her wanted to pull the trigger, shoot and shoot until she could be sure Ev would never move again. Part of her wanted to cling to Ev and never let go. Part of her, still, just wanted to die and forget about everything. There seemed to be a lot of parts of her jangling around, trying to fit back together in her body the way they had used to.

"You won't," said Ev. "Not for a long time."

"I don't believe you," Yasira repeated. "I don't. I'll never believe a thing you say ever again. I should shoot you."

"If you like," said Ev diffidently.

"I would have every right," said Yasira, shaking harder now. "No one would blame me if I did. It's up to me."

"Of course. Why do you think I gave you the gun?"

Yasira lowered her arms, very slightly, very slowly.

Shoot her, urged one part of Yasira. *Shoot her now. Before she gets free and does Gods know what else to the galaxy. You can't trust her when she says she's learned. You can't trust anything. Shoot her.*

I hate you, said another. *Shooting's too good for you.*

Don't leave me, wailed a third.

Ev smiled.

"I'll see you again, I think. I hope. Not soon. But I think I will, if you let me live. When you're ready."

She walked to the portal. Yasira kept the gun half-trained on her all the way until she'd disappeared inside. And, uselessly, for several seconds afterwards.

"What's going on?" said Tiv, standing up suddenly from the edge of the bed. "Are you all right? The console just got black and sparkly and... stopped working, and... There's blood on you."

"It's okay," said Yasira.

"But what..."

"It's okay," Yasira repeated. She could barely formulate any other words. "Just... This way. Close your eyes."

Tiv, the good girl, nodded and rose. She took Yasira's hand and followed her to the *Talon's* bridge. Her face was pale and her grip shaky. She kept her eyes closed. Yasira's shoes left tiny crescents of blood – Akavi's – on the metal floor.

He lay there, perfectly still, in a slowly-growing pool of blood. His blood, somehow, looked the same as anyone's. Yasira had expected to feel guilty, looking at the body, but she was too exhausted to feel much of anything. She'd feel guilty later. Or angry later. Or relieved later, or triumphant that he'd never be able to hurt her again. Maybe all of them. Whatever.

She had a plan – a mortal plan, now, not the Outside plan – and she needed to carry it out quickly. Tiv had to go back to Zwerfk. Back to Ship Lake. Back to a normal life – which was the one place Yasira could never go again. And she had to do it without the angels intercepting them.

But the best way to do that was to use Outside.

"You did something, didn't you?" said Tiv tremulously, eyes still closed. "You... took over the ship. Yasira, are you...? I mean, is...?"

"I'll explain everything," Yasira lied. "Later."

Tiv bit the inside of her lower lip. "Okay."

Yasira looked at the portal and visualized, as clearly as she could, the inside of the airlock in Ev's secret lair. She wouldn't go all the way in, she told herself. It was just a way point. A stop on the way out of here, which could immediately be used again to get to Zwerfk. Tiv need never see it again. Or at all.

The lair's steel walls, barer and uglier than the filigreed metal of a God-built ship, appeared out of the static. Yasira stepped through and tugged Tiv in behind her.

The familiar feeling of Outside in the air closed in around them both, and so did a feeling of relief, something Yasira couldn't immediately explain, as if her job was really done now. She wavered, the exhaustion suddenly stronger than ever. She wasn't done. Tiv wasn't safe.

Tiv breathed in sharply. "Where are we? This feels creepy."

"Just a second," said Yasira. "Just…"

Her tongue thickened in her mouth, and words stopped coming.

She knew what she wanted to say. She was losing speech, shutting down too quickly, but she could still hear the words in her head. *It's okay. This is just a step between stops. Keep your eyes closed. Turn around. Now picture, as hard as you can, your home back in Zwerfk. You're going home. Believe that, okay? Picture it as clearly as you can, and then take a step forward.*

Don't worry. I'll be right behind you.

Tiv would be sad later. When she realized that last part was a lie. That Yasira had stayed behind, and that Tiv didn't know the way back. But Yasira's life had already been destroyed. Not fair to do that to Tiv's life, too. And the only way not to do it to Tiv was to make sure that this was nothing to Tiv but a bad, surreal dream. To make sure she never came back here, never even had the ghost of a clue how.

It wasn't like Tiv was really hers, anyway.

"Tiv, this…" she tried, helplessly. "I…"

Akavi had told her she was unusually resilient. What a load of bullshit. She couldn't even keep it together long enough to do this one, simple thing.

Black spots danced in front of her eyes. Her knees creaked under her own weight like an eighty-year-old's knees.

"What?" said Tiv, eyelids fluttering open.

"I…" she said again.

Darkness reached out for her. This wasn't the darkness of non-being. That, Yasira knew, would not be an option again. This was plain, simple, shock and exhaustion. But, as her legs began to give out, it took her just the same.

EPILOGUE

Death is a lie.

FROM THE DIARIES OF DR EVIANNA TALIRR

Akavi faded in and out of consciousness. Sometimes he was lucid enough to notice the time. Occasionally he took note of the sensory warnings blaring in his internal circuitry: *Stomach and small intestine perforated. Blood loss at critical levels. Communication channels for emergency medical response not found. Seek mortal or angelic medical assistance immediately: you are in hypovolemic shock.*

Not that it mattered; he was scheduled for termination anyway. The gun had only saved some effort for some other angel.

Instead of attempting to fix himself, he considered the situation.

Akavi had not only failed. He had been set up to fail. He had been given an impossible assignment. He had spun his wheels trying to carry it out for three years, and then finally everything had spun out of control.

Irimiru, too, had been given an impossible assignment. That was how it worked. Overseers were handed down goals and told to delegate them among underlings as they saw fit. Yet Irimiru would never take responsibility for the failure. Failure was death. And failure in the angelic corps must have a cause. All things must be possible for the Gods, if they were to retain mortal faith. So any failure, even at an impossible task, was some angel or mortal's fault, and that someone must be rooted out and destroyed.

Nemesis, in the task of protecting mortals from Outside and from the heretic known as Dr Evianna Talirr, had failed. Akavi smiled very slightly, inside, at the feeling of allowing himself to think such blasphemy. *She* had failed. She had likely worked that out some time ago: certainly before Akavi sent Yasira down planetside. She could not have known how badly that specific part of the plan would go, or how much Yasira would manage to accomplish; surely, She would have murdered both him and Yasira if She'd known that. But perhaps She had known all along that Talirr was an impossible task, and that Yasira's device would do nothing good. So She had arranged to hide the failure until the right moment: to give the appearance of a possibility of success. So that, when Akavi failed, the failure would truly appear to be his.

Or maybe, in Nemesis' unfathomable mind, this wasn't failure. Maybe She had calculated everything down to the last decimal place and concluded that having Jai fail publicly in this way was the means to an end. Maybe whatever She chose to do next would depend on it.

Either way, She had betrayed him. So had Irimiru. So had Yasira. *Yasira.*

He faded to red. When he became aware of his body again, there were bots moving, touching him. Confusion. When had the bots regained function? Maybe they were another angel's bots. They manhandled his limbs, stuck things into his wrists and stomach. Pain. He was very, very cold, which distressed him even more than the pain. Someone was walking around, but he couldn't quite see.

He blacked out again.

Later, he noticed that his circuitry wasn't screaming at him anymore, and opened his eyes.

He was on his back, looking at the falcon carved in iridescent filigree on the ceiling of his own room aboard the *Talon*. One of his chairs could be folded out and converted to a stretcher; that was probably what he was lying on. There was an IV in his arm.

Elu sat at the side of the room, perfectly still, watching him.

Akavi's mouth twitched, which sent soreness spreading through his face and neck, though it wasn't as bad as before. He suspected he'd been medicated.

"You," he said, forming the sounds carefully and precisely so as not to betray weakness, "are an idiot."

"Sir?"

"What do you think you're going to accomplish here? I'm under a termination order. If I'm not mistaken, you've somehow stowed your way onto my ship in advance of the termination team, breaking every relevant regulation and destroying your own career in the process, just to heal me. Did you not read the wording of the order? It was for me alone. You were to be reassigned, not destroyed. Of course, an insubordinate action like this will change that. I would expect you to sacrifice yourself for me under normal circumstances – it's a predilection I value in underlings – but a sacrifice for no discernible gain is not sacrifice, it is stupidity."

"No, sir," said Elu. "It was a judgement call, and I made it. Didn't you tell me it's past time I stopped behaving like a child?"

Akavi looked at him sidelong.

He had not wanted to admit it to himself, but the boy had been nearly ready. Losing Akavi and being reassigned would have been hard on him, of course. But he would have survived. Probably kept his rank. Perhaps even kept growing and made a competent officer, in time.

Akavi hated waste.

"The termination team couldn't find you," said Elu. "No one could. The *Talon* just vanished off every sensor map, right after it registered Talirr's appearance, and the portal wouldn't function."

"Yes. Outside technology. So you made your way here how, exactly?"

"I'm not sure."

Akavi kept looking at him. Elu nervously wrung his hands.

"The portal wouldn't work for the termination team. It wouldn't work for any of the sell-souls, or even for Irimiru. They all said that there was no signal, that you'd completely vanished. But, sir, it wasn't *true*. I kept feeling... fragments. Connections with different people always felt different to me. Your feelings feel different from Enga's or Irimiru's. I couldn't get a proper signal from you on the ansible, but

I remembered how a signal from you would feel, and I kept getting little, twisted echoes of that feeling. I don't know how to explain."

Akavi could guess. Talirr had blocked the ansible uplinks, but she had done it very casually, likely not expecting to need the block for more than a few minutes. It made perfect sense, in such a circumstance, for cracks to appear. For something tiny, too distorted for God-built sensors, but extant nonetheless, to make its way out.

God-built circuitry had more processing power than a human. Immensely more. But there were things an obsessed, besotted, emotional human mind could do that no circuitry ever could. Like finding a tiny echo of Akavi, by feel, in data too distorted to statistically analyze. That was why the Gods bothered bargaining for human servants in the first place.

"So I said, let me try. They looked at me funny, but they let me. I focused on the feeling of you, and then I went through the portal and wound up here."

"And failed to report back. I see." He paused. His circuitry said it had been many hours since the shooting, but he didn't know at what point in those hours Elu had appeared. How long had it been? Evidently long enough for extensive robot surgery. They were, for the moment, alone.

"I don't know what happened, but the bots weren't working. Nothing was working. I had to manually reboot them all. They barely got to you in time, and then I remembered I had to manually reboot the printers, too, to get a transfusion… It was tricky. I wasn't sure you'd make it."

"And then?"

Elu took a deep breath, in and back out.

"It's up to you, sir, now that you're awake. But here's what I think. So far this Outside effect seems pretty stable. I'd make a wild guess and say we have a week or two before it breaks down. More if we're lucky. Less if we're not. But in a week's time I can uninstall the ship's ansible equipment, remove our uplinks, and remodel the ship to look like a civilian transport. I've already dismantled the self-destruct. We have a printer to see to our needs, and you can look mortal when you want to. Dr Talirr has evaded capture by the Gods for three years, and she doesn't have either of those things going for her. I think we could survive a long time. Maybe find her on our own. Maybe fix what happened today. Maybe redeem yourself."

Akavi snorted, and then wished he hadn't, as pain bloomed radially through his face and neck. Redemption. *Please*. They were angels of Nemesis.

Was it possible Elu could still turn back, change his mind? Was it possible he could reappear on the *Menagerie*, after this, and receive only a reprimand? Impossible to tell without knowing how long it had been, but the odds were against it.

Elu must have run those odds, too. He was naive, but not stupid.

"Let me make something clear," said Akavi. "What you're proposing means you will be alone with me here. Forever, or at least for the rest of our lives. You're not Vaurian; you can't make your circuitry invisible. So you can't ever risk showing yourself. You will not be able to leave the *Talon*. You will be cut off from the ansible nets. And I'm not going to love you just because you came here to save me. I *don't* love. That will never change."

Elu raised his chin. "Neither will I."

He was standing out of reach, Akavi noted. It would have been very easy for him to move a little closer, to casually touch his chest or his hands while Akavi was too exhausted to object. Yet the boy followed protocol, even here. So perhaps there was hope.

Redemption. Foolishness. It would never be that.

Yet Irimiru had betrayed him. Yasira Shien, the heretic, had betrayed him. Nemesis Herself had betrayed him. So, upon reflection, that gave him something to do after all.

"Elu, my dear," said Akavi, forcing a small smile. "How do you feel about revenge?"

Yasira woke and stared at the ceiling for a while.

She was back in her guest bed in Ev's lair. Tiv must have put her here.

Maybe that was all Tiv had done. Just dragged Yasira to bed, gotten spooked, and left. That would be nice. It would mean not actually having to move.

She stared at the plain gray ceiling for a long while before she heard Tiv's footsteps tiptoeing in.

"Oh," said Tiv, "you're awake."

Yasira said nothing.

She had failed. The pattern had succeeded, but all Yasira had wanted was to make Tiv safe, and she'd fucked it up.

"I found orange juice," said Tiv. "And toast. In that weird freaky upside-down kitchen thing. This place is *weird*, by the way. Don't know how long this stuff has been in the fridge, but it smells okay, and you need to eat, so."

"Not hungry," said Yasira.

Her words were barely working to begin with. How could she explain to Tiv that Tiv wasn't supposed to be here? That it wasn't how things could be.

Tiv was a good girl and Tiv still loved her. She'd said as much on the ansible. Tiv would be loyal, even when Yasira told her not to. Especially when Yasira told her not to.

And Yasira was secretly, shamefully glad.

"Only because you're exhausted," said Tiv. "I mean, I would be too, after… whatever just happened. But we're here. And alive. And you. Need. To eat."

Yasira rolled over and grudgingly picked up the glass of orange juice. Her joints ached, she had bruises all over, but that was nothing new.

"Then we need to talk about what in the world is going on," said Tiv.

Yasira took a sip of the juice. It tasted like juice always tasted. She swilled it in her mouth, swallowed, put the glass down.

"You weren't supposed to know what was happening," she said.

"Yeah? What was I supposed to do, get amnesia?"

"Go back to your life. Go back to Ship. Pretend nothing happened."

Tiv raised her chin, concealing the tiny quiver of her lip. "I don't take orders."

Yasira looked at her sidelong.

Did Outside care what people thought? She didn't think so. But Yasira did, and it had been Yasira's plan. Was that why Tiv had been left out of the plan? Because either Yasira or Outside knew, on some level, that she wouldn't want to be saved?

But – Tiv *had* been saved, partway. She had been a prisoner of angels of Nemesis and now she was not. Yasira remembered the relief she'd felt when Tiv left the *Talon*. Maybe that counted for something.

"All right," said Tiv. "Let me lay this out for you. You want me to pretend nothing happened? I've been trying to do that ever since the *Pride of Jai*. Fourteen months. It didn't work out so great. Nobody believes anything I tell them about you. About what happened. Not even Ship. She didn't laugh in my face or tell me I was crazy and I figured that was the best I could do. And that was after just one day of things going wrong. I didn't go through anything other people didn't, except that I loved you, and apparently that wasn't okay. What do you think happens if I go back again after all this? I can't. I know what happened to me doesn't hold a candle to whatever happened to you. But I still saw you come back from the dead, got kidnapped, watched you tortured by angels. I thought angels were good. I kind of had to rethink that. I'm pretty sure you led me past a *dead* angel back there. I don't really understand what just happened. But I get to be traumatized, too. I can leave notes for people, I can make sure they know I'm still alive. Ship deserves that much. A lot of people do. But I can't just waltz back in and pretend that nothing happened. That I still…" Her voice lowered, cracked. "That I still trust the Gods, after what I saw. Don't you get it? It would be a *lie*."

Yasira buried her face in her hands.

"You might like it more," she said, after a long moment trying to find the words. "Lying. It might be better for you than the truth."

"How about you let me decide that myself," said Tiv, and there was something cold in her voice now.

Haltingly, in small pieces, she told Tiv everything. It took a long time. Finding the words was hard, and saying them was draining.

Frequently she broke off, and Tiv fed her toast, and made concerned, comforting noises. A couple of times Yasira asked for a break, and Tiv left her in the soothing dark with her blankets until she could think again. Frequently Tiv had questions, even for the parts that Yasira thought were obvious, and she went in circles trying to explain. It was long after lunch, and into the afternoon, when she got to the end.

She had expected to cry, but any part of her that could was still buried under sheer, numb, suffocating exhaustion.

The room was silent, apart from the buzzing of nearby machinery, for a minute or so. Yasira lay on her stomach, motionless.

"So," said Tiv, sitting at the side of the bed, "what are we going to do now?"

And a new emotion rose through the numbness like bile.

There was one more reason why she'd wanted Tiv to leave. To keep Tiv safe, yes. But also…

Whatever was happening now on Jai, it was happening because of her. Without Tiv, she could have ignored that. Surely she'd done enough; the pattern had certainly thought so. She could wrap herself in blankets here in this lab that no one could find, and starve or something, and that would be the end of it. With Tiv…

Tiv would let her rest, but only in the way that normal people rested. There might not be a cure for most of what was wrong with Yasira. But Tiv would want her to rest and heal until there was strength in her bones again. Thoughts in her skull that didn't jangle and clatter and drown themselves out. Until doing something other than lying here in a puddle felt like an option again.

And then Tiv – reliable, good girl Tiv – would want to help people.

The people of Jai were not safe. Nemesis had decided not to kill them, for now. But Nemesis was not out of the fight. Nemesis was brilliant and patient. She was probably already intervening however She could, in whatever way Her circuits calculated She could get away with. Waiting until She had the right excuse.

Akavi had been right about Ev, in a way. She had tried to fight the Gods out of spite. Yasira and Tiv's fight would not be like that.

It would be a fight to save people. A fight to save their world.

But Yasira and Tiv would be fighting the Gods.

"We're going to be heretics, I guess," said Yasira, muffled by her pillow. When Tiv did not respond, Yasira rolled over slightly and looked back up at her. "I mean it, Tiv. Just by being here, we're heretics. If you want to help make any of this right, then so are you. If you stay, you'll never live a normal life ever again. You'll never get to take it back. Do you understand?"

There was another silence.

"No," said Tiv. "But I want to. And what you've said, if I even understand half of what you've said – those people need help, and there's no one to fix it but us."

Yasira searched Tiv's face. She was crap with faces, even the faces of the people she loved. Tiv was upset, sure. But Tiv had loved the Gods. She'd sat in church with her face shining. She'd said that she couldn't trust Them anymore. But surely that was just talk. Surely that faith couldn't have been broken so quickly.

Then again, it had been more then a year since Yasira disappeared. Maybe it hadn't been quick at all.

There was so much that they didn't know about each other anymore.

"Maybe not even us," said Yasira. "Maybe we can't fix it."

Tiv smiled, then. Smiled like she'd always smiled in church, though there was a sad wobble in it now. Like she'd always smiled at Yasira, before this all started.

Abruptly Yasira realized she'd had it all wrong. Tiv was a good girl, yes. She'd loved the Gods because she thought They were good. Then, swiftly and painfully, she'd learned otherwise. But she hadn't gone vengeful like Ev. She hadn't burned out like Yasira. Tiv was still good. Learning the truth hadn't taken that from her. She just knew a little more about it now.

Maybe Yasira had saved Tiv after all. Maybe taking her here, to a place where she could still believe in something, was what Tiv needed. Maybe the pattern had seen, all along, that this was how it would go.

Maybe Tiv deserved to make that choice for herself.

Tiv hesitantly took Yasira's hand. "Maybe we can't fix it," she said. "But do you want to try?"

It was stupid. This was nothing to build a rebellion on. Both of them were lies. Yasira could see them, in her mind's eye, from every perspective. Look small, and they were nothing but massive conglomerations of cells, breathing and excreting, doing nothing but their innate biological functions. Look large, and they were meaningless clumps of matter, insignificant specks in the greater pattern, which had already made up its mind. None of this was real.

But, if you looked at it just right, here they were. One small part of the pattern that could still reach out and encourage another. It was enough.

ACKNOWLEDGMENTS

None of this ever would have happened without Akavi. He started it. And Akavi would not have existed without my dear friend Virgo, who originated the character, and with whose full blessing and cooperation I created the world of this book.

Nor would Akavi be who he is without the rest of the old Santhil D&D group: Devon Doyal, James M. Eden, Michael Friesen, Zofia Melton, Midwoka, Brittany Schieron, John Vipperman, Charlie Wood, and Zeth.

As I felt my way through *The Outside's* early draft, I had A. Merc Rustad as the most enthusiastic happyraptor of an alpha reader I could ask for. Elizabeth Bartmess, Dani Alexis Ryskamp, and Maigen Turner beta read the manuscript and had useful advice. In particular, Elizabeth's comments helped me do a deep, painful dive into Yasira's character that made her live and breathe far more satisfyingly than I could have managed for her on my own. Elizabeth now works as a professional sensitivity reader and I can't recommend them highly enough.

My agent, Hannah Bowman, is simply brilliant. I've benefited greatly from her drive and business sense as well as her thoughtful editorial gaze. I owe thanks to all the people at Angry Robot who took a chance on this weird book and who kept it on track during a difficult restructuring period. In particular, I want to thank Gemma Creffield, Marc Gascoigne, and Penny Reeve for their work.

Some research did go into this book's draft and revisions. I wish I could provide a proper list of citations for further reading, but unfortunately, most of that research occurred in the form of long and aimless Wikipedia dives about mysticism. I did find Dr. Judith Herman's book, *Trauma and Recovery*, to be an unexpectedly valuable resource. I also owe an obvious debt to the many other science fiction authors doing Lovecraft subversions before me, who are too numerous to fairly name here.

I owe a shout-out to all the supervisors I had in graduate school: Dr Daniel G. Brown and Dr Charles L.A. Clarke of the University of Waterloo and Dr David Skillicorn at Queen's University. All of them are very nice people who worked well with me and who have definitely not been secret Lovecraftian cultists this whole time, nuh-uh. Nothing in this book should be construed as having any negative reflection on their character.

Finally, I am grateful to Merc (again), Tris Blackthorne, Jacqueline Flay, Dave Fredsberg, Rose Lemberg, Elial and Kalina Shadowpine, Salie Snapdragon, Bogi Takács, and Brett Tucker, all of whom were there for me during the extremely turbulent period of my life when I drafted and revised this novel. Without their patient friendship and support, I might not be here. In that eventuality, *The Outside* would also not be here. So if you have read this far and enjoyed yourself, you now owe them something, too.

ABOUT THE AUTHOR

Ada Hoffmann is a Canadian computer scientist who writes weird speculative fiction. She works as a term adjunct at Queen's University when not writing. She lives with and is supported in these endeavors by her primary partner Dave, a teenage stepdaughter, a black cat, a ball python, and a tarantula.

Ada is autistic, bisexual, and genderfluid. She is the author of the short story collection *Monsters in my Mind* and of the *Autistic Book Party* review series, which is dedicated to in-depth analysis of autistic characters in speculative fiction. Her shorter work has appeared in venues such as *Strange Horizons, Asimov's,* and *Uncanny*, and has been longlisted for the BSFA and Rhysling awards, twice each.

If you enjoyed *The Outside*, Ada would love to hear from you!

Find her online at http://ada-hoffmann.com/ or @xasymptote or on Patreon at http://www.patreon.com/ada-hoffmann, where she offers backers peeks at her writing life, cat pictures, opportunities to vote for the books they want reviewed, and other small goodies.

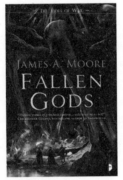
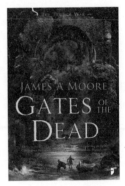